S0-ABC-847

"Strong, smart and capable, Riley will remind many of Anita Blake, Laurell K. Hamilton's kick-ass vampire hunter. . . . Fans of Anita Blake and Charlaine Harris' Sookie Stackhouse vampire series will be rewarded."
—*Publishers Weekly*

"Unbridled lust and kick-ass action are the hallmarks of this first novel in a brand-new paranormal series. . . . 'Sizzling' is the only word to describe this heated, action-filled, suspenseful romantic drama."
—Curled Up with a Good Book

"Desert island keeper . . . Grade: A . . . I wanted to read this book in one sitting, and was terribly offended that the real world intruded on my reading time! . . . Inevitable comparisons can be made to Anita Blake, Kim Harrison, and Kelley Armstrong's books, but I think Ms. Arthur has a clear voice of her own and her characters speak for themselves. . . . I am hooked!"

—All About Romance

Praise for *Kissing Sin*

"The second book in this paranormal guardian series is just as phenomenal as the first. . . . I am addicted!!"
—Fresh Fiction

"Arthur's world building skills are absolutely superb and I recommend this story to any reader who enjoys tales of the paranormal."
—Coffee Time Romance and More

"Fast paced and filled with deliciously sexy characters, readers will find *Kissing Sin* a fantastic urban fantasy with a hot serving of romance that continues to sizzle long after the last page is read."

—Darque Reviews

"Keri Arthur's unique characters and the imaginative world she's created will make this series one that readers won't want to miss."

—A Romance Review

Praise for *Tempting Evil*

"Riley Jenson is kick-ass . . . genuinely tough and strong, but still vulnerable enough to make her interesting. . . . Arthur is not derivative of early [Laurell K.] Hamilton—far from it—but the intensity of her writing and the complexity of her heroine and her stories is reminiscent."

—All About Romance

"This paranormal romance series gets better and better with each new book. . . . An exciting adventure that delivers all you need for a fabulous read—sexy shapeshifters, hot vampires, wild uncontrollable sex and the slightest hint of a love that's meant to be forever."

—Fresh Fiction

"Pure sexy action adventure . . . I found the world vividly realized and fascinating. . . . So, if you like your erotic scenes hot, fast, and frequent, your heroine sassy, sexy, and tough, and your stories packed with hard-hitting action in a vividly realized fantasy world, then *Tempting Evil* and its companion novels could be just what you're looking for."

—SFRevu

"Keri Arthur's Riley Jenson series just keeps getting better and better and is sure to call to fans of other authors with kick-ass heroines such as Christine Feehan and Laurell K. Hamilton. I have become a steadfast fan of this marvelous series and I am greatly looking forward to finding out what is next in store for this fascinating and strong character."

—A Romance Review

Praise for *Dangerous Games*

"One of the best books I have ever read. . . . The storyline is so exciting I did not realize I was literally sitting on the edge of my chair. . . . Arthur has a real winner on her hands. Five cups."

—Coffee Time Romance and More

"The depths of emotion, the tense plot, and the conflict of powerful driving forces inside the heroine made for [an] absorbing read."

—SFRevu

"This series is phenomenal! *Dangerous Games* is an incredibly original and devastatingly sexy story. It keeps you spellbound and mesmerized on every page. Absolutely perfect!!"

—Fresh Fiction

Praise for *Embraced by Darkness*

"Arthur is positively one of the best urban fantasy authors in print today. The characters have been well-drawn from the start and the mysteries just keep getting better. A creative, sexy and adventure-filled world that readers will just love escaping to."

—Darque Reviews

"Arthur's storytelling is getting better and better with each book. *Embraced by Darkness* has suspense, interesting concepts, terrific main and secondary characters, well-developed story arcs, and the world-building is highly entertaining. . . . I think this series is worth the time and emotional investment to read."

—Reuters.com

"Once again, Keri Arthur has created a perfect, exciting and thrilling read with intensity that kept me vigilantly turning each page, hoping it would never end."

—Fresh Fiction

"Reminiscent of Laurell K. Hamilton back when her books had mysteries to solve, Arthur's characters inhabit a dark sexy world of the paranormal."

—*The Parkersburg News and Sentinel*

"I love this series."

—All About Romance

Praise for *The Darkest Kiss*

"The paranormal Australia that Arthur concocts works perfectly, and the plot speeds along at a breakneck pace. Riley fans won't be disappointed."

—*Publishers Weekly*

Praise for *Bound to Shadows*

"The Riley Jenson Guardian series ROCKS! Riley is one bad-ass heroine with a heart of gold. Keri Arthur never disappoints and always leaves me eagerly anticipating the next book. A classic, fabulous read!"

—Fresh Fiction

By Keri Arthur

THE RIPPLE CREEK WEREWOLF SERIES
Beneath a Rising Moon
Beneath a Darkening Moon

THE DARK ANGELS SERIES
Darkness Unbound
Darkness Rising

THE MYTH AND MAGIC SERIES
Destiny Kills
Mercy Burns

THE RILEY JENSON GUARDIAN SERIES
Full Moon Rising
Kissing Sin
Tempting Evil
Dangerous Games
Embraced by Darkness
The Darkest Kiss
Deadly Desire
Bound to Shadows
Moon Sworn

BENEATH
A
DARKENING
MOON

KERI ARTHUR

DELL
NEW YORK

Beneath a Darkening Moon is a work of fiction. Names, characters, places, and incidents either are the product of the author's imagination or are used fictitiously. Any resemblance to actual persons, living or dead, events, or locales is entirely coincidental.

2012 Dell Mass Market Edition

Copyright © 2003 by Keri Arthur
Excerpt from *Dancing with the Devil* by Keri Arthur copyright © 2012 by Keri Arthur

Published in the United States by Dell, an imprint of The Random House Publishing Group, a division of Random House, Inc., New York.

DELL is a registered trademark of Random House, Inc., and the colophon is a trademark of Random House, Inc.

Originally published in slightly different form in paperback in the United States by ImaJinn Books, Hickory Corners, MI, in 2003.

ISBN: 978-0-440-24650-3
eBook ISBN: 978-0-345-53580-1

This book contains an excerpt from the forthcoming novel *Dancing with the Devil* by Keri Arthur. This excerpt has been set for this edition only and may not reflect the final content of the forthcoming edition.

Cover design: Lynn Andreozzi
Cover illustration: Juliana Kolesova

Printed in the United States of America

www.bantamdell.com

9 8 7 6 5 4 3 2 1

Dell mass market edition: October 2012

AUTHOR'S NOTE

THE RIPPLE CREEK werewolves differ from the were-wolves of Riley Jenson's world. While many similarities exist—such as soul mates and swearing your love to the moon—there are just as many differences. These books were the start of my journey into the werewolf realm, and it was these books that gave life to the world that became Riley Jenson's.

I hope you enjoy them!

BENEATH
a
DARKENING MOON

Chapter One

Savannah Grant climbed out of the truck and took a deep breath of the crisp fall air. Though it had snowed last night, the sky this morning was rich and blue, and the sun was surprisingly warm.

The aspen trees surrounding the small clearing glowed a rich, vibrant gold that contrasted sharply with the blue of the sky and the white of the snow-covered peaks looming high above. Leaves littered the ground beneath her feet, but the snow that had covered them earlier had melted. Now, the sunlight gleamed through the drops of water that remained, making them glow like tiny diamonds.

But this tranquil setting hid a darker heart.

She slammed the door shut and turned as a second truck came to a halt in the clearing. Three men climbed out—two deputy rangers and a brown-haired teen who looked positively green around the gills.

The teenager's gaze skirted the clearing, resting momentarily on the barely visible trail that disappeared through the aspens. Then he gulped and looked at Savannah. His blue eyes were wide and frightened—a sure sign that, for once in his short life,

Matt wasn't crying wolf. "I don't have to go back up there, do I?"

"No." She tried to give the kid a reassuring smile, but it probably looked as fake as it felt. But then, it wasn't every day that two human tourists were murdered within a week of each other inside the confines of the Ripple Creek Werewolf Reservation.

And worse, those murders were an almost exact replica of a past event—an event that still haunted her dreams.

A shiver ran down her spine. Not from the cold, though here in the mountains it was chilly despite the sun's heat. While her clairvoyance skills were sometimes hit-and-miss, she'd certainly had more than her fair share of premonitions come true, and that's what she was feeling now. The past she'd tried so hard to forget was about to be resurrected.

She rubbed her arms and stepped away from the truck. "Ike, do you want to stay here with Matt?"

"But I want to go up there with you—"

"Ike," she warned, in no mood to take any of the young deputy's crap today. "Either you do as I say, or you head back down the mountain."

"How the hell am I going to learn anything—"

"You could always sit at a desk and do paperwork," she cut in. "Your choice."

Sullen didn't even begin to describe his expression as he nodded. Guilt slithered through her, but she shoved it away and glanced across at Ronan. "Ready?"

The russet-haired deputy nodded and hitched the small backpack onto his shoulder. She spun and walked across the clearing. Sunlight filtering through the golden leaves dappled the faint path, but quickly gave way to deeper shadows as they moved into the pines.

"You were a bit hard on the kid, weren't you?" Ronan said, his deep voice seeming to resonate through the silence. "I know he can be annoying where you're concerned, but he truly *is* eager to learn."

She blew out a breath. "I know. It's just that—"

"You're dreaming again, aren't you?"

She looked over her shoulder. Ronan's gray eyes gleamed almost silver in the shadows, full of concern. But then, they'd known each other a very long time. Ronan was not only one of her few close friends, but her very first lover when she'd been a teenager just starting to explore her sexuality. And even though it went against her policy of not mixing business and pleasure, they still shared a moon dance when one of them was feeling lonely.

"What makes you think that?"

His smile lit up his eyes. "The only time you're so short-tempered is when you're feeling the heat of the moon or have been dreaming. Considering we shared a few rather energetic nights last weekend, I figured it was the latter."

She grinned. "Have you made the bed yet?"

"Yeah. Otherwise Conor would be curious."

She nodded. The cabin they used for their retreats had been in Ronan's family for years, but these days it was only occupied in spring, when the fishing was good. It was the perfect sanctuary the rest of the year, except that Conor, Ronan's younger brother, was one of those wolves who had a nose for intrigue and always seemed to be three steps behind them. While he didn't appear to know about their sometime affair, neither of them wanted him to find out—if only because the kid was a blabbermouth. Besides, their illicit meetings not only went against her own rules, but council rules as well.

The council, she thought grimly, definitely needed to pull their heads out of their collective asses. Not so much because of the no-fraternizing-with-co-workers rule, but for all the other rules they were trying to institute—like a ten o'clock curfew for anyone under eighteen. This was the twenty-first century, for God's sake, not the Middle Ages. It was rules like that that had driven her out of both her home *and* Ripple Creek when she was barely seventeen.

Of course, her views on the matter, though often aired, weren't taken into consideration, despite the fact her dad was the head of the council. He also happened to be the main force behind all the saving-yourself-for-marriage bullshit currently simmering, despite the hassle and heartache such beliefs had caused Neva, Savannah's twin, just over a year ago.

"What are the dreams about this time?" Ronan asked.

She brushed a tree branch aside, waiting until he'd passed before letting it go. "Same old, same old. Death, destruction, and mayhem."

Only this time, it wasn't in the past, but the present. And that scared her, because the man behind those murders was supposedly dead.

So how could they be happening again, here in Ripple Creek, in almost the exact same manner? The press had never been allowed to release all the details, so it couldn't be a copycat. Yet the murder—or at least, the first murder—was the same. Right down to the mutilation of the victim's genitals.

Only two things were different—this time, the victims were human, and instead of letting the blood drain into the soil, someone—or something—was lapping it up.

A shiver ran down her spine. Fear, she acknowledged. Fear of what was coming. *Who* was coming.

She swallowed heavily but didn't allow *that* particular fear any more space, because at that moment, death touched the air. She stopped, sniffing the faint breeze and tasting the scents entwined within it.

"A new death," Ronan said, stopping close enough that she could feel his body heat. "The blood is still fresh."

She nodded. "The hint of sage and musk suggests the victim is male."

"Same as the first one."

She glanced over her shoulder and met his gaze. The grim certainty reflected in his eyes echoed through her. They had themselves a serial killer—and with autumn giving way to winter and drawing in the cross-country skiing crowd, soon there would be far too many potential victims in Ripple Creek.

"Let's get up there before the scavengers do."

She followed the ever-thickening scent of death through the trees. The path became steeper, rockier, as the tree line began to recede. The clumps of snow became drifts, and the chill in the air was more noticeable. Yet, despite that, sweat trickled down her spine. The past she'd fled was merging with the present, and all she could see in the future was disaster.

She swiped at the moisture dribbling down her

forehead and tried to get a grip on her imagination. It was just a murderer—just a crazy person. The past *wasn't* coming back to haunt her. It was a weird coincidence, nothing more.

Maybe, that deep-down voice said. *And maybe not.*

Regardless of whether it *was* just a coincidence, when she'd reported the murders to the IIS—who were an offshoot of the FBI, and who by law had to be notified whenever a human was killed on werewolf land—she'd noted them as being similar to those past murders. And that meant that they just might send the same man to investigate.

And *he* was the last man she ever wanted to see in Ripple Creek.

"There're the egg-shaped boulders Matt mentioned," Ronan said, pointing to the rocks off to the left-hand side of the trail.

She nodded and made her way toward them. Beyond the stones, death waited.

Like the first victim, this man had his arms and legs stretched wide, his penis and scrotum sliced away, and his heart removed. For a moment she closed her eyes, fighting not only the sickness that churned in the pit of her stomach, but also the memories that came crowding back. Of course, they weren't actually *her* memories, but rather those of the man she'd been sleeping with. A man who'd been the very opposite of the gentle soul she'd thought him to be.

Yet even without those memories, it was doubtful that scenes like this would ever become easy, she thought, as her gaze swept around the stone circle that surrounded the mutilated body. She might have spent the last nine years as a ranger, but death was not something she'd encountered often. Which was why finding someone so brutally and methodically slaughtered still had the power to shock her.

"We have ourselves a nut-job," Ronan said, as he came to a halt beside her.

"That we have." The question was did this nut-job re-create past events by chance or by design? "You want to secure the area and take some preliminary photos? I'll call headquarters, and get them to send the coroner."

"The doc's not going to be happy," Ronan commented, as he swung the pack off his shoulder and pulled out the crime scene tape. "It's barely eight in the morning, and Wednesday is his day off."

"Obviously no one told our murderer that," she snapped, then met his sharp glance with a wave of her hand. "I know, I know. I'm going to have to stop being so bitchy."

"Or go see someone about those dreams."

She nodded and dragged her cell phone from her pocket. Then she stepped out of his way and made her call. Kelly, who was both their administrative assistant and communications officer, answered on the second ring.

"Ripple Creek Ranger's Office."

"Kel, can you ask Doc Carson to head up to Pike's Clearing at the top of Red Mountain Road? Ike will be waiting for him."

"Will do. You've a visitor, by the way."

"Who?"

"An investigator from the Interspecies Investigation Squad. He wouldn't give me his name."

Savannah swore under her breath, even as her heart

began to race. Was it him? She was tempted to ask Kel for a description, but that would only make Kel curious. And the last thing she needed was *anyone* asking questions about her connection to this man—if it was indeed the same man—especially since the men and women of the IIS had a reputation of riding rough-shod over local law enforcement and had, in the past, caused a lot of bad feelings between the community and its police officers.

"Tell him I'm coming in." At least that would give Ronan, Ike, and the doc time to do a preliminary examination of the scene and the body before the IIS charged in and took over. She glanced at her watch. "I'll be there in twenty."

"I'll tell him. I'll even offer him decent coffee."

In Kel speak, that meant the man in question was not only single but gorgeous. Which Cade *had* been. She took a deep breath and tried to calm her nerves. It had been ten years since she'd seen him. Hell, the truth be known, he'd probably forgotten all about her and moved on. It wasn't like he'd had any real feelings for her, despite their amazing compatibility in the sack.

"Thanks, Kel." She hung up and met Ronan's gaze. "The IIS are here."

He swore, long and loud.

"Yeah," she said. "Exactly. I'm heading back down. I'll get Ike to meet Carson, and he'll have to assist you here."

Ronan nodded. "He's damn good with the cameras, so he can take over that job."

"Just keep an eye on him. With the IIS involved, we can't afford any of his exuberant mistakes."

Ronan nodded and began taking photos of the body and the ceremonial ring of small stones surrounding it. She cast one more look at the victim, her gaze resting momentarily on the severed genital area, noting once again the lack of blood in the dirt beneath the body. Then she shivered and turned around, making her way back down the hill.

If history was repeating itself, she just had to hope that *everything* about that time wasn't about to make an appearance. Because there were some decisions she'd made back then that she had no desire to revisit in any way, shape, or form.

"Ike," she called, once she'd reached the clearing, "I want you to go down to the main road and wait for Doc Carson, then bring him up here and take him to Ronan. You'll be helping Ronan after that."

The young deputy's eyes lit up. "Really?"

"Really." God, was she ever that enthusiastic? Probably not. By the time she'd applied for the deputy position, she'd truly seen the darker side of human *and* wolf nature. She'd known all too well the damage some people could do to others—physical *or* emotional.

"Matt, do you want a ride back into town with me?"

The teenager nodded and climbed into her truck. She glanced back at Ike. "Do what Ronan tells you to—nothing more, nothing less."

Ike grinned and gave her a thumbs-up, his carrot-bright hair glowing like a beacon in the morning sun. Savannah shook her head, climbed into her truck, and headed back to town. By the time she'd dropped

Matt off and talked briefly to his parents, thirty-five minutes had come and gone.

Kel looked up as Savannah opened the front door of their little section of city hall, her expression a mix of amusement and annoyance. "Our dear IIS officer is not impressed with tardiness. Or so he's said every five minutes for the last fifteen minutes."

"One of those, huh?"

"Yeah. All looks and no charm." Kel placed a mug on the counter, and the rich aroma of cinnamon coffee wafted up. "Here, take this. You're going to need it."

Savannah picked up the steaming mug. "What excuse did you give him?"

"I didn't. He's not my boss and he certainly wasn't polite, so he didn't deserve an update."

She couldn't help a grin. "So what coffee did *he* get?"

"Machine blend only."

Meaning he'd really pissed her off. "Could you take all my calls while I deal with him?"

"Will do."

"Thanks, Kel."

Savannah sipped the sweet, aromatic liquid, fortifying herself as she walked around the counter and down the long hall to her office. The door was shut and the blinds shuttered, affording her no glimpse of this paragon who'd managed to annoy their administrative assistant.

She grasped the handle with her free hand and pushed the door open. "Sorry to keep you wait—"

The rest of her words died as the man inside turned around.

She stopped as trepidation, and something else—something she couldn't quite define—rippled through her.

It was Cade, just as she'd feared.

For too many minutes, all she could do was stare. This man had haunted her dreams for nigh on ten years, yet except for the crow's-feet near his eyes, his too handsome features showed no real sign of aging. He was a big man, just over six feet tall, his build lean but powerful, like a sprinter. His hair was dark brown, but the mahogany highlights she'd so adored now contrasted with the flecks of silver that gleamed in the sunlight streaming in through the window behind him. Once upon a time, his hair had been long and tied back carelessly in a ponytail—a ponytail she always used to undo, just so she could run her fingers through its gloriously silken length. Now it was short, barely even brushing the shoulders of his starched blue shirt.

Her gaze finally, inevitably, locked with his. For several heartbeats she couldn't think, was barely able to breathe. The navy blue of his eyes all but consumed her. Heat prickled across her skin and ignited a familiar ache deep inside her. She knew she had to move, had to do something other than simply stand here. Yet she couldn't tear herself away from the power of that gaze. From the memories she saw deep within it.

But there was surprise there, too. He hadn't expected to see her here, and it took her a moment to realize why—he'd known her under another name.

A slight smile touched the lips that were still as sensual as she remembered. Then his gaze rolled languidly down her body—a touch that wasn't a touch, and yet one that sent energy singing across every fiber of her being. Her nipples hardened, pressing almost painfully against her shirt, and the deep-down ache grew stronger.

His gaze completed its erotic journey and rose to meet hers again, lingering a little on the scar that marred the left side of her face. But it wasn't the heat in his look that made her tremble. It was the sudden flash of anger.

As if *he* had anything to be angry about.

"Well," he said. "Fancy finding you here."

His voice was husky, deep—and conjured memories of whispered endearments and long, sweaty nights of lovemaking. And even after all the time that had separated them, his voice still had the power to undo her. Maybe because she still heard it in her dreams—dreams in which he'd spun his web of desire and deceit around her as easily as he had in real life.

And it was *those* memories, as well as the anger that was now so visible in the depths of his eyes, that got her moving.

"What are you doing here, Cade?"

The smile that touched his lips never warmed the icy, dark blue depths of his eyes. "You reported a murder. I'm here to investigate."

She sat down at her desk and waved him to one of the visitor's chairs. He sat down, his movements still full of power and grace.

"I mean, why are you really here?" She drank more coffee, grateful for the flush of warmth it spread through her otherwise chilled system.

He raised a dark eyebrow. "As I said, I'm here to investigate the murder of a human on this reservation."

"And did you happen to tell your superiors that you were once involved with the chief ranger of said reservation?"

"How could I, when I didn't know myself?" His gaze met hers, and all she could see—all she could feel—was his cold, cold anger. The warm caring that had once attracted her to this man had long gone—if indeed it had actually existed. "I knew you as Vannah Harvey, and you certainly had no pretensions of becoming a ranger back then."

His comment had anger flicking through her, but she somehow reined it in. "And now that you *do* know that I'm the ranger here?"

"It won't make any difference. You were nothing more than a means to an end, Vannah. A pleasant way to pass the time as I tried to catch a killer."

Though she'd long known the truth, his words still hurt. After all, she'd once cared deeply for this man. Probably too deeply. To discover it was all nothing more than lies had cut to the quick. Yet his lies were not the worst of his actions. Far from it.

She leaned back in her chair and feigned a calm she didn't feel. "My name is Savannah. Kindly use it."

"*Savannah,*" he mocked. "Such a sweet name."

"So was the girl you knew as Vannah. You sure as hell cured her of that."

Something flashed in his eyes. Not anger, because that was there already, but something deeper, darker. "The girl I knew as Vannah put on a damn good show, but time sure proved otherwise."

"Time?" She gave an unladylike snort. "We knew each other less than a month."

But it had been time enough to think she was in

love. Time enough to prove how bad a judge her heart and instincts could sometimes be.

"Sometimes a month is all it takes to prove how very wrong first impressions can be."

"How very true," she said dryly. "So why don't we just drop the Happy Trails memory hour and get down to business?"

"Suits me."

He crossed his legs, drawing her eye down the powerful line of his thigh and shin to the garish blue and red of his boots. A smile touched her lips. It seemed even the starched blue correctness of the IIS couldn't break his love of cowboy boots.

"Tell me about the murder."

Her gaze came back to his. "Everything is in the report, which I've no doubt you've read."

"But I want your impressions."

"Really?" Bitterness crept into her voice. "And why would you want the opinion of a no good—what was the term you used that night? Whore? Strumpet?"

His face closed over. "I thought we were keeping this to business."

So they were. But it was harder than she thought it would be, especially when the warm mix of sage and tangerine that always accompanied him touched the air, stirring her hormones as much as it did her memories of the nights she'd spent in his arms, drinking in that same scent.

"There's been a second murder," she said, the annoyance in her voice aimed more at herself than him. God, anyone would think she was still that dizzy teenager, not the wiser woman she'd become. "Same MO."

He sat up a little straighter. "Why didn't you mention this straightaway?"

"It could have something to do with seeing the one person I never wanted to see again."

Again that darkness flared in his eyes. "Tell me about the second murder."

"As far as we can tell, it's exactly the same as the first one. My people are up there now, locking down the scene and taking preliminary photos."

"Who discovered the body?"

"A local teenager out for an early morning run."

"You've taken his statement?"

Anger flickered through her. What in moons did he think she was, an amateur? "Hell no," she drawled. "Was I supposed to?"

"Sarcasm is not what either of us needs right now." His gaze bored into hers. "If you can't handle me being here on this case, then step aside and let someone else take it."

She didn't bother answering. As the IIS officer for this region, he had no choice about being here—and as head ranger, neither did she. But he was right about one thing; she had to get a grip on herself. "The coroner should be up there by now. You got a team following?"

He nodded. "Two people. They should be here this afternoon. We will, of course, take over the investigation, though we'd appreciate your department's help in dealing with the townsfolk."

And he was going to need it, because the citizens of Ripple Creek didn't cotton to the sort of superior attitude he was currently displaying. She took a sip of coffee and asked, "How far behind are they?"

"They'll be here in a few hours."

"Are you going to wait for them, or do you want to head up to the crime scene now?"

"I'd like to get up there before the scene gets too contaminated."

That flicker of anger became a roar. "*My* people are well trained and damn good at their jobs!"

"But they aren't trained for this sort of investigation, which is why the IIS is always called in."

The IIS being called in had nothing to do with skill—or the lack thereof—but was simply a means of pacifying the humans who always seemed to think that the murder of one of their own on a werewolf reservation was the first sign of a planned uprising. Humans—or some of them, at least—seemed to live in permanent fear of wolves. Why, she had no idea—especially when humans had all but wiped out the werewolf population in America. Hell, of the twenty reservations that had been originally granted, only eleven now existed. And two of those were in jeopardy from the encroaching human population. Resettlement was currently being discussed, but she knew from her old man that *this* time the wolves were going to give the government the legal fight of its life.

But she didn't bother saying anything, because voicing her opinion wouldn't matter a damn. Cade was here, and that was that.

She gulped down the rest of her coffee and rose. "I'll take you out there now."

"Good. And on the way, you can give me your opinion about these killings."

She bit back the instinctive urge to throw another bitchy comment at him. And as she walked past him, she tried to ignore the warm scent of tangerine in her nostrils. But it wasn't so easy to ignore his familiar presence at her back, or the way his heat seemed to caress her skin, burning her like the summer sun.

It had been that way the first time she'd met him— a rush of heat, and a fever that had become fiercer the longer she'd stayed in his presence. No wolf before or since had elicited that sort of reaction, and she was damn glad of that fact. These days, she was quite content to spend her time in Ronan's arms, secure in the knowledge that the sex was good, that she was safe, and that he would never do anything to hurt her.

Kel turned around at the sound of their footsteps, and her gaze went from Savannah to Cade and back again. Though her expression was perfectly pleasant, Savannah was hard pressed not to smile. Cade had a lot of ground to make up if he expected anything more than the most basic assistance from Kel. And considering that the smooth operation of this ranger station greatly depended on the efficiency of its admin assistant, Cade was in deep trouble.

Unless, of course, he brought his own admin assistant—which, considering the sort of money being thrown at the IIS these days, was highly likely.

"Kel, I'm taking Mr. Jones up to Pike's Clearing. If anything urgent comes up, call Steve in to handle it." She glanced over her shoulder. "Have you booked rooms for yourself and your people?"

The deep blue of his eyes seemed to bore right through her. "Not yet."

She repressed a shiver and glanced back at Kel. "And arrange two rooms at one of the local lodges."

A smile touched Kel's lips. "Right away."

Savannah knew that look, and suspected that luxury accommodations—or at least, as close as they got to it here in Ripple Creek—were not in the offing. "In town," she added, just to ensure they didn't end up in some godforsaken corner on the outskirts.

Kel pouted, and Savannah smiled and led the way out the door. At least Cade couldn't berate her about the accommodations—but she very much suspected that he'd have a lot of other things to discuss. Most of them in the past, and most of them things she'd much rather forget.

But if he thought she was still that meek, mild teenager, he had another thing coming. And if he wanted a fight, he'd get one.

Because after ten years of dreaming about those events, she was more than ready for it.

CADE SHIFTED SLIGHTLY in the truck's seat so he could study Vannah's profile without being obvious. She'd changed more than he'd thought possible since he'd last seen her, and that surprised him—though why it did he had no idea. After all, he was no longer that green IIS recruit on his first assignment, so why would she still be that free-spirited teenager who'd captivated him so long ago?

The most obvious of those changes was the pale scar over her left eye, but while it caught his gaze, it didn't really detract from her unconventional beauty. Nothing could—not the scar, or the shorter cut of her once gloriously long hair, or the cold wariness in her green eyes.

He'd always expected that they would meet again

sometime, simply because his work as an IIS officer took him to many different reservations. And though he'd never really thought about how he would react, he'd expected that anger would be first and foremost. It had certainly been there—hard, deep, and furious. But what he hadn't expected was the rush of desire, or such fierce relief over the fact that she was safe, well, and whole.

And if anything, the flood of those last two emotions only served to make him angrier—at her and at himself. He'd followed the path of desire with her once before, and it had almost ended in his death. He would not go down that path again—not even for the woman who still haunted his dreams.

"Tell me your first impressions of the murders," he said again, his voice a touch harsher than necessary.

She slanted him a frosty look. "It's in the report."

"I want *your* thoughts, not the sanitized summary you wrote for the IIS."

A smile flirted with her lips—lips whose sensual touch he could still remember. "Do you *really* want to know my thoughts?"

"Do I have to put you on warning?" Maybe that would be a good idea. Two warnings and she'd be off the case, and he would be free to deal with the murders without interference from either her or the past.

"The killer uses a ritual to murder his victims," she said, voice ultra-professional yet still managing to sound tart. "Blood results showed that the first victim was drugged. And, given there's no evidence of resistance, I'd say the second victim was, too."

"The stone circle was present in the second murder as well?"

She nodded. "As were the mutilations."

"And what do you think of that?"

Her gaze met his briefly, the green depths giving little away. This reserve was new. Once upon a time, he could have read a world of emotions in her eyes. Though he'd learned the hard way that some of those emotions were nothing more than lies.

"I think we have a nut on our hands."

He raised an eyebrow. Was she deliberately avoiding any reference to the past murders, or was she simply intent on giving him the usual "this is my town and don't you forget it" crap that he generally received from rangers of small reservations like Ripple Creek? He suspected it was the latter, and that disappointed him. He'd expected more from her.

Though why, he had no idea. After all, she'd given him very little in the way of help the first time they'd met.

"And you don't see any similarities to past murders?"

She met his gaze again. "That's not for me to judge, is it? Not with the IIS here."

In other words, she wasn't admitting anything. Not to him, anyway. Which was no surprise, really. They'd done it the hard way the first time, and probably would again.

She stopped the truck beside another, in a clearing that could have come straight off a postcard, and climbed out. He quickly followed suit, breathing deeply of the crisp air. If there was anything he missed about reservation life, it was the purity of the air and the utter quiet of clearings like this.

But then, it was hardly practical for an IIS officer

to live on one of the reservations he might have to investigate. Plus, he'd grown used to city life—and as places to live went, Denver wasn't all that bad. At least there were glorious mountains within easy driving distance.

"This way," she said, and disappeared down a small path until all he could see was the occasional flash of sunlight gleaming off her golden hair.

Not that he needed to see her to follow her. Her scent was as unusual as she was—a tantalizing mix of a warm summer breeze combined with the rich headiness of exotic flowers and fruits. Even here in the mountains, with the crispness of the air and the scent of pine and snow heavy in his nostrils, her aroma was a teasing, sensual seduction.

And he had better get control of both his senses and his memories. He was here to catch a killer—nothing more, nothing less. Whether or not he and the chief ranger had a past was irrelevant, even if he still bore a scar across his shoulder blade that was the direct result of said ranger's duplicity.

As they came out of the tree line, a hint of blood touched the cold air. The rich, metallic smell made his pulse quicken in anticipation—something that always happened at the beginning of a hunt, even after all his years as an IIS agent. He ignored the sensation and swept his gaze across the barren, snow-speckled landscape. Ten years ago, the killer had carefully avoided the obvious paths, concentrating his movements across barren stone or through water—an easy enough task given that the murders always happened in the one spot, underground. Given that *this* killer seemed to be imitating the past, he very much

suspected similar caution would be employed. Only
here, the murder wasn't underground, and the sur-
rounds weren't as rocky, so there was a good chance
that they might find a print.

If the rangers hadn't walked all over the area, that
was.

Which wasn't being entirely fair. He glanced at
Vannah's stiff back, his gaze drawn to the gentle bob
of her golden ponytail, and then down the curves
of her back and rump, so lovingly displayed by the
close-fitting, pale green ranger's uniform.

He'd seen sloppy work done on many of the reservations, but Ripple Creek didn't appear to be one of
them. Her initial report to the IIS had been one of the
best he'd seen—even if he hadn't known it was hers
when he'd read it—but that didn't mean she and her
team had the ability to deal with something like this.

She led him through the rocks and stopped when
she reached a large egg-shaped stone. He stopped
beside her, his nostrils filling with her rich scent as
his gaze swept the scene before them. It was exactly
the same as the seven he'd seen ten years ago.

Two men worked near the feet of the victim. The
older of the two—and the man he presumed was the
reservation's acting coroner—was on his hands and
knees between the victim's legs, intently scrutinizing
the gaping hole that had once contained the victim's
penis and scrotum. A much younger man stood ready
with a camera and an eager expression.

A third ranger squatted at the top of the stone circle, but looked up as Cade came to a halt. The flicker
of animosity in his gray eyes was brief but nonethe-

less there. He placed a flag in the soil, rose, then carefully made his way toward them.

"We've found several footprints, both human and wolf. I've flagged them all." He came to a halt beside Vannah and crossed his arms.

Presenting a united front against the invader, Cade thought, and barely restrained a bitter smile. How many times did he have to face such shows of unity before people began to realize he was actually working for them, not against them?

"Ronan, this is Senior Agent Cade Jones, from the IIS."

The russet-haired ranger held out his hand. His grip was neither aggressive nor passive, just the grip of a man very comfortable in what he was and what he was doing.

"Pleasure to meet you, sir," the ranger said.

Like hell it was. "Please, call me Cade. I don't believe there should be any formalities between fellow law enforcement officers." Not as long as they understood *he* was in charge. He waved a hand toward the victim. "How far have you progressed?"

"We've taken photos of the victim and surroundings. We've also done an initial check for marks, but we haven't moved the victim as yet. I've ordered an ambulance to take the body to the state medical examiner."

Cade nodded. "I'll have someone waiting there. Did you find anything different from the first murder?"

"Not so far."

"What is the coroner looking at?"

"Marks in the soil," the coroner said, without looking up. "If I didn't know better, I'd say someone was lapping up the blood as this fellow bled to death. Saw it with the first murder, too."

If true, this *was* a departure from the previous murders, and it would help cement his theory that this was a copycat. He moved closer to the body. Vannah and the other ranger followed—a fact he knew only because her scent remained as strong as it had been when he'd stood beside her.

He squatted on the outside of the stone circle. This close, the aroma of blood and death was overwhelming.

"Where?" he said.

The coroner quickly pointed to several marks in the soil. He was right—it did look like lap marks. He glanced up at the kid with the camera. "Have you taken photos?"

The carrot-haired ranger nodded, his very demeanor one of fierce anticipation. First murder, Cade thought wryly, and wondered if the kid's exuberance would outlast the case. It certainly hadn't with *his* first murder.

But then, he'd been a still-wet-behind-the ears recruit into the IIS, not a mere ranger, and those murders were still the worst he'd ever seen. Until now.

"Are you ready to move the body?"

"Yes, sir. Just thought you'd prefer to be a witness."

At least the officials in this town seemed to be up on recommended procedures. He couldn't remember the number of times he'd arrived at a crime scene only to find the body already bagged and hauled away. And while it was true that he usually couldn't spot anything more than the coroner would, he liked to be present when the body was first moved—just for that one time when he *did* spot something. "Thank you."

The old man nodded and carefully moved to one side of the victim. The kid raised the camera and took a shot. Heaven only knows why, but Cade could hardly berate him when he was trying to do the right thing.

The coroner shifted the victim's arm. Then he rolled the body over, carefully avoiding the flag that had been placed in the soil not too far away from the corpse's thigh. And there, on the victim's back, was another major difference from the original murders.

Because carved into the dead man's flesh were two words: *Remember Rosehall.*

He remembered, all right. How could he not, when his very first case had been his worst? The thing was, the man behind those original murders was dead. He'd seen the body himself. He'd been at the burial and watched the casket being covered with dirt, just in case.

Most of those who'd been on the team at that time believed their felon had worked solo. He never had, but as a green recruit, his suspicions hardly rated much mention in any of the reports—especially since there was absolutely no evidence to back up his theory.

But these murders were almost exactly the same, and the man who'd committed them had been dead for eight years. Which meant his suspicions *must* have been right. There had to have been an accomplice— there was no other way these murders could mirror the first. The full details had never been released, and the trial itself had been closed to the media—not that it would have made huge headlines. Wolves murdering other wolves didn't really rate much of a mention in this human-dominated world.

These murders, however, would be an entirely different story. Vannah had done a good job so far of keeping the news contained.

Cade sat back on his heels and glanced up at her. "Was there anything carved into the first victim's flesh?"

She crossed her arms. He couldn't honestly say whether or not she recognized the importance of the message, because he could read nothing in her expression or her eyes. But she had to understand it. She'd *been* at Rosehall, for God's sake.

"No. It would have been in the report, otherwise."

He nodded, then rose and stepped back so that the kid could get clearer shots of the blood that had seeped from the cuts and stained the soil.

From the clearing below came the roar of an engine.

"That'll be the ambulance," Ronan said. "You want me to bring them up?"

"Yes," he replied curtly.

Ronan's gaze flicked to Vannah, whose nod was almost imperceptible. No guessing where *his* allegiance lay, or who he'd be taking orders from. Then again, Cade had faced that sort of response many times on the reservations. At least the rangers here were more circumspect than most.

He turned, his gaze searching the area. Half a dozen small flags dotted the ground, indicators of possible evidence that Ronan had found. He began a search of his own, but after an hour or so, he had discovered nothing more than what had already been marked.

Despite his earlier aspersions, Vannah's people obviously knew their jobs.

He rose and stretched the kinks out of his back. There wasn't much more he could do here until Trista and Anton showed up with their equipment. The site just needed to be guarded, and any of the rangers were more than capable of that. What he needed was some decent coffee—which seemed to be seriously lacking at the ranger station—and a burger or two.

Though an icy beer wouldn't go amiss, either. As the sun had risen toward noon, the heat and light reflecting off the nearby snow was fierce. He wiped the sweat from his forehead and glanced down to the tree line where Vannah stood talking to Ronan.

And saw Ronan briefly touch her face.

Anger crashed through him, territorial and instinctive. A growl rumbled up his throat, and before he even realized what he was doing, he'd taken several steps toward them. Then he forced himself to stop and take a deep breath. He released it slowly, flexing his fingers as he tried to retain some control.

But he knew, as he stared down at the two of them, that he was in deep, deep trouble.

Because the promise that he and Vannah had made to the moon so long ago—a promise that bound them to each other for the course of one full moon—was obviously still in force. And the sheer ferocity of his response suggested that the moon was not going to let them escape their promises so easily a second time.

Chapter Two

SAVANNAH GLANCED AT her watch and tried to contain her surge of irritation. Pick me up at five, he'd said. We'll discuss any developments on the case while you drive me to my hotel.

Well, it was nearly six, evening had fallen—along with the nightly chill—and he was still a no-show. What was she, his chauffeur? It was bad enough that he and his team had basically banned them from the murder site, but to have one of her own men guarding the main path—and the kid at that—was goddamned infuriating.

She blew out a breath and pushed away from the side of the truck. It was getting too cold to stand there any longer and, besides, the nightfall seemed to have woken an odd sort of restlessness in her. It was almost as if the moon stirred heat through her system. Yet, tonight, the moon would rise as a waxing crescent—about as far away from the full moon and its accompanying wildness as you could possibly get.

But still the restlessness stirred, flicking through her veins like a fire about to ignite.

She suspected the cause. Suspected and feared it,

though she certainly hadn't expected the foolish promise they'd made so long ago to still be in force. But then, the moon never was one to let promises go, and they'd never completed theirs.

However, there was nothing she could do except hope that Cade wasn't feeling the same way—and that he wouldn't enforce a completion.

She walked across to where Ike squatted. His expression was an odd mix of flustered embarrassment and determination. "Boss, I've been ordered to stop you or anyone else from going up the trail."

"Did he tell you to stop anyone from entering the forest from an area well away from the trail?"

Ike's gaze searched hers. Wanting to please her, but not wanting to get on Cade's bad side. "Well, no, but the intent—"

"I'm not talking about intent. And if I don't use the path, you're technically obeying orders, aren't you?"

"I suppose." But his voice was filled with the doubt she could see in his expression.

"You won't get into trouble," she assured him—even if she had to stand in front of him to protect him from the firing squad.

He nodded, accepting her word. She ducked through the trees and began to climb. Now that night had closed in, the shadows were thick and deep under the autumn-clad trees. Leaves crunched beneath her feet—a soft, crisp sound that echoed across the stillness. From up ahead came the soft murmur of voices—Cade's rich tone, entwined with a soft, feminine lilt. One of his officers, at least, was female.

Then another sound stirred the evening—another footstep, one out of sync with her own.

She stopped, every sense alert as she listened to the gentle stirring of the wind. The person ahead had obviously stopped, too, because the only sound she could now hear was the rhythmic rise and fall of the voices ahead. She waited, trusting what she'd heard, knowing she had nothing to lose by simply standing there. After all, that's what she'd be doing down at the truck.

Five minutes passed.

Then, from up ahead and to her right, the steps began again, edging closer to the soft conversation coming from the murder scene. Those steps were too light to be human, meaning it was either a wolf or something else—something with the intelligence or natural cunning of a hunter.

But she was betting on a wolf.

Still, she didn't move. As a member of the golden pack, she was gifted with strong telepathic abilities, and while her abilities were far outstripped by her sister, Savannah had more than enough skill to read the mind of almost anyone she chose to. And though it was a gift she didn't often use—simply because it went against all her ethics—there were times, like this, when it was simply easier to reach out and discover what she was up against before she charged in.

She carefully lowered her shields and reached out telepathically to the person ahead.

Only to be hit so hard by a seemingly unending wall of hate and violence that she staggered backward and let out a small sound of shock and pain. She quickly shored up her defenses, but the hunter must have heard her soft cry of distress since she could hear the soft steps moving away from the murder scene. And toward her.

Still shaking from the force of the other person's hatred, she quickly called to the wolf within. Power rushed through her—an electric feeling that numbed sensation as her body reshaped and re-formed. In those brief few seconds, she was without sight, without hearing, and vulnerable to attack, which is why she'd chosen to change here rather than closer to whoever was up ahead. Better safe than sorry. Then, in her alternate form, she leapt forward, seeking the scents in the air as she ran, pinning down the few that were different, foreign. Musk and mint.

Relief snaked through her. It wasn't the smell of anyone she knew, though why she'd expected to recognize it, she couldn't honestly say.

She dashed through the darkness, following the faint scent trail, chasing the rush of footsteps across the night. The other wolf was fast, but with each step she drew closer.

Then came the sound of a car door slamming and, two seconds later, the roar of an engine. She cursed, but the words came out as a little more than a rumble of anger as she surged forward. The car had sped away long before she came into the small clearing, and all that was left was the settling dust.

Cursing again, she stuck her nose to the ground and hunted around for any scent or clues. There wasn't even a decent tire track to be found. She moved back into the forest to see if she could find a footprint, but the thick cover of autumn leaves made that all but impossible. Annoyed, she turned and headed back for her truck.

The rhythmic murmur of voices was no longer coming from the murder site, meaning Cade and his crew had probably shut down for the night. Meaning *she* was undoubtedly in trouble for not being where she was supposed to.

But hey, if she had been, she might never have discovered the fact they had a watcher.

She shifted shape as she neared the end of the aspens and, in human form, strode into the clearing. Cade was leaning against the side of her truck, his arms crossed and his stance radiating annoyance.

A man very unimpressed with tardiness, Kel had noted. For once in her life, it looked as if Kel had actually understated that fact, because he was certainly more than unimpressed.

"I hope you didn't reprimand Ike. He was only obeying *my* orders," she stated, coming to a halt five steps away, out of immediate arm's length. But she was still within range of his heady, masculine scent, and it twined through her senses as like a caress, causing the wildness within to churn in greater agitation.

"My orders should have countermanded yours." His voice was edgy, rough, as if he were feeling the heat of the moon as much as she. "This is *my* investigation now, *not* yours."

She snorted. "And here I thought we could work as a team."

Something glittered in his eyes—something she couldn't quite catch. Or maybe it was simply the reflection of starlight. "We have several problems on that front."

"Yeah, you think I'm a no-good slut, and I think you're a lying, devious bastard." And right now, she wasn't inclined to tell him *anything*. He'd need to know about their watcher, but now that night had fallen, there was nothing more he or his team could do, and she didn't need to give him another reason to yell at her.

His anger touched the air—a heat thick enough to burn. "True. But I wasn't talking about either of those problems."

She raised an eyebrow. "Then what the hell *were* you talking about?"

He hesitated. "I prefer not to discuss it here."

"Why? Are you scared of the dark?" Taunting him probably wasn't a good idea, but her inner bitch just couldn't let the moment pass. And after all, wasn't he the reason the bitch was born in the first place? She might have been a rebel before she'd left Ripple Creek and headed to Kansas and Rosehall, but she'd been a sweet one. Or so Neva had declared. And if she couldn't trust her twin to give an honest opinion, who could she trust?

"And shouldn't I be?" His gaze ran down the length of her—a slow, sensuous perusal that sent heat flaring across her skin. But when his gaze finally rose to hers again, the dark depths were touched with a bitterness that almost outshone the lust. "After all, I learned the hard way that devils mostly come at night, and the most dangerous of them all is the one who looks like an angel."

"I wasn't the one who went into our relationship lying, Cade, so don't get all high and mighty with *me*."

His expression was contemptuous. "But you learned to lie, didn't you?"

"If I did, it was because I had a damn good teacher."
She crossed her arms, refusing to back down, even
though common sense was screaming to just give up
and forget about it. "All those pretty words, all those
promises made in the dark. All of them lies. But I
guess you're right. I guess I did tell the biggest lie of
all."

His anger lashed at her, as fierce as the gleam in
his dark eyes. Yet that gleam wasn't bitterness now.
It was simply desire, and it burned as savagely as it
ever had, crashing through her like a storm, making
her tremble.

God help her, she wanted him. Wanted him as
fiercely as she had back when she was a stupid teenager doing nothing more than rebelling against the
restrictions of her childhood. And it *wasn't* just the
moon promise. It never had been. Some things, it
seemed, never changed, no matter how much time
and hurt had passed.

"And which of your many lies was the biggest?"
he asked.

That he didn't even remember the words she'd said
just before he'd torn everything apart hurt more than
she thought it would. But then, how stupid was she to
think he even *would* remember? He'd been too intent
on invading her mind to listen to anything she might
have said—but in doing so, he'd left his own defenses
open. In that moment, she'd learned not only who he
was, but the fact she'd been little more than a means
of finding a killer.

"It doesn't really matter now, does it?" It had never
mattered. She shrugged and turned away, suddenly
tired of arguing. No matter how much she might

have dreamed of letting all her frustration, all her anger, loose on him, it didn't feel as cathartic as she'd thought it would now that the dream had become a reality.

All she was really doing was dragging up old hurts, old pain, and it simply wasn't worth the trouble. *He* wasn't worth the trouble.

But she'd only gone three steps when his hand caught hers and spun her around.

"Don't ever walk away from me again when we're in the middle of something!" he said harshly. "Not again."

"We weren't in the middle of something *last* time—we were at an end. And I didn't walk. I ran." From him, and from what he'd done. She pulled her hand from his, her fingers still tingling from the contact. "And I'll do whatever I want. You're not my boss."

Or lover. Or friend. Or anything else important, she thought, spinning on her heel and walking around the back of the truck.

"That's where you're wrong," he said. "Want me to prove it?"

"I don't want anything from you." Her gaze met his over the back of the truck. "Nothing but a quick result, so you can get the hell out of my town."

"There are forces preventing that, despite how much either of us might wish otherwise."

"I don't want excuses. Just get it done, and get out."

"Savannah . . . stop."

His voice was so soft she barely heard it. And yet his words seemed to hang in the air, surrounded by an energy that whisked across her skin and burned into her mind, becoming a compulsion she had no choice but to obey. And even though she fought the order with every ounce of strength she had, her feet stopped and her hand stilled.

She knew why—he was using their pledge of commitment against her. And, of course, the moon, in all her wisdom, generally gave that power to the male of the species rather than the female. There was little she could do other than accept it. But that *didn't* mean she had to like it.

Fury burned through her, momentarily obliterating the desire. "Bastard!"

He gave her a lopsided smile that tugged at her memories and snagged at old hurts. God, how she'd loved that little-boy smile . . .

"I never forced you into that promise, Vannah."

"Savannah," she bit back. "And you're forcing it now, aren't you?"

"Yes."

He walked around the truck, each step so full of effortless grace that he could have been walking on air. Which was what made him a good IIS officer, she reminded herself fiercely. He could sneak up on people all too easily, and just as easily misinterpret what he'd heard.

But he wasn't sneaking now. He was boldly going where few men had dared go before, and there wasn't anything she could do to stop it. Not right now, anyway.

But later, he would pay. Somehow, she'd make sure of it.

In the darkness, his handsome features were shadowed, and his eyes were little more than obsidian stone, though the occasional spark of navy still gleamed. A spark that was so hot. So hungry.

And it echoed through every inch of her, until her whole body felt stretched taut with desire. Part of her wanted to run, to somehow break the bonds of magic and just flee. But that other part, the wild part that had been contained for so long, wanted to stay and savor the delights this man could offer. *Had* offered, in the past. But she had no idea which part would have won, simply because the choice had been snatched from her. And that, more than anything, infuriated her. If she was going to leap into the abyss, she wanted it to be of her own free will.

His gaze swept down her body, lingering on her breasts, making her nipples grow taut. Then his gaze slipped further down, following the curve of her waist, stopping again on her groin, as if he could actually see the heat pooling there. But he didn't really need to see it, because the scent of her arousal hung on the air—an aroma as sweet as the fierce musk of desire emanating from his skin.

His smile, when his gaze finally rose, was that of a predatory wolf who had his prey in his sights. A male who knew that the prey was ready to be brought down and consumed.

"Don't do this," she warned, even as part of her screamed for the warmth of his caress and the heat of his body on her skin.

He stepped closer, until all she could smell was the heady aroma of lust and man. "Do what?" He raised a hand, his fingers brushing her cheek. His touch was a fire that burned through skin and muscle and bone, until it seemed her very soul quivered.

"Don't use force," she somehow said. "Not again. Not in any form."

"I'm not forcing you to respond, Vannah. I never have."

"Savannah," she corrected. But it came out little more than a husky whisper as his face drew closer. Then his lips brushed hers—a kiss so sweet, so full of memories, that tears touched her eyes.

She squeezed them shut, fighting the desire coursing through her limbs. Praying for the sanity to resist his seduction when all she wanted to do was return the tenderness of his touch.

"Using the moon magic *is* force, because you leave me no choice."

"True." His breath brushed her lips as he spoke, sending a warm shiver of anticipation across her skin. "But I can't let you go without seeing if our kiss is as good as I remember."

With that, he wrapped his arms around her, crushing her close as his lips found hers. It was a kiss as wild as she remembered, and as erotic as those that had haunted her dreams. It was also a very unapologetic affirmation of what he wanted. What he intended to do.

With their bodies pressed so close, she couldn't help but be aware of every part of him, from the rapid rise and fall of his chest pressing against her to the heated hardness of his erection. Part of her longed to arch into that hardness, to press it firmly against that part of *her* that throbbed so fiercely. To rub back and forth until the moon's madness took over in a surge of heat and desire.

The saner part—the part that ached from past hurts

rather than desire—was fiercely glad that his compulsion still held her motionless, if only because she couldn't succumb to her baser instincts.

Then he broke their kiss and stepped back with a suddenness that surprised her. But for too many minutes, his gaze bored into hers, his breath a rasp that flowed over her like a fierce summer storm. And though she could have broken their eye contact, she didn't—simply because she needed him to see she was not that silly teenager anymore. That this time she knew him for the bastard he was and would not be fooled by pretty words or the promise of tenderness in his kiss or his touch.

"So, was it?" she said, forcing a note of indifference into her voice.

He frowned. "Was it what?"

"As good as you remembered?"

His smile was almost grim. "Yes. And you can move again now."

Energy tingled across her skin, unlocking the force of his earlier command. Her fingers clenched against the truck's door handle and, for an instant, she debated the pros and cons of punching him. If it weren't for the fact that she loved her job and didn't want to risk it, she might have succumbed.

She flung open the door instead and then stopped, unable to let the moment pass without at least saying something. "If you ever—*ever*—use the moon's power against me like that again, I'll report you to your superiors and make damn sure you're never allowed out on field investigations anymore."

As threats went, it was far better than anything

physical, simply because all he cared about was catching his man. He'd proved that long ago.

He snorted softly. "You think I'd be transferred to a desk simply because of a kiss? Step into the real world, Vannah."

"I am." She climbed into the truck and glanced back at him. "Oh, and by the way, my father is Levon Grant."

The smug, condescending amusement fled his face. Her father might be considered a joke in certain sectors of Ripple Creek, but he had some pretty powerful friends—friends that had spread his puritan views far and wide. Friends who were highly placed in many government departments, including, she believed, the IIS.

And while she might disagree with her father's views, she wasn't above using his contacts if Cade didn't heed the warning.

He didn't say anything, just spun on his heel and walked around to the passenger side of the truck. Once he'd climbed in, she started the engine, turned the truck around, and drove back to Ripple Creek.

The air in the truck was thick with tension and simmering rage—his *and* hers—but, underneath it, desire still burned—and it wasn't *just* the pull of the unfulfilled promise. Which meant, she thought grimly, now that this man had stepped back into her life—no matter for what reason or how briefly—she would be fighting this insane attraction to him at every minute of every day. Despite how little she now trusted him.

It was infuriating. And dangerous. Because the longer she resisted this fire between them, the more risk she stood of succumbing to the moon madness—

a condition that afflicted any wolf who ignored the proximity of his or her moon-sworn partner. With distance, it was survivable. But if the two were close . . . it was literally a case of surrender or lose your mind.

She grimaced. The truth of the matter was, there was only one thing she *could* do. And at least there were only five of the seven days she'd promised him left—surely she could survive that? Especially given that her reaction—or attraction—to Cade was as strong as it ever had been. Dancing with him wasn't going to be a hardship.

But giving in *would*.

And it would undoubtedly dredge up memories and emotions she'd much rather forget, and that would also be a problem.

"What are we going to do?" she said, as the stoplight ahead turned red and she braked.

He glanced at her—something she felt rather than saw. "As I said, we need to talk. Is there somewhere decent to eat?"

"Yeah." Several places, including her old man's diner. But there wasn't a snowflake's chance in hell she was taking him there. Not only because Ari would be all over him like a wolf in heat, but because Neva would be all over her with all sorts of telepathic questions. Right now, she didn't feel up to confronting either woman. "But in case you've forgotten, small towns have big ears, and what is brewing between us is not something I want the world to know."

"Ashamed of me?" he asked dryly.

"No, ashamed of the fact that the stupidity of my past is coming back to haunt me. My body may be clamoring to dance with you, Cade, but I don't have to like it." She met his gaze squarely. "Or you."

His lips twisted bitterly. "I'm no happier about the turn of events than you are, believe me."

"So why did you force the kiss?"

He stared at her for a moment longer, his expression giving little away. "Because," he said eventually, "I had no choice."

"Bullshit. The moon heat isn't *that* strong." Not yet, anyway.

He grimaced. "Not everything I say is a lie."

She bit back another bitchy comment and swung the truck into the ranger station's parking lot. The building was dark—Kel and Ronan were long gone, and it was Bodee's week to handle any night calls. "We can get takeout," she said, as she stopped the truck, "and talk without fear of anyone overhearing."

"Or suspecting," he said, bitterness and anger entwined in his rich voice, "that the head ranger and the head of the IIS investigation team have a bit of moon madness going."

She climbed out of the truck and locked the door. "Precisely."

He followed her to the main doors, the heat of his body an almost tangible force even though several feet separated them. She unlocked the doors and switched on the lights. Then she picked up the phone and dialed the nearby pizza joint. They often delivered to the station, so they wouldn't think there was anything odd about the request, despite the late hour.

He had walked over to the bulletin board, the tension riding his shoulders giving lie to the air of casualness he was attempting to project.

"It'll be ten minutes," she said, after she'd hung up. "The conference room is the second door to the right. You want to wait there while I make coffee and wait for the food?"

"Feel the need for breathing room?"

"Yes," she said bluntly. "It's not every day I have my worst nightmare stepping back into my life."

Amusement glinted briefly in his eyes, and his mouth curved into a bittersweet smile. But he didn't say anything, just shoved his hands into his pockets and sauntered down the hall.

She blew out a breath and got down to the business of making some decent coffee. By the time she'd finished, the delivery kid had arrived. She paid him, adding a good tip, and locked the door behind him. No sense taking the chance of someone walking in—especially since she had no idea what would happen.

She collected the steaming mugs and their dinner and carefully made her way into the conference room. Cade was studying the mug shots of everyone who worked at the station and the brief histories underneath.

"This is an unusual idea," he said, without turning around.

She didn't answer immediately, letting her gaze linger on the tight fit of his shirt across his shoulders and the way his muscles rippled under the soft material. Then she gave herself a mental kick and said, "Yeah, but it's a good way of introducing everyone."

"So every time someone new comes in, he or she hits the wall?"

"Yes." She placed his pizza and coffee in front of

the nearest chair, then retreated to the far end of the table.

"There hasn't been much staff turnover since you took over."

"No." Because they all got on extremely well. "And that's not what we're here to discuss."

"I guess not." He sat, tackling his food with a gusto that suggested he hadn't eaten in a while.

She ate at a slower pace, even though she was no less hungry. But the way tension was riding her body, she'd probably have indigestion if she gulped down her pizza too fast.

When he'd finished, he picked up his coffee and leaned back in his chair. Surprise flickered through his eyes at the taste. "Decent coffee."

"A rare thing in this ranger station if you piss off our admin assistant," she replied, tossing the remnants of her food into the trash. "So are you going to step away from this investigation or not?"

His smile was wolfish. "You'd love me to, wouldn't you?"

"Yes." She returned his look steadily. "And isn't there some sort of protocol that prohibits an IIS officer from being intimately involved with a reservation's rangers during the course of an investigation?"

"It's one of those unwritten rules—and before you ask, there *is* no one else. I am the one most familiar with the past murders, so this case is mine. Whether we like it or not."

And she didn't like it. She definitely didn't like it. She didn't like the way he made her body sing with desire. Or how desperately a part of her wanted to succumb. The sooner she could get rid of him, the better. "So what's the other problem you mentioned?"

He pushed away from the table and rose. "Hart, the third member of my team, called me this afternoon with the results of his own autopsy on the first victim. He found something the medical examiner didn't."

She raised her eyebrows. "What?"

"A sliver of paper inserted into the index finger of the victim's left hand."

"Why would anyone do that?"

"To taunt us." He began to pace back and forth. His steps brought him close to her end of the table, washing the scent of desire across her senses as he turned and retreated. In such a confined space, his energy and masculine aroma were almost overwhelming.

"Hart actually thought it might have been a sliver of wood when he first pulled it out." His gaze caught hers briefly. "Miniature crosses had been inserted into the same finger of the original victims."

"I didn't know that."

"No, I suppose you wouldn't."

She let the maliciousness in his voice slide past. "What did the note say? And did the crosses have anything written on them?"

"No. The crosses were made of silver, and were obviously meant to prevent the shapechange during the blooding ceremony. This note said, 'Vengeance tastes sweeter when the cooking is slow.'"

She raised her eyebrows. "So our lunatic is poetic?"

"Apparently so."

"Jontee wasn't." Although he'd certainly had a way

with words, and a presence that was so sweet—so powerful—it was spellbinding. That he was also a killer wasn't something she'd discovered until close to the end.

His gaze speared her again. She sipped her coffee, trying to retain an air of indifference while the two halves of her soul waged a war inside her. Fuck or fight, to put it crudely.

"Jontee McGuire is dead," Cade said.

"You're sure of that?"

"Yes. I watched them bury him."

"Was there anyone from Rosehall at the funeral? Or anyone from his family?"

"No. I was watching for either."

"Then tell me how *this* murderer is copying *those* murders so precisely?"

He stopped at her end of the table, placing his hands on the wooden surface as he leaned toward her. His scent washed across her. She wouldn't last another five minutes in his presence, let alone a couple of hours. Passion had always been a madness that flared to life between them like a fire about to rage out of control—and, in many ways, just as dangerous. Nothing this fierce, this powerful, could be without consequences—and she really had no intention of letting him stick around until those consequences were revealed.

But until he *did* leave, she had no choice but to face up to the results of her actions so long ago. Still, there was one thing she was sure of. Any dance they might share would be on *her* terms. Not his, and not the moon's.

"You tell *me*." He glared at her for several seconds,

then added, voice curt, "I never entirely believed you when you said that you knew nothing."

"But you never actually *asked* me about what I knew, Cade. You just charged right in and took what you thought you needed." Not that she *had* known much—only what she'd caught in Jontee's thoughts when sleeping with him. And, at the time, she'd thought them to be little more than nightmares. It wasn't until Cade had tried ripping the information from her mind that she'd realized the truth—about Jontee, *and* about Cade.

"I was trying to stop a murderer."

And in the process had destroyed something so very fragile, so very rare. Or so she'd thought at the time. But it seemed that she was the only one who'd thought what was happening between them was worth anything.

"Then I guess you got what you wanted, didn't you?" she taunted.

He stared at her for too many minutes, his gaze so intent, so full of heat and anger, that she felt like a schoolkid under the glare of a stern principal again. And that only fueled her fury. Damn it, she'd done nothing wrong ten years ago. If he could accuse her of anything, it was naïveté.

She pushed away from the table and stood. He straightened as well—and though the table was still between them, he was far too close. But retreat was the one thing she wouldn't do. This was *her* turf, *her* home, and this time she would not give him the upper hand. "I understand why the moon heat will cause problems, but why do you think the murderer leaving notes is such an issue?"

"Don't play obtuse, Vannah. You know as well as I do that they're personal messages, aimed at the two people who were at Rosehall."

She raised an eyebrow. "There were lots of us at Rosehall. It was a commune, for God's sake."

"But not everyone there believed in free sex. Some had a taste for blood."

"Only one," she corrected. "And stop using that condescending tone. If I remember correctly, you were more than ready to partake of the free sex."

"I still am," he said, reaching for her.

She stepped back and punched his hand away. "This murderer *can't* be going after people who were at Rosehall. There were no humans at Rosehall."

He flexed his fingers as if her punch had hurt him, which she hadn't intended to do. "What if these murders are merely a means of drawing together the two people responsible for bringing Rosehall down?"

"I never—"

"By association, yeah, you did. You announced the moon promise, remember? Given what I was there to do, it would be easy enough to assume that you were aware of my actions, and even working for me."

"I was young and stupid, but not everyone else there was. And that's a rather large logical leap."

He snorted softly. "How logical was it for a half-breed wolf to be murdering other half-breeds because their blood was unclean?"

Not very. She finished her coffee and put the mug back on the table. "So I guess we *should* be extra cautious until we understand the motive for these murders."

He nodded. "Do you live alone?"

"Yes, and you are not spending the night with me." That would suggest an intimacy that went beyond just sex, and she wasn't willing to go that far. Not with him.

He gave her that bittersweet smile again, and it made her ineffably sad. "Once you would have begged me to stay."

"As I said, I was young and stupid." She hesitated, but she knew she had to lay down some ground rules before this fire between them got completely out of hand. "We may not be able to master these feelings, but I do have some conditions."

"Conditions?" He made a contemptuous sound. "How can you put restrictions on something neither of us has any control over?"

"Because I'd rather succumb to moon madness than ever put myself at your mercy again."

"It wasn't that bad, Vannah . . ."

"Savannah," she amended angrily. "And yes, it was."

He stared at her for a moment. Then he spun on his heel and returned to his pacing. "So what are your conditions?"

"No one knows about us. If we mate, we do so late at night and where no one can see us."

His nod was short and sharp, and as angry as his steps.

"Second, do not touch me in any way, sexual or not, during the day."

He gave her a savage glance. "We do what you must to assuage the moon, but nothing more?"

"Exactly."

He came to a halt at her end of the table, pressing his palms against the wood and leaning forward again. "I'll agree to your two conditions if you agree to two of mine."

She raised her chin. "What?"

"First, we dance tonight."

She supposed it was inevitable. If the lust that burned between them was this bad just past the new moon, what would it be like as each passing day brought them closer and closer to the full moon? Neither of them would be able to function, let alone catch this killer. But as much as she wanted him, she also *didn't* want him. She didn't want to lose herself in his arms when it was nothing more than the heat of the moon's promise driving them together.

"What else?"

His sudden grin was all territorial, and all wild wolf. "*This* time, you'll lie with no other for as long as I'm here, or I'll report you and Ronan to your prudish little council. Then I'll stand back and watch the fireworks."

Chapter Three

THOUGH CADE HAD expected an immediate and fiery response to his admittedly outrageous demands, she didn't say anything. She just stared at him with those coldly luminous green eyes of hers, making him feel like pond scum that wasn't even worth scraping off her shoe.

Which is what he figured her opinion was right now.

It shouldn't have mattered. He wanted her, she wanted him, and the promise they'd so stupidly made ensured the outcome would be gratifying for them both. What she thought about him, or what he thought about her, shouldn't enter into the equation.

Yet, for some reason, her opinion *did* matter.

Maybe exhaustion had addled his brain. Or perhaps the sun and the heat reflecting off the snow this afternoon had burned away a brain cell or two. Why else would he care about the opinion of a lying, cheating snippet of a wolf who had almost succeeded in not only getting him killed, but also letting a murderer go free?

"How did you know about Ronan and me?"

Her words, low and somehow sexy, sent lust surging through his veins. He fought the urge to reach for her and merely said, "I'm trained to read body language, remember?"

And right now, hers was practically screaming with the desire to belt him.

She nodded and crossed her arms. "Then I agree to your terms."

Exaltation ran through him. She was his. *Again.* "Where do you plan for us to . . . meet?"

She considered for a moment, then said, "I recently bought an old lodge as a long-term renovation project. It's called White Peaks, and it's out on Meadows Road, which is at the western edge of the reservation. My nearest neighbors don't arrive until ski season opens, so we should remain undiscovered."

His mouth twisted. "So you were serious about not inviting me to your home?"

Contempt flashed across her features. "Absolutely."

That was a shame. While he might never trust her again, he certainly wouldn't have minded uncovering more about the woman who'd once had him so hooked he couldn't even think straight. He glanced at his watch. "Shall we say midnight?"

She hesitated, then nodded once. "Is there anything else we need to discuss?"

"Other than the need to be extremely cautious, not at the moment."

"When will the second autopsy be in?"

"Sometime tomorrow."

"So you want to go back to the hotel now?"

"Yes. Thank you."

She gave him a look that could have frozen boiling

water and led the way out the door. The short journey to the hotel was so tense the air practically crackled.

She stopped in front of his assigned quarters in what looked like the less than luxurious end of town. He glanced at her, but she wasn't looking at him, just staring straight ahead with deliberate determination. Yet the tension riding her shoulders suggested she was aware of his every move.

Just as he was endlessly aware of hers.

He opened the door. The night air swept in, bitingly cold. Yet it did little to cool the warmth flooding his skin.

"One thing," she said, before he could move.

"What?"

"There was a watcher in the forest." She glanced at him, her cool green eyes seeming to glimmer in the truck's shadowed darkness. "That's why I went in— I thought I heard something. Unfortunately, she or he heard me and fled."

Anger surged. "Why didn't you mention this earlier?"

"What was the point? It was pitch black, and there were no tracks to be found."

"Says you," he retorted. "You'll take me there tomorrow. Clear?"

"Fine," she said, pulling her gaze from his. But not before he'd seen the stain of anger in her cheeks.

He climbed out of the truck and had barely slammed the door closed when she took off, tires squealing and pelting him with a rain of gravel.

"Bitch," he muttered, yet he couldn't help smiling. She'd always been spirited. In fact, that was what had first attracted him to her. That, and her glorious golden hair.

He spun on his heel and headed for the room Trista and Anton were sharing. Both were sitting on the carpeted floor. Anton was staring at the laptop while Trista was looking through the old case files Cade had brought along.

"You're right," she said, her pale caramel eyes warmed by the fire burning in the hearth. "There's very little difference between the past murders and these."

He reached for the autopsy report Hart had faxed over. "Except for the fact these victims are human, and have notes carved into their backs."

"Not to mention the fact it appears someone is drinking the blood."

"Yes. Last time the victims were simply bled out." And the cavern had reeked with the scent—it had taken weeks to clear the stench from his nose.

"It's unusual for a wolf to like the taste of human blood," Anton mused without looking up from the screen.

"Jontee McGuire wasn't a full wolf, but a half-breed." Cade quickly scanned the autopsy report, but other than the note inserted in the left index finger, Hart had found nothing new.

Trista frowned and pushed her fingers through her short brown hair. "Wolves don't often mate with humans."

"In this case, the half-breeds' mothers were drugged and raped by human males on a dare."

She grimaced. "There was a rash of such attacks about thirty years ago. Psychologists reckoned it was some sort of stupid coming-of-age thing. You know, take the werewolf and prove you're a man." She snorted. "Like drugging a victim is the act of a *real* man. I tell you, there's something to be said for keeping humans out of the reservations."

"Many of the smaller reservations survive on tourist income," Anton commented, brown eyes flat with annoyance as he looked up. "Without it, they'd be in real trouble."

"I know, but—"

"Let's not get into *that* argument again," Cade said, knowing from past experience that the two of them could debate the subject for hours. And the fact that Trista came from one of the biggest reservations—and one of the two threatened by the encroaching human population—while Anton came from a small, barely surviving reservation, only inflamed the situation. Cade threw the report back onto the table and paced the small room. "What are your thoughts on the lap marks?"

"Either our copycat wasn't aware of the procedure in the first murders," Anton said, "or he likes the taste of warm blood fresh from the body."

"Why are you both so convinced it's a copycat?" Trista asked. "So okay, Jontee is dead, but didn't he have twelve mistresses?"

" 'True believers,' he preferred to call them," Cade said. "There were four wives and eight mistresses, all of whom he shared with the enlightened." And one of those mistresses had been Vannah—which was the other reason Cade had targeted her. That and the fact that he'd wanted her from the moment his boss had dropped twelve photographs on the desk and told him to pick one.

"Couldn't it be one of them, then?" Trista asked.

"Two wives and six mistresses took lie detector tests, as well as being read by psychics either before or after we'd caught Jontee. None of them knew anything about the murders."

"What about the other four?" Anton picked up a folder and flicked over several pages. "Nelle James, Fee Mays, Vannah Harvey, and Joanna Noles. Did you manage to track them down as well?"

Cade stopped near the window, studying the darkness. "No. We had Jontee, and since the evidence we found confirmed that he *was* the killer, we called off the search." Though *he'd* kept looking for Nelle. And Vannah.

Outside, the sliver of the moon was rising, riding low in the clear night sky. The heat of it seared through him, and his body ached with desire. He wanted Vannah—wanted to hold her, caress her, and lose himself deep in the hot, wet warmth of her body. Wanted it *now,* not in a few hours. He scrubbed a hand across his rough jaw. He couldn't stay in this room. He had to get out, had to walk, before the fever became too obvious.

"You want me to run a check on them all now? See if I can find anything new?" Anton asked.

"Vannah Harvey was my entry into the commune and knew nothing." Which wasn't exactly true. She'd known enough to give him Jontee. Known enough to almost get him killed. "And I've already checked the others—there's no record of any of them after they disappeared that night."

Which wasn't really that much of a surprise. Half the people living in the commune weren't using their real names. Like Vannah, for instance. And that was the reason he'd never been able to find her, no matter how hard he'd tried.

"Was everyone at the commune either wolves or half-breeds?" Trista asked.

"Yes," he said, spinning away from the moon and the night to resume his pacing.

Trista arched a brow. "Interesting."

He glanced at her. "Why?"

"Because if Jontee was killing in revenge for his mother's rape, why was he killing other half-breeds? Why not go after the humans behind such acts?"

"You've read the reports."

She grimaced. "'As an offering of peace and restoration to the Goddess herself.' That doesn't exactly make sense."

"It did to Jontee. He believed half-breeds were tainted, and that by spilling their blood into the soil, he was cleansing their souls for future lives."

She snorted. "So why not off himself?"

"Because he was the tool of the Goddess, and therefore immune from the taint."

"Well, he was certainly a *tool*." She studied him for a moment, her pale eyes knowing. "So what's our next move?"

"Tomorrow you can grab one of the rangers and start visiting all the hotels, motels, etcetera, to collect the names of anyone who has checked in during the last two weeks."

"Why new?" Anton asked. "There's nothing to indicate this isn't being done by a local."

No, but if a local had been at the commune, then surely Vannah would have mentioned it. After all, that person would be the obvious starting point.

"It's easier to eliminate visitors first." He glanced back at Trista. "Ronan would probably be a good choice as a guide. He seems to be a bit more personable than the kid."

And knowing Trista's more-than-predatory ways, the handsome Ronan would soon be less of a problem for him. Or rather, for his access to Vannah.

While bedding reservation rangers might go against the unwritten code of conduct, he'd turned a blind eye to it in the past and he'd certainly do so now. Especially if it got him what he wanted—time alone with the one person he'd never been able to shake from his thoughts, no matter how hard he'd tried.

Trista nodded. "Since it's almost cross-country ski season, we could end up with quite a few names to cross-check."

"Then draft the kid as well." Cade looked at Anton. "You can run the fingerprints we found at the murder site through the system. Tomorrow, I'll run back to the site with our head ranger. Apparently we had a watcher this evening. She gave chase, but lost him."

"Then we could be right in thinking that this is all a setup to get you here."

"Probably." Vannah was here, after all, and now so was he.

"If that's the case, it might be better if you step down—"

He cut Trista off with a curt, "I'm not going anywhere."

"That's not—"

"I know. But if the bastard behind these murders is after me, then they're welcome to give it a try."

"The IIS doesn't approve of its agents acting as bait," Anton said dryly. "It's considered a waste of good training when they get killed."

Cade grinned. "I have no intention of getting killed." Especially when sex was in the air. "I'm off to scout the town and see if I can hear any gossip in the bars. Call if Hart sends the second autopsy report in."

Anton reached for his briefcase, grabbing something, and tossed it to Cade. "Emergency tracer," Anton said, as Cade caught it. "If you get into trouble, press it and we'll come running."

Cade turned the button-sized bit of technology over in his palm. It had a small loop at one end so that it could be threaded through a chain. He could wear it without being obvious. "What's the range?"

"Ten miles."

"Even in the mountains?"

Anton nodded.

"Amazing."

"It could be more than amazing. It could be lifesaving," Anton said, voice still dry. "So make sure you have it with you at all times. Even in the shower."

"It's waterproof?"

"And shockproof."

"Good." He undid the gold chain from his neck and threaded the tracer on to it. "Call me if anything happens."

Anton nodded.

Then Cade spun around and headed into the moonlit night.

* * *

SAVANNAH PUSHED OPEN the diner door. Warmth rushed out at her, followed quickly by the familiar scents of homemade bread and the richness of fried onion. Her dad might have some crazy ideas about what was and wasn't proper for young wolves, but he sure could cook a mean burger—and the best darned bread she'd tasted anywhere.

The place was packed, as usual. Ari, the head waitress, flitted between her tables, her spiky golden hair glowing in the warm ambience of the diner's interior. More than one customer followed her movements with longing, and Savannah smiled. Though Levon kept warning Ari about flirting with the customers, there was no doubt that they enjoyed it—or that it was good for business.

Her gaze scanned the rest of the room, coming to rest on the well-rounded figure at the far end of the room. Neva straightened, a smile touching her lips as her gaze met Savannah's.

Hey, welcome to the madhouse, Sis.

Thanks. Aren't you supposed to be resting?

I was, but Jacci called in sick.

Does Duncan know?

Neva's amusement bubbled through Savannah's mind. *He's helping Dad cook burgers.*

Will wonders never cease. She'd never expected that Levon would reach even grudging acceptance of her sister's soul mate after only a year. *You got a spare table, or do I retreat to the kitchen?*

Dad will rope you in to help if you do, and it doesn't feel like you're up to that. Come down here.

Savannah wound her way through the tables, smiling so many hellos that her cheeks began to ache. Half the town seemed to be in the diner tonight. While some small part of her wanted to retreat, mostly she wanted to wrap herself in familiar surroundings and the warmth of family in an effort to ward off the chill of Cade's return.

Neva was resetting a small table at the far end of the counter. Savannah kissed her sister's cheek, then bent and did the same to her bulging belly.

"How are the brats treating you?" She placed her hands gently to either side of Neva's tummy and smiled when she felt the responding kicks.

Neva grinned. "I've decided they are going to be athletes, because they don't ever seem to stop moving."

"It's their father's fault. The Sinclairs have a reputation for being extremely active."

Her twin's green eyes sparkled. "You don't have to tell me. How do you think I got pregnant in the first place?"

"Well, that's what happens when he goes off the fertility control shots and the two of you go at it like rabbits."

"Neither of us actually expected his fertility would kick in this quickly. It usually takes at least a couple of months for a male's sperm count to come back to normal." Neva's smile certainly didn't suggest she minded—quite the opposite, in fact. "You want the usual?"

"Just coffee and some banana-nut bread tonight. Thanks, Sis."

Neva nodded and waddled toward the kitchen.

Savannah reached for the newspaper sitting on the counter and got down to the business of catching up on the local news. Ten minutes later, Neva was back with her order, complete with an extra cup for herself.

"So," she said, stretching out her legs and wriggling her feet with a sigh of relief as she sat. "What's up?"

Savannah smiled. She should have known she couldn't come in here seeking a moment of serenity without her twin sensing something was wrong. She picked up a slice of the rich-smelling bread and munched on it as she figured out how best to phrase her question.

"Did you ever regret making that first promise to the moon?"

Neva frowned. "How could I when I did it to save you?"

"But if you had to do it all again . . . would you?"

"Yes. Because, at the time, it was my only option." Neva paused, speculation growing in her eyes. "This is about a promise you made, isn't it? That old history you once mentioned but wouldn't explain."

Savannah nodded. "Let's just say it's come back to bite me."

Neva's concern flicked through Savannah's mind. "And you'd rather avoid being bitten again?"

She sighed. "I'm not sure what I want—and that's half the problem." God, they hadn't even made love yet, and her thoughts were all but consumed by him. She couldn't afford that, not a second time. And certainly not with a murderer running loose.

Neva reached across the table and wrapped her hand around Savannah's. "Do you like him?"

"I did once."

"And are you still attracted to him?"

A smile touched her lips as she remembered the heat of his kiss, and the way she'd ached to arch into him. "Yes."

"And are you going to dance with him?"

"Yes. But only because I have no real choice."

"Why not?"

Promises made.

Ah. Neva lightly squeezed Savannah's hand. *You want me to touch his thoughts and blast away any memory of the promise?*

No, because this is an unfulfilled moon promise.

Well, shit.

Exactly.

Neva leaned back in her chair and rubbed her belly with her free hand. *I'm here if you need me, Sav. Anytime, night or day. Just call me.*

She knew that, but hearing it said was comforting. Most people considered her the stronger of the two, but that had never really been the case. Neva had shown more gumption and courage in the last year than Savannah had ever shown in her entire life. Walking into the Sinclair mansion during the moon dance, tying herself to the wildest of the Sinclair brothers, and finally, inevitably, rejecting their father's demands—that took nerve *and* strength. Hell, when Savannah had rebelled, all she'd done was leave town. And while she may have joined a left-of-center commune and done things that would have given her old man a heart attack, in the grand scheme of things they didn't really count, because no one here knew about them. And while she'd forced the final confrontation between her sister and her parents so that Neva could claim the man she loved without fear of parental backlash, she had no such courage when it came to her own life. Nor when it came to Cade and the history between them.

There's no shame in being scared of confronting your past, Sav.

I'm a ranger, she said, mind-voice dry. *We're supposed to be able to control our fears.*

But you're also a woman. So why not just enjoy the sex and to hell with the rest? If worse comes to worst, pretend he's Ronan or something.

Savannah almost choked on her bread, and Neva grinned mischievously. *Did you really think you'd be able to keep a secret like that from me?*

No one else knows, do they?

Hell, no. This town runs on gossip. If anyone knew, it'd be public knowledge in an instant.

That was all too true—which made the fact they'd kept a lid on the murders all the more amazing. Even Matt had kept his mouth shut—a miracle in itself.

Neva glanced back at the crowded diner and sighed. "I guess I'd better start helping again." She hesitated. "You're seeing him tonight, I gather?"

Savannah nodded.

"Then come for breakfast tomorrow morning, and tell me all about it. And remember . . . it's what *you* want that's important. Not the past, and not him. And remember, too, that while you may be forced into the dance, you can probably control the way events unfold."

"Oh, I've already laid down the ground rules."

Neva grinned and squeezed Savannah's hand again. "That's my girl." She quickly finished the rest of her coffee and pushed to her feet with a groan. "No one told me pregnancy was a backbreaker."

As she waddled away, Savannah sipped her coffee and considered her sister's advice. As usual, Neva was right. To get through this, she not only had to keep to the ground rules she'd already set, but she also had to keep it just about the sex. Hard, fast, long, or slow, it didn't matter, as long as it remained detached. All about physical sensation, and not about feelings or emotions.

He'd done it the first time—and he'd done it so well that she'd thought it *had* been real. Until the last night. Until he'd shown his true colors with that one, unforgivable act.

But then, those events—both her foolishness with Cade, and not seeing what Jontee truly was—had, in many ways, led to her becoming a ranger. So, in some ways, she owed a debt of thanks to the past. She loved what she did, and she probably wouldn't have thought to become a ranger if not for those events.

A bell chimed as the diner door opened, and she looked up to see Ronan walk in. Though he didn't often eat here, she wasn't entirely surprised that he'd come tonight. She'd been avoiding him for most of the day, but it was inevitable he would catch up with her.

Thanks to the aftermath of the dreams he'd witnessed so often, he knew a little about Rosehall. He would have recognized the intent behind the words carved into the victim's back—and he knew those words had been aimed at her.

She picked up her coffee, meeting his gaze squarely and watching him move through the tables. Ari caught him halfway, flirting more outrageously than she usually did. Ari had had the hots for Ronan, and had for as long as Savannah could remember. As far as she knew, he'd never returned the interest—but maybe that was *her* fault. After all, Ronan had been hurt by the past as much as she had, and she was just as much a crutch for him emotionally as he was to her.

He dragged out a chair and sat down opposite her. "So," he said simply. "Explain."

She did—briefly.

"And Cade?" he asked.

"Became sexually involved with me to get close to Jontee and stop him."

"So you were one of Jontee's lovers?"

"I was Sunday and Wednesday." Though she hated the fact that she'd been involved with a killer, she couldn't actually regret the rest of her Rosehall experience. If nothing else, it had been a wild, amazing ride. "Cade was under the impression that, as one of Jontee's lovers, I had to know something about the murders. I didn't." Not through firsthand knowledge, anyway. No one had. Jontee had kept the dark intent of the commune well and truly hidden from *everyone*—something she'd told Cade over and over, but he'd never believed her. Never trusted her.

"And the murders here?"

"The MOs seem to indicate that someone didn't take too kindly to Cade's part in bringing Rosehall down."

"And what of your part in it?"

"I didn't *have* a part in it, but someone obviously thinks I did."

He studied her for a minute, his expression caring and his gray eyes concerned. "And Cade? What does his presence here mean?"

She knew he meant on a personal level rather than a professional one, so she sucked in a breath and blew it out slowly. "We made a promise to the moon at Rosehall. Apparently, because we never actually fulfilled that promise, the power of it still holds." Her gaze caught his over the rim of her cup. "For the next five nights."

He gave her a sweet half-smile. "I figured something was going on between you two." He reached across the table and lightly pressed his fingertips against her hand. A brief but tender touch—all they dared here in public. "He hurt you once. Don't let him do it again."

She smiled, wishing she could lean across the table and kiss him. Wishing she was free to love him as he deserved to be loved.

Then he leaned back in the chair, creating space between them once again for the sake of those who were undoubtedly watching. "If this madman is planning to come after you, you may need protection."

"What I need is to catch this person before he can kill again."

He nodded. "Still, I'll start looking at security precautions for your apartment, just in case."

"Fine." He'd do it anyway, even if she told him not to.

He rose. "You know my number if you need me."

She nodded, watching him walk out the door. Why couldn't fate allow her to fall for someone like Ronan? Someone who had more caring and tenderness in his little finger than Cade had in his entire body? It wasn't fair. But then, who said life had to be fair?

She glanced at her watch and grimaced. Time to go meet the man she couldn't quite hate, as much as she might want to.

THERE WERE TWO bars in Ripple Creek, and Cade was surprised to discover that neither was buzzing with news of the murders. Somehow, the rangers had kept a lid on it, even though towns like this usually thrived on gossip.

He finished his beer, taking his time as his gaze scanned the semi-crowded room, his foot tapping to the thumping beat of music. Everyone here in the Blue Nights seemed to be after nothing more than a good time, either chatting in large groups or squeezing onto the already crowded dance floor. Besides himself, there didn't appear to be any loners, or even anyone his cop senses would have labeled as suspicious. But then, in all his years as an IIS officer, he'd never had a suspect who actually looked suspicious. They'd always been average Joes, or family men. Someone who didn't beg more than a cursory glance.

Someone like Jontee.

Whether the same pattern would apply here in Ripple Creek was anyone's guess, but he suspected the murderer would be as hard to catch as any other. But, in some ways, he couldn't be sorry about that. Sure, he wanted this case solved before anyone else got killed, but he was more than willing to draw out his time with Vannah. They'd always been sexually compatible—and he had the five nights of the moon promise she still owed him.

He placed his empty glass on the table and rose, nodding good night to the bartender as he strolled outside.

Under the cold light of the barely visible moon, the heat in his veins seemed to sharpen until his whole body ached with the fierceness of desire. He glanced at his watch and cursed softly when he saw it was only eleven. He was tempted to call her and demand that they move up their meeting. He *could* do it. The moon gave the male that power.

But he'd made her a promise not to use the moon magic again—and until it suited him to do otherwise, he intended to keep that promise.

He turned right, heading for Meadows Road, even though he still had an hour to kill. If she was feeling the moon anywhere near as strongly as he, she'd be there already, waiting. And arriving early would give him more time to enjoy her luscious body.

He shoved his hands into his pockets as he strolled down Main Street. Ripple Creek, unlike many of the reservations, hadn't moved with the times, and still retained much of its old-fashioned architecture. And, if what he'd heard about the council was true, they'd also kept many of the old-school ideals when it came to sex. Which was odd, considering a Sinclair pack lived on the reservation—and the Sinclairs had a wild, hedonistic reputation that he knew was thoroughly deserved.

Which, in turn, probably explained Levon Grant's popularity. Licentious behavior often existed hand in hand with old-fashioned conservatism.

It was hard to imagine Vannah being Grant's daughter, though—especially since she'd been one of Jontee McGuire's mistresses. In fact, her main duty at the commune had been to welcome newcomers and introduce them to the sexual ways of Rosehall. There'd been over one hundred people at that commune, and even though she'd apparently arrived there almost a year after the commune had been set up, that was still a lot of welcomes. Still a lot of men.

He supposed that, by Sinclair standards, it was pretty tame. He'd put a stop to it pretty quickly once they were an item, but he'd never been able to stop her from going to Jontee. And despite the fact that her relationship with Jontee was the only reason he'd been there—to read her thoughts and, through her, Jontee's—sharing her had always eaten at him.

But there was no sharing this time. She was his— only his—and would remain so as long as he was in Ripple Creek. As he turned onto Meadows Road and made his way up the steep incline, it began to snow, and there was something almost magical about the soft flakes falling in the deep silence of the night. He walked past a music auditorium that looked more like a series of conjoined tents, and then he passed several large concrete structures that claimed to be the Ripple Creek School of Music. Then the trees began to crowd closer as the buildings and houses gave way to parkland. The road narrowed. And, without streetlights, the shadows grew thick. With his breath steaming in the night air, and the soft gurgle of water coming from his left, it was easy to imagine he was in an untouched wilderness rather than the outskirts of a thriving town. He passed several small roadside mailboxes that gave lie to that impression, and finally came to one that said White Peaks.

He stopped, looking up the steep driveway. No lights beckoned ahead, and there was no hint of exotic fruit or flowers warming the air. She hadn't passed this way yet. Annoyance, tinged with a disappointment, swept through him. Still, there was no point going back to town. She'd be here soon enough.

He walked up the sharp incline. By the time he'd reached the top, his legs ached. He stopped, sucking in air as he scanned the run-down building. He'd been expecting a small house, but this was, in fact, an old ski lodge, probably capable of holding up to thirty couples. It was shaped like a flat-bottomed V, with the flat, front section the main office and the sides the accommodations. There was nothing pretty about it. Half the windows were smashed, the roof in the right wing had partially collapsed, and one side of the steps leading up to the main doors had fallen away.

Then he caught soft flickers of orange light reflecting through the cracked front windows, and anticipation surged. Because those flickers were flames. From a fireplace.

She *was* here.

He strode toward the main door, avoiding the snow-covered steps and leaping directly onto the covered patio. His footsteps echoed across the stillness and, as he opened the door, a bell chimed softly.

The front room was small, holding a reception desk on the right side and a curved staircase that led up to the first floor landing on the other. Straight ahead, through an open set of doors, was a huge communal room filled with sheet-covered sofas and chairs. At the end of the room was the fire he'd seen. And the fireplace was huge, dominating half the back wall.

The scent of dust and age teased his nostrils, but underneath it was the erotic aroma of woman. *His* woman.

She wasn't in the immediate area, though. Her scent would have been far stronger if she were.

"Vannah?" His voice seemed to hang in the quiet, a note of fierce longing and desire.

"If you want me, you have to find me." Her voice had a tinny quality, yet it still contained a heated promise that sent his pulse racing. He looked over his shoulder and saw the small two-way radio sitting on the window frame.

He picked the unit up and pressed the button. "And what do I get when I do?"

"As long as you're naked, whatever you want."

His pulse surged. He wanted her now, not in ten minutes. Not in two minutes. *Now.*

"Why the games, Vannah?"

"Why not? Don't expect things to go easy, Cade, just because I once was."

There wasn't much he could say to that, simply because it was the truth. "When I find you, I intend to take you." A floorboard squeaked and he glanced at the first-floor landing. She was moving. "Be ready for me."

"The moon makes me ready." Her voice was little more than a low, taunting murmur. "And if you don't hurry, I'll tend to my own needs." She paused, then added, "Or find someone else to ease the ache."

"You promised—"

"And we both know how much esteem you place on promises, so you might want to hurry."

Anger swept through him—the rage of a wolf whose turf is being threatened. "You are mine, Vannah. And I'm coming to claim what I own."

"You don't own me. You never have."

You never will. The unsaid words seemed to form in the shadows, as powerful as the attraction that had always existed between them. But she was wrong. He *did* own her—at least for the next five nights. He kicked off his boots and socks, then padded barefoot up the stairs. At the top he stopped, tasting the air, searching for the rich headiness of her scent. He'd expected her to be on the left, simply because that way was safer. But as ever, she did the unexpected. Her scent was coming from the right.

He followed the darkened hallway, passing closed doorways without bothering to stop and check them. She wasn't there. He'd feel her, smell her, if she was. The air got colder, the smell of dust and age gradually replaced by the crispness of the night. Ragged glimpses of sky appeared above him and he slowed, knowing he was coming to the most unstable section. In the middle of the hall, highlighted by starlight, was a pale mauve bra.

Lust surged through him—an ache so fierce he thought he was going to explode. God, anyone would think he'd been celibate for the last ten years. But in some ways, he supposed he had been. Certainly, sex had never achieved the same intensity since Vannah left.

He bent, grasping the bra and raising it to his nose. The silky material was still warm from the heat of her body, and rich with the luscious scent of her. He breathed in deeply, filling his lungs with her fragrance. It affected him in ways he couldn't even begin to describe, and it wasn't just her scent. It was her.

He shoved the wisp of material in his pocket and pushed open the nearby door. It was a stairwell, leading down. He followed it and opened the door at the bottom.

"You're not naked, wolf," she said through the two-way. "I'm guessing you're not as eager as you claim."

"You can see me?"

"Obviously."

"Then judge the state of my desire for yourself."

His clothes hit the stained carpet in rapid succession. His erection slapped his belly, pulsing with heat and desire.

He glanced at the ceiling, but he couldn't see any mirrors or cameras. She had to be close.

"I think," she said, her voice a low purr touched with amusement, "that you'd better hurry. You look ready to explode."

He glanced right, seeing nothing but shadowed furniture, and went left instead. Air stirred past his nostrils, tickling his senses with lush femininity. He grinned in anticipation. She was close. Very close.

The hall was dark, but many of the rooms were open, allowing a whisper of moonlight to filter in. The ceiling was lined with cracks, probably caused by the roof's collapse onto the floor above, but he had no doubt it was safe, if only because she was here, too.

His gaze fell on another wisp of material sitting in the doorway ahead, and the heat in his loins became a fiery ache. He picked up the panties and raised them to his nose, drawing in the rich scent of her desire.

It only increased his own, and he hadn't thought that was possible.

The room beyond was empty, holding only dust and cobwebs. But there was an interconnecting door midway down the left wall, and it was open. The darkness beyond was lit by a soft golden light that flickered and gleamed like a jarful of fireflies.

He strode forward. The room he entered was small, and heated by a fire burning in the hearth at the far end. There was no furniture other than a large sofa, and Vannah leaned against its back. She was motionless, her arms crossed over her breasts, her honey-colored skin caressed by the flames until she seemed like a glorious golden statue. He forced himself to stop and drink in the sight of her, even though every inch of him quivered with the need to lose himself in all that rich, golden warmth.

She was much more lovely than he remembered.

"So," she said, a mocking glint in her green eyes, "you've found your prize. Do you intend to claim it, or are you just going to stand there?"

A low rumble of annoyance rose up his throat. In response, a cool smile touched her lips, and she turned her back. Another deliberate taunt that only fueled the fire.

While some part of him recognized and acknowledged what she was doing, he was more than willing to play along. After all, he was here for the sex—and that's exactly what she was offering. Nothing more, and nothing less.

He slid his arms around her waist, pulling her warm,

naked flesh back against him. Her butt rested against his erection, teasing him. He pressed forward a little, so that her cheeks wrapped around him, encasing him in warmth, tormenting him with possibilities he felt no temptation to explore. Not when heaven itself lay so close.

A quiver that was all desire ran through him. He brushed a kiss across one bare shoulder, running his tongue over her skin, tasting the familiar, tangy richness that was all Vannah.

"How do you want me?" he whispered, and lightly nipped her ear.

A matching shudder ran through her, and the tempo of her breathing became ragged. "Hard. Fast."

He was rigid against her, aching for release, but he fought the need pounding through his veins, wanting to prove to her that while it might be fast and furious between them, it was never going to be without passion.

"How fast?"

"Very fast." Her voice was little more than a gasp.

"Good." Because fast was really the only option this first time—she'd made very sure of that.

He pressed her forward over the back of the sofa and gently kicked her feet apart. As she braced herself, he slid a hand over her rear, enjoying the feel of her silky skin under his rougher fingertips. Then he was delving into the warm, wet part of her that he ached to enter. He caressed her for several minutes, then slid first one finger, then two, into that hot wetness—stretching her, readying her. She pushed back against him, riding his hand with increasing urgency as her muscles pulsed around him. Her skin was feverish, flushed with desire, and the smell of her arousal tested his strength, his will, until he was all but shaking with his need.

He pressed his thumb against her clit—stroking her, teasing her inside and out, until her breathing was little more than gasps of pleasure. As the tremors of her orgasm began, he grabbed her hips, holding her still as he thrust deep inside her. She groaned— a rich sound of gratification he could only echo. But as much as he wanted to, he didn't move, just enjoyed the moment of being deep within her, her flesh pulsing around his, her scent filling his every breath.

Then the urgency of the moon bloomed, and he began to rock, gently at first, then harder, faster. He claimed every inch of her, delving so deep her whole body shuddered with the force of his movements.

She was moaning, twitching, and the sounds of her pleasure had the red tide rising until it became a wall of desire he could not deny. He came—a hot, torrential release whose force tore a groan from his throat.

But the moon and he weren't finished yet. Not by a long shot. When he regained his breath, he withdrew and tugged her around to face him. Her eyes were aflame with a mix of hunger and annoyance, though what she was annoyed about he had no idea. But before she could say anything, he claimed her lips. He kissed her, caressed her, licked every inch of her, until her scent and her taste were once more imprinted on every fiber of his being.

He made love to her, over and over, until the long hours of the night began to fade into the dawn of a new day.

Then he left her—but only because she demanded it.

Chapter Four

SAVANNAH WOKE TO the shrill, annoying sound of ringing. She muttered an obscenity and hugged her pillow over her ears, willing the noise away so she could sleep.

But it didn't stop. She tossed the pillow aside in frustration and groped for the phone.

"Hello?" she said, her voice as groggy as she felt.

"You forgot to set your alarm again, didn't you?" Kel said, her tone far too chipper for this early hour.

Savannah squinted at the clock. So okay, it wasn't actually as early as she'd guessed, but considering she'd crawled into bed at five a.m., it meant she'd only managed four and a half hours of sleep. And *that* was nowhere near enough. Not after all the energy she'd spent over the long, and admittedly glorious, night. Cade might be many things, but an indifferent lover certainly wasn't one of them.

She yawned, and then realized Kel was saying something else. "What?"

Kel sighed dramatically. "I said, Ronan's been drafted into helping that caramel-eyed floozy collect names, and that starched boss of hers is sitting in your office demanding to know where you are."

Cade was up already? Good God, the man had stamina. She blew out a breath and threw the covers off. "Tell him I'll be there in ten. And have a cup of coffee ready."

"Will do."

She replaced the receiver and padded to the bathroom for a quick shower. It was only when she was getting dressed that she realized Cade still had her mauve bra. In the rush to get home, she'd forgotten to ask for it back.

Last night had been as hard and fast and detached as she'd hoped—and the best darn sex she'd had in a long time. She and Ronan were good together, but there wasn't that spark that made the sex between her and Cade so very intense. She and Ronan were just good friends, and that's exactly how they made love.

And I can hear you purring all the way from my side of town. Neva's amused thoughts whisked into her mind. *I'm gathering last night went well?*

Very well. Unfortunately, though, I'm not going to make it for breakfast. I've been called into the office.

You're the boss. Can't you make them wait?

Amusement ran through Savannah. *In this case, no.*

Well, damn. I wanted to hear all the juicy details.

And there were plenty to tell, but she pulled her thoughts away from the enticing images of Cade's naked, sweating body, and said, *I'll come into the diner tonight for dinner. We can talk then.*

I'm not going into the diner today. My feet are ballooning, and Duncan has commanded me to stay home and rest. She gave an unladylike snort. *Nor-*

mally I'd tell him where to shove such a command, but unfortunately, he's right.

Savannah plopped down onto the bed and shoved on her boots. It had to be wonderful to be loved like that, she thought. To have a man who adored you so much that he'd lay his life on the line for you.

Your turn will come, Sav. It's only a matter of time.

Yeah, so she kept telling herself. Only she had a horrible suspicion that fate had already given her a chance, and that maybe there were no more chances left for her.

I'll drop by after dinner then, and bring along the foot bath.

Oooh! Thanks.

Savannah cut the connection, then grabbed her keys and ID off the dresser and snagged her handbag off the back of the door as she headed for the stairs. She lived above the florist shop at the western end of the main shopping strip. Most days she walked to work. But with two murders in the last week, she'd begun taking the truck. Just in case.

She breathed deeply of the lush scents drifting from the shop, but she didn't bother to say hello to Anni, the latest in a long line of managers—and probably the least successful. Mainly because Anni loved to chat and often forgot to charge customers for the flowers they walked out with. But as much as Savannah enjoyed the older woman's company, she couldn't afford to waste any more time today. She buzzed open the back door and stepped out, wincing a little as the sunshine hit her eyes. She raised a hand to shade them and saw a piece of paper barely visible under the sprinkling of snow gathered around the truck's wiper blade.

"Goddamn, not again." She'd warned the local pizza place three times now about coming onto private property to shove their flyers under car wipers. For as much as she understood that they were new and needed to advertise, they were technically breaking the law.

She ripped the paper from under the blade, hit the remote to open the truck, and climbed inside. She gave a cursory glance at the paper as she threw her bag onto the passenger seat and then froze.

It wasn't an ad for the local pizza place.

It was a threat.

Against her.

You'll pay for your part in Rosehall's destruction.

Several words immediately sprang to mind, but none could be said in polite company. Or with Anni hanging out the back window of her shop, trying to catch her attention.

She ignored the old woman and stared at the note, letting the implications sink in, feeling fear stirring in the pit of her stomach.

Ronan was right. They were coming after her as well as for Cade. And while she'd suspected as much, she'd been hoping she was wrong. She'd loved Rosehall—at least until she'd become aware of the true reason behind its existence. It wasn't a celebration of life as everyone had been told, but rather a temple to death and vengeance.

She dropped the note on the seat and climbed back out of the truck. Then she grabbed her phone out of her bag, calling the station as she knelt, and took a careful look under her truck.

"Kel," she said, as soon as the call was answered. "You want to get Steve over to my place straight away with a fingerprint kit."

She had one in her vehicle, but she wasn't touching the truck any more than necessary. The fact that she'd already jumped into it and nothing had happened suggested she was being overly cautious, but it was better to be safe than sorry.

"Trouble?" Kel asked, concern in her voice.

"Yeah. You'd better tell him to bring Mr. Jones along, too."

"Will do."

Savannah hung up and glanced across at Anni, who was waving frantically. With a sigh, she approached. "Sorry, Anni. I really haven't got time to talk today."

"It's all right, dear. I just wanted to tell you I saw the Harvey kid sneaking about your truck when I drove in this morning. I chased him off, but I thought you'd like to know."

There were definite benefits to living above a shop run by the town busybody. "You're talking about Honor Harvey's kid, Denny?"

Anni nodded, sending her long gray curls bobbing. "It was about six."

"Did he do anything to my car?"

"He was shoving a note under the wiper. Squealed like the baby brat he is when I yelled at him."

And she'd slept through all of it. Some ranger she was. She glanced around at the sound of a car pulling up and saw it was Steve and Cade. "I have to go. Thanks for letting me know, Anni."

The older woman nodded and made a show of retreating. But Savannah knew she'd still be paying attention to the events unfolding in the parking lot.

Sighing, she walked across to the gate. Steve had circled around to the trunk of his car, probably to retrieve the fingerprinting kit, but Cade was stalking toward her, all grace and power.

She flared her nostrils, drawing in the wild scent of him, letting it fill her senses. Heat flicked through her veins—a warning that the moon's call had not eased with the coming of day. Desire sparked deep in his eyes, letting her know he was more than aware of what she was feeling. Then that flicker was gone, leaving his expression cool and blank.

He was keeping his end of their deal. She had to wonder if she could do the same.

"What's happened?" He stopped in front of her, swamping her senses with his tangerine scent and overwhelming masculinity.

"Someone left me a note."

"Where?"

"Under the wiper. I didn't read it until I was in the truck. That's where I left it."

He nodded, his gaze sweeping her, leaving her tingling. "They left nothing else?"

"I had a quick look under the truck, but that's about it."

He nodded. "I called Anton. He was on the bomb squad before he transferred over."

She raised an eyebrow. Going from the bomb squad to the IIS was an unusual step. "I don't really think our killer wants to blow me up. At least not this early in the game."

"No," he agreed. "But he does seem to enjoy taunting us. Any idea when the note was left?"

"The lady who runs the flower shop caught Denny Harvey, a local kid, leaving it this morning. You want to come with me to question him, or would you prefer to wait here?"

"A *kid* delivered the note?"

She nodded. "Our local hoodlum, who's into scaring human visitors and swiping their cars for joyrides."

"Sounds like a charmer."

"Oh, he is." All leather and attitude, but little true toughness.

Cade glanced around as a second car pulled up. "Anton's here now. I'll go talk to him, then I'll come with you." His navy eyes seemed to gleam briefly with amusement, and his voice dropped as he added, "It's always such a pleasure."

"Don't play on words," she warned softly. "Not here."

His lips twisted. But whether it was a smile or a grimace, she wasn't entirely sure.

"That wasn't in the rules we agreed on."

"But keeping this thing a secret was." She crossed her arms. "I hate this whole situation, Cade."

Which was both the truth and a lie, because she didn't actually hate being with him. Couldn't, when his very presence seemed to bring her senses alive in a way no other wolf ever had. But her hormones weren't the sum of her, and she had no intention of being fooled a second time.

"I don't care if you hate it or not." Though his voice was even, there was a gleam in his eyes that suggested annoyance, and the force of it seared her skin. "There's no escaping the moon this time. Or me."

"So you've said." She stepped back from his presence, and suddenly the air seemed so much cooler. "I'll just go get the keys from Steve."

"I'll meet you at the car." He spun away, every step radiating anger.

Well, that was just too bad. He was here to catch a killer, nothing more. The fact that she seemed to be part of the bargain was a quirk of fate neither of them could alter. And even if she didn't like the fact that the moon gave her no choice, she'd enjoy the sex. But if he was expecting anything more than sex, then he needed his head checked.

Steve was walking through the gates, fingerprint kit and notebook in hand. "What's up, boss?" His deep voice was more gravelly than usual, and his hair looked like it hadn't seen a comb in a month.

Too many cigarettes and beer last night, she thought, and wondered when he was going to start taking his health seriously. "Someone left a threatening note on my car this morning. After Anton checks the truck for devices, I want you to go over it with a fine-tooth comb."

"I dare say the IIS will, too."

"Probably. So keep an eye on what they find and let me know." She held out her hand. "I need your car keys to go visit Denny."

"Don't tell me that stupid little punk is involved?"

"According to Anni, he delivered the note."

"Idiot." He handed her the keys then coughed heavily as he walked away.

She resisted the urge to order him to the doctor and

headed over to the car. Cade joined her a few minutes later. "So tell me about this Denny," he said as he buckled himself in.

She shifted gears and pulled out of the lot. "His dad died in a car accident about eight years ago. His mom has spoiled the kid since, and believes he can do no wrong. Denny, of course, now figures he can do whatever he wants and get away with it."

"A brat, in other words."

She nodded. "And not the brightest of bulbs, either."

"Will he be at home?"

"Unlikely. His usual haunt is the basketball court over on Monarch Street."

"He doesn't go to school?"

"He quit when he was sixteen." She glanced at him. "He's now eighteen, but he looks at least twenty-four."

He fell silent for a few moments, but his gaze was something she could feel—a heat that slid through her veins as smoothly as his hands had slid over her skin. And it stirred her just as quickly.

Why hadn't the moon fever faded with the daylight? Was that the price she had to pay for running before the promise had ended? Or was it simply a matter of being close to the one man who had affected her in a way that no other man ever had? Either way, however, it was going to present problems. Could she really do her job and hunt down a murderer when her hormones had her as jumpy as a bitch in heat?

She really didn't know, and *that* was the major problem—not the unfulfilled moon promise.

"What?" she said, when she couldn't stand the growing silence any longer.

"Have you kept in contact with any of your friends from Rosehall?"

She slanted him a cool glance which was nothing but a brave front, but he didn't know that. "According to you, I didn't have friends. I just had bedmates."

"What about Nelle James?"

Nelle. So that's what this line of questioning was about. "I didn't sleep with Nelle."

His expression suggested he very much doubted her, and *that* was infuriating. She hadn't shared herself with *everyone* at the commune, no matter what he thought, and she most definitely hadn't slept with women. Not that she had anything against those who did; it's just that it didn't rock *her* boat.

"But you were close," he said. "Very close."

Yes, because Nelle had taken her under her wing when she'd first arrived at the commune, showing her the ropes and quickly introducing her to Jontee. She'd barely even been there a month when she became one of his "true believers"—a position that was highly sought after but rarely gifted, and one she'd thoroughly enjoyed. And then Cade had come along and wrecked it all. "What of it?"

"You warned her to run, didn't you?"

His voice was flat, but she shot him a quick look. His expression was just as flat as his voice, but his eyes glimmered with the faintest hint of fury.

"Yes, I did."

"Why?"

"Because she was my friend."

"And your friend was involved in murder."

The anger that had been bubbling under the surface surged to life, and it was all she could do to keep it in check. Goddamn it, was he trying to destroy every good memory of those times? "Why would you think Nelle has anything to do with Jontee's schemes?"

"Because there *was* someone else involved. There had to be."

"Why?"

"Think about it, Vannah. Did Jontee really seem capable of pulling off the sheer amount of planning those murders would have taken?"

"No, but he obviously did."

"But I don't think he did it alone."

"Well, Nelle couldn't have been involved." Damn it, she hadn't been *that* bad a judge of character, surely, even if she *had* been young. "Besides, once the news of the murders had leaked, we *did* discuss it, and Nelle had been as shocked and as disbelieving as everyone else."

"So why, in all the years since, have we never been able to track down Nelle James?"

"That one fact makes you jump to the conclusion that she had to have been involved? I mean, it couldn't be something as simple as her using a false name at Rosehall, now could it?"

"Like you, you mean?"

"Yes." She glanced at him. "And you always did think I knew more than what I was saying."

"That's because you damn well did. It's thanks to you—or rather, the information I pulled out of your mind—that I caught Jontee."

"Pulled being the operative word." She hesitated and took a deep breath, trying to calm the old anger. "That hurt, you know—physically *and* emotionally. You might as well have raped me."

His brief look was almost contemptuous. "I've pulled information out of suspects' minds many times before, and most of the time the person I was with wasn't even aware of it. Let's not get so dramatic about what actually happened."

"But were most of those others telepathic, like you? Like me?"

"No . . ."

"There's your answer, then."

He frowned. "But why would that make any difference?"

She shook her head. He couldn't see the harm in it, even all these years later. And why would he? He'd been there to catch a murderer, and she was no more than a means to an end with whom he happened to share an amazing sexual relationship.

She just wished she could have said the same about him. Life would have been so much easier—then and now.

She stopped the car as close to the basketball courts as possible and pointed across the road. "There's Denny, in the blue and black. Let me talk to him first."

"Afraid I'll hit him?" Cade said, voice edged with contempt.

She snorted softly. "You're not the type. But raping his mind? You've already proven yourself more than capable of that."

He grabbed her arm, his fingers digging into her flesh, bruising her. "It wasn't rape of *any* kind, Vannah."

"Then what else would you call forced entry into another telepath's mind?" She wrenched her arm away from his and climbed out. The cool wind ran fingers through her hair, chilling her scalp but not her anger.

Damn him for being here, she thought as she slammed the door closed. And damn her for letting him get to her. She was a ranger *and* a grown woman now. She ought to know better.

She walked around the car and across the road without bothering to see if he followed. But his footsteps told her he wasn't far behind. It was like being trailed by a storm cloud; his presence was that dark, that furious.

Denny glanced up, his face paling a little when he spotted them. He caught the ball and, for several seconds, looked as if he was going to run. Then a smirk touched his lips.

"Morning, Ranger Grant." His gaze went past her, and his bravado slipped a little.

If Cade looked as scary as he felt, then Savannah couldn't actually fault the kid for being a little frightened.

"Who paid you to drop that note under my wipers?" she said.

"I didn't—"

"Denny, Anni saw you."

"Sneaking cow," he muttered, then sniffed. "And what if I did? It was only a joke . . ."

"Did you read it?"

"Yeah."

"Then you know it was a threat."

"No, it wasn't. She told me—" He stopped abruptly. Something in her stomach clenched, but before she could say anything, Cade demanded, "She who?"

Though his voice was flat, there was an undercur-

rent that suggested violence. Denny swallowed and
went white, which was not an easy thing for a brown
wolf to achieve.

"I don't know. I never saw her before."

"Was she young? Old?" Cade snapped.

Savannah crossed her arms and resisted the temptation to tell him to take it down a notch. After all, he
was getting answers more quickly than she usually
did.

"Young," Denny stammered. "Late teens, maybe
even early twenties. She said she'd meet me later tonight and pay me."

"Where?" Savannah asked, obscurely relieved. The
age meant it couldn't have been Nelle, as Cade had
undoubtedly believed.

"At Club Grange."

"A local rave room," she said for Cade's benefit.
And it was a venue that had caused more than its
share of problems over the last few months. For some
strange reason, people seemed to think out of town
meant safe from the rangers. "Give me a description,
Denny."

"About my height. Blond hair. Blue eyes. Big tits."
He shrugged.

"Wolf?"

He snorted. "When they look like that, who cares?"

"You'd better start caring," Cade said, "because
you're in deep shit this time."

"For a note?"

"Threatening an officer of the law is a crime."

"But I wasn't—"

"But you did." Cade paused. "Of course, if you
were to go to that club tonight and point the woman

out to us, I might consider letting you off with a warning."

"And miss out—"

"Would you rather have sex or a firsthand view of a jail cell?"

If the kid's expression was anything to go by, it was a close run thing.

"All right," he muttered eventually. "I gotta meet her at ten."

"In the main room or the moon room?" Savannah asked.

He half-sneered, then his gaze shot beyond her and his bravado fled again. "Moon room."

"Then we'll be there, too," Cade said. "And if you're not—"

He let the words hang, but Denny's expression suggested he definitely got the message. "Can I go now?"

Savannah nodded, and the teenager scampered, leaving her alone with Cade once more.

Oh, joy, she thought sourly. After taking a deep breath to fortify herself, she turned around. His expression was every bit as dark as she'd expected.

"If we go there tonight, the news will spread like wildfire and our suspect *won't* show."

"So is this place just for teens?"

"No, but it's recently become the must-go place for the late teen and early twenties set." Mainly thanks to her old man's attempts to shut the place down. Nothing like a good bit of council outrage to make the inquisitive sit up and take notice.

"And what is the moon room?"

She half-smiled. "Just because the leaders of this

town are against the moon dance doesn't mean all its citizens are."

"Naturally, seeing as there's a Sinclair clan living on the reservation." He crossed his arms, and she clenched her fingers against the urge to run her fingers across all the muscles that gesture revealed. "But what has that got to do with the moon room at this club?"

"It's outside city limits and on private land. Just as the Sinclair mansion is."

"Ah. So the moon room is, in fact, a safe place where wolves can celebrate." He frowned. "But Denny is underage. He can't legally be at a bar."

She snorted. "Like teenagers all around the world don't get past that problem? Anyway, his mom lives and works at the bar, and her brother owns the place, so technically he's under the supervision of his parent and on home ground. And he doesn't drink."

"Just . . . celebrates?"

She nodded. "The problem with us going there tonight is that everyone knows me. And that'll alert our quarry."

His gaze slid down her body and heat prickled across her skin, igniting the ache deep inside. Her nipples hardened, pressing painfully against her shirt. She licked her lips, trying to remain calm and collected when her pulse raced so loudly it seemed to roar in her ears. Lord, how she wanted him. Wanted to run her hands over his warm, hard flesh, feel the press of it against her breasts, her belly, her thighs. To drink in his scent and his arousal and lose herself in that place that contained only pleasure. No memories, no lies, just pure, unadulterated bliss. They'd had that last night and could so easily have it again, here and now.

Had she been anywhere else but the middle of a very public park, the sheer force of her need for him might have had her crossing the line she'd drawn between them. But thankfully, they weren't alone. Or secluded.

When his gaze finally rose to meet hers again, there wasn't only the thick heat of lust in his eyes, but the need to hurt, to accuse. She braced herself against his words.

"I'm sure you can change your appearance," he drawled. "After all, that was one of the things you were so good at, wasn't it? Changing your appearance to match each newcomer's needs?"

The barb cut deep—not so much because it was true, but because he still clung to the belief that she'd bedded every male at the commune. But she forced an eyebrow upward, feigning a calm she didn't feel. "I never had any complaints."

"Oh, I'm sure you didn't. You were so very good at your work, after all."

"Yes, I was, wasn't I?" She stepped around him, then briefly stopped and met his gaze again. "And tell me, who is the biggest whore? The woman who sleeps with a man for the sheer pleasure of it, or the man who sleeps with the woman for the sole purpose of getting information?"

"I was working undercover," he bit back as he followed her. "That was part of the job."

"I'm sure it was, but that doesn't actually answer the question." She unlocked the car and strode around to the driver's side. "Where to next?"

Part of her was hoping he'd say the forest. The saner part was praying that he didn't.

His gaze met hers, blue eyes cold. Yet a shimmer of excitement ran through her. Because those eyes, for all their glacial indifference, spoke to the wildness within her.

They would go to the forest. And that wildness would be released.

"Take me," he said, "to the clearing where you heard the car."

Her pulse rate soared and sweat broke out across her palms. He could smell her desire as much as she could smell his, so there was no point in feigning disinterest. And what he was *really* saying was that it was up to her to break their agreement. Her choice; her decision. But once she did, it was all bets off.

God, she'd barely been in his presence for half a day, and already she was breaking down. Where was her strength of will when she really needed it?

Trying to regain control, she simply nodded and climbed into the car. He took his cell phone out of his pocket and quickly dialed, issuing orders to Trista as Savannah drove out of town and up Red Mountain Road. She turned into the side road, but stopped a short way in.

"The snow hasn't melted up here yet," she said, when he looked at her. "And we haven't got chains on."

He nodded, and they both climbed out. She breathed deeply, letting the scented but cold mountain air fill her lungs, hoping it would wash the heat and the smell of this man from her lungs and kin.

But it didn't.

Even with the car between them, her senses were filled with his presence. She wasn't going to survive the entire day without touching him, or begging him to touch her.

She glanced at the sky, silently swearing at a moon that was currently shining its cold light on another side of the world. Then, shoving her hands into her pockets, she began the long climb up the road. After a few minutes he joined her, walking so close that the warmth of his body caressed hers, yet not close enough that their arms were brushing.

And suddenly, she was aching for the simple pleasures they'd once shared—like walking up a mountain hand in hand. She could still remember the gentle way he'd twined his fingers through hers, the way he'd gripped tight, holding her upright as she'd slipped.

She blinked away the sudden sting of tears. Damn it, she had to stop doing this. The past was gone. She needed to get over it—and over *him*.

Yet she very much suspected that in order to do *either* of those, she had to sit down and confront him. Ten years ago, she'd run rather than take him to task for his actions. *That* had been her biggest mistake. The years had not eased the pain or her feelings for him, because there'd been no true end between them.

Now, she needed that ending to put it all behind her.

Yet even now, the thought of *really* challenging him over what he'd done scared the hell out of her. Because as long as she *didn't* go there, some small part of her could still believe that—despite his words, despite the fact that she was just a means to an end—some small part of him really *had* cared.

And the mere fact that she still clung to that hope spoke of how much she needed to exorcise those feelings if she was ever to get on with her life.

Once they reached the parking area at the top of the road, she led him across to the spot from which the car had taken off. He squatted, studying the ground, carefully moving leaves about with a pen he'd drawn from his pocket.

"Looks like it could have been a truck rather than a car," he said, after a few minutes.

She frowned. "You found a track?"

His quick look suggested she should have found it, too, and that annoyed her. It wasn't as if she'd had the benefit of daylight.

She squatted beside him and did her best to ignore his rich, enticing aroma. "Where?"

He outlined what was little more than a wide smudge in the mud.

"No wonder I didn't spot it last night," she muttered, then tilted her head as she studied the vague impression. There was something odd about it. "They didn't have chains on."

"No, otherwise the imprints would have been deeper." He glanced at her, his navy eyes cool. Dangerous. The gaze of a cop rather than a lover. "Why?"

She frowned. "Well, this road isn't surfaced and, because it's so steep, getting up here without chains would have been pretty much impossible."

"The perp could have had a four-wheel drive."

"Even a four-wheel drive can have trouble on a steep, slushy road."

"Your point being?"

His curt tone had her fingers clenching. She flexed

them, but it didn't do much to ease the annoyance. "The very fact that this impression is so faint suggests that the driver not only didn't have chains, but he didn't, in fact, drive up here yesterday. The ground that was under the truck is drier, which is why he didn't leave much of an impression when he first sped off."

He ran his pen over the ground beside the faint impression. "It does seem firmer." He glanced at her. "A good observation, ranger."

His voice was patronizing, as if he hadn't expected something like that. Her inner bitch rose to the surface, but she somehow managed to quell the instinct to snarl at him. "Meaning," she said, her voice surprisingly even, "that our quarry was probably here before the snow had fallen."

"It also suggests you might have heard him moving positions rather than trying to sneak up on us."

She rose and walked around the tire impression, then down the hill a ways. The air was noticeably colder this far from Cade, but at least she could take a breath free from the enticing spice of his presence. "It also means we should be able to find more tracks. If he didn't have chains, he would have had little control going back down that road."

"If he'd hit something, we would have seen it."

"But the road is straight. What if he managed a controlled slide most of the way down and just sideswiped the trees at the bottom?" She certainly hadn't noticed any sign of damage, but she hadn't been looking for something like that.

Which was just more proof that Cade's presence was rattling her more than it should.

"With that sort of impact, he'd still be down there."

"Depends on how bad the slide was, how fast he was going, and how quickly he was able to recover once he hit the main road. But even a small bump might have left paint."

He nodded. "Go check. I'll get Anton up here with some plaster."

She resisted the urge to salute and continued down the hill. The road dropped sharply away from the viewing point, and soon she was alone. The wind moved through the pines lining the road, making them sway and whisper. Yet, beyond that, the day seemed hushed. Intense.

Too intense.

She continued on down the hill and eventually found what she was looking for—tree damage. She couldn't see any paint, but that didn't mean there wasn't any—she cut the thought short as the breeze stirred around her. Mixed within the scents of balsam and pine and the oncoming storm came two other aromas.

Ginseng and sandalwood.

Jontee's scent.

The small hairs on the back of her neck rose. Jontee was dead, so he couldn't be out there now, following her. Watching her.

But someone definitely was.

Chapter Five

As soon as Vannah left, Cade felt the wrongness. He glanced up and scanned the trees, half-wondering if it was nothing more than missing her presence, the warmth of her body so close to his—missing her exotic scent teasing his nostrils, fueling the fires already raging in his body.

They were going to have to do something about this moon fever. Neither of them could afford to get distracted when there was a madman running around. But to ease the fever, they had to make love, and that could be just as dangerous.

She knew that as much as he did. He'd seen it in her green eyes when he'd all but dared her to break the promises they'd made last night.

Which wasn't the sanest thing he'd ever done, but he hadn't exactly been in a calm, rational frame of mind at the time. Where in hell did she get off accusing him of mind-rape? He'd been well trained in probing a suspect's mind. He had been so damn good at it that even the men who'd trained him hadn't been aware of him rummaging through their thoughts.

He *hadn't* raped her mind, though he most certainly *had* read it.

And in doing so, he'd caught his killer. He'd pulled not only details about the cavern and the path that led up to it, but brutal flashes of bloodshed and gore. Whether they had come from Jontee's mind, as she'd claimed, or whether she'd somehow witnessed them, he couldn't say—though he *did* truly believe she'd never been involved. She hadn't even been present at the commune when they'd first started.

Something flickered through the trees to his left. A fragment of green darker than the pines that swayed and dipped in the gathering wind. He frowned. It wasn't a tree or bush set deep in the forest, because the movements were too furtive, too human.

Anticipation shot through him. Could it be their watcher from last night?

It was certainly a possibility—though surely the person who'd watched them yesterday would be a little more circumspect.

He watched the green patch for a moment longer, then shifted shape and padded after it. The hush of the pine-filled forest enclosed him, and the dappled light and deeper shadows provided good cover for his dark brown coat. He pricked up his ears, listening to the soft steps ahead as he nosed the air, tasting the scents riding the breeze. The man smelled of stale cigarettes—an easy scent to follow in the crisp mountain air.

He increased his pace, loping quietly through the undergrowth, drawing ever closer to the stranger. The man didn't appear to notice his approach. He was too busy following the soft sound of steps from up ahead.

Vannah, Cade thought suddenly. The man was following Vannah.

A red wave of anger surged through him. And without even thinking about what he was doing, he charged out of the shadows and straight at the stranger.

The man swung around at the last moment, his squawk of surprise becoming a grunt of pain as Cade plowed into him from the side. As the man hit the ground, Cade shifted shape, grabbing the stranger by the throat and pinning him down. The growl that rumbled up from his chest was all wild wolf. For several seconds, he knelt there, teeth bared and breathing fast as he fought the territorial need to rip open the stranger's neck. To protect what was his.

"Wait," the man gasped, blue eyes wide and frightened. "I meant no—"

Cade tightened his grip on the man's throat, cutting off the rest of his words. "Tell me who you are and what you're doing here."

Then he relaxed his fingers a little, and the stranger gasped. "Alf Reeson, reporter from the *Ripple Creek Gazette.* Who the hell are you?"

A reporter? That was the last thing they needed, if it was true. "Cade Jones, IIS. Where are your credentials?"

"Top pocket."

Cade reached in and pulled out a worn leather wallet. Inside, he found a smoke-stained press card and photo. Though press cards were easily faked, he suspected this one was the real deal, because it was grimy, faded with age and smoke, and dog-eared in a way only time could achieve. He flipped the wallet closed and put it back. "Why are you here?"

"I heard there were some problems at Ranger Grant's place this morning. Someone left a threatening note." The small man shrugged—a movement that looked awkward with Cade still gripping his neck. "Thought I might find a story if I followed her."

And he had—or at least, he'd caught the whiff of a story, if the gleam in the reporter's blue eyes was anything to go by. The Ripple Creek rangers might have kept the murders out of the news, but by attacking Reeson the way he had, Cade had all but blown the case wide open. And though he doubted he could save the situation, he certainly had to try. The last thing they needed was a repeat of the hysteria that had plagued the public ten years ago.

"The so-called threatening note was a prank left by a kid," he said, removing his fingers from the reporter's neck and reaching into his pocket for his badge. "However, given the fact that Ranger Grant is assisting with my investigation, sneaking around after her is not a smart move."

Cade rose, and the reporter eyed the badge as he sat up and rubbed his neck. Even in the hazy light of the forest, it was easy to see the red finger marks ringing Reeson's neck. Still, Cade knew, it could have been so much worse.

Where had that fury come from? He'd never blown up like that before. Never.

"I wasn't sneaking. I was following." Reeson paused. "So tell me, what are you and the ranger investigating?"

"Nothing I can talk about at the moment."

Reeson's grin was all reporter. "Is that on the record?"

"No. And if you quote me on it, I'll give someone else the exclusive when there is something to report."

Reeson raised a graying eyebrow. "Is that a promise, Agent Jones?"

"Yes."

The reporter grinned again and rose, brushing the leaves and pine needles from his clothes. "Expect to see me waiting at the ranger station for my exclusive, then."

"As long as you don't get in our way. Where's your car?"

"Parked on the main road."

"I'll escort you."

"Don't trust me to leave, huh?"

"You're a reporter," Cade said dryly. "And remember, if I catch you following us again, you'll lose the exclusive."

Blue eyes regarded him steadily. "And is the exclusive worth it?"

"It could be."

"Then I'll just head back to my car."

"Good." Cade grabbed Reeson's shoulder and turned him around. "The road is that way."

"You've had dealings with the press, I see," Reeson commented, amusement in his voice.

"It's part of the job."

THE SCENT LED Savannah deeper and deeper into the forest. Though there was little to be heard beyond the sound of her own breathing and the whisper of the wind through the aspens and pines, the sensation that she was not alone in the dappled semidarkness was as strong as the aroma of ginseng and sandalwood. And as strong as the memories they evoked.

She'd never loved Jontee, but she'd enjoyed making love with him—at least until Cade had swept her off her feet with his bristling ideals and overwhelming machismo.

But Cade wasn't the only reason she'd begun to distance herself from Jontee in their last weeks at Rosehall. She'd seen a change in him—a darkness she couldn't explain and hadn't liked. When she'd talked to Nelle about it, her friend had merely laughed and shrugged, reminding her that running a commune wasn't as easy as it looked.

And maybe it wasn't, but over the days that had followed, she'd realized something was very wrong. And not just with the commune, but with Jontee himself. Because of his dreams. Because of what she'd seen in them.

And that was the information that Cade had pulled from her mind.

In the sudden silence, Savannah stopped and glanced around. The wind had momentarily dropped, and the shadows seemed thick and threatening.

Imagination and memories, she thought, and rubbed her arms against the chill that raced across her skin. It had been nothing short of stupidity to come so deep into the forest alone—especially given the threatening note left on her windshield. Ronan would be disappointed, and Cade would just be plain furious. Still, she *was* a ranger, and she'd be damned if she'd let one little threat stop her.

"Vannah." The voice was soft, drawing out her name.

She resisted the surge of fear that made her long to retreat and said, in a curt voice, "Stop playing games and show yourself." Not that she had any hope of her words being obeyed.

"You will pay for what you did."

The voice didn't sound either male or female. It just sounded . . . odd. And it came from her left, so she took a cautious step in that direction. "I didn't destroy Rosehall. Jontee did that all by himself."

"You were the betrayer. You gave Jontee away."

Gave him away? How, when all she'd really known was that something was wrong? Despite the darkness she'd seen growing in Jontee, never in a million years would she have guessed that *he* was the force behind the eighteen murders that had occurred in and around Wichita.

She stepped closer. The tang of ginseng and sandalwood got stronger but, oddly enough, she could find no trace of a man. Or a woman, for that matter.

"Jontee was a killer. He deserved exactly what he got." And she couldn't see anyone hiding in the shadows beyond the trees. Yet they had to be there, somewhere.

Suspicion snaked through her.

"He took you in, Vannah," the strange voice continued. "He taught you, loved you, and you repaid his kindness with betrayal."

She stepped past the pines, into the deeper shadows from which the voice seemed to be emanating. There was no one there. Just a ratty-looking tape recorder sitting on the ground. She blew out a frustrated breath. She was being played; no doubt about it.

"I will kill you, Vannah, just as I will kill your lover, but it won't be a fast death. You will suffer, as Jontee suffered."

A chill ran down her spine as the voice on the tape fell silent, then the wind seemed to spring back to life, as if it had been holding its breath while the message played. Behind the small machine, something yellow fluttered.

She squatted in front of the tape recorder. Ginseng and sandalwood swamped her senses, and memories rose. Jontee's teasing smile as she'd come to him on her allotted nights. The warmth of his touch, so good and yet so distant. Cade's thunderous expression every time she left him for Jontee.

Frowning, she took a pen from her pocket and carefully pinned the yellow strip of ribbon to the ground. There was no message on the part she could see, but a good half of it had been buried under the soil.

She dragged the ribbon sideways with the pen, gently pulling the rest of it out. The dirt fell away, revealing a beaded bracelet, and the fear that had all but vanished returned tenfold. Because she knew the bracelet. She recognized the emblem sitting in the middle of it—a yellow rose entwined around the peace symbol. Rosehall's signature.

It was Jontee's bracelet. One that should have been buried with him.

He *couldn't* be alive. Cade had assured her of that, and she believed him. So why was this bracelet here? And how did it get here?

She pulled her cell phone out of her pocket and

dialed Cade's number. "Where are you?" she said, the minute he answered.

"Just escorting a reporter back to his car."

She groaned. "Not Alf Reeson?" The man had the nose of a bloodhound. If he'd sensed there was a story unfolding, there'd be no getting rid of him.

"The same. And where the hell are you?"

She masked a surge of anger at his peremptory tone. "Grab the kit from the car and walk back up the road until you see a wild raspberry bush on the right side. Then head north into the forest."

"Don't move."

"Don't worry. I have no intention of going any-where."

His grunt suggested he didn't believe her. Grin-ning slightly, she hung up and rose. Since ginseng and sandalwood weren't exactly everyday aromas, there had to be something here permeated with those scents. The scent was too strong to be just the ribbon.

She took a cursory look around, but didn't find anything. No other source for the scent, and no foot-steps. Nothing to suggest anyone had been here but her. So whoever was behind the threats was either a shifter who could take to the wing, or was someone damn good at tracking.

Unless . . . Savannah glanced upward, studying the branches above her head. In the pine to the right of the tape recorder she saw something white. She moved to the tree and carefully pushed the branch to one side. The handle of a white metal cup had been nailed to the thick part of the branch, and inside it was a cloth. She didn't have to go closer to know the cloth had been soaked in ginseng and sandalwood. The two scents were overwhelming.

Then she stepped away carefully and let the branch swing back into position. She couldn't touch anything until Cade got here with the kit. But rather than just standing idly and waiting, she did a wider search around the perimeter of the small clearing, trying to find some trace of the person who'd left the recorder. But all she found was a slight scuff in the soil, as if someone had slipped on the leaves.

She shoved her pen in the soil to mark the spot and moved on. Soft steps rode the wind and, seconds later, Cade appeared. Just watching him walk through the trees with such easy, effortless grace had her heart slamming against the wall of her chest.

"I found where the truck hit a tree," she said, before the anger so evident in his eyes could erupt. "And someone left me a message."

"They might have done more than that," he said, approaching far too close for comfort. The heat of him swamped her, sizzling across her nerve endings. "Coming here alone was pretty stupid."

"No more stupid than walking down a lonely mountain road alone," she shot back.

"*I* am more than capable of protecting myself."

"And so am I. But neither of us can do anything about a long-range rifle."

He took a step closer, and suddenly the air seemed thicker. She licked her lips, but resisted the urge to retreat.

"Maybe," he agreed softly. "But I don't think our would-be killer is interested in taking the easy way out."

"No. Whoever this is, he intends to draw it out. He wants us both to suffer."

His gaze met hers—so very angry, and yet so very aware of what was burning between them.

Moisture skated across her skin—tiny beads of perspiration that had nothing to do with fear and everything to do with the man who stood too close. "Whoever it is, they know about us."

One dark brow flicked upward. "Indeed? What, precisely, does the tape say?"

She told him, then added, "No one followed me last night."

"Nor me." He frowned. "So whoever it is knows about the moon promise."

"And I haven't exactly gone spreading *that* little bit of stupidity around, believe me."

Something deep and dangerous flared in his eyes. "It's not exactly a moment I'm proud of, either. But we did it, and now are stuck with it."

Such a nice way of putting it. Still, it was hardly any worse than calling it stupid. Albeit, for all of twenty-four hours, she'd once considered it the best damn thing she'd ever done.

And Neva wondered why she never took chances anymore.

"We'll probably have to tell our people what's happening," she said. Ronan knew, but everyone else deserved the truth as well, if only because they could be stepping into the line of fire. Who knew who this madman would go after next?

The thought terrified her.

Neva. She hadn't actually intended to reach out to

her sister so sharply, and she winced when she heard her sister's mental gasp.

What?

Call Duncan now, then both of you get to the Sinclair mansion and stay there.

I hate that place—

I don't care. It's safe. No one would get to either of them there. Not without confronting the wrath of the whole Sinclair pack.

But why?

Because you both might be in danger.

Danger? Sav, what's going on?

Long story, and one I can't really explain right now. But it's very possible someone might come after you just to get to me. Just promise you'll call Duncan immediately and get yourselves over to the mansion.

I'm contacting him as we speak.

"Savannah?"

Cade's sharp question made her jump. "What?"

"What just happened?"

She drew in a shaky breath. "I have a sister here. A very pregnant twin sister. I just ordered her to the Sinclair mansion."

Surprise etched his voice. "You have a twin?"

She nodded. "And if this person intends to come after me, Neva is a good target. She's all I really care about."

He raised an eyebrow. "What about your parents?"

"I care about them, of course, but we haven't seen eye to eye for ages. Most people know that."

"So you're presuming this person is from Ripple Creek?"

"No, I'm simply presuming this person has done

their homework. Neva is the most logical target if someone really wants to hurt me."

"And what about your lover?"

Her gaze narrowed at his derogatory tone. "What about him?"

"Isn't he also a logical target?"

"Not when no one in town knows about us."

"Supposedly no one knows about you and me, either."

"Ronan does."

He raised an eyebrow. "You told him?"

"Of course I told him. I refuse to sneak around behind anyone's back."

His grimace was touched with sadness. "Yeah, I know."

Her gaze searched his. "Sounds as if you would have preferred me to sneak."

"I would have preferred you not to go at all."

Her stupid heart did an odd little dance, though heaven only knows why. It wasn't as if he'd been jealous. To be jealous, you had to actually care, and he never had. "That was never an option."

"There are always options, Vannah."

She snorted. "Like you had the option of telling me the truth?"

"*That* wasn't an option I had."

Too many things weren't an option when it came to her, it seemed. "Look, let's not get into this here."

"No." He studied her for a second, his gaze hot and heavy. The smell of his desire washed across her senses, teasing her, making her more ready for him than she'd ever been with anyone else. And all without even touching her.

The worst thing was, she knew it wasn't the moon but the man himself. He was the fuel to her fire.

And he knew it, damn him.

He stepped so close that, if she hadn't been breathing in as he breathed out, they would have touched. Each breath he released was a warm rasp of air that flushed a tingle across her body—tiny pinpricks of desire that eventually pooled low in her body. "Don't," she said softly.

"I made a promise, and I intend to keep it." His eyes glittered at her. Dared her. "But you made no such pledge. You can touch me anytime you want."

And she did want to touch him. Badly.

"I intend to stick with the conditions I set," she said stubbornly.

"The moon will make that impossible, and you know it."

Maybe she did. But that didn't mean she had to give in the minute he crooked his little finger. Sure, she'd probably be a needy mess by the end of the day—if she made it to the end of the day—but she sure as hell wasn't going to be easy. Not this time.

And certainly not with the possibility of a reporter running around.

"We have work to do," she said resolutely.

A condescending smile touched his lips. Lips she ached to kiss.

"You can't hold out forever, Vannah."

No. But she was going to hold out for as long as she could. At the very least, it was one way of showing him she wasn't the person he thought.

And right now, she had no desire to explore why it was so important that he realize that.

* * *

SOMEHOW, SAVANNAH MADE it through the long afternoon and into the early evening. But, by God, it was hard.

She rubbed a hand across her eyes and leaned against the side of her car. She was so tired her eyes felt ready to close, and so damn hungry she was ready to shift shape and hunt rabbits. And that was something she hadn't done since she was barely a teenager.

But both of those problems were nothing compared to the fever. It felt like her skin was on fire. She couldn't go back to the office when she was radiating desire like this; it wasn't fair to anyone on her team. And especially Ronan.

Of course, there was one very simple cure: make like a bunny with Cade. She'd stop emoting the minute her lust was sated.

She blew out a breath and glanced up the road. Anton had driven up earlier, and he and Cade had made a plaster mold of the smudged tracks they'd found and checked out the area where the truck had sideswiped the tree. Then the two men had proceeded to search the nearby forest to see if they could find exactly where the watcher had been lurking. She'd been sent down to this end of the road like some underling to stop anyone from coming up—an order she couldn't exactly rail against, because she knew the reason behind it. The fever—and the fact that Anton would undoubtedly become aware of it if he spent more than a few minutes in her company.

And even though her past relationship with Cade was something they would have to reveal to everyone on this case, the fact that the two of them were once again involved *wasn't*.

Which meant she had one choice, and only one choice, about what to do next, and the wild part of her was more than a little excited about it. Truth be told, the saner part was, too.

She crossed her arms and glanced up the mountain again. Dusk was settling in, and the evening chill was already frosting the night air. Surely the men would be down soon. They wouldn't be able to see much in this gloom.

Even as the thought crossed her mind, the sound of an engine cut across the hush, then headlights hit her, pinning her in brightness. She raised her hand to protect her eyes, squinting as she watched the four-wheel drive approach. Even though it hadn't rained recently, the truck was still sliding a fair bit on the steep road.

It would have been much worse with the snow falling the night before, which meant that the driver of the vehicle last night was either highly skilled or damn lucky.

Another point in Nelle's favor. She couldn't drive— or at least she couldn't ten years ago.

Anton slid the truck to a stop, and Cade stepped out. The quickly fading light caught the flickers of mahogany and silver in his dark hair.

He didn't approach her, didn't even look at her, until Anton had disappeared down the road that led back to town. "The day has gone," he said, his voice a low vibration that had her hormones skipping excitedly. "I can now officially touch you."

Please, the wild part of her practically begged. "I

will not make out in the forest like some oversexed teenager."

His eyes gleamed with amusement, reminding her of the times they *had* made out like oversexed teenagers. "Then where?"

"My lodge." Where else could they go? It was the only place that was in any way secure. Although, if the murderer had done his homework, it wasn't exactly safe, either.

"Now?"

"Now," she confirmed, and unlocked the car.

"Good."

His voice was little more than a growl, and a tremor of anticipation ran through her. It was going to be good. Fast, but good.

The drive back to town was quiet, but it was filled with a simmering tension that had sweat breaking out across her skin. Yet, despite the urgency that beat in time with every thump of her heart, she wasn't about to make the mistake of driving straight to her lodge. Town gossip was not something she needed to deal with on top of everything else.

She stopped at his hotel and glanced at him. "If I don't see you in ten minutes, I'll start without you."

"Don't even think about it," he all but snarled.

Oh yeah, she thought with a smile. He was feeling the moon every bit as badly as she. She took off, the wheels skidding on the stones, and made it to the lodge without seeing anyone she knew. Still, she did take a quick look around to ensure the place was safe. Then she headed down to the small room they had used last night.

She felt Cade's arrival long before she saw him.

His presence was like a fierce wind before a summer storm, and it battered her senses just as badly.

The rich aroma of sage and tangerine swirled around her, and footsteps echoed on the wooden floors—firm, deliberate steps, drawing ever closer. She stripped off her clothes, laying them across the arm of the sofa, then turned to face him as he entered.

His gaze skidded down her body, then rose to meet hers. "You smell ready, Vannah."

She walked toward him, watching the heat and desire flare brighter in his eyes. "You have no idea."

She tangled her hands in his silky, almost too short hair and drew him down so she could kiss him. But there was nothing gentle about their kiss. It was hard, urgent, and fierce. And utterly glorious.

He wrapped a hand around her rear, lifting her up then moving her backward. She grunted as her back hit the wall, then wrapped her legs around him, pushing against the heated stiffness of his erection. He thrust against her, sending shivers of delight racing across her skin. She groaned, reveling in the glory of it and yet needing to feel so much more.

She unwrapped her legs, letting them slide down his body until her feet touched the floor. Then with shaking, urgent fingers, she undid his shirt, his pants. He kicked off his boxers and lifted her again. She'd barely wrapped her legs around his waist before he was in her, filling her.

Then he began to move, and thought became impossible. All she could do was move with him, savoring the sensations flowing through her. As his strokes became fierce, so did hers, riding him hard, until the power of their mating shook her entire body. The rich ache spread like wildfire through her, becoming a kaleidoscope of sensations that washed through every corner of her mind. Then the shuddering took hold and she gasped, grabbing his shoulders and thrusting him deeper. His movements became more urgent, his body driving deep inside hers, touching that *one* special spot, over and over and over.

She came as he did, his roar echoing through her ears as she twitched and moaned.

When they were both able to breathe again, he leaned his sweaty forehead against hers and sighed. His breath was warm, almost sweet, as it caressed her, stirring her barely sated hormones to sluggish life.

"Dear God," he said softly, "I don't think I could have held off a moment longer."

A smile touched her lips. "Lost some of your laudable control over the years, have you?"

He pulled back a little. The odd seriousness in his dark eyes made her pulse skip, then race. "There was never anything controlled about us. Not once we actually met, anyway."

Part of her desperately wanted to believe that statement, to believe that he'd been as much a prisoner of passion as she. But the truth was, his actions denied his words—then and now.

"Everything about us was controlled—from the minute you walked into the commune to the moment you raided my mind. All of it was planned to achieve one goal."

"To catch a killer," he agreed.

"So how can you say it wasn't controlled?"

"I didn't say the situation wasn't controlled. I said *we* weren't."

She raised an eyebrow. "And there's a difference?"

He slid his hands under her rump, supporting her as he moved away from the wall and walked toward the sofa. "A big difference."

"I wouldn't have thought so."

He kicked the lever that folded down the back of the sofa and placed her on the worn cushions. He stretched out beside her, throwing one leg over hers and drawing her so close that skin pressed against skin, letting her feel every beat of his heart, every intake of breath. It felt good. Almost too good. But the sofa wasn't all that big, and there was no point in trying to retreat because there just wasn't room.

And if she told herself that often enough, she might even believe it.

"Different or not, it doesn't really matter anymore, does it?" he said.

"No." But it did, if only because one tiny part of her was still so desperate to hold on to the dream, even if that dream wasn't one he'd ever share. "But that doesn't mean there's no need to talk about what went on between us."

He leaned back a little and idly flicked a nipple with a gentle finger, an almost insolent smile touching his luscious lips. In the sharpening cold of the night, it was an almost painful sensation. And yet, at the same time, very arousing.

"Leave it in the past, Vannah. Opening old wounds won't achieve anything."

His head dipped and his teeth grazed her aching

nipples. She shivered, barely resisting the urge to arch her back and raise her breasts for his pleasure.

His teeth skimmed her areola, then caught a nipple and lightly pulled. She gasped, caught between pleasure and pain, and loving every unexpected minute of it.

"I need to move on with my life," she somehow managed to say. "And I can't with this lying unfinished between us."

He didn't answer, but simply shifted his position and grazed his way up to her neck, her ears, her lips. Then his gaze caught hers, and again, there was an energy, an anger, gleaming in those navy depths that stirred something deep inside her.

Cade had hurt her once, and if she wasn't very careful, he could do so again. And the anger that burned deep in his gaze suggested that, while the moon was driving them together, it was a more basic need that was fueling him now: the need to fully reclaim what was once his.

His next words confirmed her thoughts. "There will be no moving on until the moon and I are done with you."

"The moon only gives you four more nights," she said bluntly. "And if we survive this, *I* want to move on. From the past and from you."

Something dark and dangerous flashed in his eyes. He didn't answer, just claimed her mouth with a kiss that was fiercely possessive and so damn hot it felt like she would explode into flames.

From then on, there was no talking, just touching and caressing and tasting. She explored his body, reveling in his scent—and his salty, seductive, and oh so masculine taste—until all she could feel, all she could smell, all she wanted, was him.

He returned the favor, leaving no part of her body untouched or unexplored. He nipped her, caressed her, licked her, discovering erogenous zones long ignored and bringing her to the edge of orgasm time and again. But he never let the wave crest. He backed away each time, waiting until the tremors eased before starting all over again. He did this until her skin was slick with sweat and desire, and all she could think about was the rigid length of him sliding deep and hard into her.

But if he sensed her need, he was ignoring it.

When his tongue flicked over her clitoris, she jumped, and a whimper that was part frustration and part a plea escaped her lips. He chuckled softly, his breath hot against her skin. Then he suckled on her, and she came with such a thunderous roar that her neighbors would have surely heard her had they been home.

The tremors hadn't even begun to ease when he shifted. His flesh was as slick as hers, and his body trembled with his effort at control. She wrapped her legs around his hips, trying to force him closer, desperate to feel him inside. And when he pressed himself against her, she whimpered, wanting the whole damn length of him and not just the tip.

"Vannah," he said, and in his voice there was an edge of command she could not ignore.

She opened her eyes and met his gaze. The depths of his eyes were filled with that dark danger she'd glimpsed earlier, and in that moment she knew what he was about to do.

"Don't," she said quickly.

He either didn't hear her, or he didn't *want* to hear her, because energy touched the air, fluttering across her skin like a thousand tiny sparks. The power of the moon, coming to life once again.

All he said was "You are mine, and only mine, until I say otherwise."

Oh God, oh God . . . What the hell was she going to do? He was using the moon to bind her past the time of their first pledge, and thanks to the promise she'd so innocently made, there wasn't a damn thing she could do about it.

Damn the moon, she thought viciously. And damn *him* for taking the moon-given power and twisting the spirit of it to his own ends.

"I am only yours until the power of the moon ends. No longer."

"No." His voice was full of unforgiving determination. The dance of energy became more emphatic, enforcing his words. "Say it."

Goddamn it, he was getting what he wanted—and what the moon demanded—so why ask for more?

"Bastard."

"Say it. You will be mine until I say otherwise."

"No, damn you. *No."* She arched her hips and captured him, driving him deep. He shuddered, and for a moment he moved with her. Then his breath hissed between his teeth and he withdrew.

He didn't say anything, just stared at her with hungry, demanding eyes as the energy burned brighter, wrapping her in heat and the need to obey.

"Damn it, why?" she all but yelled.

"Because I have no intention of sitting on the sidelines and watching you dance with your lover if this case should last more than four days." He raised a hand and caught her chin, his fingers close to bruising. "Say it."

"I *hate* you." But she didn't, not badly enough. Not then, and not now.

"But you want me, don't you?"

"Yes." And that was the whole problem. When it came to Cade, control was something she'd never seemed to have enough of.

"Then that's the only thing that matters. Say the words, Savannah."

She knew that fighting the compulsion was useless, yet there was no way in hell she would give in without a fight. So she fought, and the dance of energy became thick and fierce, until it felt as if her entire body was on fire with the compulsion to obey. Eventually, she had no choice but to say the words. "I'm yours, and only yours, until you say otherwise."

His grin was quick and predatory. "Until I say," he repeated fiercely, and drove deep inside her, claiming her with his body as thoroughly as he had claimed her with his words.

And as much as she hated his actions, with the moon driving them so fiercely, she had no desire to fight or push him off. She wrapped her legs tighter around him, holding him close as he began to move. She moved with him, relishing the sensations flowing through her. Right now, that's all she really had, because his actions tonight had smashed the tiny spark of hope that had lingered in her heart. All he cared about, all he'd ever cared about, was his satisfaction. She'd been a fool to hope for anything else.

His strokes became stronger, faster, and once again the sweet pressure began to build until it seemed her whole body ached with the need for release.

When he came, she went with him, his roar drowning out her own strangled groan as his body slammed into hers so hard the whole sofa shook.

But as the power of her own release faded, and the reverberations of his roar grew fainter, she heard the footsteps.

They were no longer alone in the lodge.

Chapter Six

EVEN THROUGH THE red haze of satisfaction, Cade heard the sound. He froze, listening, as the night air began to chill the sweat on his skin and tension rippled through Vannah's warm body beneath him.

"You expecting someone?" he whispered, glancing down. Her green eyes glowed like an angry cat's in the darkness.

"No." Her soft voice was curt. "And get off me."

He did. She rolled swiftly upright, clambering off the sofa and padding to the door. The moonlight filtering in from the next room caressed her, making her skin gleam like porcelain.

Desire stirred anew, but he ignored it and rose to stand behind her. Another heavy step echoed across the silence, then another. Cade frowned. Those weren't the steps of someone trying to sneak up on them. Quite the opposite, in fact.

"I think—"

"It's Ronan," she said at the same time, then added, "I'll go talk to him."

"Not naked, you won't."

She turned around. The fury in her eyes should have

been warning enough, but he was too busy watching the flicker of the moon's cold light in her glorious golden hair to actually watch what she was doing. He barely had time to register the fact that she'd raised her fist when the blow crashed into his chin with surprising force, snapping his head back and dropping him to the floor. He hit with a bone-crunching grunt and, for a moment, couldn't even breathe.

"Don't you ever use the moon's magic on me like that again!" She stood at his feet, her fists clenched, her body quivering with the force of her anger.

His own anger crashed through him, but desire came with it, so thick and fast it overrode his fury. God, she looked so beautiful standing there, with the heat of her rage warming the moon's silvery glow on her skin. And though anger still burned, he wasn't exactly sure who he was angry at—her for punching him, or himself for being decked so easily.

"Or what?" he retorted. "You'll shoot me?"

"Shooting is too good for a bastard who abuses the moon gift." Her gaze skated down his body and came to rest on his cock. "I think a well-placed cut or two might be more advantageous."

"You'll never get *that* close with a knife, sweetheart, so drop the idea."

She bared her teeth. "Who needs a knife?"

He laughed, even though he knew her threat was real. "Who'd have guessed that the sweet wolf I promised myself to was such a hellion?"

"Sweet?" She snorted softly. "I was many things, but I was *never* sweet. As you've already noted." She glanced over her shoulder briefly and said, "Wait here."

Wait here when she was out flaunting her charms to another wolf? Not damn likely. He scrambled to his feet, but the sudden movement had pain shooting through his jaw and cheek. He winced and carefully touched the side of his face. Bruised for sure, and at least one loose tooth.

She sure could pack a punch—both physically *and* sexually. Which was why he wasn't about to let her go before this case was solved. As much as he understood the risk of getting involved with her again when a madman bent on revenge was on the loose, he just couldn't help it. The moon had him in its grip, and there was no fighting it.

But that didn't exactly explain why he'd prolonged the situation by forcing her to agree to a longer term, other than the fact that he wasn't about to let another wolf have what he wanted. Not this time, when he could actually do something to stop it. The first time it would have endangered his mission. This time, there was no such restriction—and he'd be damned if he'd share her again.

He didn't care about the anger his demand had caused. She'd never denied her desire for him, and as long as that desire was still there, he was going to take full advantage of it. Besides, given the events that had unfolded ten years ago thanks to her decisions, his actions tonight barely began to approximate payback.

The murmur of conversation dragged him out of his thoughts and got him moving. He strode through the moonlit room and out into the corridor. Savannah and Ronan were standing down the hall, and far too close for his liking. They were talking so softly he couldn't make out the words, but if body language was anything to go by, Ronan wasn't telling Vannah anything she wanted to hear. As Cade approached, Ronan looked up, his gaze locking with Cade's.

And what Cade saw in the other man's eyes didn't really surprise him. He'd expected anger and possessiveness, and they were both there, though not in the volumes he'd expected. But what he didn't anticipate was what he found when he skimmed the ranger's thoughts. The reason for those emotions wasn't the fury of a wolf whose mate had been poached, but rather concern for Vannah herself. Beyond that, one clear and definite thought echoed—and it was a warning very evident in the clear gray depths of Ronan's eyes.

Hurt her, and you're a dead man.

Cade halted behind Vannah and crossed his arms. "What do you want, ranger?"

Ronan's gaze skimmed the bruised side of Cade's face, and amusement touched one corner of his mouth. "Trista and Anton are looking for you. Since neither of you are answering your phones, I thought I'd better come up here and warn you before someone else thought of it."

"If my team wanted me, they could have easily found me. I'm tagged with a locator."

"Then you wouldn't have minded them finding you like this?"

Ronan's tone suggested *he* minded very much, and Cade resisted the impulse to bite back a comment on who actually had rights when it came to Savannah. He simply growled, "What do they want?"

"How would I know? Your people play their cards

very close. Anyone would think we were on opposing sides, rather than partners in this investigation."

Cade ignored the barb. After all, Ripple Creek's rangers weren't exactly forthcoming with information, either. And given the tension emanating from the woman who stood so close to them both, he very much suspected the news about his team wasn't the only reason Ronan had come up here. "How did the name collecting go today?"

"A total of fifty-three people checked in during the two weeks before the murders began. I believe Trista intends to run the names through your system."

Cade nodded. The IIS had access to a greater range of information than the rangers did.

"Any likely suspects?"

"No." Ronan glanced at Vannah. "I'll see you outside?"

She nodded. "Give me five minutes to get dressed."

"What's going on?" Cade said, the minute Ronan left.

She gave him a contemptuous look. "Town business." Then she pushed past him and headed for her clothes.

Annoyance flared. Damn it, he had the *right* to know what was going on—with the case, and with her and Ronan. He followed her, trying to keep his thoughts away from the enticing sway of her hips, the erotic way silken strands of her hair caressed her shoulders and back.

"What sort of town business?"

"Not the sort of town business that's any of *your* business."

"Savannah," he warned.

She grabbed her bra and began putting it on. "Oh, so now you remember my name?"

"Is it anything to do with our case?"

"If it was, I'd be reporting it, like the good little lackey I am."

"You are not a lackey."

She snorted. "Get real. Reservation rangers are always lackeys for you guys. Hell, IIS seems to think we haven't the training to tie our boots properly."

"I've never treated—"

"So why is Ronan playing guide to Trista?" She hesitated, and her gaze widened. "You bastard. You were getting him out of your way, weren't you?"

She was *far* too quick—which was probably the reason she'd been made head ranger at such a young age. That and the fact that her daddy was the head of the reservation council. "It's always better to have a local on those sorts of information-gathering missions."

"Please credit me with a little intelligence." She shook her head and grabbed her pants. "You disappoint me, Cade."

He laughed. "*I* disappoint *you?* Sweetheart, disappointment is one of the milder emotions I felt when you ran away ten years ago."

"I told you why I ran."

"Because I read your mind?"

"Because you forced yourself into my mind!" She looked up at him, and something deep inside him stilled when he saw the sheen of tears in her eyes. "No telepath should do that to another. Not ever."

Part of him wanted to step forward and wrap his

arms around her, soothe away all the hurt, all the tears. The other part—the angry, hurt part—rejoiced.

She was right; he was a bastard. "In whose world?"

"In my world. In the world of telepathic wolves."

"Well, there is no such rule in *my* world."

"Which is why you and I would have never worked out."

He snorted. "We work out just fine in the only place that matters."

She stared at him, and the pain in her expression gradually faded until there was nothing left except an odd sort of emptiness. And for some reason, that made him think he'd made a huge mistake, but what exactly that mistake was, he didn't know. Yet something inside wanted to retract the words and ask for forgiveness.

"There was a fire over on the east side," she said, her voice matter-of-fact. "The fire department thinks it could be suspicious. Ronan and I are heading over."

"Why you two? I thought Bodee was on evening call?" Damn it, why was he arguing? What did it matter? Or was it simply the fact she was heading off with her usual lover when, by the right of the moon and the night, she should be with him?

Was he *jealous*?

Of course he was. She was his mate, no matter how temporary or unwillingly. And no wolf shared what was his.

"Bodee *is* on call. After eight." She glanced at her watch. "It's barely seven."

"What about Denny and Club Grange?"

She bent, picking up her boots and putting them on. "I'll meet you there. And I suggest you put on a disguise yourself because, by now, half the town will know you're here, even if they don't know why."

With that, she brushed past him and walked out the door. He was tempted to drag her back into his arms and kiss her until the ice was erased from her expression, but that wasn't practical or sensible. The moon fever would ensure she'd be back in his arms before long and, right now, there was work to be done.

He dressed and headed back to his room—or rather, his team's room. Anton was again sitting on the floor with the laptop perched in front of him, but he glanced up as Cade entered.

"Have you got your phone turned off, boss?"

"No, but I've had signal problems. What's up?"

Anton's expression suggested he wasn't buying it, but he kept his thoughts to himself, for which Cade was extremely thankful. He didn't need any more problems right now.

"Hart faxed over the autopsy report on the second victim." Anton picked up a folder and tossed it across the coffee table toward Cade. "The MO is much the same."

"Is the note included?" Cade picked up the folder and looked through it. There'd been a note there, all right.

"*As was stolen from me, so shall I steal from you,*" Anton quoted, and met Cade's gaze squarely. "Savannah Grant is Vannah Harvey, isn't she?"

"Yes." There was no point in denying it. Anton and Trista would have to know anyway, given the threats against her. "What made you suspect?"

"The notes themselves. I mean, why leave one at the head ranger's when she was never at Rosehall?

Unless, of course, she was there under an assumed name." He paused, brown eyes filled with annoyance. "When were you going to tell us?"

"That's what I came back here to do." He handed over the evidence bag that had the tape in it. "Once you listened to that, her alter ego would have been evident, anyway."

"Which is why you insisted on keeping this bag rather than me bringing it back here with the rest of the evidence?" Anton paused. "That's not good legal form, you know."

"This killer is never going to be brought to justice, and you and I both know it."

Anton raised his eyebrows. "If you're telling me—"

"All I'm telling you," Cade cut in, "is that this killer has no intention of being caught like Jontee was."

"And why would you think that?"

"Because we didn't catch him the first time." Cade walked across to the minibar and pulled out a beer.

"You're obviously not talking about Jontee . . ."

"No." Cade popped the top of the beer and took a long drink. "Jontee was behind the killings, but I always thought it was impossible that he'd be working alone."

"There's nothing like that in the files."

"Because the man in charge of the investigation believed there was only one killer—the one we caught." He shrugged. "The opinions of a raw recruit didn't matter."

"Sometimes the ramblings of the inexperienced hold grains of truth a more experienced eye have missed."

"Now you sound like your philosopher father."

Anton smiled. "Are your notes on file somewhere?"

He nodded. "In the notes attached to the main case files, but I have the originals with me."

"Good." Anton paused, then asked, "Have you questioned Ranger Grant about Rosehall?"

"There's no need. I read her mind at the time. That's how I caught Jontee, remember?"

"That doesn't mean you got every scrap of information she possessed."

"Believe me, I read her mind quite thoroughly."

Anton frowned. "But isn't she from the golden pack?"

"Yeah? So?"

"Well, the golden pack are among the strongest telepaths ever recorded. Even the weakest can generally run mental circles around telepaths from other packs."

It was Cade's turn to frown. "I caught her at a very open moment, though."

"It shouldn't have mattered. The minute she felt you invading her mind, she would have slammed down as many shields as she could." Anton's frown deepened. "You might have caught information about Jontee, but I very much doubt you'd have caught everything she knew."

But you never actually asked me about what I knew, she'd said to him yesterday. *You just charged right in and took.*

And he'd been too busy fighting desire and trying to defend his past actions to even pursue the admission.

Maybe she was right. Maybe this investigation *did* need another leader. One with a clearer head who was not so intimately involved. "Where's Trista?"

"She's with the kid, cross-checking the names she and Ronan collected today."

Cade nodded. "What time is Hart due in?"

"He's returning to Denver to grab one of the mobile forensics vans, so I wouldn't expect him until morning."

Cade nodded and glanced at the bagged and tagged items strewn across the table. "Discover anything yet?"

"Nothing helpful. The partial tire tracks match those sold as standard on at least three different makes of four-wheel drives. The shoe tracks we found in the forest don't appear to match the partial print found near the tape recorder. I've scanned both through to the labs to see if they can come up with a shoe make or anything else useful."

"Let's hope they find something." Cade rubbed a hand across his still aching jaw. "I'm going out with Ranger Grant later tonight to find and question the woman who paid the kid to leave the note under her wiper."

Anton raised his eyebrows. "A woman? Did the kid give you a description?"

"Average height, late teens to early twenties, blond, blue eyes, and buxom."

Anton snorted. "Every teenage male's wet dream."

"Exactly, which makes me suspect she was also paid to bribe the kid."

Anton nodded in agreement. "You intend to question the ranger while you're at it?"

"Yeah." Whether he actually got any information was another matter entirely. She wasn't exactly happy with him at the moment. He tossed the empty beer bottle in the trash can. "Call me if you get anything."

"I will. Just make sure you've got the phone turned on this time, or we *will* use the locator."

Cade ignored the barb, but he heeded the warning as he headed for the door.

"I CAN SMELL him on you, you know."

Savannah glanced at Ronan as they walked toward the blackened remains of the old house. "I'm sorry. I don't mean to continuously shove it in your face."

His smile was almost a grimace. "I know. It's just a warning. I may be more sensitive to your aroma, but the others have worked with you for a while and they will notice as well."

"They're going to know sooner or later that Cade and I were once lovers."

He nodded. "But you don't want them to know the relationship has blossomed again, do you?"

"Blossomed is definitely the wrong word," she said dryly. As was *relationship*. "And no, it's not something I want everyone in town to know."

The old gate creaked as he pushed it open, and he stood aside to allow her through first. At the back of the blackened wreckage of the house were two fire engines, their red and blue lights washing the night with an eerie brightness. She couldn't see Manny Johnson, the head of the local fire department, but she knew he was here somewhere. Ripple Creek didn't get many emergency calls, and as gruesome as it sounded, she knew Manny wouldn't have missed it.

"Can I ask why?" Ronan asked softly.

She frowned up at him. "Why what?"

"Why don't you want the town to know about you and Cade?"

"Because it's against the code of conduct."

"Not really. We are, but you and Cade are not."

"He's here on a case. A murder case. *That* makes it against the rules."

Ronan's expression suggested he didn't think it was. "Are you ashamed of what you did with him?"

Startled, she glanced up at him. "Of course not."

His gray eyes were intent, yet his expression was touched by something close to sadness. That made no sense, considering what they were discussing. "So are you ashamed of what you did at Rosehall?"

"No. But, by the same token, I don't want the whole town finding out about it, either."

"Why not?"

"Because I am no longer that person. She died long ago."

"Did she?" he mused. "Or did circumstances merely force her into hiding?"

She opened her mouth to deny his statement, but the acrid smell of smoke and death swirled around her, catching in her throat and making her cough, which was probably just as well. She couldn't deny something she knew deep down to be true, as her reaction to Cade these last few days had proven. That part of her *hadn't* died. It had merely waited for the right person to bring it back out.

It was such a goddamn shame that the right person just happened to be Cade again.

A big man stepped from the side of the ruined house, smiling grimly when he saw them.

"We'll finish this discussion later," she murmured to Ronan, then held out her hand to the approaching fire chief. "How have you been, Manny?"

"I've had better days," the older man said wearily, shaking her hand, then wiping a sooty forearm across his brow. "Old Lana Lee died in the fire."

Savannah swore softly. She'd known this was Lana's house, but she'd thought the widow had gone to the Bitterroot reservation to visit her daughter. She had said as much to Manny.

"Yeah," he said. "Apparently she returned yesterday."

"Damn." She'd gotten to know the old woman over the years, simply because it was Lana who owned the flower shop below Savannah's apartment. While they'd never been more than pleasantly polite, she'd liked the older woman. Liked her style. "Has the coroner been called?"

Manny nodded. "And the state fire marshal. The body has been bagged and sent to the medical examiner for the cause of death ruling."

"Your guess?"

"Asphyxiation."

"So the body showed no sign of trauma?"

"Not according to the coroner. Doc Carson's home, if you want to talk to him."

Savannah glanced at Ronan, who nodded and reached for his cell phone as he stepped away from them. "And the fire?" she said, looking back at the fire chief.

"Suspicious."

"Why?"

"It started in the bedroom—a lit candle left too

close to the lace curtains. The fire quickly moved into the roof, and from there—in an old house like this—it was only minutes before the whole place was ablaze."

"But Lana hated candles." She'd hated them since her son had died in a similar accident when he was five years old.

"Exactly," Manny said. "So how did the candles get there, and who lit them?"

And why would they want to light them? Who'd want to kill Lana, for God's sake? She might have been independently wealthy, thanks to her dead husband's insurance policies and the regular income she got from the flower shop's lease, but she lived frugally, and she had few material possessions. She hadn't even stepped into the TV age, let alone the DVD years. She'd preferred her music and books to all those "newfangled toys," as she called them. "Is the building safe enough for us to poke around in?"

Manny nodded and swung into step beside her as she moved toward the skeletal remains of the house.

"Were the front and back doors locked?" she asked, stepping carefully through the remains of what was once the living room wall. The ceiling in this section was gone, leaving the living room open to the elements. Burned rafters arched skyward like broken fingers reaching for the stars. Her gaze followed the burn line across the rafters to the wall—which, though it still stood, was skeletal, revealing the bedroom next door. The roof had collapsed there, too.

"The front door was locked," Manny answered. "The back door wasn't."

"Meaning Lana had let someone into her house?"

"Possibly. The old girl was meticulous about locking her doors, and she even held conversations through the closed door."

Savannah grinned. "I had a ten-minute discussion like that with her last year. It was snowing, and she was afraid opening the door would let out too much heat."

"She always was a bit of a character," Manny agreed. His gaze swept around the room, and the amusement in his expression faded. "But she was a gentle old soul who wouldn't have harmed a gnat. She didn't deserve this."

"No." The question was, why had her life ended like this? "Where'd you find her body?"

He pointed toward the end of the house that still had most of its roof intact. "In the kitchen, slumped over the table with her coffee."

"Were smoke detectors installed?"

"Yeah, but the batteries were dead. Or at least, the one in the kitchen was."

Savannah headed down the hallway. "Wouldn't she have smelled the smoke? Seen it?"

"One of the boys was telling me that Lana's sense of smell was pretty bad. Apparently she'd left the gas on a few times without knowing it."

"But still, the smoke would have been fairly thick, wouldn't it?"

"This old house exploded pretty fast. Given the fact it was dusk and none of the lights were on, she might not have seen the smoke until it was too late."

And she obviously hadn't if she'd been found at the table. Savannah stopped just inside the kitchen doorway and looked around. Most of the damage in here was either smoke- or water-related. Her gaze swept the small room and came to rest on the table. Soot had outlined where Lana had slumped in death, and anger slithered through Savannah. Why would someone do this to a harmless old woman?

"When was the fire reported?"

"Seventeen-forty-five. By that time, it had reached the roof and pretty much destroyed the house."

"Who reported it?"

"Rex, the neighbor to the right, saw the smoke and gave us a call. Apparently it wasn't long after that the living room roof collapsed."

Meaning there might have been accelerants involved, as well as the candle. But they wouldn't know that for sure until the fire marshal arrived. She walked over to the sink. There were no extra cups, no spoons, nothing to indicate that Lana had shared her coffee with anyone else. She walked toward the back door. Old slippers, summer sandals, and a worn pair of lined rubber boots stood in a tidy line to one side of the doorway. In the doorway itself, mud tracks proliferated. Most were from the boots of Manny and his men . . . except for one. She frowned, stepped to one side, and squatted in front of it.

The footprint wasn't small, nor was it as fresh as the others. And it had a different print pattern. She pointed at it as she glanced up at Manny. "Any of your men wearing different boots today?"

He frowned and shook his head. "Regulation down the line."

She picked up one of Lana's boots and flipped it over to study the heel and sole. There was mud caked on, indicating Lana had gone outside earlier, but the pattern was different from the muddy ones on the floor. "You want to keep your men away until we can get a photo of this?"

Manny nodded. Savannah rose and headed back out to the car. Ronan met her at the gate.

"The doc confirmed what Manny said. There doesn't appear to be any obvious signs of injury, beyond those related to the fire."

She nodded. "But Lana had a visitor before the fire started."

"Did the neighbors tell you that?"

She shook her head and opened the door. "No. I found a boot print that didn't match either Lana's boots or the ones used by Manny and his men."

Ronan reached into the back and grabbed the crime scene kit. "That doesn't mean it belongs to the person who set the fire."

"No, but it might. You want to go interview the neighbors while I take a few photos? Rex, the neighbor on the right, reported the fire."

"I'll start with him, then." Ronan hesitated and looked around, as if to see who was near, then added softly, "There's something I need to say."

Her stomach clenched. She knew it was about Cade, about what they'd been talking about before, without even skimming his thoughts—not that she ever did that with Ronan. Or any of the other rangers, for that matter. "Can't it wait?"

He shook his head. "I know you think Cade coming back into your life is a bad thing, and if I'm looking at it from a purely selfish point of view, I tend to agree. But I really don't think it is."

She raised an eyebrow. "Why on earth not?"

His gaze met hers, and once again there was a

touch of sadness in those clear gray depths. Yet there was also determination, and on some inner level that frightened her. Her life was about to change, and she wasn't entirely sure she was ready for it.

"Because until now, you and I have been living like sleepwalkers, just going through the motions. Both of us have been afraid to experience the depth of true emotions again, so we keep to the safety of each other."

She opened her mouth to deny his statement, but he raised a warning finger, stopping her.

"His arrival here has awakened something in you, Savannah. Don't let it go back to sleep, because it's beautiful to see."

"Ronan—"

He smiled and caught her hand, then raised it to his lips and kissed it gently. "There's no need to say anything. There never was."

He released her, handed her the kit, then turned and walked away.

And she knew it was as much a symbolic retreat as it was literal.

She took a deep, shuddering breath and tried to control the swirl of . . . not hurt, but at the very least, regret. Yet, deep in her heart, she knew that what he was doing was right for them both.

Even when Cade finally left Ripple Creek, there would be no going back to the easy camaraderie she and Ronan had once shared, if only because the wolf within her had indeed woken again. *That* part of her—the part she'd subdued for so long—had always wanted more than just a comfortable existence. She wanted lust, and passion. She wanted the unquenchable fire of needing to be with someone so badly it felt like she'd die without him. But most important, she wanted to know what it was like to be the object of one man's undying love.

And those were things she could never find in Ronan's arms, no matter how much either of them might want it.

But she'd found most of it with Cade—then *and* now.

Fate, she thought as she brushed the heel of her hand across her eyes, had to be a woman, because it sure as hell was a bitch.

Chapter Seven

CADE COMBED THE remainder of the temporary color through his hair, then stepped back to study the effect.

Bright red definitely didn't suit him. It made his skin look sallow rather than tanned. But when combined with the silver-gray contact lenses, it went a long way toward disguising his identity. Add faded denims, black T-shirt, and a worn black-leather jacket, and he looked nothing like his usual suit-wearing official self, even though he'd done nothing to disguise his features.

But then, he didn't need to. Few people really stopped to examine faces. Most folks just scanned the surface, making basic assumptions based on little more than clothing and skin color. That had been proved time and again in lineups and undercover operations the world over.

He picked up his keys, wallet, and coat. As he headed for the door, anticipation rose. What sort of disguise would Vannah wear? At Rosehall, she'd worn all sorts of costumes—from the prim and proper librarian to a leather-clad whip-mistress, both of which he'd enjoyed immensely. Neither of those was suitable for tonight's venture, but he had no doubt that whatever she came up with would be equally exciting. If there was one thing Vannah could never be accused of, it was lacking imagination.

So why had she settled for being a ranger?

The world of police work, with all its rigid rules and regulations, was something he would never have thought she'd be comfortable in. The Vannah he'd known had been a free spirit and would have chafed at the restrictions she now worked under.

But then, how well had he really known her? He hadn't even known she was using a false name, for heaven's sake. Which, now that he actually thought about it, was pretty slack police work on his part—and that of his supervisors.

Why hadn't they known?

The thought niggled at him and, instead of heading for his car, he turned and walked to his team's room.

"Hey, pretty sexy look you have happening there, boss," Trista said, her expression amused as her gaze swept him.

"Apparently, if I don't wear a disguise to this nightclub, our quarry will run."

"You sure our chief ranger isn't pulling your leg?"

"No, I'm not." And worse yet, he hadn't even thought of the possibility. He glanced at Anton. "Have you had a chance to go through the files and find my notes?"

Anton shook his head and raised the slice of pizza he held. "Thought I'd have something to eat first. Why?"

"Because I want you to uncover what identity

checks were done for Vannah Harvey and Nelle James in the early stages of the original investigation."

Anton frowned. "There must have been checks. I mean, you didn't go in blind and randomly select a target, did you?"

"No, but there wasn't much in the folders I was given on Vannah and Nelle, other than photos, names, and position in the group."

Trista reached across the table and picked up a slice of pizza of her own. "But it's standard procedure that all possible cross-checks are done before sending an agent undercover. If they came up empty, it would have raised suspicions."

Anton's frown deepened. "And considering you were the one going undercover, I would have thought someone would have told you if there were doubts about your target's identity."

"I'd have thought so, too." He rubbed a hand across his jaw, wincing when he hit the darkening bruise. Still, a bruise added to the cover, because people would focus on that more than his actual features. "While you're checking the files, do a cross-check on Oliver James, too."

Trista raised her eyebrows. "Why? Oliver quit the IIS with a spotless record, didn't he?"

Cade nodded. "Eight years ago. He's apparently living in Florida nowadays."

"So why run a check on him?"

"Because I'm curious." He glanced at Anton. "And because if I was right all those years ago and there *was* a second person involved, then maybe Vannah wasn't the only reason it almost went to hell."

"Hang on," Trista said. "I'm missing something.

How did our head ranger almost cause it to all go to hell?"

Cade grimaced. "Nelle was Vannah's best friend, and I believe she warned Nelle that I was going after Jontee. I think Nelle then warned Jontee, who ambushed and almost succeeded in killing me."

"So why wasn't she charged for impeding an investigation? Why wasn't a warrant issued for her?"

"Because there was no evidence that Nelle was involved with Jontee in any way other than sexually. You can't get a warrant without evidence. Besides, Oliver had his man and a confession, and that's all he cared about."

"That's not good policing—if there was even the remotest possibility that someone else was involved, it should have been pursued."

"Yes. But I'm not casting doubts on Oliver or his part of the investigation. I just want to know why there was no serious background information on Vannah and Nelle, that's all."

"Because you have a hunch," Anton said.

"And in the past," Trista muttered, "those hunches have proven amazingly accurate. You realize the problems this will cause? Oliver has a lot of friends in the department."

"I'm just asking you to check, nothing more. I don't expect to find anything." He glanced at his watch. "Now I'd better get going. Buzz me if anything urgent comes up."

"Enjoy the club," Trista said, her voice dry.

He glanced at her. "It's for work."

"I'm sure it is," she said, and took a bite of the pizza. Unfortunately, it didn't quite hide her grin.

Obviously, he hadn't been as discreet about Savannah as he'd presumed. But knowing that saying anything would only make it worse—and deepen Trista's amusement—he simply turned and walked out of the room.

Snow had begun falling during his brief time indoors, and it coated the road with a slushy mix that quickly froze under the evening's chill. He hesitated, glancing at the car—knowing that if the weather continued like this, the roads would quickly become as icy as a skating rink. He glanced at his watch. He still had forty-five minutes before their target was due to arrive. And even though the night was freezing, he felt the sudden need to run, to stretch his legs and feel the chill ruffling his coat as the snow drifted past his nose.

He glanced at the sky a final time, then shifted shape and loped toward Main Street.

THE BASE-HEAVY THUMP of music rode the night, and the smell of sweat and lust mingled freely in the air, stirring Savannah's memories as much as her senses.

Rosehall had smelled much like this.

It was the freedom to be yourself, to follow your desires, without having to worry about the consequences your actions might have on others.

In her teenage years, there'd been few places where a young wolf with moon fever could go other than the dances at the Sinclair mansion. And as much as she'd wanted to rebel against her father's strictures, she hadn't wanted to ruin his standing in the community.

When she'd heard of Rosehall, it had seemed an ideal way to satisfy her deeper hungers without having to worry about her dad's reputation—or his anger. And it *had* been a magical, liberating experience—at least until Cade had arrived, taunting her with possibilities that could never be.

She shivered as she shifted back to human shape in the shadows leading up to the nightclub's front entrance. But it wasn't the chill of the night that had caused the shiver, but rather the direction of her thoughts. Why couldn't she stop thinking about Cade and all that had transpired in the past? Why did she have to keep tormenting herself with the pain of dreams long since dead? He cared for nothing more than his own needs, as he'd amply proved tonight. So why couldn't she let it all go and simply enjoy the moment?

Because the heart is a funny creature, Neva's voice whispered into her mind. *And often a stubborn one. Part of you loves him still, Sav.*

No, part of me still loves the idea of love. It loves something that, in reality, was little more than a shadow and a lie.

Neva's doubts swam through Savannah's thoughts, but all she actually said was *You need to talk to him.*

I know, but right now I'm a little busy trying to catch a murderer. She paused. *Are you and Duncan safely ensconced in the mansion?*

And a breezy goddamn hole it is in this weather, too. Duncan's had to set roaring fires in both the fireplaces in his rooms just to warm me.

I'm surprised he didn't warm you in a more intimate manner. . . .

Oh, he did. Neva's mind-voice was filled with amusement. *But as good as we are together, sex can only last so long. Especially when the kids start kicking. How long am I expected to stay here?*

Until we catch our killer.

And why is this killer coming after you?

As revenge for something he thinks I've done.

Rosehall?

Savannah blinked, though she wasn't sure why she was surprised at how much her sister knew. After all, Neva had always been the stronger of the two of them when it came to telepathy. *Just how much have you been reading in my mind lately?*

Neva's laughter swam through her, warm as summer sunshine. *Not much. Certainly not when it started getting interesting.*

Just as well, or I'd have to warn the pups their mom's a voyeur.

Neva's amusement deepened momentarily, and then fell away. *What about Mom and Dad?*

Savannah blew out a mental breath. *I haven't warned them yet.*

You've been avoiding it.

Yes. Although she wasn't ashamed of her actions at Rosehall, her dad would be. And as contradictory as it was—especially since she'd gone to Rosehall in rebellion *against* her dad's rules—she didn't want to lose his respect. Rosehall was in the past, and the rebellion that had driven her there had since died.

Hadn't it?

I'll talk to them later tonight, she continued, trying to ignore the thought that maybe the problems she'd had with her father were no deader than the wildness. *It might be wise for them to get out of town for a while.*

Dad's never going to do that willingly.

Whatever his faults, he loves Mom. He'll do it for her.

I hope you're taking similar precautions with your own safety.

Ronan's looking into it.

That man is a gem.

And one she loved, but not in the way he deserved to be loved. He was right to end it now. The simple truth was that they were both using the other as a crutch, finding safety in each other's arms rather than facing life and love again. She was going to miss their particular closeness, and yet part of her rejoiced.

Maybe, after ten long years, she was finally ready to face it all again.

But was she, for all her tough words, ready to face up to Cade and everything he'd done—and everything *she'd* done? Because there was no doubt she had to do both of those if she wanted to move past the hurt.

But could she really do it? Move past all he'd meant to her and just get on with her life?

She didn't know. But maybe it was time to at least find out. If Cade's arrival had shown her one thing, it was the fact that she could no longer drift along. She loved her job, but her job was not enough.

She wanted what Neva had. A man who loved her. A man to share the ups and downs of life with, to have children with.

But are you ready to fight for that? Neva asked softly. *Like you forced me to fight for it?*

Savannah frowned. *What do you mean?*

You once loved Cade. Perhaps you still do. What if the reason you haven't moved on is the fact that your heart doesn't want to? What if Cade is the one?

He doesn't love me, Neva. He never did. I was just a means to an end.

That's not what I asked.

No. She paused. *And I guess the answer is, I don't know.*

Then you'd better start deciding before he walks out of your life for a second time.

He didn't walk out on me the first time.

You know what I mean.

Yes. And she hated it when her sister was right. Neva's amusement swam through her mind again, and Savannah smiled reluctantly. *Gotta go do some work. I'll talk to you tomorrow.*

After you talk to Mom and Dad.

Duncan's right. Marriage has turned you into a nag. Savannah broke the connection between them in the midst of her twin's laughter and strode toward the front steps, although, after ten years of *not* wearing five-inch spike heels, it took a lot of concentration not to fall flat on her face.

The heels tapped against the concrete as she climbed the steps—a soft tattoo that seemed to carry easily over the thump of the music. The security guard near the door leisurely looked her up and down, and a wide grin split his lips.

"Ain't seen you here before, darling," he said, his voice as deep as his gaze was appreciative.

A warm flush of satisfaction swept through her. In that moment, she felt both extremely feminine and utterly sexual, neither of which she'd felt since leaving Rosehall.

And that made her angry—at herself, more than anything. Damn it, she *was* a woman—a sexual, sensual woman—and she occasionally *deserved* to be the object of lust. Yet that was something the ranger part of her never had been, not in all the long years she'd been back in Ripple Creek. And it was a sad indictment of how badly she'd been burned by Cade that she'd let such a vital part of her be buried for so long.

Still, better late than never. And if Kel's brother didn't recognize her in this outfit—an outfit Nelle had once labeled "the erotic biker"—no one would. Hell, she'd gone to school with Tane, had actually had a major crush on him between ninth and tenth grades, and had kissed him more than once in eleventh. A flirt? Oh yeah, she had been a flirt back then, as Ronan could attest.

With a grin tugging her lips, she exaggerated the swing of her hips as she sashayed toward Tane. The chains dangling from her skirt chimed in time with the rap of her stilettos, and the cool breeze caressed the parts of her bare legs and stomach not covered by her long leather coat. Given how little she was really wearing, she should have been freezing, but she wasn't. The exhilaration of strutting her stuff again was more than enough to keep her warm.

"You may not see me again," she purred as she neared him, "so enjoy the experience while you can."

"Oh, I am." He chuckled softly as he opened the door. "Enjoy your night, miss."

"Clara," she said. "And thank you."

He nodded, his gaze lingering, causing a heat she

could feel way down to her toes as she walked into
the semidarkness of the nightclub. Even though there
was only one man she wanted, that didn't stop her
enjoying the attention of—

She stopped short. Cade might be the only man she
could have right now, but he certainly wasn't the only
man she wanted, because he didn't want what *she*
wanted.

But what if he did?

No; she pushed the thought from her mind. Why
entertain the idea when it was never going to happen?

She paid her entrance fee and handed over her coat.
Then she moved to the shadow-filled corner between
the cashier and the long black, steel, and chrome
bar that dominated the left side of the room. The air
was thick with the scent of desire, sending an ache of
anticipation through her. She wondered if Cade was
here yet. Wondered if she'd recognize him—or if he'd
recognize her.

The heavy beat of the music was louder inside, and
when combined with the frantic pulsing of the multicolored lighting, it had an almost hypnotic effect.
She found herself tapping her foot despite the fact she
normally hated techno.

There was a good crowd tonight, too. The dance
floor was packed, and they were standing three deep
at the bar. She saw several people she recognized,
and a few teenagers who certainly didn't meet the
eighteen-year-old entry requirement. Still, given her
own experiences, she wasn't about to make a fuss.
Especially not tonight.

At the end of the long room were the heavy pan-
eled doors that led into the moon dance room. Two

security guards were stationed there, and she knew their job was to check IDs and ensure that no alcohol was taken into the smaller dance room. She also knew that the ID check wasn't as well enforced as her father would have wanted.

She looked upstairs, checking the balcony that ran around the room. Shadows moved in the darkness above, some obviously doing more than just dancing to the techno beat. Others leaned on the railing, either catching the action in the shadows or watching those on the dance floor. She couldn't see Denny upstairs, so maybe he was among the gyrating mass on the dance floor.

She walked along the bar side of the room, so close to the moving mass of men and women that the air felt like liquid heat, and the musk of desire was so sharp that it fueled the fires of her own need.

Yet she couldn't sate those needs, not even when she found Cade. They were here to catch the woman who'd paid Denny to leave the note, and nothing more.

She found Denny at the back of the room, to the right of the entrance to the moon room. He was dancing with a spike-haired wolf who seemed to have more piercings than Savannah had toes and fingers, and who looked at least ten years older than Denny. Like most of the dancers, they seemed to be ruled by the music, their bodies moving in sync with the frantic rhythm rather than each other. She continued on, trying to find Cade, but she didn't see anyone vaguely resembling him on this level. She turned around and headed for the nearby stairs. It would be easier to keep an eye on Denny from above, and she might be able to spot Cade from there, too.

The shadows closed in around her as she climbed, and the air became so cloying tiny beads of perspiration broke out across her skin. She grabbed a coaster off a nearby table and lightly fanned herself. Her scalp itched, and it was all she could do not to rip off the short black wig. She leaned a hip against the balustrade and scanned the shadows. Couples sat at the various tables or were pressed against the walls, talking and drinking and loving. None of the women were blond or big-breasted, and none of the men matched Cade's height or build.

Relief rolled through her. In truth, she had no more desire to share him with others than he had to share her—which was odd, because she'd had no such concerns at Rosehall. But then, he never did dance with anyone else but her. She'd been the one dancing with others—at least until they'd made the moon promise. And even then, she'd still danced with Jontee. Which Cade had wanted, because all he had needed was Jontee. Not her.

And certainly not a declaration of love.

Hell, he couldn't even remember her saying it, though she could easily guess why. He'd been too busy getting ready to invade her mind.

She blew out a breath, lifting the silky black hair away from her forehead. Glancing down to check that Denny was still dancing, she pushed away from the balustrade and moved along the walkway.

A big man walked toward her, his red hair catching the flicker of the lights and gleaming like fire in the shadows. She let her gaze drift over him, taking in the gleam of his silver eyes as he scanned the shadows, the oh-so-kissable lushness of his mouth, the way his leather jacket emphasized the width of his shoulders and the strength of his arms, while his faded jeans paid homage to the long, lean strength of his legs. He moved with such effortless grace that he could have been walking on air . . .

She blinked.

He walked like *Cade*.

Her gaze shot upward. Aside from the gray eyes, it was Cade's face. The bruise darkening his chin was evidence of that, if nothing else.

A smile tugged at her lips. Would he recognize her? There was only one way to find out. She strolled toward him, accentuating the swing of her hips, watching his expression, waiting for the moment of awareness. His gaze briefly scanned her and moved on. Then he did a double take, and a grin split his lips.

"Well, well," he said, stopping so close the heat of his body surged over her in a wave. He wrapped a hand around her waist and drew her closer. "Don't you look luscious."

"So do you," she purred, running her hands down his leather-clad arms and enjoying the press of his hard body against hers. "And I do like the contacts. I always did like a man with silver eyes." Not to mention leather. Too bad he was wearing jeans. As good as he looked in them, just the thought of leather pants sent her pulse running. There was something very sensual about running a hand over a leather-clad butt.

The muscles under her fingertips tightened so suddenly that it felt as if she were caressing steel. She glanced up in time to see the amusement fade from his expression.

"You found Denny yet?"

His voice was clipped with annoyance, and she frowned. "He's downstairs, dancing with a spike-haired wolf." She hesitated, then added, "Why the attitude?"

"We'd better find someplace to watch from."

She nodded toward the balustrade. "We can do it from there."

His hand slid from her waist to her arm, and his grip was a little too tight as he propelled her forward. "Let's get over there, then."

She pulled her arm from his grip and stopped. "I asked you a question. Answer it first."

He continued on to the balustrade. "How many wolves do you know with silver eyes?"

She stared at his back, more than a little perplexed. "What?"

"So you weren't thinking about Ronan when you said that?"

She laughed. She couldn't help it. He was *jealous*. He had to be. Why else would he make a comment like that? "Ronan was the last wolf on my mind, believe me."

He gave her a withering look. "We're here to work, so let's concentrate on that."

"I'd much rather talk about your reaction."

A grunt was his only reply. How was she supposed to interpret something like that? God, for a man who was so damn willing to throw opinions around, he was mighty closemouthed when it came to anything personal.

Still, she leaned on the railing beside him, close enough that the heat of his body caressed her skin, yet not close enough that they touched. Despite her earlier resolution, despite the doubts she'd expressed to her sister only moments before, she really wasn't sure *what* she wanted anymore. Even when she wasn't with Cade, he filled her thoughts. But wasn't that a natural consequence of the way they'd ended their relationship and what still lay unresolved between them?

Maybe.

And maybe not.

Maybe she still cared for him more than she wanted to admit. But was she willing to risk the utter devastation of realizing he didn't love her a second time? Especially since his actions certainly indicated he was enamored with nothing more than the power of their lovemaking?

I don't know, she thought. *I just don't know.*

But one thing she was sure of. They couldn't stand here like statues, and if they weren't going to make out, they might as well discuss the past. And better here, where her emotions had to be restrained.

Frowning at her cowardice, she glanced down to check that Denny was still where she'd left him, then said, "We need to talk."

"About what?"

Cade wasn't looking at her, but scanning the crowd below. His stance was casual, yet tension touched the corners of his eyes and rode his shoulders. Residual anger over her comment, she thought, rather than any real concern about what she wanted to say.

She took a deep breath, gathering her courage.

"About Rosehall. About what happened between us."

He glanced at her briefly, his expression closed, giving no hint as to what he might be thinking or feeling. "What's there to talk about? We both know what happened."

"Maybe. But we've never talked about how it affected us."

"It was a long time ago. Why dredge it up now?"

"Because, in one way or another, that past is still affecting us both."

"The only effect it's having on me is that you're mine, and only mine, until I say otherwise." He gave her a territorial grin. "And you had better believe that, this time, I will defend that right."

She raised her eyebrows at the anger so evident in his words. "Did you hate sharing me with Jontee that much?"

"Yes."

"But wasn't that why you chose me? Because I was sharing Jontee's bed?"

He looked away. "Yes." But his answer came out clipped, as if she were tearing the word from his lips.

"Then your anger makes no sense."

"We shared a moon promise, damn it!"

"A moon promise that named Jontee as the exception."

"Yes." His voice was a growl.

She stared at him for a moment, then said, "If I didn't know you better, I'd say that you were jealous of Jontee."

He gave her a look that could only be described as glacial. "Don't be ridiculous."

Amusement, and perhaps just a touch of elation, ran through her. Maybe the emotional side of their relationship wasn't as one-sided as she'd thought. She turned to face him, propping her hip against the railing. "You *were* jealous." Then *and* now.

"I was there to do a job. Sharing you was part of that job."

"But that doesn't address the question of jealousy."

"But it's the only answer that matters."

"Not to me."

His gaze searched hers. "Why?"

Because I loved you. Because I need to know if you even really liked me. She shrugged, feigning a casualness she suddenly didn't feel. "Because jealousy suggests I was more than just a means to an end."

He didn't move, didn't seem to react in any way. Yet the air between them suddenly crackled with tension. "And why does it matter to you?"

She stared at him for a moment, wondering how any man could be so obtuse. Did he really not know how she'd felt? Had he never really heard *any* of the things she'd said to him? "Because you were more than just another dancer to me."

His sudden and all-too-brief smile was edged with a wistfulness that made her soul ache. Then he reached out and brushed her cheek, his touch a fire that seemed to burn deep into her flesh. His eyes were filled with an intentness that made her bones feel weaker than water.

"Do you know how I chose you as my target?" he said softly, moving his hand down her neck and across her shoulder.

"No." Her voice came out breathless. She could

barely even breathe, let alone talk, because every inch of her thrummed with desire. She needed him—and it wasn't the heady atmosphere of the club or the demands of the moon. It had never been the moon. Not then, and not now. It was the man.

"My boss handed me twelve folders. Inside were photos and information about each of Jontee's women." He slid his hand around her waist and tugged her toward him, crushing her close. Heat pooled where their bodies met.

"So you could have chosen any one of them?" She briefly closed her eyes, enjoying the warmth of the night and the way the air-conditioning brushed her skin with fleeting coolness. Enjoying the caress of his fingers across her spine and the way his body seemed a perfect match for hers, touching all the right places with heated hardness.

"Twelve beautiful women, and I had to choose only one." His lips were so close that his breath whispered across her lips, making them ache for the touch of his. "But for me, there was only ever one choice."

Her gaze rose to his again. "Why?"

With his free hand, he caught several strands of the wig's short black hair, tugging on it lightly. Amusement ran fleetingly across his luscious lips. "Because I loved the look of your hair. And because there was something in your eyes that spoke to the wildness in me."

"It was just a photo."

He nodded. "A luscious photo of a nymph on a balcony."

"So it was lust at first sight?"

He hesitated. "What else could there be?"

What else, indeed? And even though she'd known what his answer would be, his words still scraped old hurts. "Then why agree to the moon ceremony?"

He shrugged. "I wanted you to be mine, and only mine. At least, as much as possible without endangering my mission."

"And there was nothing more than desire and an alpha's need to possess behind your decision?"

"There was no time for anything else."

They'd had two weeks together—which was more than enough time if everything felt right. And it had for her. "And if we'd had the time?"

He shrugged again. "Who knows?"

"Then you would have continued seeing me, if things hadn't happened the way they did?"

"If you hadn't disappeared off the face of the earth, you mean?"

"If you hadn't abused my trust the way you did."

He snorted softly. "I only read your mind. Hardly an abuse of trust."

She pulled out of his arms. The night felt cooler without his touch. "You really have no idea, do you?"

He reached for her again, but she slapped his hand away. He sighed, a sound filled with annoyance. "Any idea of what?"

"Are your parents or pack telepathic?"

"I cannot believe we keep coming back to this. And no, none of my immediate family is telepathic. What has that got to do with anything?"

"Nothing, other than the fact no one has taught you common courtesy."

"I'm an IIS officer. Part of my job is entering the

minds of others to read them. I've done it lots of times and, believe me, no one has ever been the wiser."

She raised a skeptical eyebrow. "Those other telepaths being the people who trained you?"

"Yes. And what difference does that make?"

"They were ready for you, Cade. They had to be, because when a telepath raids another telepath's mind, it's never pretty, and it's never easy."

"Unless you have the training."

"Training? I was raised in one of the strongest telepathic wolf packs there is, for Christ's sake. Even my low-end shields are stronger than the average telepath's. What you did was nothing short of brutality."

"Quit being so melodramatic. I didn't force my way in, and I didn't rip through your shields, because there weren't any."

"Really? Are you willing to bet on that?"

His eyes narrowed at the challenge. "Yes."

"Right here, right now?"

"Yes."

Her sudden grin undoubtedly had a nasty edge, because right at that moment she was feeling particularly nasty. She might not have Neva's mental strength, but she was her father's daughter, and her father was the head of their pack simply because he *was* the strongest. "And what price would you be willing to pay? How about, if I'm right, you revoke your little addition to the moon promise?"

"No." His answer was immediate and obviously instinctive.

She felt like baring her teeth and growling in frustration. Why did this man always take without ever being willing to give, even just this once? "Are you afraid you'll lose?"

"You're mine, Vannah, and you will remain mine until I say otherwise."

"If you were so damn sure I belonged to you, you'd be letting *me* make the choice. But you aren't sure, are you?" She snorted softly. "I never took you for a coward—"

She stopped, glancing down as movement near the door caught her eye. A big-busted blonde had entered the club. Dressed in a short skirt, a white tube top that flared brightly under the strobe lights, and what looked to be six-inch stilettos, the blonde definitely fit the description Denny had given them.

She mentally cursed the woman's timing, but added, "I think our quarry just arrived."

He made a low rumble that sounded as ominous as thunder, but he glanced downstairs. "She's definitely as Denny described."

She nodded, briefly watching the woman as she teetered on the edge of the steps. "How do you want to play this?"

The dark look he cast her way suggested that this was the last game he wanted to play right now. "We wait until she makes contact with Denny."

She nodded and leaned on the railing, her arms crossed as she watched the woman totter around the bar side of the dance floor. "Some women just shouldn't wear stilettos. She looks like she's going to topple over at any minute."

"Are you sure it's not a function of how . . . top-heavy she is?" he commented, his voice hinting at amusement.

Savannah glanced over at him. Laugh lines crinkled the corners of his eyes, lending his face a sudden warmth. Though still angry with him, she couldn't help smiling. "You're a breast man?"

"*Any* man is a breast man, and don't let them tell you otherwise." His gaze slid from her face down to her chest. Her nipples puckered under his scrutiny, and warmth flushed across her skin. "However, I have always been of the opinion that a nice, plump handful is all that a man really needs."

"Just as well, seeing that a plump handful is all you're going to get from me."

He raised an eyebrow. "Have I ever complained?"

"No." She frowned as the blonde stopped and reached into the small bag slung over her shoulder. "But you've never complimented them, either."

"Remiss of me."

"Very."

He glanced downstairs, then back at her. "What if I say you have the most luscious breasts I've ever seen?"

"I'd say you were full of shit."

His sudden grin was unexpected, and made her heart do an old, familiar dance. "Is that the cop speaking, or the woman?" he asked, voice so low it seemed little more than a warm vibration across her skin.

"Both." The blonde had gotten out her phone and was searching the upper balconies as she talked. Looking for Denny, or for someone else? Savannah frowned as the woman's gaze seemed to snag on her and Cade, lingering for too many seconds before moving on. "We've been made."

"What?" He looked down. "How?"

The blonde was still talking on the phone, and though her gaze seemed to be on the dancers in front of her, the sudden tension in her stance suggested she was ready to flee given the slightest provocation. "I don't know, but she's seen us. Or me, at least."

"Odd that she answered the phone before she made us." He glanced at Savannah. "It suggests an accomplice."

"Or that the person behind the threats is in this room." Yet if Tane didn't recognize her, why would anyone else, especially disguised as she was? "Shall we wait or move?"

Before Cade could answer, the woman made the decision for them, slipping her phone into her bag as she turned and headed back toward the door. "You go left; I'll go right," he said, thrusting away from the railing.

She nodded and headed left. Her stilettos clattered against the metal stairs as she ran, making enough noise that the dancers closest to her glanced up. And though Denny was one of them, there was no recognition in his eyes. At least that meant he'd probably still be here if she and Cade missed their quarry.

Ahead, the blonde was climbing the stairs and walking toward the door. She didn't seem to be in a hurry, meaning they either had the wrong woman or she knew she had plenty of time to escape. Savannah was betting on the latter. If this woman was involved in the murders, then there would have been provisions should something go wrong. The fiend behind the recent murders was too well organized to leave anything to chance.

Savannah ran along the edge of the dance floor, dodging the occasional overenthusiastic dancer or drunk patron. By the time she got to the steps, the blonde had already left the building. Cade was two steps behind her as she pushed the door open and ran out.

"There," he said, pointing left to the flare of reversing lights.

They ran toward the truck as it reversed out of the parking spot. Savannah glanced at the plates, noting the number and the fact they were from Arizona. Before they could get any closer, the truck sped off, leaving them in a cloud of burnt rubber and exhaust.

Cade swore and thrust a hand through his hair. "Our first solid connection to the murders, and we let her get away."

"I wouldn't call her a solid connection as yet," she said as she tried to catch her breath. "And at least we can track down the truck via the plate number."

"Not when it had false plates."

She raised her eyebrows. "How do you know that?"

"Because the second plate wasn't stuck on too well. I saw the corner of the real plate sticking out one side."

She grimaced. "At least we still have the truck." Even if that make and color was one of the more popular ones in Ripple Creek. She tugged off her wig and scratched irritably at her scalp. "Of course, the question is what—or who—tipped her off?"

Cade glanced at her. "Did anyone see you coming over here?"

"I was in wolf form, so it wouldn't have mattered."

"Maybe they were watching your apartment."

She frowned. "They could just as easily have been watching your rooms. It's no secret now that the IIS is in town, even if no one knows why."

"I would have noticed a shadow."

Irritation swept through her. "Meaning I wouldn't have?"

The guard glanced their way. "Keep it down," Cade said, as he waved a reassuring hand toward the guard. When he looked back at her, Cade's expression was a mix of annoyance and frustration. "Meaning, you've had less experience at being tailed than me."

"Less experience doesn't mean no experience," she bit back. "And I wasn't followed."

"Then how the hell did that woman—who I've never met and I presume you haven't either—make us?"

"I don't know."

"Someone *must* have followed one of us."

No one had followed her; she was sure of it. So what had given them away? She frowned, remembering the way the blonde's gaze had lingered on them—or, more particularly, her. It suggested that she'd been the one recognized, but how? With the wig and the costume, she looked nothing like herself. Someone from Rosehall might have recognized the shoes, but the darkness of the club precluded that.

Rosehall . . .

Oh, shit. She'd never worn this costume at Rosehall, but she had gotten it there.

"Someone recognized my outfit," she said, her voice empty of the anger boiling inside. Anger aimed at herself, at her own thoughtlessness. Yet, how could she have known that there was *any* chance of the costume being recognized?

"What?"

"This outfit," she said, lightly flicking the chains wrapping the skirt. "I got it at Rosehall."

"From who? Jontee?"

If only. "No. Besides, Jontee's dead, and hardly in a position to recognize anything."

"Then who?"

She took a deep breath and released it slowly. "Nelle James."

Chapter Eight

CADE STUDIED HER for a long moment, then said slowly, "Nelle James gave you that outfit?"

"Isn't that what I just said?"

Her voice held a mix of anger and defiance, and he smiled grimly. There was no need to reprimand her for her stupidity, because she was kicking herself hard enough. "Meaning she's here in town?"

"I would have told you if she was," she snapped, her green eyes flashing.

"Would you? I'm not so sure." After all, how well did he actually know her? The report Oliver had given him had contained very little information, and she'd pretty much kept mum about personal details in the brief time they'd been together at Rosehall. The only thing he knew for sure was the fact that she and Nelle had been very close friends. And close friends didn't rat each other out, did they?

"I'm a *ranger*," she said, voice deceptively calm given how white her knuckles had suddenly become. "Don't you ever accuse me of not doing my job properly!"

"I didn't—"

"Then what the hell do you think making an accusation like that was?"

"I was trying to elicit an honest response, which I got."

"Bastard!"

"I'm an IIS officer. That's what we do." He reached into his jacket pocket for his cell phone. "Why don't you go talk to Denny while I see if I can track down that truck?"

She stared at him for a second or two, her fingers flexing, as if debating whether to slug him or salute him. In the end she did neither. She simply shoved the wig back on before walking away. He called Anton, but as he waited, his gaze was drawn to the enticing sway of her hips as she stalked toward the club. There was, he noted with amusement, something very alluring about the way a woman walked when she was angry.

"Hey, boss," Anton said, by way of hello. "What's up?"

"I want you to head up to Main Street and cruise around for a dark blue truck being driven by a blonde in a short skirt and a white tube top. She'd be in her early to mid-twenties."

"Not exactly an unpleasant task." He paused, and Cade heard the sound of keys jingling and the quick murmur of conversation before a door slammed. "Why are we looking for the blonde?"

"She was the woman who apparently asked the kid to leave the note on Ranger Grant's windshield."

"And she spotted you? Dressed as you were?"

"It's a long story. So, what's Trista doing?"

"Going back through the files, like you asked."

"Good. Give me a call if you spot the blonde, but don't pull her over. Just tail her."

"Will do."

Cade hung up and called Trista, asking her to come down to the club's parking lot with her crime scene kit. Given the stench of burned rubber when the truck had taken off, there would surely be skid marks. Even if they couldn't pick up the tread pattern, they'd at least get an idea of tire width, which, in turn, might give them some idea if the tracks left in the forest were a possible match. As he hung up, Savannah stalked back out of the club. Just watching her made him ache.

It was, he thought, a bitch of a situation. Yet one he couldn't—or wouldn't—relinquish. Not this time.

So was it jealousy, like she'd claimed?

He didn't know. How could he, when he'd never experienced anything remotely like this before he'd met her? But if jealousy could be classified as wanting to be the only one holding her, the only one loving her, then her accusation was probably right. He'd never been good at sharing—as many of his brothers would undoubtedly testify.

She stopped well beyond his reach, but the cold night seemed to amplify her scent. It swam around him, warming him as quickly as any caress. Lord, it was just as well they'd taken the edge off the fever earlier; otherwise he'd be tearing her clothes off like some frenzied teenager.

"I've asked Ike to come down and tail Denny." Her voice was cool, professional, and totally devoid of the heat he could see in her eyes.

Cade nodded. "Could be he'll lead us to the blonde."

"I wasn't worried about that. I was worried about Denny's safety."

"I doubt he'd—"

"You're willing to risk his life?" she cut in, the heat in her eyes now anger rather than desire.

"No." He paused. "But if that's the case, then why use Ike to tail him? The kid's a little inexperienced, isn't he?"

"Maybe, but he's also closer to Denny's age than the rest of us. He won't look so out of place at some of Denny's haunts."

"But people are going to recognize him, especially with that red hair."

"He'll wear a cap. Quite the fashion amongst teenagers at the moment—or so he tells me."

Cade wasn't convinced, but he kept his doubts to himself. After all, she knew her people better than he did. "Did Denny have anything else to give us?"

"He did say that I looked hot." Amusement touched her lips, but it quickly faded. "And he didn't meet her here at the club, but rather at the burger joint on Galena Street. He said she'd worked the night shift there, off and on, for the last couple of weeks. I thought I'd head over there now and check it out."

"It's rather convenient that he remembers all that now."

"Denny has only ever said as much as he needed to keep everyone happy."

"Next time, I'll push the brat a bit more." His gaze drifted down her leather-clad body, and his erection swelled painfully. "If you go dressed like that, they're never going to look at you the same way again."

"And that could be a good thing," she muttered, blowing out a breath that lifted the silky black strands from her forehead. "I'll change, naturally."

"Good." He didn't want anyone else ogling her any more than he wanted anyone else making love to her. And was that a wolf's natural predatory instincts, or something else entirely? He didn't know.

He didn't *want* to know.

Her eyes narrowed dangerously. "Just because the moon is on your side, don't think you can control all my actions."

"I wouldn't dream of it."

She snorted softly. "Yeah, right."

He glanced at his watch and saw it was barely eleven. Thankfully, there was a lot of night left. "Shall we meet back at your lodge by two? That gives us a few hours before dawn."

She opened her mouth as if to say something, then obviously thought the better of it and simply nodded. Then she walked away, calling to the wolf within. He watched the fluid beauty of the change, as attracted to the golden wolf as he was the woman.

When her form was finally claimed by the shadows, he walked over to where the woman's truck had been parked. Moisture gleamed wetly on the road surface. He squatted, and dipped a finger into the fluid. Oil. He scanned the rest of the immediate area, but couldn't immediately see anything else.

As he rose, lights swept into the parking lot, blinding him. He threw up a hand to protect his eyes and tried to see if it was Trista.

The vehicle cruised slowly toward him, as if intent on keeping him pinned in the light. He frowned, an odd sense of unease creeping up his spine. He took a step back. As he did so, the engine gunned and, with a squeal of tires, the truck came hurtling at him. He waited until it was clear that the truck wasn't going to swerve, then threw himself sideways. His shoulder crashed into the side of a nearby car, sending a shock wave of pain down his left arm. The truck clipped the car, metal screeching, and then the car skidded in his direction, jarring his arm a second time. Pain lanced through him, but he ignored it and backed away quickly. As the truck swung away, the high beams no longer pinned him and he caught a glimpse of the wild brown hair, dark glasses, and small pinched mouth of the woman driving before his gaze focused on something else—the small crossbow hanging out the window. A crossbow armed with what looked like a wooden arrow.

He swore, spun around, and ran for the back of the car. Almost immediately, he heard the soft twang as the arrow was released, then the hiss of air as the weapon hurtled toward him. He wasn't going to make it to the end of the vehicle, even though it was less than a pace away. He threw himself to the ground in the hopes that the woman had aimed high rather than low.

He wasn't fast enough.

The arrow hit him just below the back of his knee, cutting through skin and muscle. Pain rose like a tidal wave. *White ash*. The thought sliced through the pain as quickly as the arrow had sliced through his body, and with it came the taste of fear. White ash was

particularly deadly to werewolves and shapeshifters. With the arrow in his flesh, he couldn't move in
human form, and he couldn't shift to his wolf form.
He couldn't do anything but grit his teeth against the
urge to scream.

Yet despite the pain, his senses were still working,
because sound assaulted him: the deep rumble of the
truck, which was still too close. Shouts coming from
the direction of the club. Laughter, high and wild and
oddly familiar. The growl of a wolf in attack mode.

He forced his eyes open and saw a golden wolf in
mid-flight, arrowing toward the truck. I'm hallucinat-
ing, he thought, blinking to clear the image. But it
didn't fade. Instead, the wolf crashed into the driver's
door. Teeth flashed, shining white in the black night,
and blood spurted. The warm, rich scent rose swiftly
on the breeze. There was a yelp of pain, then the
driver gunned the engine and the wolf dropped back
to the ground as the truck sped away.

He closed his eyes and let his head fall back to the
asphalt. Quick steps approached, but the pain was
all-consuming and he couldn't find the energy to force
his eyes open a second time.

Cool hands touched his forehead, and the smell of
Savannah swamped him. It did nothing to ease the
pain, but by God, he was glad she was here.

Not that he could ever tell her that.

"Tane's gone to fetch the medikit and to call an ambulance," she said, her voice distant yet filled with
concern.

Tell him to hurry, he thought, then her words im-
pacted on his drifting consciousness. *Who the hell
was Tane?* No one he knew, that was for sure. "White

ash," he hissed, shaking his head a little to try and keep himself from sliding into unconsciousness.

"I'm glad I managed to sink my teeth into the bitch," she muttered. "And at least the arrow missed anything vital."

There was no such thing as missing something vital, and they both knew it. With the white ash in his flesh, he was as helpless as a day-old pup. And if the wood remained in his skin too long, it would poison him as surely as arsenic.

"Take it out," he ground out between clenched teeth. God, why was she even hesitating?

"The arrow's barbed," she said, her voice seeming to come from farther and farther away. "I can't take it out. I can only push it through."

"Do it." It had to be better than the burning touch of the wood.

"You'll be maimed for days . . ."

"And I'll be worse than maimed if you don't god-damn remove it!"

"Cade, if one of the barbs breaks off—"

"I know," he interrupted, his words little more than a gasp of air, his flesh like a furnace. "Just do it."

She took a deep, shuddering breath and said, "Tane, give me the knife you always keep down your boot."

Tane again. He sure as hell was going to find out who this person was. Considering she'd supposedly never come here before, she seemed awfully familiar with the man.

So, you are jealous, a voice whispered inside his mind.

A female voice, familiar and yet not.

No, he replied.

Then why claim her as you have? Why react so protectively when she talks to another male?

Because she is mine.

She will never be yours unless she gives herself freely. And you're too afraid of losing her to give her the chance.

Anger swept through him. *Who is this?*

Someone who will annihilate you if you hurt my sister again.

You're Vannah's twin?

Yes.

How the hell did you get into my mind? He had shields. Good shields. Even the instructors at the academy could never touch his thoughts unless he lowered some of his protection.

A distinctly unfeminine snort ran through his mind. *Your shields are little more than what a pup would have in the golden pack.*

But Savannah—

Trusted you, which is why her shields were so low. And you abused that trust. For that pain alone, I should whip you.

And does Vannah know you're in my head now?

A chuckle ran through his mind, and then another voice, as cool as the hands that were now on his flesh, joined the first.

Goddamn it, Neva, you promised to behave.

Vannah? Never, in all his training, had anyone told him it was possible to hold a three-way telepathic conversation.

Yes. Now shut up and brace yourself. Ready, Neva?

Yes.

Alarm ran through him. *Hang on, ready for wha—*

The rest of the sentence was cut off as a force swept through him, capturing his mind, his control, and wrapping him in a net as strong as iron—yet as gentle as silk.

Go, the steel that was Neva's presence said.

The white ash sliced through his flesh. It should have left him screaming, but it didn't. Though he felt the arrow's path, the cocoon around his mind shielded him from all hurt, all agony, all sensation.

Vannah swore, but it was a far-off sound that held no meaning. As were the words that followed. *Cade, you have to shift shape to stem the blood.*

Shift shape? Why should he? He was content—

He's incoherent, Neva said. *I've shielded him from the pain, but the shock is still there. You want me to . . . ?*

No. It had better be me. Vannah's voice held a grimness that sent a distant shiver of warning down his spine. *He hates me anyway, so it won't matter.*

He doesn't hate you, Sis.

Lust doesn't count. It's quite possible to hate someone and still want them sexually, you know.

Ladies, he wanted to scream, *I can still hear you.* But the words in that part of his mind never reached the two women.

Do it, Neva said. *It's getting harder to hold him.*

Do what? he wondered.

Then he knew, because Vannah was in his mind, in his soul—invading his very essence as she called to the wolf within. He wanted to rage against the intrusion, but his thoughts were still held in that cocoon of silky steel, and he could only scream in silent frustration as his body obeyed. Muscles and bone became fluid as his flesh reshaped itself. He'd barely even achieved wolf form before Vannah was calling to the magic in his soul once again, restoring him to human form.

Sleep, she whispered, somehow making it an order he had no choice but to obey. *Sleep for now. We'll talk later.*

You bet we will, he thought, then sleep overtook him and he knew no more.

SAVANNAH TOOK A deep, shuddering breath and sat back on her heels. Forcing him to change shape had several advantages. For one, it had proved there were no white ash barbs remaining in his flesh. And second, it had stopped the blood pouring from the wound. And the hole in his leg, while still bad, had at least partially closed. Another change or two and he'd be able to put some weight on it. But for now, it was enough to get him to the hospital—because she wouldn't put it past the bitch who'd fired the weapon to have tipped it in poison, just for the hell of it.

She brushed the sweaty strands of hair from her forehead and mentally reached for her sister. *Thanks for the help.*

Anytime. But he's going to be angry.

Nothing new there.

Neva's sharp snort made Savannah wince. She hadn't gone that deep into someone's mind in ages, and it had taken a toll. Her head was booming, she felt weak as a newborn kitten, and sweat still trickled down her forehead. All she wanted to do was go home and sleep, but she couldn't see that happening for a while.

Take care, Neva said. *And remember to have your shields up when he wakes.*

I've had my shields up since he arrived.

Good. Neva faded from Savannah's mind, and she glanced at the slightly shell-shocked Tane. "Thanks for helping."

"I didn't do much, except hold his leg steady." Tane's gaze skated down her body, then leapt away again. Heat flushed across his cheeks. "Damn, Savannah, you should dress like that more often."

"Hardly practical for a ranger, is it now?" she said, gently reminding him of her position. She reached for the coat he'd retrieved for her only minutes ago. "And since my reason for being here is an official one, I'll have to ask you to keep my presence to yourself."

He glanced past her for a moment. "We've drawn a crowd. Someone will figure out who you are." He smiled slightly. "Especially given the way you yelled at them all to shut up and get back."

She smiled. "Or, since I'm dressed like a nasty biker chick, maybe not."

He grinned. "You might be right. Do you want me to do anything else?"

"Yeah, call the ambulance and find out what's taking so long. And tell the crowd to piss off before the sheriff gets here and decides to arrest them all."

He raised an eyebrow. "Would she do that?"

"If she's angry enough."

His grin widened. "Tell me again why we never went out?"

"Because you preferred Genny with the legs that didn't end."

"More the fool me, then."

He trotted off before she could reply, which was probably just as well. Glancing down, she brushed the sweaty hair from Cade's forehead, smiling a little when she saw the streaks of red staining his skin. The hair dye was coming out already, which was good, because she really did prefer his regular color. She let her fingers trail down his still heated cheek. Even in his sleep, he looked angry. Didn't the man ever relax?

Her fingers dropped to his lips, remembering the way he'd kissed her, devoured her, only hours before. What was it between them that always made sex so good it was almost off the Richter scale? Hell, she'd always enjoyed sex, but with Cade there was something else. Something special.

Lights swept into the parking lot and she looked up. Relief ran through her when she saw the ambulance. A second car followed it in, and she recognized the gray Ford. Trista. As Cade's assistant climbed out of the car, Savannah rose, getting out of the paramedics' way as they tended to Cade.

"Could you cordon off the area?" she asked before Trista could say anything. "A square up to that blue car should do it."

Trista's eyebrows rose. What that meant, exactly, Savannah wasn't sure.

"Cade called me here to check out a crime scene. Didn't sound like he was a part of it at the time."

"At the time, he wasn't."

"Someone shot him?"

Savannah nodded. "With white ash."

Trista's gaze flickered to the bloodied arrow, which lay on the ground next to a gleaming pool of Cade's blood. "He or she means business."

"It was a she. And she didn't mean to kill him, just maim him." She pointed to both the crossbow and the specks of blood still gleaming wetly on the roadside. "I tore that from her grasp as she sped off. The blood is hers."

Trista glanced at the weapon. When her cool, golden gaze met Savannah's again, it was tinged with surprise. "You attacked a moving car in wolf form?"

"Yes."

"Why?"

"Because wolves are faster." A fact Trista undoubtedly knew.

"Then you weren't in the immediate area?"

"No." Savannah bit back her impatience as her gaze followed the stretcher bearing Cade away. "I was heading back toward town."

"Then how did you know he was in trouble?"

She hesitated. How *had* she known? She shouldn't have, not with her shields on full. Yet she'd felt his desperation, his fear, and had almost fallen in pain the moment the arrow had rent his flesh. Only anger and her own fear had kept her going. And the worst of it was that she would have killed the woman if she'd had the chance. Would have ripped out her throat as easily as she'd torn through the woman's arm. A wolf defended its mate at any cost, and she'd been more than ready to do just that.

Except Cade wasn't her mate. Not in *that* sense, anyway.

She shrugged with a casualness she didn't really feel. "I just did. Do you want to go with your boss to the hospital while I seal off this area?"

"No, you go. I'll start proceedings here." Trista

reached down into the bag she was carrying and pulled out the crime scene tape.

Savannah climbed into the back of the ambulance and studied Cade as the doors were closed and the ambulance took off. If she was certain of anything, it was the fact that she wasn't anywhere near over the man.

So the question was, like Neva had asked, what was she going to do about it?

Fight for him, the wild part of her said. *Fight to keep him, and don't let him go. Not this time.*

But the part of her that had offered him her heart only to have him abuse it trembled in fear. Was she really ready to do that to herself again?

I don't know.

Was that the truth, or was she just lying to herself?

She braced herself as the ambulance sped around a corner, wincing a little as the siren's howl seemed to echo through her aching head. But it couldn't stop the questions tumbling endlessly through her.

Was she lying to herself?

Maybe.

Was she ready to be hurt again?

Not really.

But if she didn't open herself up to the possibility of hurt, how could she open herself to love? She'd spent the last ten years cocooned in the safety of Ronan's arms, but the time had come for her to take a risk again.

And maybe the simple truth was that she had to take that risk with the one man she'd never been able to forget. While Cade might not feel anything more than simple lust, she owed it to herself to find out. No matter how much the end result might hurt.

Because she still loved him. She could lie to her sister. She could even try lying to herself. But her instinctive reactions tonight showed the truth.

Despite the ten years that had passed, despite her anger at his actions—then *and* now—her heart still lay in his hands.

Fate *was* a bitch; there was no doubt about it.

AWARENESS RETURNED SLOWLY. Pain hit first—not a sharp pain, but a muted, constant ache that thumped in time with the throbbing in his head. But gradually, sounds impinged and he stirred. Somewhere to his left came the soft ticking of a clock and, from directly ahead, the squeak of a trolley and the murmur of distant voices. Close to his right came the slow inhale and exhale of someone sleeping.

It was a sound Cade would have recognized anywhere. He'd once spent his nights lying beside Vannah, just listening to her sleep. Wondering when the job had become a dream come true—and when it would all come crashing down.

Which it had, all too soon, because of the lies that had stood between them. Because of who he was and what he had been there to do.

He opened his eyes. She was curled up in the chair next to him, wrapped in a blanket that covered her from neck to toe. She'd taken off the black wig, and her golden hair fell around her face, a silken shower that made his fingers itch with the need to touch her. Even though ten years had passed, in sleep she was still that innocent-looking woman he'd met so long ago. And she was just as beautiful, even with the scar. Only when she was awake could you see the real change. Once, her green eyes had been filled with life and laughter. Now the only thing there was wariness and distance. And that made him sad. He might have been at Rosehall to do a job, but he'd tried to shield her as much as he could, even if she'd thought otherwise.

Part of him wished they could just start over—wished the history between them could be swept away so that all that was left was their intense attraction. It would have been wonderful to explore just where that attraction might have led. But he was who he was, and she was who she was, and the way they now interacted was never going to change. He was too hotheaded, too possessive, and she was too free-spirited. It wouldn't have worked back then. It probably wouldn't work now.

He forced his gaze away from her and looked around. He saw white walls, white-sheeted beds, and white-coated men and women walking past the door. He was obviously in a hospital . . . but why?

Memory hit even as the question went through his mind, and he realized what had happened. What she'd done.

Anger surged through him, and his gaze jumped back to her. As if sensing his fury, her green eyes opened and she stared back at him. And the defiance so evident in her gaze only fueled the fires of his anger to greater heights.

"You had no right to do what you did!" Though he tried to keep his voice carefully neutral, anger crept through. Raiding his mind was one thing—he could hardly rail against the intrusion when he did it for a living himself—but raiding his psyche, his very soul, was another matter entirely.

"I did it to save your life." Her voice was as cool as her eyes, yet he sensed an anger that was equal to his own.

As if *she* had anything to be angry about! "You accuse me of mind-rape, yet all I did was read your mind. What you and your sister did last night was far worse."

"You didn't just read my mind, Cade. You broke through several shields to do it."

"And you didn't?"

"We didn't break anything. We merely eased them aside."

"There's a difference?"

"There most certainly is."

He snorted. "And you're sure you're not trying to justify your own actions?"

"No. And I can show you the difference, if you want."

"I hardly think you could invade my mind now that I'm awake and fully aware."

"Cade, what you know about telepathy is laughably small. The golden pack has had centuries of training behind them. We've forgotten more than your instructors at the academy will ever learn."

The academy had some of the best telepaths in the States. Granted, none were from the golden pack, but that didn't mean they were any less capable. "You have no idea what you're talking about."

Her eyebrows rose. "Meaning you're willing to partake in a little demonstration?"

"Anytime, babe."

She snorted softly. "If you weren't still recovering, I'd give you a lesson right here."

"Oh, don't worry. I'm feeling fit enough not only to repel an intruder, but to give her a lesson in true psychic strength."

Her gaze narrowed, her beautiful eyes becoming little more than green slits. "Maybe I should have let you bleed to death."

"So why didn't you? At least then you'd be free of the moon promise."

She flung the blanket away and stood up. He caught a brief flash of long golden legs before the black leather coat she was wearing fell into place.

"You know, you're right," she said. "I'm a fool for not thinking of that."

"I'm surprised it wasn't your *first* consideration."

She stopped near the window and crossed her arms. The rising daylight warmed her skin and made her hair shine. "My *first* consideration was actually marking the bitch who'd shot you."

"And did you?" Hopefully, something good had come out of this mess after all.

"Of course." The look she threw his way was almost caustic. "I shredded her arm and retrieved the crossbow. Trista is running a check on the prints she pulled off it."

"Has anyone come into the emergency room with wolf bites?"

"No. And Ronan's contacted the local doc and asked him to inform us if anyone comes his way."

"Good. Do we have a line on either of the trucks or drivers yet?"

"Not from my people. But your people are hardly likely to inform me if they have, are they?"

"We are a team—"

"No, you and your people are the team. My staff and I are just the convenient lackeys. And it's working against us, Cade. We need to pool resources and work *together* to catch these people."

"The IIS has more than enough experience—"

"This *isn't* your normal case. This is about you and me, and making us pay for Rosehall. These people *know* us—"

"Of course they know us," he broke in, arguing the point even though he knew she was right. "Nelle James is behind the attacks. She was your best friend, the one you confided in. She knew why I was there."

"It wasn't Nelle James in that truck."

"Are you sure? Or are you still trying to protect her?"

Heat warmed her cheeks. Anger, he sensed, not embarrassment. "Unless Nelle had a face-lift that has taken more than twenty years off her appearance, then yes, I'm sure."

He frowned. "What do you mean?"

"Nelle was twenty years older than me, which means she'd be close to fifty right now. The woman in the truck had to be in her twenties. She was also blond underneath the wig."

His eyebrows rose. "So it was the blonde who was there to contact Denny?"

"No. Different truck, different blonde." She crossed her arms. "I gave a description to Trista when she was in earlier. I presume she'll inform you if she finds a match. In the meantime, I have to go home and change, then go check out that burger joint."

He flung off the blankets. "I'll come with you."

"I don't think so."

"You are not wandering out there alone!"

"I won't be alone. Ronan will be with me."

"No, he won't." He forced himself into an upright position, but even such a small movement had him puffing like he'd run a marathon, and his head spun dizzily.

"You lost a lot of blood last night. You need rest."

"I need to find out who this killer is." And he needed to be with her as much as possible, while the moon was on his side.

She walked across to the bed, and her steps beat a tattoo that seemed to echo through his head. "Stop the macho act and just be sensible." She pressed a hand against his shoulder and pushed him back. The ease with which she did it was humbling. "If you rest, you can get out of here tonight."

He caught her hand and raised it to her lips, kissing her fingers. Desire stirred the air—his and hers. "I intend to be. We have a night to make up for."

She raised an eyebrow, a teasing light in her eyes. "You've been shot, we have no idea who the killers are, and you're worried about sex? You're incredible."

He grinned wolfishly and tugged her toward him. She resisted for a second, and then allowed herself to be pulled onto the bed. Her body pressed into his side, and even the fiercer aches of abused flesh gave way to the quick burn of need for her.

"Oh, I intend to be incredible," he said softly, the rich scent of flowers filling his nostrils as his lips brushed hers.

She raised her free hand and ran her fingers down his cheek. "You always were."

"Then why did you keep going to Jontee?" Even as the words left him he realized his stupidity. Yet it was something he needed to know.

She pulled away, her tender expression fading. "Because I made a promise."

"You made a promise to me, too."

"Yes, but my promise to Jontee predated the one to you."

He shifted position, trying to get comfortable, trying to control the anger running through him. Because if he let that anger loose, he'd never get an answer to the one question that had haunted him over the years.

"But if what we shared was so good, why did you even need to fulfill your promise to Jontee?"

"Because I don't believe in breaking promises."

"Even at the risk of losing something that could have been special?"

She studied him for a moment. Her expression gave little away, yet he could feel the tension in her, the indecision. "Was it special?" she said eventually. "For you, I mean?"

"It was good," he said. "Good enough that I didn't want to share it—or you—with anyone. Yet you made me." His gaze caught and held hers, demanding that she put to rest the one question he'd asked every night for the last ten years. "I just need to know why!"

She crossed her arms. "Part of the ceremony of becoming one of the true believers was a promise to share his bed for a year."

"Was it a magical bond?"

"No, but Jontee was very powerful. Very . . . hypnotic. You wanted to please him, wanted to do as he asked."

"So why make a moon promise with me?"

She didn't answer for several minutes. She just stared at him, as if debating with herself. Then she blinked and looked away. "You have to understand," she said softly. "I wanted to be with just you, but I was also afraid."

"Of what? Of me?" He couldn't help the incredulity in his voice. "While you and I might never agree as to what happened the night I read your mind, you surely had to know I'd never hurt you. Not physically. And not even mentally—not intentionally, anyway."

And he would have killed any man who did.

Her gaze returned to him. "I wasn't so much afraid of you but of what I was feeling."

"And yet you claimed to love me. That's a strange sort of love, Savannah."

Something flickered in her eyes—something he couldn't identify. "I didn't think you heard me say that."

"Oh, I heard it. I just didn't believe it."

Her eyes widened. "Why not?"

"Because how can you love one man when you continue to fuck another?"

It was a harsh thing to say, yet he didn't regret it, even when he saw the flash of hurt in her eyes. Because it was the truth. Love wasn't just words, it was actions—and her actions hadn't matched what she'd said. If he ever said he loved a woman, it would be because he was utterly and totally sure. It would be forever.

"That's unfair," she said softly, the hurt he'd seen in her eyes leaking into her voice. "You're six years older than me. You'd already done all your exploring when you came to Rosehall. You cannot expect the same degree of maturity from someone who has only just begun to experiment."

"Love doesn't change according to a person's age, Vannah. It just is."

"So I was supposed to give my heart, my soul, and my body to a man who was only there to catch a killer, even though he never once admitted to any feeling other than desire?" She shook her head. "I may have been young, and I may have been emotionally immature, but I wasn't a fool."

"So why did you say you loved me when you weren't even sure?"

She didn't answer, just glanced at her watch and cursed. "I have to go meet Ronan to interview the diner's owner." She hesitated, then added, "Steve's on guard outside your door. He'll keep all but your team and the assigned nurse and doctor out."

"And me in?"

"Most definitely," she said. "And we *will* continue this conversation, Cade. It's important for both of us." Then she walked out before he could reply.

He blew out a breath, and wondered why he felt more drained than he ever had chasing after criminals.

"Jeez, I wouldn't mind a bit of that action," Anton said, walking through the doorway while looking over his shoulder. Cade had no doubt as to who he was looking at.

"Don't even try it," he warned.

Anton's grin flashed. "Looks like Trista's won the bet."

Cade bit down on his annoyance. "What bet?"

"I said our ranger wasn't your type. Trista said it was obvious the two of you were at it like wolves in moon heat. It looks like she was right."

And here he'd thought he'd been discreet. "I do not appreciate my love life being the focus of attention when we have a murderer to chase down."

"Hey, if you play on work time, then it's fair game. Your rules, not mine."

Damned by his own words—though he'd never actually thought they'd ever apply to him. For ten years he'd managed to keep his sex life and his work life separate. Until now. Until he'd again encountered the one woman who'd always blurred the lines between what he had to do and what he wanted to do.

"What's happened while I've been out?"

"The tests came back on the arrow." Anton's voice was deceptively mild. Meaning, Cade knew, he was amused. But then, Anton had a warped sense of humor. "You'll be pleased to know the tip wasn't poisoned."

Considering he was still here and not dead, that was pretty obvious. "What else?"

"We got no prints from the arrow, but we did pull several from the crossbow. And we found a match." Anton held out a file.

Cade opened it up. This blonde wasn't the one who'd walked into the nightclub, though there were certain similarities. Her name was Lonny Jackson, and she was a member of the cream pack from the Merron reservation in Wyoming. Later addresses included Laramie, Wyoming, and Colorado Springs, and each of those cities had outstanding warrants against her for failing to pay minor fines. He glanced up at Anton. "Have the rangers seen this yet?"

"I just downloaded it, so no."

"Show them. They can do the footwork again. Ranger Grant is checking the diner where the other blonde was apparently working."

Anton's eyebrows rose. "So we *do* have two? I thought Trista might have heard our ranger wrong."

"She didn't. Although the woman who bribed the kid to leave the note looks enough like Lonny Jackson to be her sister."

"According to the file, Lonny Jackson doesn't have a sister."

"Dig deeper, because I'm sure there's a connection between them. It's just too much of a coincidence, otherwise. And while you're digging, do a background check on Lonny Jackson's mother. Get me a picture, if you can."

Anton grinned. "Another itch, huh?"

"Just a suspicion." In truth, the only thing he *was* sure of was the fact that Nelle James was somehow involved. She might not have shown herself yet, but he could feel her presence. It was like an itch he couldn't quite scratch. There'd always been something malevolent about the woman—something not quite right. Whether she was the force behind both the original murders and the current ones was open to conjecture but, regardless, he still believed there was more to

Nelle James than the motherly front she'd presented to the world.

"Did you find the truck last night?"

"Half this town drives a blue truck. And none of the ones I found was being driven by a nearly naked blonde, unfortunately."

"It was worth a shot." He glanced down at the file again and frowned. Then he picked up the photo, shifting it a little closer to the light. "You know, Jontee McGuire also came from the Merron pack."

"Or at least his mom did. Jontee left when he was quite young."

"Fifteen isn't that young." Not when it came to someone like Jontee, who was far more mature than his years. Of course, much of that was due to his upbringing. It seemed the cream pack weren't all that tolerant of half-breeds—even if the wolf in question was the result of force rather than choice. Jontee had no choice but to grow up fast. And, according to the psych guys, he didn't really know the meaning of reality—though that hadn't saved him in court. Nor had the innate charm that Savannah had talked about. "Maybe it's my imagination, but there is something in this woman's face that reminds me of Jontee."

"Jontee never had kids, as far as we know."

"There were none at Rosehall, that's for sure." Rosehall had been all about dreams and freedom, and children represented a reality that most there didn't want to face. "But that doesn't mean Jontee couldn't have had kids before. He was close to forty by the time we caught him, so he was certainly old enough."

And revenge for a father was certainly a good motive for murder.

"If he did have kids, why weren't they listed as next of kin?"

"Who knows? Maybe he didn't want his choices impacting his kids' lives."

Anton's expression suggested he wasn't buying that. "Well, I'll contact the ranger in Merron and see if he can add anything to what we have."

Cade nodded. "Any word from Hart yet?"

"He's due to arrive in a couple of hours."

"Get him to set up the van at the ranger's station. It'll be more secure there."

"You don't think this pair will go as far as destroying evidence?"

"Who knows, but I'm not taking any chances. I want everyone to pair up—with the rangers, if you have to—whenever you're on the street."

Anton nodded. "You realize that'll mean letting them in on the investigation?"

"This case is somewhat different than our usual case. Actually, call a general meeting of both teams for eight tonight. It's time we started cooperating fully."

"I can hear the IIS upper management having apoplexies at the mere thought."

Cade smiled. "Have you done the cross-check on Oliver?"

"Yes. Nothing out of the ordinary so far." He hesitated. "I did find one interesting snippet though. Oliver James is apparently good friends with Levon Grant, which may just explain why there was no background information on Vannah Harvey."

It certainly would—and it also meant that Savannah hadn't hidden herself from her father's prying eyes as well as she'd thought. Though if Levon had realized exactly what his daughter was up to at Rose-hall, he would have gone down there and dragged her back by the scruff of the neck. From everything he'd heard, he was that sort of man.

"Keep checking—it might be interesting to see if he has any connection to the other women we can't find."

"You don't think he's involved in the murders, do you?"

"No, but someone else was. I'm sure of it."

"But you never saw this other person?"

"Never. Not even in Jontee's memories."

Anton frowned. "So were his memories faulty, or erased?"

"Knowing what I know now, I'd say deliberately smudged. Erasing them totally would have been too obvious."

"So who do you think was involved?"

"The one woman we could never track down." He took out a photo and handed Anton the rest of the file. "Nelle James."

"The great unknown." Anton tucked the folder under his arm. "Have you talked to Ranger Grant yet?"

"I intend to, once I get out of here."

"Good. Because I think she might be able to give us some clues."

So did he. The trick was going to be resisting the moon fever long enough for her to answer his questions. He swung his legs off the bed, waited until the quick bout of dizziness passed, then stood and walked—or rather limped—over to the small ward-robe to retrieve his clothes.

"Boss, I don't think getting up is a good idea."

"Lying in bed while a killer runs loose isn't, either."

"Ranger Grant has left orders—"

"Ranger Grant's orders don't override mine." He glanced at Anton. "I need your truck."

Anton studied him for a moment, then handed over the keys. "Ranger Grant is not going to be happy."

"Right now, keeping Ranger Grant happy is not my first priority. Finding this killer and ensuring we both survive *is*."

The time to worry about happiness could come later. Until then, he wasn't even going to consider the possibility.

SAVANNAH PUSHED THE diner's door open, and was immediately assaulted by the mouthwatering aroma of frying bacon. She breathed in deeply as her stomach rumbled a noisy reminder that she hadn't eaten anything since the pizza yesterday.

"Now, there's a smell that always makes me hungry," Ronan said as he followed her inside. "How about we take a break? My treat."

Savannah grinned. "My father understands the need for me to eat takeout when I'm working, but if I actually sit down to eat at a competitor's place, there will be hell to pay."

"What are people going to think," he said, imitating her dad's voice, "when they spot you eating at the competition? It's just not good enough, Savannah."

She chuckled softly. "It's never good enough, apparently."

"His trouble is that he runs his family the way he runs this town—autocratically."

Her amusement died. "True. But he means well."

Ronan propped his butt on one of the counter stools and gave her a look. "*Meaning well* almost caused Neva to lose Duncan. *Meaning well* drove you from town when you were seventeen."

She shrugged. "That's different."

"It's not, and you know it." He picked up a toothpick from the small container on the counter and fiddled idly with it. "Are you ever going to confront him about it?"

"I have."

"I mean for you, not for Neva."

She grimaced. "It really doesn't matter anymore."

"It does when it stops you from jumping into a relationship you desperately want."

She glanced at him sharply. So now even he could see it?

"But," he continued, "that doesn't answer the question. Do you intend to tell your old man about Rosehall and Cade?"

"Definitely about Cade."

"But not about Rosehall?" He caught her hand and squeezed it gently. "You never were a coward, Savannah. Don't start now."

"I've always been a coward," she refuted softly. "I ran from Cade ten years ago rather than face up to what we'd done. Instead, I came straight home and buried the wilder part of me deep, afraid of what others might think. And I'm still afraid of telling my old man about Rosehall and my time there."

"You did nothing wrong."

"He won't see it that way."

"Maybe he needs to. Maybe if he realizes it was his rules that drove you from town in the first place, it might make him rethink his current views."

"My dad? I don't think so." She laughed and glanced past him as a short woman with graying hair came through a doorway wiping her hands on a tea towel.

The woman smiled brightly. "What can I do for you two?"

"We wouldn't mind a couple of eggs sunny-side up with that bacon you're frying up," Savannah said, deciding after everything she'd said that she was hungry enough to risk annoying her father. "And we'd like to speak to the owner or manager, if that's possible."

"Two bacon and sunny-side eggs, Frank," the woman yelled, then rested her fleshy hands on the counter as she studied them. "And I'm both manager and owner—how can I help you?"

"Rangers Grant and Harris," she replied, showing the woman her badge even though the uniform made it obvious who they were. "We believe you've had a young blond woman working the night shift for the last few weeks?"

The woman snorted. "Working isn't exactly what I would call it, but yeah, she was here. Why? What has she done?"

"We believe she might be able to help us with an investigation." Savannah hesitated. "Can you tell us a bit about her?"

"She said her name was Candy Jackson. And what mother in her right mind names their kid Candy, I ask you? No wonder the girl was a flake."

Savannah resisted the urge to smile. "A flake in what way?"

"Always chatting up the customers, always asking stupid questions, never actually doing half the things she was supposed to."

Savannah shared a glance with Ronan. Maybe they'd just gotten their first good lead.

"What type of questions?" he asked.

The woman shrugged. "About the different packs, who ran them, and who was on the council." She hesitated and frowned. "You know, I heard her asking about you and your family, Ranger Grant. She seemed awfully interested in where you all lived and what you all did. Not that it's hard information to find out. All anyone with half a brain had to do was pick up a phone book or check out the town's website. You and your dad are fairly prominent."

True, but whoever committed the recent murders obviously wasn't overburdened with a logical mind. "Have you seen her recently?"

The woman shook her head. "She was supposed to report in last night, but she didn't show. She's officially fired if she does actually show her face. Help may be hard to find, but I'm not *that* desperate."

"I don't suppose you can give us her address?"

The woman considered them for a moment, then nodded. "I don't owe her any loyalty. Hang on a sec, and I'll get her records."

She was back within a few minutes. "Someone's been through my files," she said, her expression angry. "Everything I had on her is gone."

Savannah blew out a frustrated breath. They were

always one damn step behind. "I don't suppose you can remember her address?"

The woman frowned, then leaned back and yelled, "Frank, where did Blondie live again?"

"Summit Street," a rough voice replied.

Savannah exchanged another glance with Ronan. Summit Street happened to be where Lana Lee had died as her house burned down around her. Coincidence? Her gut said no.

"I don't suppose she mentioned anything about her personal life? Friends? Family?"

The woman screwed up her nose. "Not really. I think she was from Merron, but she never mentioned kin or anything. Though when she wasn't out here chatting, she did seem to spend an awful lot of time on her phone."

Meaning they had better try to get hold of her phone records. "How come you didn't fire her earlier if she was so bad?"

The woman handed them their meals. "Bad help is sometimes better than no help. And she did bring the men in. Customers are customers."

Savannah nodded. "Thanks for your help."

"Anytime, rangers," she said, and left them to it.

Once they'd eaten and paid for their meal, they headed out. "So what next?" Ronan said. "Do we cruise over to Summit Street and hope to get lucky?"

"Candy was driving a blue truck last night. If we don't find that, we can knock on doors." She paused. "And perhaps we should revisit Rex and see if he ever saw a blonde visiting Lana."

"You think there's a connection between the two?"

"Yes—although there's no logical reason for thinking so at the moment."

"Well, we've all learned to trust your illogical hunches. I mean, all of us except Ike, but he's still green."

His words sent a chill running through her. For a moment, it felt as if death itself had reached out and caressed her soul. "Has Ike reported in yet?"

Ronan shook his head. "Not that I know of." He hesitated, eyeing her—his expression suddenly concerned. "You want me to call the station?"

She nodded. "If he hasn't reported in, get Bodee to drive around and see if he can spot him. I'll call his mom."

She grabbed her cell phone from her pocket and dialed Ike's home number. "Maureen," she said, when his mom answered. "Is Ike home?"

"No," she said, her concern evident. "He didn't come home at all last night."

Oh fuck . . .

She closed her eyes and tried not to panic. Ike, for all his faults, was a ranger. And he *could* protect himself. "He was working late last night. He's probably fallen asleep somewhere. Tell him to call me as soon as he gets home."

"Will do, Savannah."

She hung up and swung around. And saw two things.

Cade was limping toward them, and a big blue truck was hurtling down the street.

Not at Cade.

Not at her.

At Ronan.

Chapter Nine

"RONAN!" SHE SCREAMED. "Watch out."

He swung around at her warning, and in one of those snapshot moments where everything seemed to stop, she realized he'd never get out of the way in time. The truck was too close, and going too fast.

Her best friend was going to die if she didn't do something to stop it.

"No," she screamed—to the driver, to fate herself. She dropped her phone, the protective plastic casing smashing as it hit the pavement, the tiny shards glittering like tears as the sun caught them. She picked up the nearby metal trash can and, with a grunt of effort, heaved it at the approaching truck.

The trash can spun in the air, spewing rubbish everywhere. In extreme slow motion, like a dreamer caught in the middle of a nightmare, she saw the brown-haired driver's mouth drop open and her fingers clench and haul at the wheel. She watched the trash can smash into the windshield, sending hundreds of spiderlike cracks webbing across the glass. She heard the squeal of tires as the truck turned sharply. She saw the fender hit Ronan. She heard his grunt of pain. She watched him fly backward like a broken sack.

Then everything snapped back to full speed. The truck was gone, people were screaming, and all she could see was Ronan lying on the pavement.

Not moving.

No, no, no. God, no! He can't be dead. He can't—

Someone grabbed her shoulders. She blinked and looked up. Cade, white-faced and terrified.

But she couldn't allow herself to think about that. Not yet.

"I'm fine. *I'm fine.*" But Ronan wasn't. She knocked away Cade's hands, ducked under his arms, and ran to Ronan. Dropping to her knees beside him, she touched his neck, feeling for a pulse. It was there—racing, but strong.

Relief ran through her, leaving her momentarily weak. She closed her eyes and took a breath. But that didn't do much to ease the sick churning in her stomach as she said, "Someone get an ambulance."

Her voice sounded so calm, so official. Odd when she felt so fragmented.

A hand touched her shoulder and squeezed it gently. She knew who it was without looking. The heat of him—the scent of him—filled her senses, even as strength seemed to flow from his fingertips.

She looked up and smiled. His expression was as stony as his eyes, and it only took her a moment to realize why. Her reaction had reinforced his belief that she loved Ronan.

Which she did, but not in the way he suspected.

But before she could say anything to Cade, Ronan groaned and opened his eyes.

"Forget the ambulance. I'm fine." He rolled onto his back, his breath hissing through clenched teeth. "Well, except for the fact that it feels like a hundred elephants have been racing up and down my body."

"You're lucky," Cade said, moving around to squat opposite. "If Savannah hadn't thrown that trash can, you probably wouldn't be alive right now."

Ronan's gaze met hers and he smiled over the wail of the approaching sirens. "I owe you, then."

"Anytime, my friend." She grabbed his hand and squeezed it gently, more to reassure herself than him. "But you are, however, going to the hospital to get checked out, and then Steve is going to escort you home and watch over you while you rest."

"Steve? God, he smells worse than a distillery these days."

"He doesn't drink on the job," she said mildly. "And it's either Steve or you get out of town."

"I'll take Steve."

She figured as much. Ronan wasn't one to leave a job half-done. Or her unprotected.

"But," he continued, "you'd better follow up on our lead."

"I will." She glanced up at Cade. "The blonde who bribed Denny went by the name of Candy Jackson, and she apparently lives over on Summit Street."

He raised an eyebrow. "Interesting. It seems the other blonde goes by the name of Lonny Jackson."

"Sisters?"

"They could be." He glanced past her as the approaching ambulance came to a sudden halt. "Except, according to records, Lonny doesn't have a sister."

"Merron doesn't always register half-breeds, or

even their get," Ronan said. "So if she's not a full wolf, maybe that explains why there's no record of a sister."

"What?" Savannah and Cade said together.

"That's illegal," she added. "All wolf births have to be registered. The reservation's fined by the government otherwise."

"Law or not, it happens. Merron's a big reservation, and the government head counters never see half the people living there." He paused to cough, and winced in pain. When he continued, his voice was a little hoarser, but he squeezed her hand reassuringly. "The head of the council is crazier than your old man, Sav, and has a thing against half-breeds. If you're not pure, you're not a wolf, so he doesn't believe they should be registered."

"But even human births have to be registered!" Savannah said.

"He doesn't consider them human, either, but rather an abomination."

"Oh God, you're not saying he condones infanticide?" This time, there was horror in her voice.

"Let's just say that those who keep their half-breeds are not supported by the council in *any* way."

"But how do you know this?" Cade asked. "It's certainly not something I've heard, and we've handled several investigations out at Merron."

Ronan's gaze met Cade's. "A friend of mine grew up there." He looked back at Savannah. "Mikel. It might be worth talking to him."

"I will." She looked around as the EMTs approached, then squeezed Ronan's hand again and released him.

"Meeting like this is getting to be a habit," the first of the men said cheerfully as he bent over Ronan.

"One I hope to break." Her voice was dry as she stepped back to give him more room.

Cade rose and stood beside her. His arm brushed hers—only lightly, yet little shocks of electricity seemed to run up her arm and tingle down to her fingertips.

"Steve needs his ass kicked for letting you out," she said, without looking at him.

His grin was something she felt deep inside—a warmth that spread like wildfire through every nerve. "I threatened to charge him with obstruction if he didn't move."

"Not even the IIS can make a charge like that stick."

"So he said. I asked him if he wanted to risk it. He apparently didn't."

"You don't play nice."

His expression was hard. "I'm not paid to play nice."

"And do you not play nice on all your missions? Or are there some that tempt you to do more than you should? Want more than you should?" She raised her eyebrows, silently challenging him to answer honestly.

He studied her long enough to make her think he wasn't going to answer. Then he smiled somewhat sadly and said, "There was one that became more than a job."

"How much more?"

He shrugged and looked away. "It doesn't really matter."

"It does to me."

"Ronan's in the ambulance. We'd better get moving." He walked away from her, heading away from the truck, but she grabbed his arm and tugged him back. "I'm driving. And why won't you answer the question?"

"Why did you run from Rosehall?"

"I've already told you. I was afraid."

Which was a lie. She hadn't been afraid. Not back then. She'd fully intended to commit herself wholly to Cade once her promise to Jontee had ended, but then Cade had done what he'd done, and she'd learned altogether too much about Rosehall, Jontee, and Cade himself. Was it any wonder she'd run?

She unlocked the truck and opened the door for him. He climbed in awkwardly, wincing a little when he put weight on his injured leg.

"If that starts bleeding," she added, "you're going straight back to the hospital."

"Not before we catch this killer." And as she climbed into the driver's side and started the engine, he added, "If you really did love me, you would have stayed."

She swung into the traffic, heading toward Summit Street. "Let's try a little reverse psychology. Let's say you were eighteen and just beginning to explore the boundaries of your sexuality. You fall for a much older woman—"

"Six years is not *that* much older."

"When you're eighteen it is." She grinned, but it faded quickly. "So, you thought you loved that woman, but then she turned around and did something your upbringing tells you is abhorrent. You're left thinking there's no way she could have done that if she'd felt even the tiniest bit of real affection for you." She glanced at him. "Would you have stayed, or would you have run?"

His gaze raked her, but his expression gave little away. She was tempted—so very tempted—to just ease into his mind and uncover his thoughts, but that was something she'd sworn never to do. Not without good cause, anyway. And no matter how badly she might want to know what he was thinking, he had the right to his privacy.

Something those at that academy of his never thought to mention.

"If I have to answer honestly, then I don't know. I'm not you, Vannah. I will never react to a situation the same way you would."

"So you've never been in love?"

"No. And I don't believe you were, either. I read your thoughts, remember? Or raided them, as you keep insisting."

"You read *some* of my thoughts," she refuted softly. "My shields are constructed in interwoven layers rather than the straight levels of power that you have. It works better, simply because it's harder to break through." She glanced at him. "You have only three levels. I have nearly eight."

Incredulity touched his eyes. "Why would any telepath need so many?"

"You try living in a pack that's totally telepathic! It's a requirement, believe me."

"But I thought your pack didn't believe in raiding another's mind."

"We don't. But that doesn't mean it doesn't happen." She hesitated, then said, "Was Rosehall the job that became more?"

"You know it is."

"No. If I knew, I wouldn't be asking. You gave me nothing, Cade. Well, nothing except fantastic sex."

"I gave you three days."

She frowned. "What do you mean?"

He blew out a breath. "I had a job to do and a time in which to do it. I missed that deadline by three days, simply because I was afraid of the consequences. And because of that, another person died."

As the lights ahead changed from green to red, she slowed and shot him a glance. "You can't be held responsible for that."

"If I'd done what I was there to do, when I was supposed to do it, that person might not have died."

"And you might not have caught Jontee if you'd gone after him earlier."

He shrugged, and she asked, "What other consequences are you talking about?"

"Jeopardizing the first piece of happiness I'd found in a long, long time." His gaze held hers, seeming to burn right through her, until it felt as if he were reaching into her very soul. "You were more than a job to me, Savannah."

She licked her lips, her throat dry and her heart pounding unsteadily. Not from fear, not from excitement, but rather from an uneven mix of the two. Because what he was admitting wasn't a guarantee of a future, nor was it an admission that he cared now. But he *had* cared, even if only a little. And for now, that was a good place to start.

"And yet you still invaded my mind."

He nodded, his gaze still intent, still burning deep, as if he were trying to make her see past his words and make her believe. But believe *what* was the question—and one she wasn't sure she should ask. Not yet. Not until they'd cleared the air.

"Eighteen people had already died. In the end, duty *had* to take precedence over my own desires." He hesitated. "I never meant to hurt you—not emotionally, and not psychically—and I'm sorry if I did."

Something inside her melted. "So why didn't you just ask?"

A car beeped behind them, and she glanced ahead to see that the red light had changed to green. She drove on.

"Because of Nelle," he said. "And your relationship with her."

"Nelle was my friend."

"Your friend probably gave you away last night at the club."

She shook her head. "It doesn't make any sense. If Nelle was in town, she'd contact me."

"Not if she thinks you were partially responsible for Rosehall's downfall."

She shot another glance his way. "Nelle is not behind the murders."

"Which murders are we talking about? Rosehall's, or these?"

"Both. Besides, she hated the taste of blood."

"And you know this because she told you?"

She hesitated. "No, I witnessed it. She cut herself once and wouldn't suck the wound to clean it. Said it was unclean."

"Which is the exact reason Jontee gave for committing these murders. He said the victims needed to be cleansed of their taint so their souls could move on freely."

She stared at him for a moment, a mix of disbelief and horror running through her. "Really? *That's* why he was killing them?"

"Yes." He paused. "So why did you warn her about the raid later that night?"

"Why do you think I warned her?"

"You were the only other person besides me who knew about that raid. Why else would she have run?"

"If you were so afraid of my relationship with Nelle, then why tell me in the first place?"

"Because I didn't want you caught in the net. I owed you that, if nothing else."

Something inside her softened. He'd gone against all the rules to let her walk away. That one action spoke far louder than words. If only she'd had the sense to realize it at the time, her life might have turned out differently.

"So why did you warn Nelle?" he repeated softly.

She took a deep breath and released it slowly. "Nelle came into my room not long after you'd left." She hesitated, her thoughts drifting back. "I was packing to leave, and I was so hurt, so angry. She asked me what was wrong and I told her. It just all came pouring out."

"So you both decided to leave?"

"All I know was that I left. I wasn't really sure what Nelle planned to do. She did say she had things to finish."

He flashed her a frown. "What things? She was just another of Jontee's women, wasn't she?"

Savannah shook her head. "She never slept with him. She was more of a mother figure, and she handled the day-to-day running of the place. Jontee was never in the real world long enough for that."

"And yet you were quite happy sharing a dance with him?"

She looked at him. Though his expression was flat, his eyes seemed to burn with a navy fire.

"He was an amazing man," she said. "A gentle man, a man who wasn't always there mentally, but still a very good lover."

"He was a killer."

"Yes, but I didn't know that at the time. Only later." And those murders were the only reason Cade was at Rosehall, and the reason they'd met.

"But you loved him."

"I've already said I didn't."

"Yet you did love me?"

His disbelieving tone made her raise an eyebrow. "Look, I'm not denying my actions gave lie to my words. But at least try to understand where I was coming from. I was eighteen, and I had escaped a very strict upbringing to explore my sexuality. I didn't want, or expect, to find love, and it scared the hell out of me when it all went so wrong."

He scrubbed a hand across his eyes. "If you love someone, you're faithful to them. It's as simple as that."

"Love is never simple. It's different for every single person. And you've no right to judge my actions until you've fallen in love yourself."

He didn't answer, and that made her even angrier. She turned onto Summit Street and slowed. There was a blue truck in the driveway of a house four doors down from the burned wreck of Lana Lee's old house.

"Well, well," she said softly. "Look what we've found."

"No proof it's the same truck. But pull over."

She pulled in behind an old Ford wagon and stopped. The window curtains of the house in question moved slightly. "We've been made."

"So she'll run?"

"Maybe not. After all, she must have been pretty sure that she wouldn't be recognized if she tried to run Ronan over in broad daylight." She glanced at him. "Did you get the plate number?"

"Same false plate as last night."

"Which she'll have no doubt removed by now."

"No doubt."

She leaned her forearms on the steering wheel as she studied the house. "How do you want to play this?"

He reached into his pocket and pulled out a plastic-covered photo. "Go to a few houses and ask if they know this woman. Then go ask her. But before you show it to her, take it out of the plastic."

"I doubt whether she'd be dumb enough to touch it." She glanced at the picture. It could have been Candy's sister. The only difference was that this woman had smaller, meaner eyes. "And in the meantime, you'll be doing what, precisely?"

"Coming in from behind."

"On one leg? I don't think that's wise."

"A wolf has four legs, which gives me three to walk on." He raised a hand and gently cupped her cheek.

"That woman just tried to kill Ronan. You're not going to go anywhere near her alone."

"You sound as if you care."

"Maybe I do."

She raised an eyebrow and said, "Are you sure it's not the moon promise?"

His dark gaze rested on hers, and something inside her wanted to relax into his warmth. But all he said was "It might be."

It wasn't the declaration she'd been hoping for—though why she hoped, she had no idea. He obviously wasn't a man who verbalized any emotion save anger. But it wasn't an outright denial, either. And right now, she was happy with that. She opened the door and got out. A cool wind stirred her hair and sent a chill racing down her spine. She glanced at the sky. Dark clouds were racing toward them, and part of her hoped it wasn't an omen of things to come. Then, thrusting the thought away, she zipped up her jacket and walked over to the nearest house. It just happened to be Rex's.

"Morning, ranger," he said, his eaglelike gaze flicking past her briefly. "Looks like there's a hell of a storm coming. What can I do for you?"

She held out the photo. "Have you seen this woman?"

"Candy Jackson? Sure, she lives down the street, in seven—" He paused. "That's a really bad photo of her though. She looks meaner."

"That's because it's not actually Candy. Have you seen this woman around?"

"Well, hard to say, because this woman and Candy

sure look alike. It'd be hard to tell 'em apart from a distance."

Or if you had bad sight, like Lana did. Goose bumps ran over her skin, and in that moment she knew who had set the fire that had killed Lana. But knowing it was one thing, and proving it another.

"Did Candy ever visit Lana?"

"Yeah, twice a week. She used to clean up for the old girl—do her housework and the like. Lana said it was easier to pay someone than to do it herself."

"I'd heard the old girl was a bit tightfisted."

"Oh, she was, but over odd things. And it seemed she liked a clean house more than saving money." He handed her back the photo. "Candy was there the day of the fire, cleaning up."

Savannah raised her eyebrows. "What time?"

He shrugged. "I wasn't really looking at the clock, but it was after lunch."

Interesting. She wondered what Manny and the fire marshal had made of this information—and if they'd interviewed Candy. "How long has she been living here?"

He frowned. "It'd have to be three or four months, at least."

"I don't suppose she said where she came from?"

"Why? Is she in trouble?"

Savannah shook her head. "No. Just curious."

He shrugged. "She never really said, but then, we don't talk all that much. If you want to know more about her, why not ask Anni Hawkins?"

"Anni? The lady who runs the flower shop over on Main Street?"

He nodded. "I've seen her visit Candy a few times.

She delivers flowers, like, but always seems to stay for a chat."

Savannah smiled. While Anni delivering the flowers herself was a little unusual, her stopping to chat certainly wasn't. And if there was any dirt to dig up on Candy Jackson, Anni would have uncovered it by now. "Thanks for your help."

He nodded and glanced skyward again. "Be sure you're inside by four, ranger. This storm is going to be a doozy."

He closed the door, and she glanced up as she walked away. The clouds seemed to be getting darker by the minute, and the swirling wind was bitterly cold as it tugged at her ponytail and caressed her skin. But the shiver that ran down her spine wasn't caused by either. Something bad was going to happen. Maybe not now, not here, but soon.

She glanced across to her car, but Cade had already gone. She scanned the street, but she couldn't see a limping brown wolf anywhere. But the curtains in Candy Jackson's house were still hitched slightly open, meaning someone was still watching.

She pulled out her cell phone as she walked across the road to interview Candy's immediate neighbor.

"Kel," she said, the minute the woman answered, "has Ike reported in yet?"

"No."

Damn. Worry began to gnaw at her insides again. "If he hasn't reported in within the next hour, could you let me know? We'll have to start a search."

"Will do."

Then she hung up and called the fire chief.

"Manny," she said, when he finally answered. "Has the marshal finished his investigation yet?"

"Not yet," Manny replied, sounding like someone who was barely awake. "Why?"

"I just wondered what you made of Rex's statement that Candy Jackson visited Lana the afternoon of the fire."

Manny yawned. "Rex needs his eyes checked. Ms. Jackson was sharing coffee and cake with three friends at your dad's diner all afternoon."

Another chill ran through her. Candy was at the diner? That wasn't good. She really did have to talk to her parents, and as quickly as possible.

"Did you know she cleaned Lana's house twice a week?"

"Yeah, but she said she'd changed that day's appointment so she could meet her friends."

"Then you're not putting much stock in Rex's report?"

"Not when so many people saw her at the diner."

"What if I told you there's a woman in town who could pass as Candy's twin?"

"Then I'd have to say the marshal wouldn't mind talking to her. You're going to question her?"

"If we can find her."

"If you do, let me know."

"Will do."

She hung up and rapped on the front door. Candy's neighbor turned out to be a woman in her early thirties who had three screaming kids hanging off her apron, and who didn't seem to realize the woman in the photo resembled Candy. Savannah tried several other houses, more for effect than any real desire to ask questions. Then she finally moved toward Candy's house.

The curtains closed as she opened the front gate. Music played softly inside—classical rather than modern. The melody sounded vaguely familiar, though she couldn't quite place where she'd heard it before.

She walked up the front steps, scanning the front windows and the glass panels beside the front door. No movement could be seen, but someone was home. The delicious scent of baking bread filled the air.

There was no doorbell, so she rapped on the door. The sound seemed to echo, as if the house was empty. There was no immediate response, but just as she was about to knock again, footsteps approached. She slipped the plastic cover from the photo, holding it carefully by one edge as she shoved the cover into her pocket, out of sight.

The door opened, and Denny's wet dream appeared— complete with micro skirt and barely there red top. There was, Savannah noticed, no bandage on her left arm, so it definitely wasn't Candy who she'd attacked last night. But it *was* easy to see why the teenager had been willing to do anything this woman asked. He must have thought all his Christmases had come at once.

"Candy Jackson?" She flared her nostrils, taking in the scents flowing from the doorway. Aside from the rich aroma of baking, the air itself smelled musty and damp, like an old cellar that had been closed up for a very long time. There was also a hint of ginger, but it didn't seem to belong to the house but rather to someone in the house. Odd, given Candy smelled of a mixture of citrus and cigarette smoke.

"What can I do for you, ranger?" The blonde caught a small rose-shaped pendant between two fingers and began running it back and forth across a gold chain.

"I was wondering if you knew this woman." She held out the photo, but she held no real hope of getting Cade a fingerprint, for Candy obviously had no intention of opening the screen door, let alone touching the photo.

Candy's gaze dropped briefly. "She looks like me."

"Yes, she does."

"It's not me, you know."

"No. Her name is Lonny Jackson. Is she your sister, by any chance?"

With the grubby screen door between them, it was a little hard to judge the woman's reactions. Yet Savannah was certain she caught the flicker of amusement in the woman's cold blue eyes. But her voice was as flat as ever as she said, "If she is, then she's one I don't know about."

"So she could be a half-sister?"

Candy shrugged. "Possibly. My dad didn't mind spreading it around. Of course, he's been dead for quite a few years, so you can't really ask him. What do you want her for?"

"To question her about an incident at Club Grange last night."

"I was at the movies last night with several friends, so I'm afraid I can't help you."

Won't, not can't, Savannah suspected. And for someone who had just been presented with a mirror image of herself, she was acting a little too calmly.

"Can I ask the names of those friends?"

Amusement briefly touched Candy's pink-painted lips. "You don't trust me, ranger?"

Not as far as I can throw you. Savannah forced an apologetic smile. "It's just routine. After all, this woman does look like you."

"Ah." Candy paused. "Arianne Marshall and Lisette Gordan."

Another chill ran down Savannah's spine. Candy had made friends with Ari, and Ari was the one person in town, besides Ronan, who knew just about all there was to know about her family.

"Weren't you supposed to work last night?"

"Yeah, but the job sucks. I'm not going back. The old cow and her touchy-feely hubby can go to hell." She hesitated. "Did she give you my address?"

"No. Apparently your employment details have gone missing from her files."

"More likely the old bat's misplaced them. Couldn't organize herself out of a snowstorm."

Candy didn't look as if she could, either, but Savannah suspected that looks were deceiving. "Thanks for your help."

Candy nodded and closed the door. Savannah shoved the photo back into the plastic cover and retreated down the stairs. As she passed the truck, she ran her hand over the hood. It was still warm. And the fender was dented.

But the windshield wasn't smashed.

It wasn't the same truck, even if she was sure it was the same driver. So where had Candy dumped the other truck, and how had she gotten this one?

Savannah took note of the plate number, then headed across the road to interview a few more neighbors. Again, more for effect than anything else. Then she headed back to her truck. Cade was already inside, waiting. His face looked a little pinched. He was clearly in pain but refusing to admit it.

She resisted the urge to lecture him, knowing he'd only bite back, and slammed the door shut. "Anything?"

"Several interesting possibilities." He shifted slightly and absently rubbed his leg. "The garage is a drive-through, and there's a small alley at the back of the property that's been well used."

She started the engine and did a U-turn. "Nothing unusual in that."

"It is when the inside of the front garage door has been chained shut."

She frowned. "Why have a drive-through garage if you're going to chain it shut at one end?"

"Exactly. The thing is, while that lock is rusted, the garage itself is still being used. There was a huge puddle of fresh motor oil on the floor."

"There was a puddle in the parking lot last night, too." She paused. "But none on the concrete at the front of the house."

"Meaning she either uses the alley to get in and out most days, or there are two trucks."

"Two blondes, two trucks. Makes sense."

"And both living in that house."

She glanced at him. "That's a bit of a leap, isn't it? I mean, surely the neighbors would have noticed."

Though given the people she'd just interviewed, maybe not. Rex seemed to be the only one interested in neighborly goings-on.

"There were cigarette butts on the back porch—two

different brands." He reached into his pocket and drew out several plastic evidence bags. "What do you want to bet we find different DNA on the butts?"

"That doesn't mean there's a second person sharing the house."

"There are two bedrooms, and both of them are being used."

She gave him a look. "I thought you were there to protect my back."

"I decided you could protect yourself. And Candy didn't have a weapon on her."

"There was nowhere to put it, for a start."

Cade chuckled. "There certainly wasn't."

Amusement ran through her. "And here I thought you were busy peering through bedroom windows."

"Not just them. One of the living room windows gave me a really good view of both you and the woman. Once I knew she wasn't armed, I moved on."

"Why? Hot blondes not your type?"

"It depends on the blonde." He reached out and lightly tugged her hair. "Why did you cut it?"

"Probably for the same reason you cut yours. It was impractical for my line of work."

"That's not the reason I cut it."

"It wasn't? So why did you cut it?"

"Because I was angry."

"Angry?" she said, surprised. "At who?"

"You."

"You cut your hair because you were angry at me?" She shook her head. "And they say women are strange."

The sweet half-smile that twisted his lips just about

melted her heart. "Men can be just as illogical, believe me."

Oh, she believed him. Especially since some of his dealings with *her* weren't exactly high on the sanity list. But then, he'd been reacting in much the same manner as she had—with anger and in bitterness over the past. For her, that had finally begun to dissipate now that they were actually beginning to talk about it. Maybe it was for him, too. "So why were you angry?"

"Because you left Rosehall and I couldn't find you."

"But you wanted me to run, didn't you?"

"Yes, but not to hide."

"So you cut your hair when I didn't reappear. A totally understandable reaction." *Not.*

He tugged gently on her hair again. "The light's green."

She glanced ahead and saw that he was right, then lifted her foot off the brake and cruised on. "Stop ducking my questions."

"I'm not." His fingers moved from her hair to her neck, his fingertips grazing her skin. Yet even that slightest of caresses had little shocks of excitement trembling across her body. "I'm just trying to decide the best way to phrase it."

"Just give me an honest answer, however crazy it sounds, and I'll be happy."

"I cut my hair because you loved it, and I wanted to rid myself of everything that reminded me of you."

"A very female reaction, I must say."

"I got drunk first. Then I smashed up my house."

"Ah. Well, that makes all the difference." She glanced at him. "You know, you could have saved us both a lot of heartache if you'd only mentioned the fact that you liked me—maybe even cared for me—at some point during our time together at Rosehall."

"Not on a job. Not until I knew there was going to be a decent outcome." He glanced at her. "That hasn't changed, you know."

"So you're willing to admit that you cared for me then, but you're not willing to admit you care for me now because the outcome of our current case is unclear?"

"Basically, yes."

She grinned. "Which is essentially an admission anyway."

His gaze met hers. "Yes."

"I do so love a man who can express his emotions."

He smiled. "We're not ready for that yet, Savannah."

"Be still my heart—he remembered my name."

"Has anyone ever told you that you can be a bitch?"

"Many times." Her grin widened as she pulled into a parking space a few doors down from the diner. Her dad's car wasn't there yet and she frowned, glancing at her watch. It was barely nine, but by now the diner should have been open and bustling for hours. She was just about to contact Neva when she vaguely remembered him saying something about getting the brakes checked.

Cade pulled his hand away from her neck. "Why are we stopping here?"

"My dad's diner is just ahead and I need to talk to him."

"It's closed."

"Yeah. But he should be here soon, and in the meantime we can help ourselves to coffee." She glanced at the apartment above the diner, just to make sure no one was home. The lights definitely weren't on, which meant her mom had also gone out. Good. The last thing she needed right now was a motherly third degree about Cade—especially when Cade was present.

"I like the sound of coffee," he murmured, but the wicked gleam in his dark eyes suggested he had something other than breakfast in mind.

Excitement trembled through her, and for an instant she felt like a giddy teenager again, unable to wait for the touch of a newfound love. But it wasn't practical. Not here, anyway. "There's no fooling around in *this* diner."

"Vannah, you're nearly thirty. I think your dad knows you're not—"

"My dad is Levon Grant, remember." She climbed out of the car and headed toward the diner.

"Ah, yes." He slammed his door closed and hobbled along behind her. "The man behind the ridiculous no-sex-before-marriage push."

"He thinks it'll make us all better people."

"The only thing it'll make us is frustrated. The moon's effect on us werewolves will never go away, no matter how much he might want it to."

She flashed him a grin, but her smile faded when she saw how badly he was limping. Blood was beginning to spot his jeans. "You've opened the wound up again."

"Yeah." He shrugged. "It's nothing much."

"I have a feeling that wound could be gushing blood and you'd say the same thing." Exasperation filled her voice as she found the key and opened the diner's door. There was, indeed, a note on the door, explaining that the diner was closed for the morning, but would reopen for lunch. "Grab a seat while I get the medical kit. And no arguments," she added, the minute he opened his mouth.

"And you're bossy, too."

"I haven't even begun to get bossy. So change shape to stop the bleeding, then sit down."

She waited until he obeyed, then headed across the room and through the swinging doors into the kitchen. Even with the blinds pulled down, the diner was filled with murky light, but the kitchen itself was darker than hell. Even the advantage of wolf-keen sight didn't help a whole lot. And the medical kit was across the far side of the kitchen, through a maze of counters, stoves, and sinks. She fumbled for the light switch.

"Don't," Cade said from directly behind her.

She jumped and spun around. "What the hell are you doing here?"

The doors swung shut behind him, cutting off the little bit of light filtering in from the kitchen and dropping them back into almost total darkness. "Disobeying orders and following an enticing bit of tail."

"You should be resting that leg of yours." She placed a hand on his chest to stop him from moving closer. She might as well have tried to stop the moon from rising.

He caught her hand and pulled her against him. "It's only blood."

All that was visible in the blackness was the white flash of his teeth as he grinned. But she could feel him. Feel the warm hardness of his body pressed so intimately against hers. And the racing of his heart, as wild as her own.

At Rosehall, she couldn't have given a damn where they made love or who was watching, as long as they were together. But that was a long time ago and she wasn't at Rosehall, but rather her father's diner.

"Cade, we can't. Not here. Besides, your leg—"

He brushed a kiss across her lips, stopping the rest of her protest in its tracks. "My leg is fine. If you care to look, you'll see the bleeding stopped when I shifted shape."

"I can hardly check that statement when it's pitch black and you're so close your belt buckle is digging into my belly."

He kept pressing her backward until she hit something solid. One of the counters, she realized, as the chill of the metal pressed into her spine.

His soft laugh was decidedly wicked as he released her hand, then placed his on either side, neatly corralling her. "You sure it's a belt buckle?"

She was sure it wasn't. "You need that leg tended to."

"I have lots of needs that require tending. And some more urgent than others."

As if to emphasize his point, his mouth claimed hers. It wasn't the urgency-filled kiss she'd expected, but rather a slow and tender exploration that left her breathless. Dizzy.

Or maybe that was a side effect caused by the spicy mix of his scent filling every ragged breath as he pulled away. She couldn't say for sure, and she didn't really care. Not when the air was so thick with the heat of their desire that it seemed to burn like flames across her skin.

He kissed her chin, her neck, and the caress of his breath against her skin seemed almost cool compared to the heat melting her insides.

"I want you," he said softly, his gaze somehow capturing hers in the darkness. Or maybe it was just the gleam of need—a need that was as fierce as the flames burning inside her. "Here. Now."

It wasn't safe, she wanted to say. Her dad could walk in at any moment, and that would be a nightmare. But the denial wouldn't form on her lips. How could it, when every nerve ending was trembling for his touch, and the recklessness she'd buried so long had risen with a vengeance? She wanted him, regardless of the situation or the consequences.

And it wasn't the moon or the fever. It was simply the man, and what he did to her. What he'd always done to her.

"Yes," she said, her voice little more than a pant of air.

"Thank God."

"*He* had nothing to do with the decision."

He laughed softly and skimmed his hands down her sides. "Then thank you, Ms. Grant. I shall endeavor to make the experience worthwhile."

She ran her hands up his body, then cupped his face so she could drop gentle kisses on his nose, his lips. He tugged her shirt free of her pants, but as he moved to undo her buttons, she stopped him. "It occurs to me that since you're injured, I should be doing all the work."

He shook her off and continued undoing her shirt. "I don't believe in letting a woman do all the work."

She smiled and ran her hand down the muscular planes of his chest and stomach, enjoying the contrast of the silky material under her fingertips and the hardness just behind it, not to mention the contrasting coldness of his belt buckle as she leisurely undid it. "What if I promise to make it worthwhile?"

His fingers slipped under her bra and he cupped her breasts. A tremor ran through her and, for a moment, she arched against him, pressing into his touch, savoring it.

"I just might be tempted."

She placed a hand against his cheek, ran a thumb across his warm lips. "So why don't you step back and take off those jeans?"

Though she couldn't see his smile, she felt it, deep inside. "You have something in mind?"

She kissed him, softly, sweetly, then said, "I certainly have. Take off those jeans and I'll go lock the door and find us a chair."

"Now, that sounds like something I might enjoy." His fingers touched her cheek, ran fleetingly over her lips. "Don't be long."

She wasn't. Once she'd found him in the gloom again, she put the chair behind him and lightly pressed a hand against his chest.

"Now park that sexy butt." When he had, she straddled him, her thighs pressing against the outsides of his. "And undo my pants."

"I'm tempted to say 'yes ma'am,'" he said, his voice a heated mix of amusement and desire.

"I don't care what you say as long as you do as you're told."

"A woman after my own heart." He kissed her belly, sending a ripple of longing lapping across her skin, then undid her zipper. "Just remember, I control events next time."

"Maybe."

"Definitely."

Smiling at the hunger so evident in his husky tone, she stepped back, kicked off her pants, but not her panties, and straddled him again, this time sitting. As the hard length of him rested against her, she sighed. Lord, he felt so good, even like this. She rocked her hips back and forth, gently rubbing the silk of her panties across the hard length of him, teasing them both. He jerked, then groaned.

"Oh *God*, that feels good." His hands were on her hips, pressing her down, but not restricting her movements. "But it would feel a whole lot better if you were completely naked."

She leaned forward, wrapping her arms loosely around his neck and taking a nip of his earlobe. "So you're not enjoying the sensation of silk against skin?"

"Oh, I'm enjoying it." His breath was hot and quick against her neck, his fingers warm as he slid one hand from her hip to her stomach. "But skin on skin is so much better."

"But leaving the panties on means I can get dressed much faster if the need arises."

"Sensible, one supposes."

"I'm nothing if not sensible these—"

The rest of her words were lost to a gasp as his fingers slid past the elastic and into warm wetness.

She shuddered, arching her back, momentarily losing herself to the pleasure of that firm stroke. Combined with the heat of him throbbing beneath her—a heat she so desperately needed to feel deep inside—and she was just about in heaven.

But she didn't want to get there quite so fast. She wanted to play a bit longer.

She shifted, pulling away from his touch. "Did I give you permission to do that?"

"No. And I don't care."

She smiled. "Do I have to tie you up?"

"It's an option that has interesting possibilities."

"Then maybe it's something we should explore when we have more time."

"Only if you remember that what you do to me I will do to you."

"Another idea that has interesting possibilities."

She settled on top of him again and began rocking, this time a little harder. He quivered beneath her, the heat of him seeming to sear her flesh.

"I am not going to last long if you keep doing that," he groaned.

"You'll last as long as I want you to."

"A nice idea in theory . . . but in practice?"

Grinning, she stopped rocking and dropped a kiss on his neck, then worked her way down his chest. She circled his nipples several times with her tongue, then captured one with her teeth, biting lightly.

He shuddered, and she felt perspiration break out across his skin. She tasted the tiny droplets, savoring them as she ran her tongue over his flesh. He tasted of salt, of desire, and of everything she'd ever longed for in her life, everything she'd thought she'd lost.

"Vannah," he warned softly.

She trailed kisses up his neck then captured his mouth, kissing him with growing urgency. Both of them were trembling by the time she pulled away, their bodies hot and slick where flesh met flesh, and even wetter where flesh met silk.

But she didn't give him what he wanted—what she wanted. She just continued to rock.

He groaned again, and this time it was a sound of deep frustration.

"I want to be inside you," he ground out. "I want to feel your hot, wet heat wrapped around me."

"Not yet," she murmured. "But soon."

She ached for him—ached so fiercely it hurt. He pulsed against her, a promise of satisfaction that was so close and yet so far away. Still, his hard flesh touched all the right places as she rocked back and forth.

Then the deep-down quivering began, spreading like wildfire across her skin. She rocked harder, and he gasped—a short sharp sound of desperation. Desire. The trembling in his body grew stronger and she knew he was battling for control.

But the ache in hers was growing, flooding across her senses, until it became a kaleidoscope of sensations that washed through every fiber of her being. Then the shuddering took hold and she gasped, grabbing his shoulders, trying to hold on until he was inside. She reached between them and thrust her panties to one side. Then she captured him, driving him deep, until it felt as if her very soul was being invaded by the thick heat of him. His groan was a sound of ecstatic relief. It was a sound she echoed as she held still, despite the urgent demands of her body, wanting to prolong the urgency and enjoy their intimate connection. Then he moved, and she could do nothing more than move with him, gently at first and then with growing urgency, until she was consumed by the sensations and need flowing through her. She came even as his body went rigid against hers and the hot rush of his seed spilled into her.

Almost immediately she collapsed against him, resting her cheek against his sweaty chest as she battled to catch her breath. He wrapped his arms around her, holding her close as he pressed his cheek against the top of her head.

"That beats coffee any day."

She chuckled softly but didn't move, enjoying the moment of closeness while she could. "You wouldn't be thinking that if my dad chose this moment to walk in."

"Your dad doesn't scare me."

"You haven't met him yet."

He tucked a finger under her chin and raised it. He kissed her, and it was a kiss unlike any she'd ever felt from him. Sweet but possessive, heated and yet oddly filled with intent.

"You're mine, Savannah, and I won't share you with anyone. Not even your father."

Annoyance flickered through her. So they were back to *that*. "Don't be ridiculous. Besides, the moon magic doesn't make me yours. It just holds me to a promise."

She rose from him and shuffled around in the darkness until she found their clothes. She tossed him his, then got dressed herself.

"I meant what I said." His voice was little more than a rumble of annoyance coming out of the darkness to her left.

"So did I." She zipped her pants and buttoned her shirt. "And you had better be aware that my sister is very much a part of my life, and that will never change. Not for anyone."

"I didn't mean that."

"I don't care what you meant. The truth is I won't ever be yours until I make that choice freely." And the fact that she *had* made that choice wasn't something he needed to know right now. Not when he was still choosing to hide behind the safety of the moon magic and his work.

She strode across the room, guided by the glimmer of light seeping through the edges of the swinging doors, and brushed a hand across the wall, feeling for the light switch. She flicked all of them on, but nothing happened.

"Damn."

"What?" he said, instantly alert.

"Nothing. Just a blown fuse."

"The kitchen has more than one light. Try the others."

"Gee, why didn't I think of that?" she said sarcastically.

Footsteps echoed, coming toward her. "You mean they're not working, either?"

"Nope."

"Where is the circuit board?"

"Near the storeroom at the back—" She hesitated

as she caught the sudden flash of a light under one of the benches. Red light, like something had been left on.

Nothing unusual in that, as her dad had a habit of not turning off the appliances he used regularly, like the toaster. But why hadn't she noticed it before?

"What?" Cade said, his hand touching hers briefly.

"Something's been left on, I think." She took a few steps closer and bent to get a clearer look.

Something inside her froze. It wasn't a warning that an appliance had been left on, but rather numbers, counting down.

Fifteen . . .

Fourteen . . .

Thirteen . . .

Realization clicked in. It was a bomb, primed and ready to explode—clearly activated the moment she had tried to flick on the lights.

"Oh, fuck," Cade said. He grabbed her hand, pulling her out the kitchen door and toward the front door. The *locked* front door.

She thrust a hand into her pocket, fumbling for her keys and dragging them out. But she wasn't fast enough. *They* weren't fast enough.

Even as she reached for the door, there was a rumble of sound that became a blinding flash and suddenly there was nothing but heat, terrible, terrible heat, as the world went red around her.

Chapter Ten

CADE GRABBED SAVANNAH and thrust her under one of the booths, knowing the protection provided by the table and the seats might be their only chance of survival. He dove in on top of her, covering her body with his as the roar and the heat and the sheer force of the explosion hit. It was accompanied by debris and thick, unbreathable dust. Bricks, glass, and God only knew what else became deadly missiles. The table above them shuddered and cracked as it was hit with debris and metal and remnants of furniture. He cocooned Vannah against him, her body shuddering against his, her heart racing as fiercely as his own. Yet she didn't make a sound, keeping the fear he could almost taste tightly leashed. Several large chunks of glass speared into their small space, one so close to his arm that it sliced his shirt and skin. Another cut past her cheek, drawing blood before embedding itself into the cushioned vinyl seat.

Then silence fell, filled only with the crackle of fire. For a long moment, he didn't move, wanting to be certain the main explosion was over, that it was safe.

Savannah was struggling and coughing beneath

him. "It's okay," he said, smoothing her dust-covered hair. "We're okay."

She shook her head, her body racked by coughs. "The gas," she said hoarsely, twisting around. Her eyes were filled with fear as she pushed her bloodied hair from her face. "The explosion might have ruptured the lines. We have to get to the cutoff valve."

Fuck. He hadn't even thought of that. Kneeling, he scrambled out from under the table and held out a hand to help her. "Where is the valve?"

The fingers she placed in his were bloody and trembling, yet there was nothing resembling fear in her voice as she said, "Out the back, near the generator."

He looked over. Half of the inner wall had come down in the explosion. They'd be scrambling over it to get to the valve. He rose and helped her to her feet. "Lead the way, before that fire gets any worse."

She nodded, her green eyes shocked as her gaze skated around the restaurant. "Oh God—"

"Savannah," he prompted softly.

She glanced at him, then half-ran, half-scrambled, over the bricks and rubbish, through the twisted remains of tables and chairs.

Yet despite all the damage, they'd been lucky. This section of the diner remained relatively untouched, even if all the windows had blown out. Most of the booths, while covered in debris, were still standing, and several tables near them were even relatively unscathed. It was the booths, tables, and counter on the kitchen side that had taken the force of the blast—and, therefore, had the most damage.

He turned his gaze to the devastation that had once been the kitchen. The bomb had been powerful enough to destroy the immediate area and blow off that section of the ceiling, revealing the rooms above. Yet it wasn't strong enough to bring down the main walls.

But if they'd been in the kitchen, or had turned on the lights earlier, when he was more interested in making love to Vannah than drinking coffee, they would be dead.

That bomb had been aimed at her father, not her. Not them.

The back door still hung on its hinges, but only barely. Vannah grabbed his arm, balancing herself as she kicked at the door. It gave way on her third blow.

"Over here," she said, then started coughing so violently she was almost doubled over. He touched her back, wanting to comfort her, yet knowing there had to be priorities. And right now, no matter what his instincts might be saying, she wasn't it.

He found the gas valve and turned it off. Then he got out his cell phone and checked to make sure it was still working. It was, thankfully. He dialed Anton's number and grabbed Savannah's hand, pulling her away from the smoke and dust into the fresh air.

"Anton," he said, the minute his associate answered, "I need you to get over to the diner near the corner of First and Main. Someone just tried to blow it up."

"Hell. Is everyone okay?"

"Yeah. Just get here fast."

"Will do."

He hung up. The wail of sirens split the air, approaching fast. He and Vannah should head around to the front to clear the gawkers that always gathered after a major drama, like gulls drawn to a tasty morsel. But right now, he didn't give a damn about the gawkers or any remaining danger. Not when Savannah was still coughing.

He glanced around until he found a tap. Luckily, it had a hose attached. "You want a drink?"

She nodded and leaned against the rickety back fence, scrubbing a hand across her face and smearing blood everywhere. "That bomb wasn't aimed at us."

He turned on the tap and brought the hose over. "No."

She washed her hands under the dribbling water, then grabbed the hose and took a long drink. "Thanks," she said, handing it back.

"Your face is cut." He reached up with a free hand and wiped the blood away. Not that it helped much. The cut was relatively deep and bleeding heavily. "I think you'll need to shift shape to stop the flow."

"It's only blood," she said, repeating his earlier words with a shaky smile.

"Cheeky wench." With his hand still cupping her cheek, he leaned forward and kissed her. And while passion was evident, there was none of the urgency that had so filled their kisses only a few minutes ago—just a vibrant mix of tenderness and relief. She was okay; he was okay. Everything else didn't much matter.

When the approaching sirens stopped, he pulled back and dropped his hand. "We'd better get around to the front."

She half-nodded, took several steps forward, then stopped and groaned. "Dad's around the front."

"How do you know?"

She tapped a finger to her head. "He's seen my truck and is impolitely knocking. We'd better get going."

He followed her as she walked off. "How does one impolitely knock, telepathically?"

She glanced at him, merriment dancing in her green eyes. "Do you really want to know?"

"I've a notion I should say no, but I'm feeling reckless."

She arched an eyebrow, the glint in her eyes deepening. He threw up his strongest mind-shield as a precaution—for all the good it did him. The noise hit like a hammer and made him feel like he was standing inside a ringing church bell. A church bell that oddly sounded like someone screaming his name. His whole body vibrated with the ungodly noise, but thankfully it cut off as abruptly as it started.

"That," she said smugly, "is what I meant."

And she'd done it when his shields were on full. If she could do that so easily, then she could probably do everything else she'd threatened. Maybe he *did* have a lot to learn when it came to telepathy.

"And you have to put up with intrusions like that all the time?"

"No. Most people just ask." She paused, and her voice, whisper soft, said, *Like this,* in his thoughts. It was a quick caress of sunshine that had him hungering for more. God, conversing with his teachers had never felt so good . . . so intimate.

Though considering his teachers had been male, it would have been a bit of a worry if it *had*.

If your pack is so strong, how do you keep anyone out? Or keep a telepathic conversation private?

We usually don't have to worry about either. It's

considered impolite to read the thoughts of others un-invited or to use private telepathy in groups. Plus, including too many people in a mind-conversation can lead to a major headache for the one coordinating. She paused. *The only person I can't actually keep out is my twin.*

He hesitated, but couldn't stop himself from asking, *And Ronan?*

She glanced at him, her expression unreadable. Yet amusement seemed to run around him—a gentle wave of delight that somehow made him feel foolish. Though why, he had no idea. After all, what was so damn wrong with the question?

"What is it about Ronan that you dislike so much?"

He's had you for ten more years than me, he thought. *He knows you better than perhaps I ever will.* None of which made sense to say. Yet. "I don't dislike him. It's just a territory thing."

"That's implying I'm a territory that can be won, and when did you decide to make it a contest?"

She raised an eyebrow, silently challenging him. It wasn't a question he could answer—not until he'd actually had time to think about it himself. To think about what he actually wanted, beyond as much time with her as he could get.

"And why is it," she continued, "that when male wolves hit a question they don't want to answer, they resort to the old 'it's a territory thing' excuse?"

"Because we're one-dimensional and can't think of any other excuses," he said dryly.

"So true." Her gaze left his at the sound of voices—one in particular, loud and gruff. She shook her head and added, "Dad's organizing the troops again.

Heaven forbid that they actually be allowed to do their jobs without his input."

"I'll take care of him if you like."

She gave him a wry look. "I don't really need your protection. I never have."

No, he thought. And it was that independence that had hooked him when they'd first met. She *didn't* need him—and yet, she'd wanted to be with him, wanted to share all the delights of her life with him, whether they be large or small. And he couldn't even share something as simple as the truth. He *was* a bastard. There was no doubt about it.

But he was a bastard who was going to keep her alive, no matter what.

"If these people are going after your family, you'd better get your parents out of here."

"Yeah. I'd been meaning to talk to Dad. It was stupid of me to delay, but I didn't think they'd be targeted so fast."

"Whoever is behind all this is playing by rules we don't understand. Better to account for all possible outcomes than be sorry afterward."

She looked at him, her expression unreadable, and nodded. "You're right. I kept my sister safe, but I didn't do the same for my parents. Stupid, as I said."

Maybe. But then, she'd probably been working on the same assumption he'd been—that the killer would come straight after them now that they were both in town. Obviously, her game plan was bigger than that.

As they walked around the corner onto Main Street, a big man with thinning blond hair and angry-looking green eyes was coming toward them.

"Sav," he all but barked. "Are you all right? What the hell happened here?"

He stopped several feet in front of them, giving them both a glare. Cade felt invisible hackles rising. It was that, more than the sudden tension tightening Savannah's shoulders, that told him this aging, leathery wolf was her father, Levon Grant.

"I'm fine," she said, voice cool. "But the diner was bombed."

"Why the hell would someone bomb the diner?"

"It was meant for you, but Cade and I got there first."

Green eyes fastened on Cade. "And who the hell might Cade be?"

She stepped to one side, and waved a hand his way. "Cade Jones, from the Interspecies Investigation Squad."

"Really?"

The old man looked him up and down, then offered his hand. But his expression, when it met with Cade's, was shuttered, giving very little away. Even the anger had disappeared, which was to be expected. He wouldn't be the pack alpha and town leader if he wasn't strong *and* a damn good politician.

"What are you here for, Agent Jones?"

Cade shook the offered hand, noting the power in the older man's grip and returning it in kind. "I'm investigating two murders on the reservation."

"Indeed." The old man's gaze returned to Savannah, and the air fairly crackled with hostility. "Why wasn't I informed?"

Again, those invisible hackles rose. Cade wasn't sure if it was a natural reaction to the man's antagonistic body language, or simply an instinctive need to protect what he deemed his. But either way, he was going to have to watch it. Levon Grant was not someone he wanted as an enemy. Not—given Levon's apparent contacts within the IIS—if he wanted to remain in his chosen career. "I asked Ranger Grant not to tell you."

Those sharp green eyes came back to him. "And why wouldn't you want to tell a reservation's council that a murdering bomber was in town?"

"We had no idea they'd go to these extremes," Savannah snapped, then grabbed her father's arm. "You and I need to talk. Now," she added, when the old man didn't move.

Cade watched her drag him away. As he saw the tension so evident between the two, one thing became obvious—his earlier assumption that Vannah had won the head ranger's position because her dad was head of the council was totally mistaken. If what he'd just witnessed was any demonstration, Levon Grant didn't support his daughter in *any* way.

Odd for a man who was supposedly so keen on family values.

A gray truck pulled to a halt beside the fire trucks, and Anton climbed out. Cade walked over to him.

"Hell of a mess," Anton commented. "If you and the ranger were in there, you were extremely lucky to get out."

"Very," Cade agreed, his gaze on a green ranger's truck coming down the street fast. "The bomb was set in the kitchen, and wired to the light. When the scene is declared stable, I want you to go in there and see what you can uncover."

Anton nodded. "Wiring the bomb to the lights suggests some electrical skills that our pretty blond suspect likely does not have."

The truck stopped and two rangers climbed out—one Steve, the other a dark-haired man in his mid-forties. Not Ronan, as he'd half-expected. "There are two pretty blondes, and we have no idea what skills Nelle James has."

"Or if she's even involved," Anton said.

Cade met Anton's gaze. "She's involved."

"If she was here in town, surely Ranger Grant would know. After all, they were good friends."

So he would have thought. But then, ten years had passed since Rosehall. When combined with a twenty-year age gap, the Nelle he and Vannah remembered might not even remotely resemble the Nelle of today, particularly if those years had been harsh ones.

He frowned. "How is the cross-check going on the recent arrivals?"

"Everyone has checked out."

"What about Lonny Jackson's mother?"

"Her name is Frankie Jackson. She married one Kenneth Jackson some eighteen years ago."

"So he's not Lonny's natural father?" Or the sister's, if indeed Candy was Lonny's sister.

Anton shook his head. "On her birth certificate, the father is listed as unknown."

Damn. "Any other information on the mother?"

"Yeah, she and her husband died in a car crash ten years ago."

Cade scrubbed a hand through his dirt-encrusted hair. This case was getting more and more complex. Every damn time they seemed to find a lead, it vanished. But they were on the right track, he was sure of it. "And what happened to Lonny after their deaths?"

"That we're still trying to find out. We found a picture of Frankie. It's in the car, along with all the other information we've collected, if you still want to look at it."

It couldn't hurt. Given the way this case was going, he'd probably spot the dead Frankie walking around Ripple Creek. "The second blonde's name is Candy Jackson," he told Anton. "Ronan said that Merron doesn't always register half-breeds, so maybe that explains why she looks like Lonny and yet isn't listed as a sister."

"Trista's calling the Merron ranger this morning." Anton paused and added dryly, "They did get on extremely well."

Cade snorted softly. It would have been more accurate to say that Trista and the Merron ranger had been going at it like rabbits. But if they could use that past relationship to get more information out of the man, then he was all for it. "I'll talk to her."

He glanced across to where Vannah and her father were still arguing, noting that she seemed to be giving as good as she got. Part of him ached to go over there and defend her, but he had no rights beyond those he'd snatched with the moon magic. Besides, as she'd said, she was more than capable of looking after herself.

But it was interesting that she was doing so against her father. While most wolf packs held a modern view of women's rights, they were also very much a patriarchal society. An alpha male always ruled, never an alpha female—except in his family, of course. Since his father had died when he was young, his mom had ruled the house. But she'd still obeyed the edicts of the pack's alpha.

So maybe the real reason Vannah and her father didn't get on was because they were very much alike, and she refused to acknowledge his right of rule over her.

"She's going to need round-the-clock protection," Anton said softly. "You both are."

"We don't have the staff to run protection and keep up with the investigation. The best we can do is change where we stay—and don't advertise it."

"You could leave town."

"No. These bitches are mine."

"If indeed they are bitches and not bastards."

He didn't bother answering. He was pretty sure his rookie guess about there being more than one killer at Rosehall had been right, and he was damn sure he was right now. All he had to do was find the proof.

"If you don't run, hiding isn't going to do much good," Anton continued. "Gossip has a way of getting around in a town like this. Especially if the two of you shack up together."

"I have no choice, Anton." He forced his gaze from Vannah as Steve and the second ranger began talking to the fire chief. He frowned, suddenly wondering who was protecting Ronan. "I'm afraid the chief ranger and I have unfinished moon business."

"We gathered that." Anton paused. "You'd better be careful that it doesn't distract you."

"That's one warning I don't need. Let me know as soon as Hart arrives."

Anton nodded. Cade headed for Anton's truck. By

the time he got there, his leg ached fiercely, and the dried spots of blood on his leg had been flooded with a brighter, fresher red. He shifted shape again, knowing it would stop the immediate flow, but it wasn't going to help long term. Not if he didn't stop moving around on it.

There was no way in hell he was going back into the hospital, but he could rest for a while. He grabbed the folder from the backseat and limped over to Vannah's debris-covered truck to wait for her.

SAVANNAH THRUST A hand through her blood-stiffened hair and tried to ignore the urge to scream at her father. He was frustrating at the best of times, but when it came to taking orders he refused to see the sense in, she might as well bash her head against a wall.

Which, to be honest, was half the reason she'd delayed talking to him. She just had to thank God that her mom hadn't been home and paid the price for her reluctance to confront her old man.

"Look," she said, barely managing to keep the exasperation out of her voice. "I'm not arguing any more about this. I'm assigning Bodee to keep you company while you collect Mom from the hairdresser's, and then he will escort you both out of town."

Her father's green eyes flashed with anger. "I won't be forced out of my own damn town!"

"Have you actually looked at the diner? Half the top floor is gone. If Mom had been home as usual, you'd be down at the morgue right now identifying her remains." She stopped to take a deep breath, trying to calm the anger and guilt surging through her.

"Look, I know you don't want to leave, but I can't do my job and find these people if I'm constantly worried about your safety. And I simply haven't the manpower to put you under a full-time guard."

"You said that these people are after you, not me."

"But they'll try to get to me through you and Mom. I sent Neva to the mansion for her safety. Either go there, too, or get out of town."

"I refuse to go anywhere near that den of depravity."

"Then leave town." She glanced over to where Bodee was standing, and she noted for the first time that Steve was with him. Damn it, why wasn't he guarding Ronan? "Bodee, Steve, can I see you both, please?"

The two men walked over. Steve held up his hands as soon as he neared her and said, "Don't yell at me. Ronan refused to have me anywhere near him. Said he didn't need a babysitter—only he wasn't quite that polite."

Stubborn damn man—men, she corrected, glancing back at her father.

"What's wrong with Ronan?" he asked, voice sharp.

Not that he actually cared about Ronan's safety, she thought sourly. It was more a case of his wishes being thwarted. Ever since the Sinclair murder case, he'd been maneuvering to get Ronan instated as head ranger. Not that Ronan particularly wanted the position—he hadn't even been asked about it, in fact—but that was beside the point. Her father wanted her out, having always believed it wasn't a job suitable for a woman—a belief that had been confirmed by her near death at the hands of the moon dance killer. Once she'd actually recovered and returned to the job, his machinations had begun. They hadn't been successful yet, but Savannah knew she'd only have to drop the ball once and she'd be out.

And yet, perversely, she knew he was proud of her work and the way she had handled herself. She knew because he'd told her more than once—usually right before he and Mom launched into their "it's time you settle down and have babies" routine.

And Neva's marital bliss and resulting pregnancy had only increased their fervor to see her palmed off onto some poor, unsuspecting man.

"I think whoever is behind the bombing might also have tried to run Ronan down this afternoon," she explained, then glanced at Bodee. "Someone is certainly going after everyone I care about, anyway. I've ordered my mom and dad to leave town immediately. I want you to play chauffeur and take them to wherever they want to go." She returned her gaze to her dad's. "But go somewhere you've never been, somewhere people wouldn't expect you to be."

"This is damnably inconvenient."

"Being dead would be doubly so. Just do it, and let me get on with my job."

He grunted. "Get that cut seen to, will you? It's bleeding everywhere."

As yeses went, it was grudging, but it was better than nothing. She smiled, then leaned forward and kissed his cheek. "Be careful."

"You, too, cub. You, too." He squeezed her arm, then spun around and followed Bodee to the car.

She heaved a silent sigh of relief and looked at Steve. "Any word on Ike yet?"

"No one's seen him."

"Damn." She bit her lip for a moment, trying to quell the fear knotting her stomach as she watched Anton and several firefighters enter the diner's carcass. "Call Denny's mom and see if he made it home, then contact search and rescue about Ike. Once they've been advised, head on over to Ronan's. I want him watched for the next twenty-four hours, even if all of you have to sit outside his house in your trucks."

Steve raised an eyebrow. "Why only twenty-four hours?"

"Because I have a feeling this is all going to be over by then."

"For good, I hope."

"Me, too," she muttered. The trouble was, her instincts didn't seem interested in seeing that far ahead.

"A twenty-four-hour watch is going to be hard to manage. We don't have enough staff to man the station *and* do a watch."

Savannah scrubbed a hand across her forehead. She had a major headache coming on, and she wasn't sure if it was a result of the bomb blast or simply a surfeit of stress. "I know. But he won't leave town, so we'll just have to manage the best we can."

Steve coughed, then sniffed and said in a scratchy voice, "So are the rest of us in danger?"

"I honestly don't know. But it's well known that Ronan and I are good friends, and I suspect that's the reason they targeted him."

Steve nodded. "Then it might be better for everyone if *you* got out of town."

"That'll only delay the inevitable confrontation. If these people are after me and Agent Cade, we're better off facing them here, where at least we have the home court advantage."

"It seems to me that the killers have the very same advantage. They know you, boss. They know what you do and who you associate with. That indicates they've been watching you for a while."

It did. She rubbed her forehead again. "I'm going home to change, and then I'm heading over to Ari's to talk to her. I want everyone to report in to Kel every half-hour."

"You know Alf Reeson's parked himself at the station, don't you? He says Agent Jones promised him an exclusive."

She had no idea if he had or hadn't, and right now Reeson was the last of her worries. "As long as he's not causing problems, ignore him."

Steve nodded as he squinted toward the diner. "I'd start looking closer to home for suspects."

"I intend to. Just be careful." She squeezed his arm and headed for her truck.

As she climbed into the driver's seat, Cade glanced up from a folder he was reading. "You okay?"

"I feel like shit, and I'm going home for a nice hot shower. Then I'm going to talk to Ari, one of the waitresses who works in the diner and who has apparently befriended Candy. What's that?" She pointed to the folder as she started the engine.

"Information on Lonny's mother, Frankie Jackson." He reached into the folder and pulled out a photo. "Have you seen her?"

The woman in the black and white photo looked

about forty, with pale wavy hair and dark eyes. Her mouth was as thin as her face, and had a downward tilt that gave her a sour look. "Is this a license photo?"

He smiled. "Yeah. They're always bad."

"That they are." Her gaze went to the woman's eyes. There was something vaguely familiar about them—a certain warmth that was also oddly calculating. "I haven't seen her around, but there's something about her that seems familiar." She paused, and then it hit. "Anni Hawkins, the woman who runs the flower shop below my apartment. Frankie has the same sort of eyes."

"Eyes? Not features?"

"No. Anni's plumper, with thick gray curls, and she's older than this woman."

"This photo was taken over ten years ago."

"Even so, this woman is still younger than Anni." She shrugged and handed back the photo. "You know, Anni is apparently friendly with Candy, which gives us a reason to talk to her. It might be worth showing her this photo to see what sort of reaction we get."

"You think we'll get a reaction?"

"Anni's the town gossip. If anyone's seen this woman, it would be her." She did a U-turn and headed toward the other end of town. "It's odd that she was personally delivering flowers to Candy, though. She hires a teenager to do most of the flower runs."

Cade shifted in the seat until he was almost facing her. "What do you know about this Anni?"

"She's a busybody who took over the florist shop about six months ago. The previous manager had a car accident and had to quit work."

"So neither woman owns the shop?"

"No. It was owned by Lana Lee." She briefly met Cade's gaze. "She died in the fire on Candy's street."

"An accidental death?"

"We don't think so."

"Connected to our case?"

"There's no evidence to suggest that so far."

"And yet you believe they are connected?"

"Yes, I do."

His sudden smile was warm. "You would have made a good cop."

"I *am* a good cop."

"I meant a real cop, not a play one."

Irritation swept through her. "My dreams may not be as lofty as yours, but that doesn't give you the right to mock them. Rangers are cops—reservation cops—regardless of what you think. We go through training, and we have to obey the same rules."

He shifted again and touched his leg absently. It was obviously aching, and he was just as obviously not going to do anything about it. *Men.*

Still, was she any better? She hadn't done much about the cut on her cheek, either.

"And here I thought you were against rules," he said. "Wasn't that what Rosehall was all about?"

"Yeah, but it was my father's rules I was trying to escape, not society's."

"And ten years later, you're still trying to escape them."

She shot him a glance. "You try being the daughter of a man who doesn't believe in sex before marriage and see how well *you* cope!"

"I intend to achieve lots of things in my life, but being a daughter is never going to be one of them."

Humor touched his rich voice. "So why come back here at all? Why not go to one of the other reservations and train there?"

"Because Neva was here."

"And Neva was the only reason you returned?"

She glanced at him, knowing what he was asking, what he was thinking. The bitchy part of her wanted to keep him on the hook and wriggling, because he certainly deserved it after coming into her town and giving her nothing but attitude. But that wasn't fair, especially since she hadn't exactly had an angelic attitude herself. Besides, if she wanted any sort of future with this man, then she had better start being honest. Even if *he* wasn't.

"Ronan had nothing to do with it. He and I are casual lovers and good friends. Nothing more, nothing less." She glanced at him. "He's not a threat."

"It wouldn't matter if he was." His dark gaze seemed to lock hers, and for an instant it seemed like she was drowning in a sea of deep blue. "He wouldn't have a snowflake's chance in hell if I decided to pursue you for real."

"But you haven't decided," she said, somehow managing to pull her gaze away and concentrate on the road.

"Because I don't need to. You're mine until I decide otherwise."

Once again with the moon promise. Why couldn't he see he was using it as an excuse—a curtain to hide behind? "I will never be wholly yours until you can trust me enough to make my own decision about who I want to be with."

He didn't say anything, just looked away. Frustration ran through her, but she resisted the urge to thump the wheel—or better yet, him. Because as much as it would be satisfying to smack some sense into his thick skull—to make him see that what was happening between them was more than just the moon magic—she also had to accept the possibility that maybe he never would.

The simple fact was, maybe he didn't *want* anything more than sex from her. He'd placed his work before her at Rosehall, despite admitting that he'd cared for her. Maybe that would happen again in Ripple Creek. Maybe she was destined to love a man who was never going to commit to anything more than his work.

Maybe.

But until that happened, she was going to keep on pushing and hoping. Because she had to believe that what lay between them was meant to be—and that, sooner or later, he would realize it. As the song went, no man was an island. Not even one as stubbornly determined as Cade.

CADE CLIMBED OUT of the truck and studied the old, two-story brick building. He hadn't really taken much note of her home the last time he'd been here, being more interested in making sure she was okay and that there hadn't been anything nastier than a note left on her car. The building was smaller than he'd expected, and from the outside looked barely wide enough to swing a cat. The two bottom-floor windows were barred, and the building itself looked to have a decent security system.

He glanced up. No bars on the top two windows,

and the fire escape looked in good order. But since they wouldn't actually be staying here, it didn't really matter how easy the fire escape or her windows were to get to.

He followed her to the security door, trying not to let his gaze settle on the enticing sway of her hips but not entirely succeeding.

"Small place," he said, more to quell the urge to take her into his arms and kiss her senseless than any actual need to break the silence that had stretched between them since her comment about his lack of trust.

Which, he supposed, was a true enough statement. But given their past history, how could she really expect otherwise? Damn it, he didn't want to share her, pure and simple, and at least the moon magic gave him that security.

But did he want more than security? More than something short term?

Maybe. But he was here to find a killer, not contemplate the direction of his life. Until that killer was found, he couldn't let himself truly concentrate on anything else. Just being with Vannah was distraction enough. He didn't need to be thinking about the future when the present was so dire.

So why did he feel guilty? Why did he have this insane urge to say the words that would break the moon bond and leave her free to do as she pleased?

He didn't want a repeat of Rosehall. The attraction between them might still be insanely strong, but he was still an old-fashioned guy at heart, and she still seemed to be the free spirit who refused to be pinned down. As much as he might want to give her the freedom to choose, he just couldn't share her again. Nor did he wish a repeat of the emotional turmoil that had happened after she'd disappeared from Rosehall. She might have thought he was joking when he'd made the comment about getting drunk and smashing up his place, but he hadn't been.

She was the only woman who'd ever pushed him that far. The only woman he'd cared that much about.

He had no desire to go through it all a second time, but the more time he spent with her, the better the chance that would happen. They might know each other well sexually, but they knew squat outside the bedroom. At least the moon magic gave them a chance to be together, a chance to get to know each other better. A chance to discover whether or not there was the possibility of a long-term relationship without interference from other challengers.

He needed that time. *They* needed that time.

She opened the keypad's cover and pressed in her code, her fingers too quick for him to catch all the numbers. He swept his gaze over the door, looking for wires or any sign of tampering. "Why buy the old lodge if you're happy living here?"

"That's an investment in the future. I can't be a ranger forever."

"Why not?" He caught her fingers as she went to push the door open, and added, "Let me check first."

She raised an eyebrow. "Both this door and mine are security-coded. No one can get into the building."

"You sure of that?"

"Yes. Anni has the code for this floor, but not mine. Not even Lana had both."

"Who has the code for your apartment, then?"

"No one besides Neva."

He kissed her warm fingers, and then released them. "Not even Ronan?"

"Not even."

"Good."

She rolled her eyes. "Just check the door so I can get upstairs and take my shower."

Enticing images of her warm, wet body rose in his mind, making his pulse race and his cock hard. Even though they'd made love very recently, he was more than ready to go again. And it wasn't the moon magic. It was her—the way she moved, the way she sometimes looked at him, her exotic scent, and, oddly, her tender touches. He took a deep breath in an effort to quell the need surging through his veins, and said, "Yes, ma'am."

She stepped to one side. He carefully cracked the door open and ran his fingers around the frame. Nothing beyond years of dust and the occasional dead bug. He opened the door a little further, checking the immediate hall area as well as behind the door. Nothing seemed out of place.

"The florist shop is closed," he said, noting the sign on the glass door to his right. "That usual for this time of day?"

"No, it isn't." She crowded close, the heat of her breasts and body burning into his spine as she peered past him. "Most of Anni's clientele comes from the after-work crowd, but she likes to open early to catch what she terms 'the later-than-they-should-be-and-in-the-doghouse' husbands and boyfriends."

"Have you got a key to the shop?"

"Why would the killers bother snatching her?"

"Who knows?" he answered. "But at this stage, I wouldn't be surprised at anything."

"But it makes no sense. I mean, Anni and I aren't anything more than neighbors."

"We are not dealing with sane people here. Besides, she's friendly with Candy, and that might just make her a suspect."

"Anything is possible, I suppose." She paused. "And yeah, I have a key upstairs. Lana gave it to me a few years ago, just in case I needed to get in."

"So no one knows you have it?"

"The fire chief suggested it, but otherwise no." Her gaze met his, her green eyes bright in the semidarkness of the hall. "Why?"

He shrugged as he led the way to the stairs. "The fire chief didn't suggest she hold your key?"

"As I said before, I haven't got a key, and no one but my sister knows my code. So if they've snatched Anni thinking they'll get an easy way into my home, they're out of luck."

He climbed the stairs, and after she'd keyed open the door, repeated the checking process. Again, nothing. He stepped inside and closed the door behind him as he looked around.

Her apartment wasn't what he'd expected. Basically, it was one big room that encompassed the kitchen, dining, and living room. The color scheme was warm, with sandstone ceilings and walls, floorboards that were stained a rich claret, and a mishmash of autumn-toned furniture and rugs. The room had been divided near the front of the building with doors leading into what he presumed would be the bathroom and a small laundry room. Her big wrought iron bed sat between the two back windows and was covered by a patchwork quilt that looked both luxurious and handmade.

Her room at Rosehall had been all airy and New Age, but this was comfortable. Relaxing.

"Nice."

She flashed him a smile over her shoulder as she walked to the kitchen area. "Thanks." She pulled a pink-tagged key from a hook. "Here's the key, if you want to check downstairs."

He caught it one-handed. "Your security code?"

She didn't hesitate, just gave it to him, which was a little surprising given her earlier vehemence that he'd never get into her home.

"I'll be back in ten. Enjoy your shower."

"If you make it back in five, you can share it with me."

Her voice was low, seductive, and had his blood boiling in an instant. But if he started making love to her now, he had a feeling he wouldn't want to stop. Not today, not tomorrow, not ever. And while it was a delicious thought, it wasn't particularly a safe one. Not that making love to her tonight would be any safer, but at least they'd be a little harder for their murderous friends to find.

"As much as I'd love to, I don't think that's a wise course right now."

Her smile tore at his resolve. "Well, if you change your mind, you know where to find me."

"See you in ten."

He left the room before desire overrode common sense. Soft laughter followed him out.

Tease, he thought.

Coward, she replied.

He grinned and headed down the stairs. The florist shop was still wrapped in darkness and as silent as a grave. He unlocked the door and felt around the frame, looking for wire before he opened it fully. While he doubted there would be anything more than cobwebs and dust, he didn't intend to take a chance. Not with this case.

The scents of lavender, roses, freesias, and God knows what else assaulted him the minute he fully opened the door. The rich aromas tickled his nose and made him sneeze. He'd never enjoyed flowery scents—not until Vannah had come along, anyway. But then, her scent was far more exotic than the cloying smells that hung in the air here.

He scanned the dark room, looking for anything that appeared out of place. Nothing did, and there were no security cameras, either. A small counter stood near the back end of the room, and behind that was a closed door. He wove his way through the masses of color, wrinkling his nose to stave off another sneeze and half wondering how any wolf could stand to be in this place for too long. But maybe the old bird didn't have much of a nose—though it was usually sight that went first in a wolf, not sense of smell.

There was nothing behind the counter beyond curled brown rose petals and torn bits of ribbons. He tried opening the door, but it was locked. The main door key didn't fit it, either, which was a little odd. What could be so important to a florist that she kept it behind a separately locked door? Especially when most of the stock was sitting in the main room?

He didn't know, and he couldn't find out without

breaking in. And he wouldn't do that until he had a reason to—otherwise, he might only succeed in warning a potential suspect that she was under suspicion.

He turned back to the desk and began opening drawers. In the third one, he found a book containing delivery orders. He scanned through the pages, looking for Candy or Lonny. Neither of them was there. So why was Anni delivering flowers to Candy, and why weren't they being recorded? He closed the book and returned it. Then he pulled his cell phone out of his pocket and called Trista.

"Hey, boss," she said. "I just finished talking to Bryton, the ranger over in Merron."

He opened the last drawer and began looking through it. "And?"

"He was very helpful."

Undoubtedly hoping for a repeat of last summer, Cade thought wryly. "So he knew Lonny Jackson?"

"Oh yeah. Apparently, the mother was off with the fairies most of the time, and her daughter ran wild."

He pulled out some notebooks and quickly flicked through them. Nothing more than old delivery addresses. The rest of the drawer was full of loose papers. He grabbed a handful, and started looking through them. "She didn't happen to have a sister called Candy, did she?"

"No. Or at least, not during the time she was at Merron."

So why the hell did Candy and Lonny look so similar? There had to be a link somewhere, he was sure of it. "Did you get anything else from him?"

"Yeah—there's a really interesting bit of gossip about Lonny's father."

A letter in spidery writing caught his eye. It was from Lana Lee and addressed to Anni. *Pay the rent you owe me,* it said, *or I shall report what I saw you do to the police.*

It was not so much the threat, as the way it was worded that struck him as odd. Why the police rather than the rangers? And what the hell had Lana seen Anni do? Frowning, he put the letter to one side, and continued on.

"So who is Lonny's father?"

"Jontee McGuire."

Elation ran through him. Finally, they had a connection. Maybe not to the current murders, but at least to Jontee and Rosehall. "You sure?"

"Bryton is. Apparently Jontee had a real knack for seducing women, even as a teenager, but when he knocked Frankie up, her father beat both of them to an inch of their lives. Jontee did a runner, and Frankie was apparently never the same again."

From what Vannah had said, Jontee hadn't been, either. Though he'd seemed pretty damn sane when they'd caught and convicted him. "How old were they?"

"Fifteen. Jontee apparently lived next door to the Doherty household—Doherty being Frankie's maiden name."

"The time frame is right." He paused, studying a snip of paper with an out-of-town phone number on it. Probably nothing, but worth checking. "I don't suppose Jontee managed to get anyone else pregnant? The existence of a half-sister would certainly explain the similarities between Lonny and Candy."

"I asked, but Bryton couldn't say. There were none

reported, but given Merron doesn't always register half-breed births, he can't check."

"Get him to ask around anyway. Someone might know something."

"Will do. Anything else?"

"Did you find out what happened to Lonny when Frankie and her husband died?"

"She apparently went to a nominated guardian."

"Who was?"

Trista paused, and he heard the sound of flicking paper in the background. "Jina Hawkins. She was Frankie's older sister."

Frankie's sister? *That* would certainly explain the similarities in looks. "Is it possible that Jontee was bedding both sisters?"

"From what Bryton said, more than possible. I did ask if he knew any of Jontee's other lovers, though, but he couldn't give me any names."

"Well, Jina would hardly have said anything given her father's reaction to Frankie getting pregnant." He paused. "Did Bryton say much about Jina?"

"Not really. Apparently she was thirteen years older than Frankie, and left Merron not long after Frankie was beaten. She hasn't been seen on the reservation since."

"So how did they find her to relocate Lonny?"

"Bryton didn't know, but he's going to ask around."

"Good. Do a check through the system and see if you can find anything on our end, and pull up a birth certificate for Candy. And while you're there, do a check on Anni Hawkins and a Lana Lee." He gave her all the spellings.

"Is Anni Hawkins related to Jina Hawkins via marriage?"

"That's one of the things I need to find out."

"And the other woman?" she asked.

"Maybe another piece of the puzzle." He shoved the papers and notebooks back into the drawer and closed it. "Oh, and check this number for me." He grabbed the scrap of paper and read out the phone number. "Let me know who or what that belongs to."

"Will do."

Trista hung up, and he shoved the phone back into his pocket. He scanned the area to ensure everything was back in place, then picked up the two bits of paper and retreated. Vannah was dressed and brushing her hair in the kitchen by the time he got back to her apartment.

"Anni's not downstairs." His boot heels echoed against the wooden floorboards as he made his way across the room. "And there doesn't seem to be anything out of place in the shop."

"I figured as much." She picked up the coffeepot with her free hand. "Coffee?"

"Yes, thanks." He grabbed the brush from her and began to run it through the wet silk of her hair. Her sigh was filled with contentment. He wished there was a mirror close so he could see her face, see the sweet half-smile that always curved her lips whenever he'd done this at Rosehall. "What do you know about Anni Hawkins?"

She shrugged. "Not a great deal. We do the inane chat thing whenever we see each other, but it never goes beyond that."

"Do you have any idea why Lana Lee would send a threatening note to Anni Hawkins?"

"No." She paused. "What did the note say?"

"That she wanted Anni to pay rent, or she'd report what she saw to the police."

"Odd for her to say police instead of rangers."

"Exactly what I was thinking. Obviously the old girl knew something about Anni that we don't. Maybe that's the reason Lana died in your suspicious fire."

"What date was the letter written?"

"On the seventeenth."

"Two days before the fire." She took a sip of her coffee, then added, "Can I look at the letter?"

He took it from his pocket and handed it to her. As she read it, he continued running the brush through her glorious hair, enjoying the soft feel of it as it slid past his fingertips, the way the silky strands gleamed like liquid gold as the overhead light caressed them. Was there anything more erotic than brushing a woman's hair other than caressing skin to skin? It had always gotten him fired up. But then, when it came to Vannah, just one look could push him over the edge.

"It definitely looks like Lana's writing," she said. "The old girl was always writing us about the 'hoodlums' taking over her street and demanding we do something about it."

"But she never mentioned Anni Hawkins?"

"No." She hesitated. "You know, Anni's talked about a lot of things over the last six months, but I can't actually recall her ever mentioning where she came from. Odd, really."

"I've asked Trista to do a search to see if she can come up with anything."

"Good." She handed him the note, then turned around and snagged her brush from his hand. "In the meantime, we'd better question Ari."

He wrapped his arms around her and pulled her close. Then he tried to ignore how good it felt, how swiftly his body responded to the warm press of hers. But it wasn't so easy to ignore the sudden longing to be able to do this anytime he pleased, for the rest of his life. "Before we go anywhere, you need to answer that question."

She frowned. "What question?"

"Why can't you be a ranger forever?"

"Oh, that." She screwed up her nose. "Because I want to have kids one day."

"Kids and a job are not mutually exclusive."

"I know, but I don't want to be a working mom. I want to be able to stay home and watch their every little milestone. At least until they're old enough to go to school."

Surprise ran through him. "Somehow, I can't imagine the free-spirited woman I knew at Rosehall becoming a stay-at-home mom."

She wrapped her arms around his neck and kissed his nose. The brief touch sent desire shooting through every inch of his body, and it was all he could do not to press her back against the counter and give in to it.

"As I keep reminding you," she said softly, her lips so close they were teasing his with possibilities, "the me you knew at Rosehall was discovering and exploring my sexuality, and I'd certainly never planned on committing to just one man."

Which she hadn't. And it still hurt, still angered him, even if the sensible part of him was willing to accept her reasons now that he'd heard her side of it. He might not understand them, but he was willing to believe them.

"What about you?" she continued softly, her green eyes twinkling with what looked like amusement.

"Never imagined myself as a stay-at-home mom," he answered dryly. "But if my wife wants to be the breadwinner, I'm more than willing to look after the kids."

"So you're a modern man?"

"I'm a lazy man who only works because he needs to support himself."

"Raising kids ain't easy, you know."

He grinned. "Don't I know it. I helped raise my brothers after my dad died and Mom was forced to work."

She raised her eyebrows. "How many brothers?"

He slid one hand down to her butt and pressed her even closer, until the heat of her mound was pressed firmly against his erection. Gently, he rubbed back and forth against her, enjoying the sensation even if it was also the ultimate form of torture since he had no intention of taking it any further. "Four."

Her pupils dilated as desire overran the amusement in her eyes. "I would have thought that having four brothers would turn you off to having kids of your own."

"Well, it did make me damn careful about getting the fertility control injection every six months, just to make sure I was shooting blanks."

She grinned. "I hope you're still shooting those blanks, because I'm not ready to have kids just yet."

"Neither am I, believe me." Even if the thought of having kids with her made him warm inside.

And therein lay his real dilemma. He could lie to her, and he could lie to himself, as much as he liked. But the truth was, if he wanted to discover if what lay between them had the strength to end in such a dream, then he was going to have to release her from the moon magic and allow her the choice of being with him. Or not.

If he released her, he risked losing her again, and once was more than enough. Yet, by not releasing her, he faced the risk of losing her anyway. He might hold her physically, but he'd never be able to lay claim to anything more.

And he wanted that more. Wanted all she was willing to freely give.

So was it love?

Having never been in love, he couldn't honestly say what it felt like. But he very much suspected that if he didn't already love her, then he was certainly headed that way. Fast. And the more he tried *not* to think about it, to concentrate on the reason he was here rather than what he was feeling, the more control seemed to slither from his grasp. She'd had that effect on him at Rosehall, and it hadn't lessened in the ten years they'd been apart.

Maybe what he should really do was just talk about it. Get it all out in the open and let it hang there for discussion. But his gut clenched and his throat threatened to close over.

Talking about emotions wasn't something he'd ever been prone to do, and it was a hard habit to break, even for something—someone—as important as this.

She was right. He was a coward. He'd faced many a criminal with a loaded gun aimed at his face, and never once had he been as terrified as he was just now.

Her lips brushed his tenderly. "Some deep thoughts you appear to be having there," she said, the glow in her eyes making him wonder if she'd perhaps been following them. "Hope all this talk of babies hasn't made you skittish."

"Not in the least. In fact, it's nice to know the free spirit has mellowed."

"I haven't mellowed that much, as you'll find out if you don't stop doing what you're doing."

He raised a teasing eyebrow. "And what might I be doing?"

"Like you can't smell my arousal." Her sudden smirk was saucy. "That's like saying I can't feel your erection."

"It's attracted to heat, and there seems to be a lot of that at the moment." He leaned down and kissed her like he intended to make love to her tonight—long and slow.

The sharp ringing of the phone shattered the moment. She broke away with a sigh, then leaned across and snagged the handset off the wall.

"This had better be good," she said, her voice smoky with frustrated desire.

He wasn't sure what the person on the other end said, but the sudden tension stiffening her body told him it wasn't good news.

"I'll be there in ten," she said, and hung up.

"What?" he asked immediately.

Her stricken gaze turned to his. "There's been another murder. They think it might be Ike."

Chapter Eleven

SAVANNAH ENGAGED THE hand brake, then crossed her arms over the steering wheel as she stared up at the old walking trail. Despite the sun flaring against the golden aspens, the trail itself lay wrapped in a darkness as complete as the clouds gathering above.

It couldn't be Ike lying dead up there in that darkness. It couldn't be.

But what was she going to do if it was? She'd sent him after Denny, despite Cade's protests that he was too inexperienced. If Ike was dead, then she was responsible, as surely as if she'd loaded the gun and pulled the trigger.

"You okay?"

Cade's voice was soft, full of an understanding that almost unleashed the tears building inside.

She nodded, licking her lips as she battled for control. She was a ranger, damn it, and she would continue to act like one, no matter who was up there.

"Grab your coat." She wrapped a shaking hand around the handle and opened the door. "Bad weather has a habit of coming in fast."

He nodded, getting his coat and the crime scene kit

from behind the seat as she climbed out of the truck. The wind blasted around her with icy sharpness, filled with the scent of the oncoming storm. They had to get up there before the rain hit and destroyed any lingering evidence. She zipped up her coat, but the sound of a truck engine coming up the hill behind them made her spin around.

It was a red truck she recognized. Ronan's. And Steve was sitting beside him.

"Shouldn't he be in the hospital?" Cade asked, limping around to stand beside her. His shoulder brushed hers, and warmth jumped between them. She fleetingly wished he'd stand closer. Wrap an arm around her shoulder and enfold her in his heat, because right now she was chilled to the bone—and it wasn't because of the weather.

"Yeah, he should," she replied, as Ronan climbed stiffly out of his truck. She raised her voice a little. "So why isn't he in the hospital?"

"Because he has no intention of twiddling his thumbs in bed while madwomen are running around trying to murder his workmates and best friend." Ronan shrugged into his leather jacket, his face pale but determined. "These bitches are mine."

"You and Cade have a common goal, then. Fitting really, seeing you're both so goddamned stubborn."

A grin teased Ronan's lips as his gaze went to Cade. "She could teach both of us a thing or two about stubborn. You know that, don't you?"

"So I'm beginning to discover," Cade said dryly, then touched a hand to her spine. The heat of his fingers soaked through the jacket and swept across her skin like fire. "We'd better get up there."

"So says the three-legged wolf who should also be in the hospital," she muttered, but she knew she was only delaying the inevitable. She snagged the crime scene kit from him and slung it over her shoulder. "Steve, you want to grab the cameras from the back of Ronan's truck?"

"You carry cameras in the back of the truck?" Cade asked as they began to make their way up the trail.

"Specially made locked compartment," Ronan answered. "They're mine rather than the department's. I'm a would-be photographer in my spare time."

"Really?" Cade's voice held a note of surprise. "What sort of cameras do you use?"

Savannah couldn't help smiling as the two men conversed. Other than her sister, they were the two most important people in her life. Given all the hostility Cade had thrown Ronan's way yesterday, the easy way they talked now was something of a surprise—and a welcome one. But had anything really changed? Or was it simply a matter of common interest breaking down the barriers? After all, while she might love Cade, she knew nothing about his life or what he did outside his job—though he'd once told her his work *was* his life. But a man who lived for his work didn't go on alcoholic benders and smash up his place when a woman walked out of his life.

It was, she thought, a rather telling reaction to the feelings he'd refused to admit at Rosehall.

The trail ahead turned sharply to the left. If the hiker who'd found the body had his facts right, they'd find the victim not far ahead.

Her stomach began to churn even harder, and she found herself praying that it wasn't Ike, that it was somebody, anybody, else. Which wasn't entirely fair, because that somebody else would have family, friends, and loved ones just like Ike did.

When she found the twisted pine the hiker had mentioned, she hesitated. Then she determinedly swept aside the drooping branches and kept on going. And there, on the dirt and rotting leaves not far off the trail, was the naked body of a man. She stopped, her gaze sweeping his mutilated, spread-eagled body before coming to rest on his face.

It wasn't Ike.

It was Denny.

Relief ran through her, swiftly followed by anger. Denny might not have been anyone's favorite kid, but he *had* been a kid, and he deserved better than this.

The three men stopped on either side of her. "Shit," Ronan said softly. "Denny."

"Yeah. Still getting bad breaks, even in death." She hauled the kit off her shoulder and unzipped it. "So where the hell is Ike if Denny is here?"

"Hopefully not a hostage." Ronan glanced at her. "Have you contacted Search and Rescue? It's not their usual type of rescue, but still—"

"I know. And Steve did."

Cade squatted on his heels, his expression pensive as he studied the scene before them. "This is different than the other two murders. This isn't a ritual, just a killing."

Her gaze jumped back to the body and, for the first time, she saw the differences. "No stone ring."

"And while his penis and scrotum are sliced away, they didn't remove his heart," Ronan added. "We have a different killer."

"Or a copycat," Cade said grimly.

"It can hardly be a copycat when we've kept the murders out of the newspapers," Ronan retorted. "And none of us has let the cat out of the bag."

"It's not a copycat," she said softly, staring at the body. For an instant, it almost seemed like she could feel Denny's struggle for life, taste that moment of stark horror when he realized what was going to happen. Could smell the thick smell of citrus and cigarette smoke as cold steel slid into his spine and pain flared like fire . . .

Then the sensations slid away and she shuddered.

"It was the same killer," she said, glad her voice showed no sign of the shakiness growing inside, "only she doesn't believe in the ritual. She just needs the thrill, the blood." She hesitated. "It was Candy who did this."

Cade looked up at her. "What makes you think that?"

She hesitated again. "Clairvoyance, instinct . . . whatever you want to call it. It hits at the weirdest times."

"But it's usually always correct." Ronan turned around to grab a camera. "So, if this is the same killer, why the ritual on the other two?"

"There are at least two killers, not one," Cade answered, his gaze returning to the body. "The other murders were a lure to get me here. This looks almost incidental."

Savannah handed Steve the crime scene tape, then crossed her arms, trying to warm the chill from her body as Ronan began taking shots of Denny. "While

I'm pretty sure both Candy and Lonny are involved, who is the third person? You can't mean Anni."

"Why not? If she's seeing Candy regularly, then she's a suspect." Cade glanced up at her again. "But I wasn't talking about her. I meant Nelle."

Savannah frowned. "Nelle's not in Ripple Creek."

"You can't be sure of that. As you said, it's been ten years. She could have changed beyond recognition."

Ronan moved around the circle to get shots from the other side of the body. She followed carefully, scanning the ground as she walked, looking for prints or anything else that would lead them to their killer. *Killers.* "Maybe, but Nelle wasn't involved in the Rosehall murders."

"Why are you so sure of that?"

"Why are you so sure that she was?"

He raised an eyebrow as he rose and walked toward the body. The leaves covering the ground crunched softly with his every step, like the faint crunching of bones. She shivered.

"Because I've always believed Jontee wasn't working alone." He squatted beside Denny's body. "As I've said before, if he wasn't clear-minded enough to run the day-to-day operations of Rosehall, how would he be able to run something as meticulously planned as the murders? Nelle handled the day-to-day stuff, so why couldn't she have handled the darker operations as well?"

She squatted beside him. "Because she didn't have any darkness in her."

He raised his eyebrows. "And Jontee did?"

She hesitated. "Not in the beginning, but toward the end, yeah, he did. He certainly seemed to be growing more frustrated and angry over the last few weeks that I was there."

"Maybe because someone else was controlling his actions."

"I don't know. I mean, if someone *did* have control over him, wouldn't I have noticed it in his thoughts?"

"Not if you weren't looking for it. You were eighteen, remember, and looking for sexual adventure, not bloodshed and darkness."

But she'd found *them* regardless. She rubbed her arms to ward off a growing chill. "As far as I'm aware, Nelle wasn't a telepath."

"Which doesn't preclude the possibility that she was. It could just mean that she was clever enough to disguise it from you."

"Nelle had no deceit in her." She hesitated, but couldn't help adding, "Not like some others who were there."

"I was there to apprehend a killer, Vannah," he retorted. "I could hardly be honest about *that,* given I had no idea just how trustworthy anyone really was."

"People," Ronan interrupted. "Argue later. Let's find what clues there are before this storm hits."

She glanced at Ronan and saw the hint of censure in his eyes. She took a deep breath and released it slowly. "You're right. I'm sorry." She glanced at her watch. "Doc Carson should be here any minute. Steve, you want to go meet him and fetch a tarp while you're there? It'll at least protect the body and the immediate area around it when the storm hits."

He nodded and headed off down the path. She pulled on some gloves and glanced at Ronan to ensure he'd taken the shots of the body's position. When he nodded, she knelt and carefully lifted Denny's right hand.

"There are abrasions along the knuckles," she noted. "He hit something pretty hard."

"Hopefully, Candy." Cade shifted a little. "Look at the jaggedness of the genital wound—it looks ripped more than cut."

"Maybe she was in a hurry."

He looked at her. "Or she used something other than a knife."

She closed her eyes for a minute, battling the surge of sick images that rose at his words. "A blood frenzy."

It happened only rarely in the werewolf population, but it was the one thing that had led to the still common human myth that werewolves became insane killers every time the moon bloomed full. Truth was, though the desire to hunt was an instinct every wolf possessed, it was one very easily controlled. It had to be, because while wolves might be stronger and faster, the human population had always vastly outnumbered them.

But just as there were humans who snapped the bonds of sanity and rationality to become killers, so there were also wolves. Those wolves were the ones who hunted. And humans, with none of the natural cunning of a wolf's normal prey, were an easy target.

Cade looked around. "If this was a blood killing, then it didn't happen here. There's no sign of a struggle. Denny might have been a kid in lust, but even he would have seen the frenzy come over her eventually."

"Yes." She hesitated, remembering the clairvoyant images. "But she did have a knife. She drove it through his spine."

Cade's eyebrows rose, but he didn't comment as he rolled Denny onto his side. The knife wound was there, just as she'd seen.

"The smell of the blood must have sent her into the frenzy," he commented.

Ronan walked up behind her and took some shots. "If this was a blood killing, why move the body and try to make it look like the others? It would have made more sense if she'd let us think this killing was unrelated. That alone suggests the frenzy wasn't all-consuming."

"There are some blood takers who learn to control it over time. Or at least long enough to get somewhere where they can't hunt humanity."

"That still doesn't explain this," she said, indicating the way Denny was positioned.

Cade scratched his jaw, his expression thoughtful. "Maybe she was ordered to make Denny look like a ritual killing, but the frenzy started getting the better of her. Or maybe the approach of the hiker forced her to retreat or risk being discovered."

"Either way," Ronan said, "there's going to be DNA evidence on his body."

"And more wherever this murder actually happened." She glanced up as rain began to sprinkle on them. The patch of sky visible through the trees was as black as coal. "That storm is about to hit. We'd better get looking. Ronan, you wait for Steve."

He nodded and handed her his spare camera. She and Cade rose and began a thorough search of the immediate area. When they found nothing, they broadened the search. About ten minutes later, the wind dropped, leaving the forest in an expectant hush—at least until the rain began to pelt down. The icy drops of moisture hit her hard, chilling her skin and slithering past her neck and down her spine. She shivered and flicked up the collar of her jacket, but it didn't seem to help much. The splats of water against the leaf-covered ground sounded as sharp as gunshots, and despite the cover of the tree canopy, the world had become gray.

"Over here," Cade called, his voice sounding close even if she couldn't see him through the trees and the wet gloom.

She made her way toward the sound of his voice and found him squatting over a muddy footprint and a patch of disturbed ground just in front of a small cave.

She knew the cave. Most of the wolves who grew up in Ripple Creek did. Thanks to the council's views on the whole sex-before-marriage thing, it was often in places like this that teenage wolves first began exploring their sexuality. Certainly, she and Ronan had explored in a very similar place.

Someone needed to oust her dad, she thought sourly, and start getting some common sense back into the community. Then maybe a kid like Denny wouldn't have been forced to use such a dangerous place.

"The struggle started inside the cave," she said, her gaze following the scuff marks, "and continued out here."

He nodded and pointed to an area where the soil was darker. "The amount of blood here indicates this might be where she tore at his genitals. I'll need to get a sample to be sure."

She took some photos first, then handed him bags and gloves before heading into the cave. She paused in the entrance, allowing her eyes time to adjust before moving inside. There was more evidence of a struggle, though the drier soil had failed to catch any worthwhile prints. There was no clothing, meaning Candy had come back here to clean up after being spooked by the hiker.

Which definitely suggested the frenzy *wasn't* all-consuming. So did that mean Candy had become so accustomed to the attacks that she could, to some extent, control them?

She didn't know. As far as she knew, they'd never had trouble with blood frenzies in Ripple Creek. Nor did they want it now. While the reservation didn't survive on the tourist dollar, there were some residents who did—not to mention that any attack by a wolf on a human tended to affect all the reservations.

She collected soil samples from several small areas that looked to be soaked by fluid of some kind, carefully numbering and recording each one. As she rose to leave, a glint caught her eye. She walked over to the corner and brushed aside the dirt. The glint turned out to be a small, rose-shaped pendant.

Exactly the same as the one Candy had been wearing.

And, just maybe, a link back to Rosehall.

"Bingo," she said softly, bagging the necklace and tagging the area before moving out of the cave.

"What have you found?" Cade had moved to an

area sheltered by overhanging rocks, but he looked around as she appeared.

"A possible connection to Candy." She showed him the necklace. "She was wearing one like this when I talked to her this morning."

"It gives us a reason to pick her up, at least." He rose. "I've found several pieces of human tissue scattered about, but not enough to account for what the boy is missing."

God. Bile rose, and she closed her eyes, fighting it. "She's had more than enough time to clean up."

"Maybe she didn't need to." He cupped a hand to her cheek, and gently brushed his thumb across her rain-wet lips. "Have you ever seen a wolf in a frenzy?"

"No, and it's not something I ever want to witness, thank you very much."

"I have." His dark eyes were distant. Troubled. "Five years ago. It took half a dozen of us to bring him down, and none of us walked away unscathed." He moved his hand and showed her his palm. Though she'd noticed the pale, ragged scar stretching from one side to the other, she'd never gotten around to asking him about it. "I was lucky. Some of them lost fingers, hands, and even a whole arm. He tore and ate whatever he could get hold of."

She swallowed back bile. "No wonder humans are scared of us."

"Even wolves should fear those who are in a frenzy. Believe me, sanity takes a backseat, and blood and flesh is all they want. And they're not picky whose."

Her phone rang—a shrill sound in the wet wildness of the storm. She started, her heart leaping into overdrive.

Cade grinned, then leaned forward and dropped a kiss on her lips, his mouth like a furnace against hers. "Getting a little jumpy, aren't you?"

"Can you blame me?" She stepped back and answered the phone.

It was Kel. "I just got a call from a couple doing the Fitness Freaks tour."

Savannah ran a hand across her face. Fitness Freaks was a hiking group that ran guided tours along the intermediate Red Mountain trail, and Kel regularly got rescue calls from hikers who weren't as fit as they thought they were. "Tell them I haven't got anyone to spare to pick up hikers who've changed their mind. They're going to have to come back down under their own steam this time."

"This didn't come from either of the organizers, but from a couple of hikers who'd dropped a little behind. They said it sounds as if something is attacking the main group. There's a whole lot of screaming and snarling."

Oh, fuck . . . "On my way. And call the paramedics out, too, Kel."

She hung up and looked at Cade. "Sounds like Candy's still in the frenzy. There's a tour group being attacked not far from here."

"Then we'd better get there. Fast."

She nodded, slung the camera over her shoulder, and followed him back down the mountain. "Are we going to need help?"

"Probably." He had his phone out even as he answered her question.

"What about tranquilizer darts?"

"The last guy I mentioned? He took half a dozen darts and still managed to mutilate three people before he went down." He paused to talk into the phone, rattling out commands in a sharp voice.

Great. Just what they needed—to be going after a mad wolf armed only with darts that might have little or no effect.

Ronan and Steve looked around as they came out of the trees.

"What's up?" Ronan stood.

"There's a tour group being attacked on the Red Mountain trail. We think it's Candy, so you'd better come with us." She glanced at Steve. "You stay here and wait for the doc."

"Hart, our forensics guy, is on his way here," Cade said, as he shoved the phone back into his pocket. "Trista and Anton will meet us up there."

"We can't afford to wait for them."

Cade glanced at her. "No. You have those tranquilizer guns in your trucks?"

"Yes."

"Then let's go get the bitch."

DESPITE THE WEATHER, the scent of blood seemed to hang in the air, thick and rich and ripe, which, Cade thought wearily, meant it was truly bad up ahead. He rubbed a hand across his jaw and half-wished they could have done something, anything, to prevent this tragedy. Attacks like this didn't do the reservations any favors, especially since it was human habit to blame all wolves for the actions of a few. They'd be paying for this for years, economically—though Candy herself would pay with her life. There was no such thing as a second chance for a wolf found guilty of murdering a human.

He shut the truck door and flipped up the collar of his coat as he stared up the trail. There was no sound other than the howl of the wind and the drumming of the rain. Not even from the two white-faced women who emerged from the cover of several pines and ran toward them.

The oldest of the two didn't stop until she'd hit him full on. He grunted in surprise and automatically wrapped his arms around her. Her entire body shook, and her skin was icy. The other woman stopped several paces away, a haunted, almost vacant look in her eyes. Exposure, combined with shock. Their first priority had to be getting them warm. He glanced at Savannah and raised an eyebrow. She nodded at his unasked question and moved back to the truck.

"It's all right, ma'am," he said, briskly but gently rubbing the back of the woman hugging him tight. "Can you tell me what happened?"

"You've got to help them. Please." Her voice was muffled by his chest and little more than a hoarse, shaky whisper.

The strong scent of blood, and the fact that there was no screaming or howling coming from the trail ahead, suggested it was already far too late. And he knew from past experience that it was better to sneak up on a wolf in a frenzy than to jump right in.

He grimaced, and tried to keep his voice calm as he said, "Ma'am, we need to know what happened."

"A big cream wolf just came out of nowhere and at-

tacked us. It was crazy, just tearing and biting and . . .
oh God." She started to cry softly.

He gently squeezed her shoulder, feeling awkward
and knowing such gestures offered little in the way
of comfort. He doubted anything would right now.
"How long has it been quiet?"

"I don't know," she said, alternating between hic-
cupping and crying. "Not long. A minute, maybe
more. God, you've got to hurry. Please."

Then she broke down completely, her sobs shaking
her body and his. Savannah approached, wrapping a
blanket around the woman's shoulders before gently
prying her away. He couldn't help heaving a sigh of relief. He hated clingy women. He always had—which
was probably why he'd fallen so hard for Savannah.
Then he stopped the thought cold. Now was not the
time for such things.

He glanced at the second woman and touched her
arm. Her flesh was almost blue, her eyes vacant and
jaw slack. "Ma'am?" he said softly.

No response. "Ma'am," he said, a little louder this
time. "We need to ask some questions."

Savannah came back with another waterproof
blanket and wrapped it around the woman's shoulders. There was no reaction.

Vannah glanced at him. "You want me to prod her
telepathically?"

He hesitated. Technically, he should be the one
doing it, since such intrusions were in his purview
while they could get her into serious trouble. But they
couldn't let this drag on. They had to know what to
expect and get up there before Candy finished gorg-

ing herself and moved on. And Vannah was obviously a far stronger psychic than he. He nodded.

Vannah placed her fingers on either side of the woman's cheeks and narrowed her eyes. A whisper of energy teased his mind, and then her thoughts were in his head, a distant echo of the force she used on the woman.

Ma'am, we need to know how many people were in your group.

He shouldn't be able to hear her. The fact that he could meant this thing between them went far deeper than he'd presumed.

God, it was so damn frustrating that he just couldn't grab her and talk to her. *Really* talk to her—get out in the open all she was feeling, all he was feeling. Get the past and future sorted out.

But there was Candy, and the humans, and somewhere in Ripple Creek a madwoman intent on making them pay for their so-called crimes of the past.

He had to think about that—to ensure they both survived—before he did anything else.

The woman came to life, jumping like a terrified rabbit as she stuttered, "Five . . . six including Marion, the guide. Please." She grabbed Savannah's jacket with her free hand, her knuckles so white they looked almost luminescent in the gloom. "Please help them. My sister—"

"We'll go find them," Savannah said, her voice rock steady, soothing, even though she gave him a hopeless sort of look that made him want to wrap his arms around her and protect her from the madness up ahead. She eased the woman's grip from her coat and added, "But you need to get into the truck with your friend and lock the door. Do you understand?"

The woman nodded, but she didn't move. Savannah gently guided her toward the truck and helped her inside.

"Humans," Ronan said, anger in his voice as he handed Cade a tranquilizer gun. "Not wolves. It's going to be a bloodbath up there."

"Yes." No wolf, or group of wolves, for that matter, could have hoped to protect a group of humans against a wolf in bloodlust. And dart guns were going to be next to useless if Candy was still in the frenzy. Still, they had no other option but to go on. The rangers didn't carry proper weapons, and his team hadn't arrived with the silver bullets yet. He raised the small dart gun and checked to make sure it was ready to fire. Two darts. Not nearly enough if this went down badly. He glanced at Vannah as she returned. "Ready?"

Her face was pale, her green eyes determined. "No. But let's go anyway."

He smiled. His woman had a lot of courage; there was no doubt about that. "Spread out. That way she can go for only one of us at a time."

She nodded and headed to the left edge of the trail. He headed down the middle, because it was the most dangerous and he was the only one with any real experience against a wolf in frenzy. Ronan took the right-hand side.

They splashed through the wind and the rain, quickly reaching a sweeping bend that arced around to the right. At the end of it, in the middle of the road, amongst the mud and the puddles, lay the bloody, broken bodies of the hiking group. Not even whole bodies. Just parts.

And standing beside them, still consuming the warm flesh, was a cream-colored wolf. She didn't even seem to notice them, though she surely would have smelled them, if not heard them. Maybe the need to consume flesh was greater than the need to flee. He'd seen it happen many a time.

He quickly raised the weapon and fired his two darts. He heard the soft reports to his left and right as Vannah and Ronan fired their weapons simultaneously. The metal-tipped darts hit the wolf in a small cluster right in the middle of her chest. She howled—a sharp sound of fury and pain—and bared bloodstained canines at them. But she didn't move, and that in itself indicated the frenzy was still under control. She had done this to these people because she'd wanted to, not because she *had* to.

"Candy Jackson, you're under arrest for—"

Before Vannah had the chance to finish, the cream wolf attacked. Not him, as he'd expected, but Vannah.

"Watch out," he warned, and threw the spent weapon at the lunging wolf, hoping to distract her even as he sprang to intercept her. But Vannah was faster. In the blink of an eye, she'd shifted shape and launched herself at the cream wolf. They hit in midair with bone-jarring force and tumbled to the ground, snarling and snapping and tearing at each other. Crimson stripes appeared along Vannah's golden hide, and fear and anger surged through him. Cursing softly, he shifted shape and lunged into the fray, snapping at Candy's back legs in an attempt to hamstring her.

As he and Vannah attacked from the back and the front, Ronan's russet-colored form hit Candy from the side, knocking her off her feet. Vannah pounced, locking her jaws around the cream wolf's exposed neck, a low warning rumbling up her throat.

Candy stilled instantly. Vannah had her jaws locked around the wolf's most vulnerable spot, and she could so easily rip the other wolf's throat apart. Cade had no idea how she was resisting the temptation, especially given the bloody mess that lay behind them.

He shifted to human form, as did Ronan. Vannah didn't move or shift shape until the drugs in the darts had taken effect and Candy went limp. As she spat the hairs from her mouth, his gaze skated down her body, noting with relief that the wounds on her side were little more than scratches.

"That wasn't a frenzy," she said eventually, wiping a hand across her mouth but still missing several cream hairs, "or we wouldn't have downed her so easily."

He brushed the hairs away from one corner of her lips with a fingertip. "No. She killed these people because she wanted to. Because she enjoys the taste of flesh."

Her gaze flicked to the mess behind them, and her face lost what little color it had left. "God, those poor people." She hesitated, and there was a catch in her voice as she added, "I can't even see Marion."

If Marion had spiky black hair and leathery brown skin, then her head and part of her torso were lying in a ditch just off the main path. But she didn't need to know that, and didn't need to see it. He touched a hand to her chin and forced her gaze back to him.

"Can Ronan handle the cleanup? We need to get Candy contained so I can begin questioning her."

"You can't."

He frowned. "What do you mean, I can't?"

"I tried to touch Candy's mind when I was attacking her. She has extremely strong shields. I doubt I'd get through, let alone you."

"I have to at least try. If I can't, I'll let you loose on her."

Her grin was wry and at odds with the horror still lingering in her eyes. "Not sure about your use of the word 'letting.' After all, this is my town, and I have as much right to question her as you do."

She didn't, but he wasn't going to argue the point when it wasn't really *that* important.

He bent down and scooped up Candy's limp form. "Why don't we get this bitch to the safety of a cell, and then we'll worry about who does what?"

To say Candy was unhappy about waking and finding herself confined by three walls and a set of bars would be the understatement of the year, Savannah thought dryly. The pale-skinned woman, her clothes half-shredded and covered in mud and blood, paced her prison, occasionally stopping to kick a wall or fling abuse at the monitoring camera. She didn't go anywhere near the cell bars, though—mainly because they were coated with silver. Even the simplest of brushes could burn a wolf's skin.

"How long are you going to let her stew?" she asked, glancing at Cade. He was watching Candy's actions with narrowed eyes, as if every movement told him something new. And maybe they did. This is what he did for a living, after all.

"Just a few more minutes." He glanced at her, his navy eyes gleaming with cold amusement. "She hates being confined. It's getting to her."

She glanced at the monitor. Candy was back to pacing rather than kicking. "Looks like fury to me."

"It was at first, but she's starting to get fidgety. Look at her eyes. Wide open."

"But angry rather than scared."

"For the moment."

Savannah crossed her arms. "Are we leaving her in that cell to interview her?"

"Yes. I'm not taking the risk of her being able to call up the blood frenzy at will. Not when there are only the two of us here."

"And Kel."

He flashed her a grin. "Kel can't even make decent coffee."

"I heard that," Kel said, walking into the room with two mugs of coffee. "Maybe I should go back to giving you dishwater, Agent Jones."

Savannah accepted the coffee gratefully. The rich aroma had hints of cinnamon and chocolate, meaning Kel *had* given them the good stuff.

"I do so appreciate good coffee," Cade said, grabbing his cup with a nod of thanks. "I just don't get it often."

"With the attitude you fling about, I'm not surprised." Kel winked at Savannah as she left the room.

Cade raised an eyebrow, his expression half-amused. "Is she always that sharp-tongued?"

"You've actually caught her on a good week. She can be quite acidic when she's in a mood."

"Bet she's great for weeding out the callers who are just intent on wasting your time."

Savannah grinned. "That she is."

She glanced at the screen as Candy stopped in front of the monitor and glared at them. It was a god-awful sight, given her face was covered in blood, strings of flesh, and short, dark hairs. Marion's coat had been black, she thought, and clenched her free hand against the desire to beat the hell out of Candy.

She took a sip of her coffee, then leaned forward and placed a finger on the screen. "What do you want to bet that line of bruising is Denny's doing?"

"Most likely. It's certainly the oldest of her bruises." He hesitated, glancing at her. "The kid went down fighting."

"Yes." She paused and forced away the images of Candy's frenzy, even though she knew they'd haunt her dreams for years to come. "So, are you going to question her while reading her telepathically?"

He nodded. "And if that doesn't work, you can have a go."

"And if *that* doesn't work?"

He shrugged. "She can rot in the cell until she decides to cooperate."

"That's not exactly legal."

"We don't have to be legal. The reservation is not bound to obey all criminal laws."

A fact she knew. She also knew that it didn't apply to major crimes, like murder. But maybe he was banking on the fact that Candy didn't know that.

He thrust to his feet. "I think the time is right to question her."

She pressed the record button so they had a verbal record of what was going on and followed him out the door and down the short corridor to the cells. Candy swung around as they entered.

"About fucking time," she spat. "I demand my rights. I want a lawyer."

Cade leaned against the wall opposite the cell and sipped his coffee. Energy stirred the edges of her mind as he reached out mentally for Candy. "You're getting neither until you answer some questions."

Candy sneered. "That ain't legal."

"Actually, it is. This is a reservation. We don't have to abide by human laws."

"I ain't talking until I get representation."

"Then you can sit in that cell and rot for all I care." He paused. "I hope you enjoyed what you did, because it's the last meal you'll be getting for quite a while."

He pushed away from the wall and began walking to the door. *Your turn,* he said, as he passed Vannah. *You're right. I can't get through her shields.*

It hadn't taken him long to figure that out, but she was more than a little surprised that he'd given in so quickly.

Not given in, he corrected. *Just acknowledging a fact. In all my years of training, I've never encountered a shield like hers.* He hesitated, and amusement rippled through her mind, as warm as summer rain. *Or a mind as strong as yours. I'm lucky you didn't kick my telepathic ass to kingdom come that night, aren't I?*

She wondered if he realized he'd read her mind as easily as if she'd spoken. Wondered if he knew that only someone extremely close to her could ever have done that. Like immediate family. Or the man who was meant to be her mate.

I was under the impression that was the other reason you'd run that night. She flashed him a mental smile to take the sting from her words.

He paused with his hand on the door handle and turned to look at her. *I never intended to run out on you, Vannah, which is why I've spent years looking for you.*

She smiled. *Yeah, so you could give me a piece of your mind.*

His smile echoed hers. *Yes. And whatever else you feel inclined to take.*

She raised an eyebrow. *Careful. I might take that as an admission.*

And you might be right. He opened the door. *You'd better question our suspect. She's just about to blow her top because you're ignoring her.*

Tough. And there's no guarantee I'll do any better than you. Her shields feel as strong as my dad's.

It's still worth a go. If she tries anything, I'll be just outside the door.

"Hey, bitch," Candy said, as Cade walked out and slammed the door behind him. "You going to let him do that?"

Savannah sipped her coffee and pretended to ignore her. Candy slapped a hand against the cell bars, but quickly ripped it away. Anger had obviously made her forget about the silver. Or was it fear? Certainly there was something that sounded an awful lot like forced bravado in her voice now.

"Hey," Candy said, louder this time. "Don't you pretend you can't hear me!"

Savannah finally looked at her. "I'm sorry. Were you talking to me?"

"Yeah. You gonna let that bastard do this?"

She paused, as if considering the question, while she reached out telepathically to the other wolf. Candy's shields weren't actually shields, but something far stranger—a swirling vortex of power that threatened to suck her in and then spit her out. She'd felt the power of it briefly on the trail when she'd had the woman pinned, but this was like comparing a sun shower to a tornado. And it was just as impossible to pass through. Maybe the frenzy—or the bloodlust, or whatever it had been—had caused the shield to weaken earlier. If that was the case, then she had no choice but to try to achieve a similar weakening.

Can't do it, she said to Cade. *But I think there might be another way to break her down.*

Like what?

A two-pronged attack. She hesitated. *The silver bars will hold a wolf in a frenzy, won't it?*

Yeah, but you wouldn't want to get within range. Apprehension swam through his thoughts. *What do you intend to do?*

Speed things up a little. We can't afford to waste the whole day.

Be careful.

Of course.

"You gonna answer or not?" Candy snapped impatiently.

"That black wolf you tore to pieces?" Savannah kept her voice even, though it was hard when all she wanted to do was grab the bitch's face and knock her lights out. "Her name was Marion, and she was a friend of mine. So yeah, I think I am going to let him do this to you."

"Your daddy wouldn't be pleased about you breaking the rules. If he was still around to care, that is."

Savannah ignored the cold pit of fury forming in her stomach and raised an eyebrow. Her mom and dad were safe; she knew that. But that didn't alter the fact that this woman had gone after them. Pack protection was born into every wolf, and Candy should have known better than to taunt her. "And why would you say something like that?"

The other woman's smile was smug. Gloating. "Because it's the truth, ranger. Because your sister will soon be dead meat, your lover will soon be dead meat, and then you'll die, just as horribly as my daddy did."

Her daddy? Surely Candy couldn't be talking about Jontee . . . could she?

It's a possibility, Cade said.

Annoyance swept through her. Was there ever going to be a time when this man stopped keeping secrets? *And when did you intend to tell me this?*

When we knew for sure. We haven't found her birth certificate yet.

Well, there was one person who *did* know for sure. She returned her attention to Candy. "I was under the impression you were a fatherless bitch. Certainly no man wanted to claim you on your birth certificate."

She snarled softly, anger gleaming in her eyes. "Just

because his name wasn't on my certificate didn't mean I didn't know him."

"The question is, did *I* know this nameless man?"

"Of course you did. You were fucking him at Rosehall, after all."

"Ah. You must mean Jontee. I never killed him, you know. He did that himself, by doing what he did." She paused, and to Cade said, *Who's her mother?*

We think it could be Jina Hawkins, Frankie's older sister.

So Jontee was doing them both?

There's no proof, but it fits. He was only fifteen at the time.

Told you he was charismatic. To Candy, she said, "And how could you be Jontee's kid? You're too old to have come out of Rosehall and certainly your mother was never there."

"She may not have been there, but she and Jontee shared a connection. She knew things. Saw things." Candy's gaze narrowed. "You betrayed him. You and that organizing bitch."

She meant Nelle, obviously. "Is that why you set the bomb in my father's diner? As payback for my perceived part in your father's death?"

Malice glittered in the other woman's eyes. "I'm not the ranger, you are. Find out yourself."

"I will. Don't worry about that." Savannah finished the last of her coffee and pushed away from the wall. "So, tell me. Was what you did on the trail a blood frenzy or simply bloodlust?"

"What does it matter? I'm dead either way."

Savannah stopped close to the bars, just out of Candy's reach, and smashed the mug against the wall. It broke—a sharp sound that made Candy jump. Shards of china scattered across the floor, glittering starkly against the dark carpet. She ignored them, concentrating on Candy, still holding the handle and one jagged piece of china in her hand.

Candy licked her lips, her uncertainty palpable. "You can't cut me with that. It's against the rules."

"Who said I was going to cut *you* with it?" She raised her free hand and ran it across the sharp edge of the cup. The flesh across her palm parted and blood began to well, tainting the warm air with its richness. She clenched her fist, ignoring the pain as she met Candy's widening gaze. "And you didn't answer my question."

Damn it, Cade cut in, *there's no need—*

This will work! She's less afraid of me than you. Just stay where you are and watch.

Candy licked her lips. "I can't answer that question. It'll incriminate me."

Savannah snorted softly. "The three of us saw you standing over the bodies of the hikers and consuming their flesh. We don't need you to admit to anything. Your fate will be the electric chair, regardless of what you do or don't say here."

"Then what does it matter?"

It didn't matter, because the hunger in the other woman's eyes, the sudden sharpness of her breathing, gave Savannah the answer. This was bloodlust. She squeezed her hand, making the blood run faster.

"Imagine it," she continued softly. "Your home until you die will be ten feet of concrete and bars. No wind to ruffle your coat. No sunlight to warm your skin. No earth under your paws."

She paused again. The hunger was sharper, Candy's expression more avid, more haunted.

"No prey to hunt and bring down. No flesh to rend. No blood to lap, fresh and warm from the body." That last bit was a guess, but a fairly safe one. Candy had to be the one doing that, since it was the only real difference from the Rosehall murders.

But how had she known all the details in the first place? Whether or not she was Jontee's kid, she hadn't been at Rosehall. So who told her? *Was* Nelle involved?

A growl rumbled up Candy's throat. "I'd rather be dead."

"That can be arranged."

Candy snarled, but the hunger in her eyes was giving way to desperation. "You wouldn't. You were always such a Goody Two-shoes."

Savannah raised an eyebrow and raised her hand, so that Candy could see the drops of blood falling from her palm. The other woman's gaze followed it avidly, her mouth open, her breath little more than savage pants. Savannah reached out telepathically. The shields were still there, still impossibly strong.

Blood wasn't going to be enough. She was going to need help with this.

"And how would you know something like that?" she asked, at the same time reaching out mentally to her sister. *Neva?*

Still here at the mansion, and still bored shitless. What can I do for you?

Can't explain why, but I need to siphon your psychic abilities. Neva had extremely strong empathic skills, and when combined with the pack's naturally strong telepathic skills, it was a formidable weapon—one that had saved both their lives in the past.

Sure. Can I help?

No. I'm questioning a suspect, and I want you out of it in case it goes belly-up.

You're as overprotective as my damn mate.

Hey, I want to be there when my nephews or nieces are born. I don't want it to happen early through overexertion.

No chance of that, Neva grumbled. *I can't even take a walk without someone in this damn place fussing over me.* She hesitated. *Okay. I'm comfortable. Take what you need.*

Thanks, Sis. She reached deeper, forming a connection. Just for an instant, she felt other energies; bright, shiny, and new energies, bursting with life and curiosity. The babies, she realized with a sense of wonder, but shut *that* part of the connection down quickly. There was no way on this earth she was going to endanger them in *any* way. She studied Candy for a moment longer, then she said, "You and I have never met before yesterday, and you haven't been in Ripple Creek that long. So why would you think I'm such a Goody Two-shoes—especially since you know I was at Rosehall?"

Candy flashed a bloody smile. "Rosehall was a long time ago, ranger. And I hear things."

"From whom?" She raised her hand and slowly licked at the blood dripping from her palm. She'd never enjoyed the taste of blood, which is why she avoided hunting in wolf form. But she'd sucked at cuts to clean them enough times not to blanch at the taste now.

Candy's nostrils flared, and the craving in her eyes became fierce. The hunger in the air became a fire of need that burned across Savannah's borrowed empathic senses, like the electricity touching the air before a storm.

She reached out empathetically, just enough to gather the emotions burning through the air and thrust them Candy's way—soaking her, drowning her, in her own passions and fears. And under the flood, Candy's shields began to weaken. They were still extremely strong, but this was definitely working.

She raised her hand again. "Smell the blood, Candy. Smell the richness of it. Imagine never being able to taste it again."

The other woman snarled, her form wavering, changing to something more than human but less than wolf. The proximity of the silver was preventing the full change. Savannah just hoped that it would also prevent Candy from breaking out, because if that happened, she'd be dead meat.

Now, Cade said, even as she gathered her psychic forces.

She hit the other wolf as hard as she could. Hit her with not only the emotions that burned through the air, but also her own. She reached deep within herself, gathering all the anger and all the horror that had been building since that first murder, weeks ago. She gathered, too, the soul-deep loneliness that had haunted her since Rosehall—a loneliness that had been buried so deep it had only come out in her dreams. She mixed it with the despair that burned in her now—a secret despair born of the fear that her time with Cade was at an end. All of that she flung at Candy, and the force of the emotive blow hit like a punch to the chin, smashing Candy backward, making her stagger and gasp as her head cracked hard against the rear of the cell. In that precise moment of confusion and dazedness, Savannah raided Candy's mind.

And learned that the woman Candy reported to, the woman who was the brains behind it all was her mother, Jina Hawkins.

Only Jina Hawkins was the woman she knew as Anni Hawkins.

Chapter Twelve

"IT DOESN'T MAKE any sense," Savannah said, slamming the door behind her as she walked to the window. She shoved her hands into her pockets, her expression dark but eyes distant as she continued, "If Anni is behind these attacks, why wait six months? Why not just kill me and get it over with?"

Cade shrugged as he sat down on one of the visitor chairs. "She wants my death as much as yours."

"So what's wrong with one at a time?"

"Nothing, but it's easier if we're both in the same place. And think about it—the first thing we did when we got here was locate and talk to everyone who was new to Ripple Creek. Maybe she was aware of procedure and wanted to cement her place before she did anything."

"It's possible, I guess."

He studied her for a moment, seeing the tension in her and wondering if its sole cause was the knowledge that she'd lived above a crazed killer for six months. He had a feeling it wasn't. He'd felt the power of her assault on Candy, and he knew its source wasn't just a reflection of Candy's hunger for blood and her terror of being contained in a small space. Much of the fear in that assault had been Vannah's. And the source of her fear was *his* fault, because he kept throwing hints at what he wanted, but he wouldn't really talk to her. Wouldn't confirm what he was feeling, or where he thought their future might lie. And not really knowing or understanding those things himself was no excuse.

Or was that just another excuse?

"At least it explains how Candy spotted you that night at the club."

She nodded. "Anni was in the shop, so it's possible she saw me leave for the club in my disguise."

"And couldn't Anni be Nelle? It's been ten years since you've seen her. That's time enough for someone to change beyond recognition."

Vannah shook her head. "Nelle was a couple of inches taller."

"Time stoops us all, and Nelle would be over fifty by now."

She glanced at him, amusement sparking briefly in her shadowed green eyes. "Fifty isn't old for a wolf, you know that. Besides, the whole shape of her face is wrong. Anni isn't Nelle."

As much as he wanted to believe otherwise, he had to trust Vannah's judgment. Besides, he'd had a brief glimpse of Anni after the note had been left on Vannah's windshield, and he had to agree—there was little resemblance to Nelle. "Then that leaves us with no connection between her and Rosehall, other than the psychic one Candy mentioned." He hesitated. "Did Jontee ever mention his past when you were with him?"

The words tasted bitter on his tongue even as he said them. It had all happened ten years ago, and yet he still couldn't get past the hurt, the anger. Was it just his pride? Or was it the acidic taste of knowing that he'd never been good enough to hold her solely to himself?

Was that same fear stopping him from doing the right thing now?

Probably, he thought wearily. And it was wrong. Yes, he'd been hurt, but so had she. Too much had been left unsaid between them, and history was repeating itself. Unless he did something about it, he stood the chance of losing her all over again.

He couldn't face that a second time. He had to do something *now* rather than wait until after this mess was cleaned up. If he died, then at least she'd know how he really felt—the confusion, the fear, and the desperate, driving need to hold her all to himself. Now and forever.

He stood abruptly, unable to sit still, unwilling to think more than necessary. Thinking had always gotten him into trouble when it came to the emotional stuff, which is why he tended to steer away from it. But this—Vannah—was far too important.

"I mean," he continued, "you were with him for quite a while. Surely you learned a little something about him."

She crossed her arms and shook her head. "He rarely spoke about where he came from. I didn't even know he'd come from the Merron reservation."

He walked across the room and stood beside her, his arm brushing hers lightly and somehow intimately. Heat flowed between them, warming his skin, warming his soul. "So he never even mentioned that he had a daughter?"

"No." She hesitated. "Although he did say something weird at breakfast one morning—that there were people who would put things right if all this went to hell."

By murdering all those responsible for Rosehall's downfall? Was Jina or Anni or whatever the hell her name really was as crazy as he'd been? "And when was this?"

"A few weeks before you arrived." She paused again. "It was about that time I began to notice a darkness in him. A frustration. I know it sounds clichéd, but it was as if the Jontee I knew and cared for was gradually being swallowed by that darkness."

"Maybe some part of him hated what he was doing."

She glanced at him, amusement glittering briefly in her eyes. "That's the first almost nice thing I've heard you say about him."

He grimaced. "No one is ever a complete monster." And if Jontee had been, Vannah wouldn't have gone near him. He was sure of that, if nothing else. "He didn't say anything else about it after that?"

She shook her head. "He wouldn't be drawn out. He was like a kid with a naughty secret. He just kept saying that *she* knew what was going on and would make it right in the end."

"And he never said who this person was?"

"No. I did ask but he refused to say anything else, except that she was his fail-safe."

Cade grunted. "That almost suggests that he knew I was coming to Rosehall."

"Well, he certainly seemed on edge those last few weeks, and it wasn't just the growing darkness in him. Maybe he *did* know. As I said, he had an otherworldly quality about him."

She leaned into him, wrapping him in heat and her erotic, sensual aroma. His reaction was instant and intense, his erection pressing painfully against the fly of his jeans. The pain was made fiercer by the knowledge that he couldn't do anything here. Or even in the near future. So he contented himself with wrapping an arm around her shoulder and drawing her even closer.

And it felt so good, so right, that he almost wished they could just stay here, right in this office, keeping the world at bay as they concentrated on themselves.

Just for a little while.

"Did Jontee have many visitors while he was locked up?" she continued, after what seemed like a long, contented sigh. "Maybe Anni was one of them."

"Besides his lawyers, he only had two other visitors, and neither were women."

"What about phone calls?"

"Only from his defense team." He frowned, remembering the trial, trying to recall the faces. But the only one he'd been concentrating on was Jontee, and to a lesser extent, his lawyer. Watching their reactions, listening to their thoughts. Everything else—every*one* else—was a blur.

"Do you have your investigation notes here?" she asked.

"On the computer in my room."

"Then why don't we get over there and check them out?"

"Because I know what's in those notes. I've been studying them since the first murder."

"All this time you were convinced that Nelle was behind these murders. Maybe that certainty caused you to miss other clues."

He opened his mouth to refute her statement, but closed it. Maybe he *had* missed something. He'd been so certain Nelle was involved that it was entirely possible he had overlooked some key point. And while Trista and Anton had studied those files as much as he had, they hadn't been involved in the original investigation and would never know it as intimately as he did.

"Good point," he said, and tightened his grip on her shoulders to stop her from moving. "But first, I have to do something."

He turned her around to face him. Her expression was one of amused anticipation. "One of the rules we agreed to," she said mildly, "was no kissing during the day. And certainly not in my office."

"I had my fingers crossed behind my back when I agreed to that," he said, voice bland. "But I don't actually intend to kiss you."

"And why the hell not?" she asked, her voice filled with a fierceness that was belied by the twinkle in her eyes.

He grinned. "Because I have something more important to do."

She raised an eyebrow, amusement giving way to speculation in her eyes. "More important than tracking down a killer?"

"Very much so."

He caught her hand and pressed it against his chest.

The heat of her fingers, combined with the heady richness of her scent, stirred him in ways he'd never thought possible. Not just his body, but where it really mattered—his heart, his soul. If this wasn't love, then he sure as hell didn't know what was. But whatever it was, he wanted it—now and forever.

"Does my lady acknowledge the power of the moon?"

She took a sharp breath, her gaze widening in surprise. But deep in the green of her eyes a joyousness bloomed, and the power of it shimmered right through him. And he knew, right at that moment, that if there was ever one thing in his life he'd done right, then it was this. And he would never regret it, no matter what happened between them.

She took another deep breath and released it slowly. Then she said the words that were the beginning of the end for his moon-spun hold on her. "It is the power of the moon that binds us as one."

The air seemed to stir around them, and energy crackled. Desire and something else—something more ethereal—shimmered between them, warming the night. Warming him.

"Does my lady acknowledge my moon-gifted claim on her?"

She moved a little closer, so that every inch of her supple body seemed pressed against his. "I acknowledge the claim of the moon. I acknowledge the rights it has given you."

He raised her fingers to his lips and kissed each one slowly. Energy zapped between them each time his lips met her skin, making his mouth tingle and his body ache. Or maybe the ache, the magic, had nothing to do with the moon and the power they were raising, but was simply the result of having her so close.

"Then by the right of the moon, and the power she has given me, I hereby renounce my claim on you. For this night, and for the remaining nights the moon has ceded me rights to."

The air seemed to thrum, to burn, at his words. A vortex of power whirled around them, snatching at their clothes, their hair. Then it was gone and all that was left was the two of them.

She rose on her toes and kissed him slowly, softly, and it was unlike any kiss he'd ever shared with her. It was so filled with glorious promise that it shook him to the core.

"Thank you," she said eventually, "for giving me the choice. For taking that risk."

He raised a hand to her cheek and ran a finger across her lips. "Now we have the chance to uncover whether what lies between is real, or simply the moon madness."

"It may be mad, but I doubt the moon has anything to do with it." She hesitated, raising an eyebrow. "Do you think it's real?"

Though her expression was serious, amusement played with the corners of her lips, as if she already knew the answer to her question. And maybe she did. Women were always more intuitive than men when it came to the emotional stuff.

He let his hand slide around to the back of her neck, holding her still as his mouth brushed hers. "Yes," he said against the teasing, luscious warmth of her lips. "I do believe this is real."

And he kissed her, trying to impart all his feelings, all his wants and desires, in that one simple action. He knew it was never going to be enough. Knew that the words themselves would have to be said—that after all these years, she deserved to hear them, even if she knew in her heart and could feel his emotions in his kiss.

And they had to be said now, while he had the time, just in case something happened to one of them. Fate had snatched her from him once. He couldn't risk it happening again without at least telling her the truth.

He pulled back from the kiss and gently cupped her cheeks between his hands. "There's something you need to know. Two things, actually."

She raised an eyebrow again. Her eyes were shining with happiness, and the glow shimmered right through him. "And what might those things be?"

"The first is the fact that I think I love you."

"Well, good, because I think the feeling might be returned."

Relief, tension, and happiness unlike anything he'd ever experienced filled him. Just for an instant, he felt like a kid who'd been given every Christmas present he'd ever asked for. He grinned. "And the second is an apology."

"For what?"

"For being such a coward at Rosehall. For never telling you what I was feeling, especially that night when you said you loved me."

"Then I have to give you an apology—for going to Jontee. For never having the courage to follow my heart—"

He stopped her with another kiss. "Enough of the

past. Let's just agree to the fact that we both made mistakes, and concentrate on the future from now on."

"Agreed."

"Then let's go get these murdering bitches so we can start exploring that future."

She grinned. "So it's off to your motel room? With its nice double bed?"

"Please remember the fact that your snotty assistant booked our rooms," he said dryly. "There is nothing nice about the bed."

"There would be with you and me in it."

She had a point, but it was one he had to ignore for now. "Bitches first. Sex later."

"Then let's go get them so we can get down to the serious stuff." She broke away from him and headed for the door.

He pulled his shirt from the waistband of his jeans to cover the erection that just wouldn't subside and followed her. A disheveled, red-haired figure was walking down the hall toward them.

"Ike! Thank God!" Savannah caught Ike's arm, steadying him as he stumbled. "Are you okay? What happened?"

The kid winced and rubbed the back of his head. "Some bastard hit me from behind."

They'd done more than that, from the look of him, Cade thought, as Vannah eased the kid into a chair and squatted beside him. Ike's face was pale, bruised, and cut, with blood drying in streaks down the side of his face. His body seemed to have fared little better. His clothes were torn, revealing smudges of blood and bruising. Someone had given the kid a beating once they'd knocked him unconscious. If it had been Candy, she must have been in a benevolent mood. She'd let him live rather than eat him. Thank God they had her behind bars now.

"Tell us what happened," he said.

Ike grimaced. "I followed Denny to a burger joint on Galena Street. He didn't order anything, just came out of the place looking really angry. Then he went over to this house on Summit Street—"

"Was there a blue pickup parked in the driveway?" Savannah asked quickly.

Ike shook his head. "But I woke up in one."

Cade squatted beside Savannah. "So how did you get from the house to the truck?"

"A blonde invited Denny inside the house. I checked the windows, and it was obvious they were making out, so I retreated to the shadows to wait. Next thing I know, I'm tied up and lying in the back of some damn truck."

"Then what happened?" Savannah asked.

He shrugged. "I was in and out of it for a while. When I awoke for real, I was in Ashcroft hut."

Cade glanced at Savannah. "Which is?"

"An old hut hikers use if they get caught by the weather or at night." She glanced at Denny. "How did you escape?"

"There was no one there. I was hog-tied, but whoever tied the knots didn't know crap. I got out of there and came straight here."

"Any signs that the hut had been used?"

"Yeah, but I wasn't really concentrating on anything more than getting out of there."

Cade rose. "We should check it out."

"We need to check out those file notes, too. I've got a feeling you've missed something."

He knew those notes by heart, and it was doubtful *he'd* see anything new in them. But she might. "Where's Ashcroft hut?"

"About three-quarters of the way along the trail. The end comes out near the entrance of the Sinclair mansion, so that's probably the quickest access point."

None of which made any sense to Cade. "How about I check out the hut, and you check the notes?"

"You shouldn't go alone. That's just tempting fate."

"Everyone else is dealing with the hiker mess. If we go together, it's just doubling the temptation. And as you said, you need to look at those notes."

Surprisingly, she didn't argue. "Then we bring in outside help." She squeezed Ike's knee and rose. "You'll need it to find the trail and the hut anyway, so I'll call the Sinclairs and get one of them to act as a guide."

"Which is only putting them in the line of danger," Cade said.

She grinned. "The Sinclairs scoff at danger."

He raised an eyebrow. "So they have the crazy gene that seems to haunt Sinclairs everywhere?"

"Some would say that," Ike muttered, then glanced at Savannah quickly. "Except for Duncan, of course."

"Duncan is your brother-in-law?" Cade guessed.

She nodded. "But given the attempt on my father's life, I won't be asking him. I'll see if René's available. He likes the rough stuff." She glanced at Ike. "You'd better get over to the hospital and get checked out."

"I'm okay. I want—"

"Ike," she warned, in a voice that brooked no argument.

The kid scowled and Cade was hard pressed not to grin. He had a feeling the kid had heard that tone more than once. He dragged his room key from his pocket and handed it to Savannah. "The computer is on the luggage bench. The password is Vannah Harvey."

Amusement touched her lush lips. "Interesting. Someone you knew?"

"Someone I thought I'd lost." He touched a hand to her face, knowing the kid was watching and not caring. "Thankfully, I found her again."

She briefly pressed her cheek into his touch. "And this time she won't run."

"Good." He let his hand drop and stepped away from her, even though all he wanted to do was take her in his arms and never let go. Not just because he loved her, but because he had a bad feeling that something was about to happen. This case was about to reach a climax. "Be careful."

"You, too." She glanced at Ike. "And you stop scowling and get to the doctor."

"Yes, ma'am," the kid said, and scooted past them.

"I'll call Duncan now," she continued. "To get to the mansion, just head down Main until you see Park Street. That'll take you to Mansion Road."

"Okay." He half-turned to go, then hesitated. "Watch your back. And don't park in front of the motel."

"Well, gee, and here I was all set to advertise my presence."

He grinned at her sarcasm. "I know, I know. You're

a ranger and you know a thing or two about policing. But I deal with crazy people on a regular basis. You don't."

"Stop worrying and just get going, or we're never going to catch these people and get on with our life."

He raised his hands. "I'm going, I'm going."

And he did. But not without kissing her goodbye first.

SAVANNAH PARKED IN the street behind the motel and climbed out of the truck. The chill of the storm was still in the air, and if the clouds hanging like lead were anything to go by, Mother Nature hadn't finished with them yet. Though storms often dumped snow on the peaks at this time of year, it didn't always stick through the warm autumn days. But she had a feeling this storm was heralding a long, cold winter, which would make the cross-country skiing crowd happy—if they dared come back to the reservation after word of Candy's attack got out.

She glanced up and down the street to see who was near or watching, feeling a little foolish even as she did so. But Cade was right—they were dealing with nutcases, and precautions needed to be taken.

The thought of him sent a twinge of worry through her. René had readily agreed to guide Cade, but that didn't stop her from feeling that they were being played for fools. Ike was a clever kid, but she couldn't help thinking his escape was too easy. Everything Anni and her disciples had done so far was meticulously planned, so tying sloppy knots and allowing Ike to escape just didn't compute.

Unless, of course, that's precisely what they'd wanted.

Which meant that Cade and René could be walking right into a trap. Of course, if there were ever two men she'd go out of her way to avoid a fight with, it was those two. She'd never seen Cade truly angry, but she'd felt the power in his body, and seen the battle scars. And René—well, she'd never met a wolf more willing to throw himself into the middle of a knife fight and consider it clean, harmless fun. He might not be insane per se, but that gene was definitely in his system.

She climbed the fence and jumped down into the small gap between the fence and the motel's back wall. In several of the rooms to her right, she could hear conversation and running water, but Cade's room was at the other end, out of the direct line of sight of the office but close to the main road. Undoubtedly, Kel had booked the noisiest rooms deliberately, but right now, with a killer intent on revenge, it was damnably inconvenient. She couldn't get in without being seen.

A chill ran across her skin. She rubbed her arms and tried not to think about her earlier certainty that something bad would happen today. Something bad *had* happened—Candy. Surely fate wouldn't dump anything else on them . . .

Another chill ran up her spine. Fate might not, but maybe Anni would.

She grimaced. She'd driven past her apartment on the way here, and the flower shop was still closed. Very unusual, to say the least. Had Anni somehow gotten wind of the fact that she was a suspect? Or was it merely a coincidence she'd gone missing on the same day they'd discovered who she really was?

There was too damn much they just didn't know, and people were dying because of it. It had to stop. And, somehow, *she* had to stop it. Frowning, she made her way down to the end of the building. After a quick look around the corner to ensure there was no one close by, she got the room key from her pocket and walked around to the front. Still no one, either nearby or passing along the road. She opened the door and stepped inside.

Though the bathroom door was open, the little bit of light filtering in from the bathroom's windows failed to lift the gloom in the main room. She let her eyes adjust, smiling a little as she noted the clothes strewn across the bed. Cade, it seemed, was as untidy as she when he wasn't in his IIS mode. She shoved away the temptation to check out his personal stuff and learn more about the man she loved. Instead, she walked across to the laptop, which sat on the luggage rack.

She moved the mouse to snap the screen back to life and typed in the access code. Several screens popped up. She clicked the one marked Rosehall, pulled up a chair, and started reading.

It was heavy stuff.

She knew some details of the murders via the memories she'd picked up in Jontee's and Cade's minds, but she'd never known all the details. Now that she did, she could never think of Jontee as a gentle man again. How could she? A gentle soul would never have been able to do what he did to those people.

She read on through the trial notes, but didn't find

any mention of Jina or Anni or anyone vaguely connected to the current case. Yet instinct said there had to be something, somewhere.

She leaned back in the chair and crossed her arms as she stared at the screen. What had happened to Nelle? Cade had been so certain that she'd been involved, yet there had been no mention of her in the trial. Not by the IIS, and not by Jontee.

She could understand Jontee staying mute to protect Nelle, as the two of them had almost been inseparable, but why hadn't the IIS followed up on her? Granted, they'd no evidence to suggest she'd been involved in any way, despite Cade's assertions, but given her closeness to Jontee, they still should have interviewed her. Or had they tried to find her, and simply not been able to? After all, Cade hadn't found *her* until he'd come here to Ripple Creek.

She looked at the time and saw with some shock that four hours had passed. She glanced at the curtained windows. Even though they were closed, it was obvious dusk was setting in. And Cade hadn't contacted her. Worry surged anew, but she thrust it firmly away. No one had actually contacted her, which obviously meant there wasn't a problem. If there was, someone would have called.

After rising and stretching, she used the bathroom and then grabbed a bottle of water and a chocolate bar from the room's minibar fridge. As she was walking back to the laptop, a yellowed piece of paper sticking out of a small notebook sitting by the bed caught her attention. She walked over and tugged it out. It was a brief newspaper summary about the outcome of the trial, and it was accompanied by a picture of the crowd waiting outside the court. There weren't many people—she frowned suddenly and peered a little closer. One of those faces looked awfully familiar, but it was hard to be certain given the size of the image.

She glanced at the date of the article, then went back to the laptop, connected to the Net, and searched for the date of the guilty verdict. She found several small articles, and a larger version of the picture she wanted. She was right—it *was* Anni. Right there in the background, half-hidden in the shadows, looking pale-faced and grim. She'd been at the trial, had heard all the details, and, if Candy was right, had been in constant telepathic contact with Jontee, no doubt right until his death. Hell, she might even have been with him when he died. *That* could have been what tipped her over the edge.

Savannah studied the other faces in the picture, but there was no one else she knew. She scrubbed a hand across her eyes and clicked off the Net. Night was settling in, and she was getting hungry for something more substantial than chocolate. She glanced at her watch again, frowning when she saw it was nearly six. Still no word from Cade or anyone else. Worry returned, and this time it refused to budge.

She rose and took her cell phone from her pocket. No messages. She pressed the call button, but before she could dial the station, someone in the room next door hit something and cursed loudly.

A cold sensation ran through her. The room next door was the one shared by Anton and Trista, but that voice hadn't belonged to either of them. Nor had it belonged to either of the hotel's managers or the woman they employed to clean the rooms, all of whom she knew.

This was someone else.

Someone, she knew instinctively, who was up to no good.

RENÉ SINCLAIR WASN'T what Cade had expected. As a general rule, Sinclairs were tall and rangy—the athletes of the werewolf world—but René was a lot shorter than most Sinclairs, and built like a boxer, all thick muscle and attitude.

And he had an awful lot to say about Savannah—thankfully, most of it complimentary. Cade would have hated to have to hit the man. He had a feeling he'd do far more damage to his fist than to René himself.

"So what are we hunting up at the old hut?" René asked eventually.

Cade hesitated, but there was something about this wolf's no-nonsense attitude that he liked. "Ike was kidnapped and taken up there. We're going to look for possible clues."

René's dark gaze was full of a sharp intelligence that matched all the muscle. "And the reason Ike was kidnapped is the same reason Neva's forced to stay at the mansion?"

Cade nodded. "There's a killer after Savannah and me."

"Why?"

"Past deeds." He shrugged.

"And Ike is not known for his quick thinking. If he escaped, it could be because someone wanted him to."

"Yes."

"Meaning we could be walking into a trap."

"Exactly."

René rolled his shoulders and grinned. "Fantastic."

Cade raised an eyebrow. "Do all Sinclairs feel the insane need to live up to the family reputation?"

"The family reputation is merely a lust for life. We can't help it if the rest of the wolf population is dominated by morals more suited to the Dark Ages."

Cade grinned. "Wouldn't happen to be talking about an in-law there, would you?"

"The man is a jackass. His daughters, however, are amazing. Even if one of them *is* a ranger." René stopped and swept a branch aside. "Here you go."

The hut stood in a small clearing just beyond the aspens and pines that lined the walking trail. It was made with logs that looked far older than the trees around them. It had a rusting iron roof and no windows on the two sides he could see. It did, however, have a stone chimney. He raised his nose, scenting the icy wind, searching for any sign of someone being near. The air smelled of snow and pine and little else.

"I can't hear anything," René commented.

"No. But these people were responsible for bombing the diner. If this is a trap, then that's certainly a possibility."

René studied him for a moment, then nodded toward the hut. "There's a small window around the back. The last time I was here, it had been boarded over, but I know there was talk of restoring the place for the ski season."

"Let's skirt the trees, and see if there are any surprises waiting there for us first."

René nodded and led the way through the trees. The hut looked much the same from the other side of the clearing, with the exception of a door and a window. Neither was boarded up, and there didn't seem to be anything out of place.

Cade drew his gun anyway. "Wait here while I check it out."

René snorted. "Yeah, right."

"I'm serious."

"So am I. If things go bad, I'm of more use to you there than here."

Cade's cop half was inclined to argue, but instinct suggested that René had it right. If things did go bad, he *was* going to need help. He might be up against two women, but those women were currently running rings around them, and every single step had been meticulously planned—with the sole exception of Candy, who'd obviously let her bloodlust get in the way of what she was supposed to do. But one mistake that played to their advantage didn't mean there would be more.

"Keep watch, then, while I check the window."

René nodded. Crouching to present less of a target, Cade ran for the back of the hut. René followed him over, but stopped at the opposite end of the back wall.

Clear here, René said, after peering cautiously around the corner.

Cade edged around the side of the hut and carefully made his way to the window. There was no sound, other than the distant rumble of thunder, and no unusual smells riding the air. Yet his instincts burned with the sensation that something was off, that something was about to happen.

He peered through the grimy glass. The hut was small, with little more than a cot, several chairs, and a table. The fireplace across the far side of the room had been recently used, with the wood in the hearth still glowing—though the heat was obviously fading.

Why would the women who'd so ruthlessly castrated two men light a fire to keep Ike warm?

They wouldn't. They'd only do it for themselves, which meant someone had to have been close when Ike escaped. Which meant they'd let him escape. Tension rode across his muscles, and it was all he could do not to swing around and scan the tree line.

He'd been in far worse situations than this, so why was he so jumpy now?

Because for the first time, it was personal. And for the first time, he actually had something to lose other than just his life.

He glanced over his shoulder. René was crouched near the corner and studying the tree line intently.

Anything?

Startled bird to our right. René's sharp gaze met his. *Could be nothing.*

And yet it likely was not. *You armed?*

René's sudden grin was answer enough. Definitely insane, these Sinclairs.

Be careful. I'm going in.

René nodded and returned his gaze to the forest. Cade rose and turned the door handle. After ensuring there were no wires attached anywhere, he pushed the door wide open. The smell of smoke and wood rushed out to greet him, along with a staleness that suggested the cabin had been unused for long periods of time. If Jina or Anni, or whatever her damn name was, was staying here, she obviously didn't believe in airing the place out.

He stepped inside, keeping his back to the wall and his gun at the ready as he scanned the small room. Nothing. Not even the ropes Ike was supposedly bound in.

Frowning and feeling more and more like things were very wrong, he walked across to the small cot. The blankets were stacked in a neat pile at the end of the bed. Ike certainly wouldn't have bothered, and it was doubtful his captors would have cleaned up after him. Nor was there any sign of blood on the mattress itself. There would have been if Ike had lain there.

He looked around the room. No blood spots anywhere else, either.

Ike hadn't woken up here. He hadn't *been* here.

He rubbed a hand across his eyes. Christ, why hadn't he checked the kid for signs of psychic intrusion? If Candy had shields strong enough to keep him out, it was a fair bet that either she, or the others in this game, had strong psychic skills. Strong enough to imprint false memories into the kid's mind, anyway.

René? he said softly.

Yeah?

It's a trap.

Fantastic.

Cade wasn't entirely sure whether that was meant sarcastically. *See anything?*

Nope.

He walked to the side of the door and peered out. The forest around the clearing was still. Perhaps a little too still.

What's the quickest way out of here?

Run like hell for the main trail. Harder to hit running targets.

But not impossible. He had hit running targets. He suspected their hunters might be able to, too. And why let them walk into the hut and discover the lie if they weren't sure of the outcome? Or the fact that they could bring their quarry down?

Are we to be wolf targets or human targets? René continued.

He hesitated. As wolves they would be faster, but in human form they could use their weapons. *Human. You watch left; I'll watch right.* He paused, scanning the tree line a second time. *Still nothing. You ready?*

As ready as I'll ever be.

Then let's go.

He ducked out the doorway and ran for the trail and the trees, keeping low to present less of a target. René was one step ahead of him, his head turned slightly left, watching the trees as directed.

Neither of them saw their attackers.

All Cade felt was a sharp sting in his side. He looked down to see the dart embedded through his sweater, into his skin, then heard René's curse and knew he'd been hit as well. They both kept running, ducking and weaving to make hitting them harder. It did little good. Another sting, another dart. He saw René stumble, as if his legs had gone out from beneath him.

Cade grabbed his arm and tried to force him on, to run them both out of there. A third dart hit him, and the strength drained from his legs as his vision began to spin. The only place either of them went was straight to the ground.

Chapter Thirteen

SAVANNAH EASED THE motel room door open and peered out. No car stood in the parking space in front of the next room, yet she could still hear movement inside. Whoever it was, they obviously thought they weren't going to be caught, as they were making no attempt to be quiet.

Maybe Candy's attack *was* planned. Maybe it was meant to be a diversion of some kind.

The thought sent another chill down her spine, though she wasn't entirely sure why. She eased past the door and padded quietly to the next room. The curtains had been drawn, so there was no chance to peer inside. She'd have to go in.

She drew her gun, wishing it was the real thing rather than just a dart gun. Ripple Creek didn't get a whole lot of nasty criminals, and the council's ruling that only tranquilizer weapons be used by rangers generally made sense. Except in situations like this where they were dealing with nutcases who had little more than murder on their minds. She'd have to talk to her dad and get him to insert some type of clause giving them the option to use real firearms if needed.

Not that the station actually had any at the moment, but she and Ronan did. She'd never used hers and hoped she never had to, but it was there just in case.

She clicked the dart's safety off. The soft sound seemed to ricochet like thunder and, inside the room, the movement stopped.

Savannah waited, tension winding through her limbs, until every muscle felt so tightly wound it surely had to snap. For several seconds, she didn't even dare breathe.

Inside, the footsteps retreated. A second later came the sound of a window sliding open.

Savannah took a step forward, then stopped. If the intruder had heard the sound of the safety clicking off, then she'd surely have realized that the sound of a window sliding open would also carry. And maybe Savannah was *meant* to react to it.

She pressed back against the wall and waited. For too many minutes, nothing happened. Her knuckles ached with the fierceness of her grip on the gun, and sweat began to trickle down her spine.

Then the curtain moved. Not much, just enough for someone to peer out. Savannah pressed herself harder against the wall and hoped like hell the angle would prevent her from being seen.

Then, movement resumed inside the room. She breathed a silent sigh of relief, stepped back, and aimed a kick at the door.

The flimsy lock gave way with little resistance, and the door crashed back. Inside, someone cursed, and there was a blur of movement as someone ran. Not at her, but away.

"Ripple Creek ranger," Savannah said, even as she

aimed the weapon at the fleeing woman—Lonny. "Stop or I'll shoot."

She didn't stop, so Savannah followed through with her threat. The dart hissed through the air just as the woman was retreating into the bathroom, striking her in the rump. There was a yelp, a hiss of anger, and then Lonny ran screaming out of the bathroom and straight at Savannah.

She managed to fire another shot, and then the woman was on her, all fury and muscle accompanied by a sickly-sweet smell. The momentum of her attack hit with the force of a truck, and the two of them went down in a tangle of arms and legs. Savannah grunted as her back caught the door frame, but it was Lonny who took the brunt of their weight as they crashed to the floor. But she didn't react, just kept on punching, her breath short and sharp, her eyes wide and her pupils dilated.

High on something, Savannah thought, as she tried to grab the other woman's arm and, simultaneously, tried to avoid most of her blows, which was all but impossible. Whatever the hell it was, it was interfering with the dart and slowing its effects. She caught one wrist, holding it tight and half-noting the bandages, until a blow to her cheek had her senses reeling. Lonny chuckled, her voice low but filled with a coldness that sent a chill down Savannah's spine. She blinked away the pain, felt the breeze of a follow-up blow coming, and leaned back as far as she could without losing her grip on Lonny's wrist. Something sharp skimmed her chin, drawing blood, and out of nowhere anger surged. Or maybe it had always been there, and she'd merely controlled it up until now. Either way, enough was enough. She might be a ranger, but she was also the target of these madwomen. It was about time she started fighting back. To hell with the rules and her own personal restrictions. These women had to be stopped any damn way they could, or someone she loved might end up paying the price.

She gathered her psychic forces and punched into Lonny's mind. She hit a shield—a strong shield—but Savannah was pissed off and she doubted there was any shield capable of keeping her out right now. Lonny's eyes widened, and fear replaced the cunning contempt that had been so evident until now. Even though Lonny tried to shore up her defenses, it was far too late. Savannah wrapped a psychic hand around the other woman's mind and squeezed.

"Stop," she said.

Lonny stilled instantly, but the fear in her eyes blossomed. "You can't do this."

"Says who?" Savannah rose and scrubbed a hand across her bleeding chin as she looked around the room. What had Lonny been doing here?

Lonny didn't say anything, and Savannah looked down at her. "Answer the question."

"Jina says."

"Why? Because I'm a ranger?"

"Because you don't have any psychic strength."

Savannah raised her eyebrows as she knelt near the bed. No psychic strength? When she came from the golden pack? "And you won't tell her that I have, will you?" She made it an order and enforced it—not only blocking the knowledge from anyone who might make psychic contact with Lonny, but also preventing her from talking to anyone else about it.

"Why on earth would you think something like that?" she asked, once she was done.

Lonny didn't answer immediately, so Savannah applied a little more psychic pressure. Lonny cursed, and sweat broke out across her brow. "Jontee told Jina. And she checked herself."

Jontee had told Jina—Anni—that she wasn't a powerful telepathic? Why would he believe that? Then she remembered that Cade had believed the very same thing. Maybe it had something to do with never having come across someone from the golden pack before. Unless you were familiar with how pack shields worked, it could be very easy to believe a lack of telepathic strength.

Although she'd never felt Anni trying to probe her, and she would have. "Anni never tested me. She lied."

"She didn't have to—not when she could read your day-to-day thoughts with ease."

Savannah snorted. Obviously, Anni didn't know much about the golden pack, or she would have realized that most of them didn't bother keeping full shields up unless they were actually with another wolf from the pack.

She pulled up the bedsheets, looked underneath, and discovered what Lonny had been doing—planting another bomb. It didn't look as if it had been set, but then again, she knew next to nothing about bombs. Nor did she trust Lonny enough to compel her to defuse it. Any woman that attacked rather than run was mad enough to set off the bomb to kill them both.

She let the cover drop back down. "Why blow up the IIS officers? That'll only bring down the wrath of the whole organization."

Lonny shrugged. "No witnesses, no tales, no trails."

Her words came out slightly slurred, and Savannah glanced around. Lonny was struggling to keep her eyes open. Obviously the two darts were finally taking effect. She'd better get her to the car, or she'd end up having to carry her.

"Get up," she ordered.

As Lonny struggled upright, Savannah placed a quick call to Anton to warn him about the bomb.

"Bastards," he said, voice edged with a mix of exhaustion and anger. "We're just about finished here, so we'll come over and defuse it." He hesitated. "Have you heard from the boss?"

"No." And the reminder caused panic to spear through her heart again. Something was very wrong.

"I'll call him." He hesitated again, then added, "It might be best if you keep someone with you until Cade returns. I don't like the feel of things right now."

That made two of them. "I will."

She hung up and marched Lonny to her truck. The blonde was all but asleep on her feet by the time they'd gotten there, forcing Savannah to lift her up and buckle her in. But at least it meant she could release her grip on Lonny's mind.

Or most of it, anyway. She still kept a mental finger on the pulse, so to speak, just in case Anni or Candy tried to make contact with Lonny. She jumped into the driver's seat and headed for the ranger station. Ronan pulled up as she did. He looked as bad as she'd ever seen him, his clothes disheveled and face drawn.

"You look like shit," she said softly as she climbed out of her truck.

He scrubbed a hand through his damp, dirt-caked

hair. "That's because I feel like shit." He shook his head, and his gaze, when it met hers, was haunted. "I never, ever, want to see something like that again. Never want to feel anything like that again."

Oh God. She'd forgotten he could sometimes sense lingering emotions in the air, even though he wasn't actually empathic.

"I'm sorry," she whispered, and hugged him.

He held her so tightly it felt as if he was squeezing the breath from her lungs, but there was nothing sexual in it. Just one close friend taking much needed comfort from another.

After a few minutes, he blew out a breath and pulled back. "Thanks," he said softly, then his gaze went past her. "Who's that in the truck?"

"Lonny." She studied him for a moment, seeing tension in the set of his shoulders. The muscle ticking near his jaw. He was controlling the horror, but only just. "You going to be all right tonight?"

"Yeah. After a drink or two." He shrugged. "You want a hand getting her inside?"

"Yes." She hesitated. "You sure you don't want me to fudge your memories enough for you to sleep?"

He smiled and lightly touched her cheek. "Thanks, but I'm okay. Really," he added, when she lifted a disbelieving eyebrow. "Let's get that woman into a cell."

They carried Lonny inside, but the minute they were through the door, Savannah knew something had happened. There was a coldness, a stillness, to the air that wasn't usually there, and it sent a chill of apprehension running through her limbs.

"She's been here," Ronan said, voice sharp.

She glanced at him. "Anni?"

He nodded. "Recently."

Her gaze went to Kel. "Has Anni Hawkins been—" She stopped, noticing for the first time the curious blankness in their assistant's eyes.

"Fuck," Ronan said softly. "What do you want to bet that Candy is no longer our prisoner?"

"Odds on, I'd say," Savannah replied softly. "You all right to take Lonny to the cells?"

He nodded and shifted his grip to take the woman's full weight. Savannah walked around the desk and squatted in front of their admin assistant.

"Kel?" she said, touching the other woman's knee lightly.

Kel blinked, but her eyes were still curiously blank as she said, "I have a message."

It was Kel's voice, and yet it wasn't. She reached out psychically, gently probing Kel's mind. It was being held by another, and though she dare not probe any deeper for fear of being detected, it didn't take a genius to guess who that other person might be.

"What was the message, Kel?"

"Be here by seven, or else your not-so-charming lover or your sister's brother-in-law will be the next victim."

Fear erupted in her heart, and for several seconds she couldn't breathe, couldn't think. Then the anger rose again, and the force of it swept the fear away. How *dare* Anni threaten *her* family, *her* man, and attempt to make them pay for something that had happened so long ago? Something that was always going to end badly for the people involved in the true madness of Rosehall?

She glanced at the clock on the wall. "That only

gives me twenty-five minutes, and I don't even know where the fuck you are."

"Then find us. You have twenty minutes, ranger. Don't waste it chatting to me."

"Cade and René had better be alive when I get there, Jina."

There was a beat of silence, then, "So you know."

"Yes. I also know now what Jontee really did. He deserved the death he got."

"It was Nelle who believed half-breeds were tainted, not him. But she controlled him and he wasn't strong enough to fight her."

"He could have if he'd wanted to enough, Jina. You underestimate his strength."

"I underestimate nothing." Kel blinked, and the light of awareness seemed to shine briefly in her eyes. Then the blankness returned. "Time's slipping by, ranger. If you are not here by seven, one of them dies."

She glanced around as the front door opened and almost groaned aloud when she saw the two dark-haired, powerful men walking in. Zeke and Tye Sinclair—René's father and oldest brother. Just what she needed.

She motioned them to be quiet and returned her attention to Kel. The reality was, she had enough psychic strength to attack Jina right now, and either freeze her mind or fry it. But it would also hurt Kel in the process, and Candy would probably kill both Cade and René in revenge. Meaning she only had one option.

"I'll be there, Jina."

"Be sure you are. Candy is extremely hungry."

Kel blinked before Savannah could reply, awareness and horror surging into her eyes.

"Oh God, oh God," she whispered. "I'm sorry. I just couldn't stop—"

"I know," Savannah interrupted. "But I need to make sure it can't happen again, which means I need to place a block in your mind."

"Go right ahead. The thought of that woman in my mind again—" She stopped and shivered. "She's mad, you know."

Savannah's smile felt tight. "I know." She raised a hand to Kel's temple. "Close your eyes."

Kel obeyed. Savannah reached out psychically and gently encased Kel's mind in a shield of power. It wouldn't actually stop a concerted attack, but it would at least break the line of communication between Kel and Jina. Savannah pulled back and took a shuddering breath. She'd never used her telepathy so much, and with such precision, in one night, and an ache was beginning to form behind her eyes. Too much more, and she'd get a killer headache.

Which would be a small price to pay if she got everyone out of this safe and sound.

She squeezed Kel's knee again. "Why don't you go get a cup of the good stuff while I talk to Zeke and Tye?"

Kel nodded and rose. She was a little shaky, but otherwise seemed okay. Savannah turned her attention to the two men. "No, you can't come with me."

Zeke's expression was mutinous. "This is the safety of my son we're talking about. I will not—"

"You will, because one of the wolves we're dealing with is insane, and the other suffers from bloodlust.

They'll be expecting Anton and Trista, but if they scent anyone else René and Cade are dead meat."

"You know from experience that we Sinclairs do not leave pack safety in the hands of others."

"Then you have the mansion well guarded?"

He blinked. "There is no need."

"Really? Neva and Duncan are there. These people are mad enough to attempt to bomb your home just to get my sister and brother-in-law. Protect them, and let me and Ronan get these bitches."

He studied her for a moment, and then he smiled. It was the smile of one hunter acknowledging another. "This is personal, isn't it?"

"Very. Sinclairs aren't the only pack who believe in protecting their own, and these women have threatened not only my family but the man I love. They will pay, believe me."

His gaze flicked from her to Ronan, as if to check his reaction to this news. "I'm very glad I never made an enemy of you, Savannah. I think you'd be a very formidable foe."

"You bet your ass I would. Now, if you don't mind, I really have to get going."

"I'll keep Neva safe, have no fear." He glanced at his son. "What if Tye stays here? Kelly might appreciate the company."

She hesitated, then nodded. "Steve's due in at eight, but it wouldn't hurt to have an extra person here. But watch the woman in the cell. She should be out of it for a while, but when she comes to, she might attempt a psychic takeover."

Tye gave her an almost ferocious smile. "She can certainly try."

Savannah nodded, feeling a little better. As much as she trusted Steve, having Tye standing guard made her far more confident about their prisoner still being here when they returned. She glanced at the clock and fear rose like a demon in the night. She stomped it back down and looked at Ronan. "Let's get ready."

AWARENESS RETURNED IN fragmented pieces that seemed to make no sense. There were voices in his head, whispering of dark words and darker deeds. There was harsh laughter and soft music. The roar of an engine and the cold touch of steel. The chill of the night caressing his skin, and the rough feel of bark against his spine. The crackle of flames and the scent of desire.

It was *that* awareness more than anything that had Cade struggling through the layers of blackness encasing his mind. Because what he smelled wasn't the scent of someone who wanted sex. That was a mellower, infinitely sweeter, aroma. What he smelled now was somehow darker, more heated and tense. It was the scent of someone who was after something far more than just sex.

Bloodlust, rather than plain old lust.

But Candy was safely locked away, so who was emitting the scent now?

He forced his eyes open—and, for a moment, had to wonder if he was actually awake and alert or still dreaming. Before him stretched a stone-filled clearing that looked an awfully lot like the one in which they'd found the second victim. In the middle of the clearing, a huge fire blazed, and around it a naked woman danced to music he could no longer hear. A second woman, this one fully clothed, stood to one side of the flames, her arms crossed and her pale face glowing with the heat of the fire.

Anni. Or rather, Jina.

He glanced back to the dancing woman, but between the darkness and the warm, jumping light of the fire, he couldn't actually tell if it was Candy or her sister, Lonny. But he had a bad feeling it was Candy, and that could only mean something had gone very wrong back at the ranger station.

Tension cut through him, settling like a weight in his gut. He knew that Vannah was more than able to take care of herself under ordinary circumstances, but there was nothing ordinary about these women or their intentions. He was even beginning to wonder if *he* could, and he'd had far more experience dealing with the lunatics of the world.

He was standing, his feet untied, which at least gave him some means of defense if they attacked. He shifted slightly, trying to get a feel for how well his arms were tied. Rough bark scraped across his spine. He glanced up. There was no canopy above him, which meant he was tied to a stump. His arms had been pulled back and his wrists roped behind the trunk. He flexed his fingers, more to get the blood flowing than anything else, then he tried to move his wrists. The rope slid around his skin, burning sharply. He hissed at the pain, and yet he felt a slight sense of elation. They'd tied him tightly, but not tightly enough. He could move his wrists, and if he could do that, then he could escape. All he needed to do was make his hands slippery enough with blood to force them past the rope's tension.

And the only problem with *that* was the dancing woman. Or rather, the lust he could smell coming off her. The slightest hint of blood could set her off, and he had a horrible suspicion that Anni wouldn't stop her. That was why she was naked—why he was naked. No troublesome clothes to get in the way of a good party.

But it was a party that wasn't going to happen if he could help it. He wasn't about to lose the future he'd always dreamed of to some woman's belated grab of revenge.

He looked around and saw René lying on the ground near his left, as naked as he and trussed up tighter than a turkey at Thanksgiving. His eyes were closed and his expression slack, as if he were still out. But the blood beginning to stain the ropes, and the slight flexing of his leg and arm muscles, told a different story.

As Cade similarly fought the ropes, he glanced back to the two women. Jina was looking his way, and she gave him a cold smile when his gaze met hers.

"So, our chief murderer is awake."

"Jontee deserved the death he got," he said, hoping that by talking he'd keep her from noticing what he and René were attempting to do. "He was the one who mutilated and bled eighteen people and, in the end, that's the only justice anyone cares about."

Which wasn't true, not by a long shot, but if it kept her talking, kept her from noticing their actions, then that was all that mattered.

Jina hawked and spat. The globule landed close to

his bare toes, glistening softly against the darker stone underneath it. "That wasn't Jontee. It was Nelle."

"Nelle may have been the main force behind the murders, but it was Jontee performing them."

Surprise touched her weather-beaten features. "If you knew that, how come you never went after her?"

"We had no proof, for a start. It was Jontee's prints on the weapon, and Jontee whom I stopped from killing the last man. I suspected Nelle, but the suspicions of a raw recruit don't mean much without proof."

She snorted softly. "You didn't try too hard to look for her afterward, did you?"

He had. But the killings *had* stopped, they had a suspect they'd caught red-handed and who'd admitted to the crimes, and there was plenty of evidence suggesting he was the only one behind them. "We had a warrant out for her arrest. She was never found."

"Hard to find someone if you ain't actually looking for them," she sneered.

"Especially when Jontee refused to answer any questions about her."

She sniffed and looked away. "He had no choice in that."

"Because Nelle held his mind?"

"Yes." She glanced his way again, and the maliciousness in her eyes sent a chill running through him. "I watched him die, you know. I was one of the witnesses."

He had to wonder how, since Jontee's execution had restricted viewing, but he didn't doubt what she said. "I was a witness, too. You could have gotten me there, Jina."

She sneered again. "It was tempting, but you weren't the first on my list, and you had to wait your time."

"So who was the first—Nelle?"

"Yes."

"And she's dead?"

"It took me nearly ten years to find her, but yes, she's dead."

Meaning he'd wasted half his time here searching for a woman who no longer existed. Maybe if he hadn't been so convinced it was Nelle behind the murders, he might have picked up the clues sooner.

"Then how did you recognize Savannah at the club?"

She snorted. "I saw the stupid bitch leaving her apartment."

So he and Savannah had both been right—she hadn't been followed, but she'd definitely been spotted.

"I can understand you snatching me, but why take René? You know he's a Sinclair, don't you?"

She sniffed. "The Sinclairs don't scare me. Besides, Candy fancied the look of him."

"If the Sinclairs don't scare you, you're more of a fool than I thought."

"We'll be long gone by the time his pack finds this place." She glanced at her watch. "Your girlfriend has ten minutes to get here. I hope she's not late."

His gut tightened. "What do you mean?"

Her grin was cold, victorious. Counting her chickens before they were hatched, Cade thought, and worked harder on the ropes.

"Meaning I left her a little message at the station

and told her to be here by seven. If she's not here soon, I'll let Candy loose on René."

"Please let her be late," Candy said softly, and whirled to a stop in front of Cade. She ran her finger down his chest, her touch as hot as the heat in her eyes. "I feel the need to rend and tear."

Her touch drifted down to his cock. She teased him, caressed him, and though he knew his response was automatic and not desire, he still hated it.

And he'd be damned if he'd put up with it. He lunged forward as far as the ropes would allow, and smashed his forehead against hers. There was a sharp cracking sound, followed quickly by Candy's yelp. She staggered backward and touched a hand to her forehead, feeling for damage. And there was plenty. He'd hit hard enough to split her skin—and his, if the warm moisture dribbling down his nose was anything to go by.

Her fingers came away bloody, and her gaze flew to his. "You will pay for this."

"And I wasn't going to pay before?" He snorted softly. "I'm not a fool, Candy."

She studied him for a moment, the light in her eyes becoming more and more feral. Tension stirred through his muscles, but there wasn't a whole lot he could do to stop her should she decide to attack.

Thankfully, she didn't. She merely smiled and slowly licked the blood from her fingers. "I shall enjoy this," she said, dropping her gaze to his cock. "And then I shall eat you. Piece by tiny piece."

"Candy, enough," Jina said softly.

Candy sniffed, but she flounced back to the fire. She didn't resume her dancing, though. She simply crossed her arms and regarded him much the same way a hunter might study its next meal.

Jina glanced at her watch again. "Eight minutes."

"Why wait?" Candy said, her gaze drifting to René's prone form. She licked her lips, her expression one of feral anticipation. "We intend to kill him anyway, and I want to play."

Jina looked at Cade. "What do you think, Agent Jones? Shall we let her loose to play?"

"It doesn't matter a damn what I think," he said, working furiously on the ropes. Jina *had* to see what he was doing, but she gave no sign of it. Either she didn't care, or she was sure that even if he did escape the ropes, he'd never escape the two of them.

Not that he wanted to escape them. Take them down, yeah, but not escape.

"Come now, play the game. To attack, or not to attack, that is the question."

"And it's not one worth answering, since you'll do what you want anyway."

Her smile was cold. "Trust a man to take the fun out of things." She glanced at Candy, then waved a hand toward René. "He's all yours, my dear."

Candy smiled, and the changing haze shimmered over her form. Then, in wolf form, she launched herself toward the helpless René.

And there wasn't one goddamn thing Cade could do to stop it.

SAVANNAH GLANCED AT her watch as she climbed out of her truck. There were still ten minutes to go, and yet she knew she couldn't afford to place any trust in the fact that Anni would keep her word and not harm either man until seven. She wasn't dealing with a rational mind, despite the "harmless old woman" act Anni had put on over the last six months.

Tension slipped through her, and she took a deep breath, trying to calm her nerves. Nothing had happened to Cade yet. They might not have shared a great deal in the way of telepathic thoughts or emotions, but she'd feel it if he were hurt. She loved him, and she'd know.

She glanced up as thunder rumbled overhead and grabbed her thick jacket off the backseat. Not only was it warm, but it covered the bulletproof jacket Anton had insisted she wear. Once she was zipped up, she grabbed her knife belt and clipped it on. Then she tucked her gun in the waistband at the back of her pants, out of sight. Anton had given her one silver bullet to use, and though she'd pointed out that there were actually two women, he'd simply shrugged and suggested she take out the most dangerous of them. It was Trista who'd told her IIS teams were only given two silver bullets per mission, because they were too expensive to produce. They were to be used only as a last resort—and only by IIS personnel. Anton was risking his career just by giving her the bullet.

None of which made *her* feel any easier. One silver bullet was one too few when she was facing those women alone.

She blew out a breath, trying to ease the tension crawling through her. Where the hell had her courage suddenly gone? Or was it natural to be nervous before you stepped into the lion's den? Sure, she'd led the hunt months ago when a crazy woman had kidnapped both Duncan and René, but that was different. She hadn't been the target that time.

And that was the problem, she realized. Not that she was the target, but the fact that it could all go so very wrong so fast.

No, she thought sternly. *It won't. Have faith.*

She slammed the door shut and headed toward the pitch-black trail, following the tracker signal with the small device Anton had given her. Ronan, Anton, and Trista were working their way through the forest, intending to attack downwind and, hopefully, unexpectedly. They had a second tracker to guide them, so with any luck they wouldn't be too far behind.

Not that any of them could afford to rely on luck. She headed through the forest, wasting no time. She didn't want time to think, and she followed the path as quickly as she dared, seeing no point in trying to approach quietly. It wasn't as if they weren't expecting her. The trail became steeper, rockier as she climbed, and the air was chill with the promise of the oncoming storm. Yet despite that, sweat trickled down her spine. Fear, not exertion.

Soon the trees began to recede and the stretches of barren ground became longer. She slowed, knowing she was drawing close to the clearing where the first victim had been found. Ahead, light danced, sending flickering shadows of yellow and orange across the clumps of snow hunkering near the remaining trees or behind the shelter of the rocks. Two women stood close to the fire, one wearing clothes, one not. Anni and Candy, having a grand old time by the look of it. Her gaze scooted past them and found Cade. Relief surged through her. Her instincts hadn't been wrong.

He might be tied up, but he was alive and appeared unhurt. He was also very naked, and that wasn't a good sign. It meant Anni was very sure of the outcome.

But what about René? Where was he?

She swept her gaze around the clearing and found him on the ground, as naked as Cade and just as trussed up, although there was enough blood on the ropes to suggest he'd been attempting to get free for some time.

Her gaze went back to the two women. They were talking, but the wind snatched their words and flung them away before she could make out what they were saying. She shifted around until she was downwind and the words carried to her.

"Trust a man to take the fun out of things." Anni's voice was contemptuous, cold. She glanced at Candy and waved a hand toward René. "He's all yours, my dear."

Even before she'd finished speaking, the golden shifting haze shimmered over Candy's naked form, moving her from human to wolf. Then she was snarling and leaping, arrowing straight toward the helpless René.

Savannah didn't pause to think. She just grabbed the gun from the waist of her pants and fired that one precious silver bullet. Her shot was on target, hitting Candy in the middle and flinging her backward as blood and fur sprayed. Her deep-seated, hungry growl became a sharp sound of pain, but even that was cut off as she hit the ground. She wasn't dead—the twitching in her limbs and her soft whimpering attested to that—but if she didn't get help soon, she would be. Very few wolves could survive a silver bullet for long.

Savannah shifted the barrel and centered it on Anni—and discovered that Anni was also armed. Only *her* weapon was aimed at Cade.

"Drop it," she warned softly, "or I'll shoot his fucking dick off."

Something hit Savannah's shields—a furious rapping that had a definite male feel. Cade. She lowered a shield and let him in.

Don't you dare drop that weapon. His mind-voice was furious, and yet it was tinged with fear—for her. *She intends to kill us anyway, and dropping that weapon only makes her job easier.*

If I don't drop it, she'll follow through with her threat. She held up one hand and let the weapon slide around her finger. *And I am not unprotected without the gun. Anni just thinks I am.*

And if you do drop it, what's to stop her from shooting me anyway? She wants us to pay, Vannah, and that sure as hell would be one painful way to go.

He was right in *that* respect. Anni was just as likely to shoot as not.

"Drop it," Anni warned softly. "Or I *will* fire."

"You'll fire anyway," she said. To Cade, she added, *Shield René. I wouldn't put it past her to try and use him to attack me.*

Will do. Just be careful she doesn't try to attack you telepathically.

The vicious grin that stretched Anni's thin lips suggested that Cade's guess about Anni's intent had been correct.

"Maybe I will shoot," Anni said, "and maybe I won't. Either way, you have no choice."

"There's always a choice, Jina."

"Like you and that bastard gave Jontee a choice?"

"Jontee *had* a choice. He could have walked away from Rosehall or given up Nelle if she was the force behind the murders."

"He *believed* in Rosehall. In what it stood for."

"And what did it really stand for?" She carefully shifted her grip so that she was once again holding the gun at the ready. "It was all a lie. A big fat lie designed to do nothing more than gather fresh fodder for the next bloodletting."

"Rosehall was an *ideal*. It was a celebration of life and love and freedom." She eyed Savannah darkly. "But you didn't see that. You chose the destroyer over Jontee, over everything he stood for."

"He stood for death. He *celebrated* death."

"That was never part of the original idea. Nelle was the one who brought in the darkness, not Jontee. At least when you two are dead, he can rest in peace."

"He can never be at peace and he'll never be free, Jina. Not then, and not now. Especially now that you've ensured his infamy lives on."

"But that's where you're wrong—he *can* rest, knowing that the people who caused his downfall will finally join him in hell. Now drop the damn weapon."

She didn't drop it. She squeezed the trigger and fired, aiming for Jina's hand rather than the safer option of a body shot. The gun's report echoed across the brief silence, followed quickly by Jina's yelp as the bullet tore through her hand. Blood, bone, and weapon flew. Jina's face contorted with pain and fury as the shimmer of shapechanging swept over her body. In wolf form, she launched herself across the fire, teeth bared and the bloody need to rend and tear gleaming in her eyes.

Savannah braced and aimed the gun, but before she could fire, another shot rang out. Jina flopped to the ground, blood and God knows what else leaking out from the gaping hole in her head.

Anton rose from behind the boulders downwind from Jina and gave her a grim smile. "That's one fewer murderer for the courts to worry about."

Trista came out of the shadows and, a second later, so did Ronan. Savannah met his gaze, saw the relief there, and gave him a smile before she looked at Cade. The depth of feeling in his navy blue eyes echoed right through her. Tension slithered from her limbs, leaving her suddenly weak and shaky. They were all right. All the people she cared about were all right.

And in the end, it had been almost too easy to stop Jina's mad plot for revenge.

Savannah wiped the sweat from her brow, clicked the safety back on the gun, and shoved it away.

"I think Candy's still alive," she said.

Anton nodded. "We'll take care of her, since I'm sure you'll want to take care of the boss." A grin touched his lips as he glanced at Ronan. "Which leaves René to you."

"I always get the best jobs," Ronan muttered.

She walked over to Cade and lightly touched his cheek. "As if I'd let her shoot you anywhere, let alone somewhere so vital to our future."

He grinned. "So you love me only for my skills in the sack?"

"Well, at this stage, I'm not sure what more there is." She kissed him softly and sweetly, but with all the relief and love that was welling up inside her. Emotions she could feel in the warm glow of his thoughts, and in the caress of his lips. When she finally pulled away, she added, "I guess it's up to you to show me what remains."

"Hard thing to do when I'm tied up," he said wryly.

"Ah. Well, I guess I'd better untie you, then."

"It would be a good start."

She grinned and walked around the stump. His wrists were rubbed raw, and the rope was blood-soaked. "You've made a mess back here," she said, getting out her knife.

"Well, I was hardly going to stand back and watch you walk into a trap . . ."

"I can defend myself." The first strand of the rope snapped away. Two more to go. She frowned in concentration, trying to avoid cutting his flesh along with the rope.

"I know. I just didn't want you to *have* to defend yourself. A wolf likes to protect his own."

Another strand gone. "You know, Neva and I swore long ago never to fall for alphas. You guys are far too much trouble."

Amusement touched his voice. "And how old were you when you decided this?"

"Five."

"A very wise age," he commented, the amusement deeper this time.

The last strand fell away. He stepped away from the post, rubbing his wrists as she shoved the knife back in its sheath. Then she met his gaze, and she realized that the amusement in his voice didn't touch his face. That his eyes were, in fact, curiously blank.

Anni had him. Controlled him. From the grave.

Her stomach bottomed out, but before she could react, his fist smashed into her face and she was flying backward. Her yelp of surprise was drowned in the haze of pain and the rush of blood. She hit the ground with a grunt, the gun at her back digging painfully into her spine. Then he was on her, his weight pinning her body and arms, his fists pummeling her hard and fast, until all she could feel was pain.

Then, suddenly Neva was there, in her mind, frantically wanting to know what was going on.

She ignored her sister, and screamed both verbally and mentally, "Cade! It's me, Vannah!" But there was no response from him. His mind was locked, overridden by Anni's vicious last wishes, and he wasn't hearing anything else.

As she twisted from side to side, desperately trying to avoid his blows, she dropped her shields and arrowed into his mind—only to rebound off a shield similar to Candy's. Anni had protected her handiwork, which meant she had never intended to shoot her or Cade. *You chose the destroyer over Jontee,* Anni had said. Which meant she'd planned all along to let them destroy each other.

The blows kept coming and blackness washed through her, threatening to sweep her into unconsciousness. From a distance she heard Ronan shout. The pummeling stopped, and there was a click and several shots. Then she heard a cry of pain. Female. Trista.

God help her, she had to stop Cade before he killed everyone. And there was only one way to do it.

She reached out to Neva, gathering her sister's talents and strength, then flung it all—every bit of pain, hurt, fear, and love she felt—straight at Cade. The force seemed to explode into the air, and it crashed through the barriers in his mind as easily as a hurricane tore through trees, shattering not only the barrier but any hold Anni had on his mind. Awareness surged briefly between them, along with dawning horror.

The effort left her drained and weak, and she had no idea what happened next. She simply let the blackness take her to a place free of pain.

Chapter Fourteen

SAVANNAH GLANCED AWAY from the mirror as Neva waddled into the small hospital room, and she couldn't help grinning. "Sis, you're looking fatter every time I see you."

Neva grimaced as she tossed a bag on a nearby chair and eased herself onto the end of the bed. "That's because I am fatter. I swear I'm having triplets, even if the doc insists there are only two."

Savannah grinned. "Doctors and machines are not infallible. Triplets or even quads are always a remote possibility."

"Bite your tongue. Two mini Duncans are more than enough." Her smile faded a little. "Have you heard from Cade yet?"

Savannah sighed and looked back at the mirror. Her reflection wasn't a pretty sight—rainbow-colored bruises, a swollen, cut nose, fat lip, and cut chin. Her torso had fared little better, and right now she looked and felt like a punching bag. In fact, she'd seen punching bags that actually looked *better* than she did right now. But while she might be bruised, nothing had been broken. Even in the midst of a nightmare, Cade had somehow managed to have some control over his punches—enough to merely batter and not break.

But in the end, it had all been worth it. Anni was dead. Candy had survived the silver bullet, but she and Lonny were currently in custody, and weren't likely to feel the free air against their coats again. Humans *really* didn't like wolves who attacked humans, and both women would pay for their crimes with their lives.

And Alf Reeson had gotten one hell of an exclusive.

"No," she said eventually. "I haven't."

"You want me to go find him and drag him here by the scruff of his neck?"

Savannah grinned. "I'd love to see you try. But no, I don't."

"Damn it, he should be here with you!"

"I can understand why he isn't."

Neva harrumphed. "If he tries to leave town, he'll have a posse on his tail."

Her grin grew. "He won't leave."

"You're sure of that?"

"Yes."

"Then tell me why the hell he isn't here begging for your forgiveness and running after your every need?"

"Because he doesn't need my forgiveness, and because he's well aware that I'm more than capable of taking care of myself."

"That doesn't excuse him for not coming to visit you."

Well, no, it didn't. But he *had* been here, for every single moment of the ten hours she'd been out of it. And while she wasn't entirely sure why he hadn't come back to visit her in the two days since then, she trusted what they had between them enough to know he wasn't going anywhere. Whatever he was up to, he had his reasons.

"I'm going to talk to him now." Savannah finished putting her hair into a ponytail, wincing a little as pain slithered through her bruised muscles.

"You shouldn't even be out of bed yet."

"God, have you and Ronan taken nagging pills? He's currently down the hall, harassing the nurses, trying to force me to stay."

Neva grinned. "I know. I passed him on the way up."

"Then why didn't you tell him not to waste his breath?"

"Because it's his breath to waste, and because Ari is down there. She's rather keen on him, you know."

"Yeah, I know . . . but he keeps missing the clues."

Neva chuckled softly. "Well, hopefully he's realized what's been waiting for him all along. Ari's a great catch, and she'd be a good match for Ronan."

Savannah wagged a finger at her. "Don't you start playing matchmaking games. He'll only sense it and get pissed off."

"You're no fun," Neva muttered, the twinkle in her eyes suggesting the idea was neither gone nor forgotten. She levered herself off the bed. "You want a ride anywhere?"

"No. I need to stretch my aching muscles."

"And here I thought the doc had ordered you to rest."

He had. And she would, once she was with Cade. "If you keep bugging me, I'll tell Duncan to take you back to the mansion and make you rest."

"Even Duncan's not brave enough to try that a second time." Neva waddled to her and lightly touched a hand to Savannah's cheek. "Let me know how things go."

"I will."

Once Neva had left, Savannah walked over to the bed and opened the bag. Loose pants, a sweater, and flip-flops. Not the most attractive outfit, but at least it was comfortable. And she doubted Cade would be too worried about what she was wearing.

She dressed and left the hospital—and left a happy Ronan flirting shamelessly with an even happier Ari.

The day was crisp and sunny—the perfect autumn day—and yet there was a touch of winter in the breeze. Savannah paused on the bottom-most step and breathed deeply, clearing her lungs of the stale hospital air. Then she turned and walked to her lodge.

By the time she'd reached the bottom of the steep driveway, she was sweating and aching and calling herself names for not accepting Neva's offer. The beating had sapped her strength more than she'd realized, and the driveway might as well be Mount Everest, for all the hope she had of climbing it now.

But before she could call for help, Cade appeared, walking down the driveway toward her. She didn't move, just enjoyed the sight of him—enjoyed the play of sun across his lightly tanned arms, the way his thigh muscles moved under his jeans, even the easy way he walked. But most of all, she enjoyed the way his navy gaze met hers, held hers, as if she were something so precious he feared to look away in case she disappeared.

"Need a hand?" he said, as he stopped in front of her.

She smiled. "Yeah. I overestimated my strength, I'm afraid."

"You should have called."

"I wanted to walk."

"And now you're regretting it."

"And now I'm regretting it," she agreed.

A smile touched his lips, and he carefully picked her up and carried her back up the hill. She sighed in contentment and rested her head against his shoulder, listening to the soothing, steady beat of his heart.

She could have stayed there forever.

"Been fixing a few things up," he said as they approached the lodge.

Her gaze skirted across the old building. At first glance, there didn't appear to be much different from when she'd last seen it. Then she noticed that the front steps had been repaired, and the skeleton of a new roof had appeared over the damaged wing.

"So you have." She met his gaze. "You didn't have to."

"Yes, I did." He walked through the open front door, up the stairs and along the hall with the roof still intact. The air was fresh, filled with the sharpness of new paint. Not all the walls were painted, but most were at least patched. "But not for the reasons you think."

She raised her eyebrows as he walked into one of the end rooms. The old sofa they'd used the first time they'd made love had been dragged in here, and he'd started a fire. He'd been expecting her. He placed her on the sofa and squatted in front of her.

She touched a hand to his cheek and slid it down his lips. He kissed each finger as she asked, "And what might those reasons be?"

"This isn't an apology," he said, waving a hand at the freshly painted walls around them.

She knew that already, but she still asked the question, simply because he wanted her to ask. "Then what is it?"

"A promise. A commitment." He touched a hand to her cheek, his fingers warm and gentle against her skin. "What I did to you is a nightmare that will haunt the worst of my nights, but I won't let it destroy me, and I won't let it destroy us. I may not know you as well as I should, but I do love you, Savannah, and I want to live the rest of my life with you."

His emotions, so raw and deep, had tears touching her eyes. "Good, because I sure as hell wasn't going to let you go anywhere anyway."

He grinned and leaned forward, gently kissing her bruised mouth. "Had the posse ready to go, huh?"

"Neva did. I told her we wouldn't need it." She ran her fingers through his silky brown hair, then slid them around the back of his neck. "You knew I was okay. That's why you weren't at the hospital."

His grin became wry. "Actually, I wasn't at the hospital because your dad threatened to do me serious bodily harm if I didn't leave you alone and give you time to recover and think."

"I am going to *kill* my father."

Cade shrugged. "He was only protecting what's his."

"I'm not his. I'm yours."

"I told him that. He wasn't inclined to believe me."

"So why didn't you just arrest his sorry ass and come visit me anyhow?"

"Because the man is going to be my father-in-law, and that would have started our relationship on the worst possible foot."

She slid her other hand around his neck and wriggled closer, until he was kneeling between her spread legs. "That almost sounds like a proposal."

"And it just might be."

"If it is, it's not a very romantic one."

He studied her for a moment. The smile on his lips and the love so evident in his eyes made her feel safe and warm and wanted. Like she'd finally come home after a long time away.

And in so many ways, she had.

"You're wearing multicolored bruises, an old track suit, and flip-flops," he said. "Not exactly a romantic outfit."

"What if I wasn't wearing it?"

"Tempting, but for those bruises."

"I'm sure a clever man could work around the bruises."

The sexy smile tugging at his lips made her hormones sizzle and her heart feel like it was about to leap out of her chest. "Is that a challenge, woman?"

"Are you up for a challenge?" She let her gaze slide down. "It certainly looks like you are."

"I'm always ready for a challenge, but not until you've answered the question on the table."

She leaned forward and kissed him. "What question?"

"Will you marry me?"

"If I say yes, will you shut up and make love to me?"

He pulled the zipper of her top down, revealing her breasts. "Yes."

"Then the answer is yes."

"Good." He slid her top off and shucked off his own shirt. "I wasn't going to accept any other answer, anyway."

"You promised to shut up."

"And make love to you," he agreed. He took her face between his hands and kissed her carefully, but oh-so-wonderfully. "It's a promise I intend to keep every single day, for the rest of our lives."

"Then shut up and get down to it," she teased.

He did—and amply proved just how clever a man he was.

If you loved Neva and Savannah's stories in *Beneath a Rising Moon* and *Beneath a Darkening Moon*, then be sure not to miss the exciting beginning of the Nikki and Michael series!

Dancing with the Devil

by

Keri Arthur

The first book in the Nikki and Michael series will be followed by the next three Nikki and Michael titles at one-month intervals: *Hearts in Darkness, Chasing the Shadows,* and *Kiss the Night Goodbye.* Here's a special preview:

SOMEONE FOLLOWED HER.

Someone she couldn't see or hear through any normal means, but whose presence vibrated across her psychic senses.

Someone whose mission was death.

The wind stirred, running chill fingers across the nape of her neck. Nikki shivered and eyed the surrounding shadows uneasily. She'd never been afraid of the dark before—had, in fact, found it something of an ally, especially in the wilder days of her youth. But tonight there was an edge to the silence, a hint of menace in the slowly swirling fog.

People disappeared on nights like this. At least, they did here in Lyndhurst.

She returned her gaze to the slender figure just ahead. This was the second night in a row Monica Trevgard had come to the park after midnight, and if the teenager had a reason for doing so, Nikki sure as hell hadn't found any evidence of it. Her actions to date made very little sense. The only child of one of Lyndhurst's—and possibly America's—richest men, Monica had spent most of her life rebelling against her family and their wealth. And yet, ironically, it was only thanks to her father's money that she was free to walk the streets tonight. Though nothing had ever been proven, it was generally acknowledged that John Trevgard had at least one judge and several police officers on his payroll.

Nikki smiled grimly. Trevgard would probably have been better off keeping his hand in his pocket and letting his only child spend some time in jail. Maybe a day or so locked behind uncompromising concrete walls would shock some sense into the girl.

It sure as hell had with *her.*

Shoving cold hands into the pockets of her old leather jacket, Nikki let her gaze roam across the fog-shrouded trees to her left.

He was still there, still following her, the man with darkness in his heart and murder on his mind. But not her murder, or even Monica's. Someone else's entirely.

She bit her lip. With two knives strapped to her wrists and her psychic abilities to fall back on, she was sufficiently protected. At least under normal circumstances. But the man out there in the darkness was far from normal, and something told her none of her weapons would be enough if he chose to attack.

Maybe *she* was as mad as Monica. Four women had already disappeared from this particular area. She should play it safe and go home, let Jake—her boss, and the man who'd become more of a parent to her than her own damn parents ever had been— take over the case. A teenager looking for trouble was going to find it—no matter how many people her father hired to follow and protect her.

Only Jake had enough on his plate already, and his night-sight had started deteriorating since he'd hit the big four-0 several years ago.

The sound of running water broke through the heavy silence. Though the fog half-hid the old fountain from sight, Nikki knew it well enough to describe every chipped detail, from the wickedly grinning cherub at the top to the embracing lovers near the bottom. It was amazing what became interesting when you had nothing else to do but watch a teenager watch the water.

Only, this time, Monica didn't stop at the fountain. She didn't even look at it. Instead, she glanced quickly over her shoulder—a casual move that raised the hairs on the back of Nikki's neck.

Monica knew she was being followed. Tonight she was the bait to catch the watcher.

The bitter breeze stirred, seeming to blow right through her soul. Nikki swore softly and ran a hand through her hair. It was nights like this, when she was caught between common sense and past promises, that she really hated being psychic. She would have run a mile away from here had it not been for her gift, which warned that death would claim Monica's soul if she weren't protected tonight.

And because she couldn't stand the weight of another death on her conscience, she had no real choice but to follow.

They neared the far edge of the park. Streetlights glimmered—forlorn wisps of brightness barely visible through the trees and the fog—and Nikki's discomfort surged. Monica wasn't heading for the street or the lights, but rather toward the old mansion on the far side of the park. The place had a reputation for being haunted, and though she wasn't particularly afraid of ghosts, the one night she'd spent there as a kid had sent her fleeing in terror. Not from the ghosts, but from the sense of evil that seemed to ooze from the walls.

Of course, it might have been nothing more than a combination of knowing that a family had once been murdered there, and an overactive imagination. But still . . .

Monica squeezed through a small gap in the fence and cast another quick look over her shoulder. There was no doubt about it—the kid definitely wanted to be followed.

Nikki stopped and watched her walk up the steps to the back door. Her common sense told her not to follow, and her psychic sense told her danger lurked inside. She clenched her fists. She could do this. She *had* to do this. For Monica's sake.

Because if she didn't, the teenager was doomed.

She stepped forward, then froze. No sound had disturbed the dark silence. Even the breeze had faded, and the fog sat still and heavy on the ground. Yet something had moved behind her. Something not quite human.

Throat dry, Nikki turned. Out of the corner of her eye, she caught a hint of movement—a hand, emerging from darkness, reaching out to touch her . . .

Yelping in fright, she jumped back and lashed out with a blast of kinetic energy. Something heavy hit a nearby oak, accompanied by a grunt of pain. She stared at the tree. Despite the sound, there was nothing or nobody at its base.

Yet something had to be there. It didn't make any sense—bodies just didn't disappear like that. She swallowed and ran trembling fingers through her hair. Disembodied hands couldn't emerge from the darkness, either.

Had it just been her imagination, finally reacting to the overwhelming sensation of being followed? No, something *had* been there. Was *still* there, even if she couldn't see it.

Not that *that* made a whole lot of sense.

She turned and studied the dark house instead. Trouble waited inside. But so did Monica.

Ignoring her unknown watcher, she climbed through the fence and ran across the shadowed yard. Edging up the steps, she slipped a small flashlight from her pocket and shone the light through the open doorway.

The entrance hall was small, laden with dust and cobwebs that shimmered like ice in the beam of light. Faded crimson-and-gold wallpaper hung in eerie strips from the walls, rustling lightly in the breeze that drifted past her legs. The house really hadn't changed much in the ten years since she'd been here last—

except for one thing. The creeping sense of evil felt a hell of a lot stronger now than it ever had before. In fact, it almost seemed alive. Alive, and waiting.

She swallowed heavily and directed the flashlight's beam toward the stairs. Motes of dust danced across the light, stirred to life in the wake of Monica's passing. She'd gone up. Up to where the sense of evil felt the strongest.

Gripping the flashlight tightly, Nikki walked through the dust toward the stairs. The air smelled of decay and unwashed bodies. Obviously, it was still a haunt for those forced to scratch a living from the streets. It was odd, though, that there was no one here now— no one but Monica and whoever it was she'd come here to meet.

A floorboard creaked beneath Nikki's weight, the sound as loud as thunder in the silence. She winced and hesitated. After several heartbeats, someone moved on the floor above.

It wasn't Monica. The footfalls were too heavy.

Reaching into her pocket, Nikki turned on her phone. If things started to go bad, she'd call for help. Trevgard might not like the publicity a call to the cops would bring, but if it meant the difference between life or death—*her* life or death—then he could go to hell.

The staircase loomed out of the shadows. Nikki shone the light upward. Something growled—a low sound almost lost under the thundering of her heart. She hesitated, staring up into the darkness. It had sounded like some sort of animal. But what animal made such an odd, rasping noise?

One hand on the banister, the other clutching the

flashlight so tightly that her knuckles began to ache, she continued on. The growl cut across the silence again.

It was definitely *not* an animal.

She reached the landing and stopped. The odd-sounding snarl seemed much closer this time. Sweat trickled down her face and the flashlight flickered slightly, its beam fading, allowing the darkness to close in around her. Nikki swore and gave it a quick shake. The last thing she needed right now was for the light to give out.

The light flickered again, then became brighter. She moved on but kept close to the wall, just in case. At least she could use it as a guide, even if the peeling remains of the wallpaper felt like dead skin against her fingertips.

The hallway ended in a T. Moonlight washed through the shattered window at the end of the left-hand corridor. On the right, the darkness was so complete that the flashlight barely penetrated it. And while she knew it was little more than a result of shuttered windows down that end of the hall, it still seemed oddly unnatural.

It wasn't a place she wanted to go. Unfortunately, Monica was down there somewhere. But that odd sound had come from the left. Whatever it was, she had to check it out first. She wasn't about to risk being attacked from behind in a place like this. So she turned left. Two doors waited ahead—one open, one closed.

Was it just fear or instinct that warned against entering either room?

The wind whispered forlornly through the shattered window, accompanied by a low moan that raised goose bumps across her skin.

It was definitely more human than animal. And it wasn't Monica. The teenager still waited in the darkness of the right-hand corridor. Edging forward, Nikki peered around the doorframe. Nothing moved in the moon-washed darkness, but something was in there. The sense of malevolence was so overwhelming she could barely breathe.

So why don't you turn around and run?

The thought whispered into her brain, feather-light but hinting at anger. Nikki froze, fear squeezing her throat tight. Just for an instant, her mind linked with another. She tasted darkness and concern and the need to kill. This was the man she'd half-seen near the fence, the man who'd followed her through the fog.

Turn around and leave. You cannot help the child now.

No. Why could she hear this man's thoughts? Telepathy had never been one of her talents, even though she'd been able to receive Tommy's thoughts well enough. *And who the hell are you to tell me what to do?*

I am merely trying to save your life. You will not like what you find here. Not in that room, and not with the teenager.

Yeah, right. Who was this weirdo? A would-be prophet of doom? *I have never run from anything in my life, and I don't intend to start now.*

The lie gave her courage. She took a deep breath and stepped into the room.

* * *

MICHAEL KELLY HIT the fence in frustration. The little fool had gone in, despite his warning. Or perhaps because of it.

She knew that danger waited. He could taste the fear in her thoughts, despite the distance between them. So why wouldn't she run? Why did she continue this fruitless pursuit? Given the strength of her psychic talents, she had to know the child was well beyond salvation.

He let his gaze roam to the far end of the house. Hidden by the darkness, evil waited for his next meal, ably served by his young companion. Unless *he* intervened, Nikki James would become the fifth woman to go missing.

Had it been anyone else, he wouldn't particularly have cared—not given the identity of the man who hunted her, a man he'd long hunted himself. But he'd been sent here tonight to save a life rather than trap and kill a murderer, and as much as he might want to do the latter, he could not. But Nikki's abilities added a dangerous dimension to his task. It was for those abilities, more than for her blood, that Jasper hunted her.

He turned and walked to the end of the fence. The sudden movement caused pain to shoot through his head, but he resisted the urge to rub the lump forming near his temple. He had deserved that—and more—for being so careless. But he hadn't expected the fool to use her kinetic abilities against him. Why, he couldn't say. He smiled grimly. Maybe senility was finally setting in.

He walked through the gate and headed for the garage. While he generally couldn't enter private homes uninvited, that restriction didn't apply to houses that had been long abandoned. He could go in unhindered, and do what he was sent here to do.

But Jasper was not in that house alone. Not only did he have the teenager at his command, but his living dead as well. Six against one were not the best of odds, even for someone like him. What Michael needed was a distraction. He slipped past the remains of the garage door and his gaze came to rest on an old gas can. He picked it up; liquid sloshed within.

Jasper hated fire. Feared it.

It might provide enough of a distraction to save Nikki James.

THE ROOM SMELLED awful—a putrid mix of stale urine, excrement, and death. Nikki cupped a hand over her nose and mouth and tried not to gag as she swept the flashlight's beam across the room.

Something slid away from the light—a hunched, humanoid shape that smelled like death.

Nikki backed away. She didn't know what hid in the shadows and didn't really care to find out. She'd learned long ago that some things were best left unexplored, and this was one of those times. Perhaps if she closed the door, the thing would leave her alone. She knew from past experience that all the doors in this old house creaked; it was one of the things that had spooked her as a teenager. At the very least, it would give her some warning if the thing decided to move.

She began to turn away, then stopped. A prickle of warning ran across the back of her neck. The shadows parted, revealing a tangled mass of long blond hair and pale, naked flesh.

It was female. And human. And yet . . . not.

What the hell . . . ?

The grotesque figure lunged at her. Fear slammed through Nikki's heart. Stumbling backward, she threw out her hand and thrust the creature away kinetically. It slammed into the back wall, grunting in surprise. But no sooner had it hit the floor than it was scrambling to its feet, its agility surprising.

Glimpsing movement to her left, Nikki whirled. A second creature ran out of the shadows, its face a mocking image of womanhood. Nikki reached again for her kinetic energy. The heavy steps of the first creature were already drawing close. Sweat—more from fear than exertion—trickled down the back of her neck. She thrust the second creature back through the doorway, then flicked a wrist knife into her palm and spun around. The first creature charged, teeth bared and hands raised like talons. Talons that showed the remnants of red nail polish. Nikki backed away, wanting to defend herself and yet suddenly reluctant to use her knife against another woman—even if that woman appeared dead set on killing her.

Then the second creature came back through the doorway, and the choice was taken out of her hands. She threw the first woman back kinetically, then sidestepped the leap of the second and slashed with the knife. The blade cut through the creature's skin as easily as butter, and blood sprayed across them both. Nikki blanched and scrubbed at it with the sleeve of her jacket as she backed away.

The creature made no sound, gave no reaction, not

even when her stomach began to peel open and her innards bulge out. She just spun around and charged again. Nausea tightened Nikki's throat. She swallowed and kept backing away, but her feet wouldn't move fast enough. The creature lashed out, and the blow flung her backward. Her back hit the wall, the flashlight went flying, and for a moment she saw stars.

The creature made a second grab for her. Nikki scrambled away, but it caught her shoulder and pulled her back. Talonlike fingers tore into her arm, and pain shot down to her fingertips. She gasped, fighting the sudden wash of nausea. The creature snarled, its breath fetid, full of death and decay. Nikki shuddered and slammed the heel of her hand into its face. For a split second, its hold weakened and she reached quickly for more kinetic energy. A sliver of pain ran through her mind—a warning that she was pushing her psychic strength too far. She ignored it and forced the heavy creature away from her. It flew across the room and smashed through the window, tumbling out of sight with a feminine cry of surprise.

Moonlight fanned across the darkness, lifting the shadows and touching the face of the second creature as it lumbered back into the room. For an instant, it resembled Jackie Sommers, one of the four women who'd recently gone missing. But if it was, what the hell had happened to her? How could someone go from an average suburban mom to something that was barely even human in so short a time?

The woman snarled—and any resemblance to Sommers shattered. The creature took one ponderous step forward, then stopped. Nikki readied another kinetic lance. The shard of pain in her head became a torrent.

She was going to have a hell of a headache tomorrow—if she survived that long.

Blood ran past her clenched fingers and dripped to the floor near her feet. She had no choice but to ignore it. One move, no matter how small, and the creature would attack.

So why wasn't it attacking now? It simply stood in the doorway, shaking its head and snarling softly. It was almost as if the creature was fighting a leash of some kind.

And she had absolutely no desire to find out who—or what—held the end of that leash.

The creature snarled again—an angry, sullen sound. Then it turned and leaped out the nearest window.

The retreat sent a chill up her spine. She waited tensely for something else to happen. The breeze stirred the dust from the shadows, and the heavy silence returned.

After several heartbeats, she sank down against the wall and drew her knees close. For a minute she simply sat there staring at the shattered window, breathing deeply and letting the silence run over her.

Had the creatures survived the fall from the window? Given the reaction—or lack thereof—to the knife wound, it was more than likely that, even if they *had* broken bones, it wasn't going to stop them. And she wasn't about to walk over to the window to find out, if only because she had no idea just what they were capable of. For all she knew, they might be crouched down there on the ground, ready to spring up and drag her outside the minute she showed her face.

But if both creatures had been desperate to destroy

her, why did the last one retreat? The desire—maybe even the need—to shed blood had been all too evident in its eyes. Yet it had leapt out the window rather than attack.

Which could only mean it had been *ordered* to. Because whatever lurked in that darkness on the other side of the corridor wanted her for itself.

Moonlight played across the glass that lay scattered around her. Glass that was stained with bright splashes of red. She wasn't sure if the blood belonged to the creatures or to her, but she knew in the end it wouldn't really matter. *He* would come for the blood. *He* would smell it and come for her.

Who *he* was, she didn't really know. Or care. She had to get out of this crazy house. She had to escape, while she still could . . .

Then the thought stalled. What about Monica? Did she really want to leave the teenager to face her fate alone?

Yes.

No.

At sixteen, Monica had barely begun to live. She had so much yet to learn, so much more of the world to see. And yet it wasn't as if Monica hadn't already had her chances. Time and again, her willful—and often violent—tendencies had gotten her into trouble, and time and again, her father's wealth and influence had gotten her out of it. Yet she never seemed to learn. She just plunged headfirst into one catastrophe after another, seemingly hell-bent on a path of destruction. Was it really worth risking her own life to save Monica's?

She took another deep breath and pushed upright.

Ten years before, while still just a teenager herself, Nikki had left another another teenager just like Monica to his fate. He'd been a hell of a lot more capable of taking care of himself than Monica would ever be, and still he had died. This time around, she was not letting fate get the upper hand.

She eased off her jacket and studied the wound on her forearm. While the three gashes were bleeding profusely, the creature's talons obviously hadn't severed anything vital. She could still move her fingers, even if it did hurt like hell. She dug a handkerchief out of her pocket and wrapped it around the wound. She hoped it would stem the flow of blood long enough for her to find Monica and get out of this house.

After putting her jacket back on, she walked across to retrieve her flashlight, only to find that it no longer worked. The reason was easy enough to discover— the battery cover must have popped when she'd dropped it and the batteries had fallen out. She had a quick look around, but couldn't find the damn things.

"That's just great," she muttered, thrusting the now useless flashlight back in her pocket. She'd have to cross the threshold into that utter darkness with only instinct to guide her.

Instinct that had proven somewhat unreliable in the past.

The hallway was quiet, but her gaze was drawn to the far end of the hall. Monica was down there somewhere. But so was the presence that tasted so evil.

She took a deep, calming breath, then walked back to the intersection. A tingle of awareness ran across the back of her neck as she neared the stairs. She hesitated, studying the shadows that hid the staircase.

The stranger had entered the house. *Michael Kelly,* Nikki thought. *His name is Michael Kelly.*

Nikki rubbed the back of her neck. Why could she read this stranger's mind? And why had he entered the house? Was he here to help her, or did he have something more sinister in mind?

No answers came from the darkness, and the spark of awareness flickered and died. Nikki frowned but continued on. The rapid beat of her heart seemed abnormally loud in the silence. Her senses warned her of another door, even though she couldn't see it. She ran her fingers along the wall and touched a door frame, then the cold metal of a knob. Stopping, she listened to the silence.

Evil was near, maybe even in the room beyond this door. She clenched the doorknob so tightly her fingers almost cramped and wondered why in hell she was doing this.

Except that she already knew. Monica reminded her of Tommy, the teenager she'd left to die so long ago. To appease his ghost—and to appease her guilt—she'd follow Monica through the flames of hell itself if that's what it took to save her, simply because she'd been unable to save Tommy.

Swallowing, she opened the door. Laughter greeted her—laughter that was young and sweet, yet somehow cold.

Monica.

The teenager stepped forward, her smile clearly visible despite the shadows that hid her face.

"If you wish to talk to me," she said, her voice melodious yet holding a touch of menace, "you must follow me first."

Then she turned and walked into yet another room. Instinct urged Nikki not to follow—told her to run as far and as fast as she could. Told her Monica wasn't worth dying for.

Yet it also told her that, if she ran, Monica would die in her place. And that was a burden she just couldn't bear. Taking a deep breath, Nikki followed the teenager.

Straight into the arms of the devil himself.